THE UNTHINKABLE BURIAL

A covert operation political thriller

By Edward L. Lanner

Published in 2025 by FeedARead.

"Edward L. Lanner" is a nom de plume of the author.

British Library C.I.P.

A CIP catalogue record for this title is available from the British Library.

This book is a work of fiction and, except in the case of historical fact, any resemblance to actual persons, living or dead, and events is purely coincidental. The commercial organizations are fictional. The described workings of public bodies are fictional, too.

Although some geographical settings are loosely based on real-world locations, these have been heavily fictionalised and as described are products of the author's imagination.

To my sisters.

PART ONE

Chapter 1

It was almost 8.30 a.m. Next to Paul Avery's ringing telephone was an emergency bulletin bearing today's date: Monday 18 July 1983. Copies had been placed on the surrounding desks too, and could be seen pinned to notice boards throughout the south Oxfordshire headquarters of the Radioactive Substances Monitoring, Storage and Disposal Agency, whose initials RSMSDA were often truncated by commentators – many insiders thought this was done pointedly rather than for brevity – to RSMS.

According to the Head of Site Administration, hundreds of Cruise missile protestors, in sympathy with those demonstrating outside the Greenham Common RAF base in neighbouring Berkshire, were expected to arrive this morning. The types of disruptive activities that should be anticipated were listed in the bulletin. Not mentioned was the likelihood that had the executive committee been more open about the agency's diminished role in the handling of nuclear weapons, the attention of these disarmament campaigners might have been avoided.

The early-morning sunlight streaming through the open-plan office of the Permanent Storage Solutions Department was as energising as an espresso, not that Avery needed a caffeine boost. He was still feeling the adrenalin surge from his motorcycle ride to work. During summer months, he enjoyed noisily overtaking sedately-driving colleagues – whereas during the winter the hedge-lined Oxfordshire lanes harboured black ice. This morning he'd let his restored 650 c.c. Triumph off its leash.

He was a little above average height and of medium build. The curliness of his blond hair required him to keep it cut short to avoid it turning into a comb-defying pad that made putting on his crash helmet painful. With a dimpled smile, high cheek bones and an eye colour that alternated between bluish- and greenish-grey, depending upon metabolic meanderings that he'd noticed correlated with his sense of wellbeing, his face was once artlessly described as that of the most handsome man on the planet – by Ann, who was tipsily disinhibited from the imbibing of numerous cocktails at the student-hall party where they met. Ann and he married two years later, following her graduation and the completion of his doctorate.

While still contemplating the bulletin's prominent instruction – "DO NOT TALK TO PROTESTORS OR TO THE PRESS WITHOUT ADMINISTRATION APPROVAL" – Avery, tie askew and with his shirt sleeves folded back to the elbows, shot out his hand to pick up the telephone receiver. At that instant a bang came from a close-by window. He swivelled on his chair, expecting to see a salvo of rubble hurtling from the site perimeter. Instead he noticed only the oily impression of a bird, most likely a pigeon, which had just crashed, wings spread, against the floor-to-ceiling glass pane.

This was his first day in the newly created position of Deputy Team Manager for "Dry Waste Storage", a position that represented a notable promotion for someone twenty-seven years old; barely three years had passed since he'd completed his doctoral research in nuclear physics. His direct boss, the actual Team Manager, would now be the eminent Professor Benedict Sykes – Sykes was the holder of a Visiting Professorship conferred by the Hull School of Advanced Energy Science – who in his late fifties had become increasingly distant from "hands on" work and spent most of the year attending conferences or visiting his opposite numbers around the globe. Although the responsibility for the development of large metal canisters to permanently store the radioactive waste that was accumulating at UK nuclear power stations was now Avery's, Professor Sykes would remain the public face of the work and expected to be kept informed of progress, particularly any results he could use in lecture slides or submit for publication in the scientific literature.

The rest of the immediate team – most of whom were older than Avery – comprised twenty-six graduate- or doctoral-level scientists, and thirteen support staff, such as workshop technicians, laboratory assistants and clerical assistants.

The goal of the team was to develop containers capable of withstanding, throughout several millennia, corrosive reactions, thermal- and radiation-induced metal fatigue, and the build-up of pressure from gases such as the helium arising from alpha particle radiation.

An agitated voice emanated from the telephone receiver – "Hullo! Hullo! Is anyone there?"

"Paul Avery here," Avery said, speaking louder than he'd intended.

"Good morning, Dr Avery. My name is Auberon Morrison. It falls to me to oversee certain sensitive matters here in Whitehall. I have been given to understand that you are particularly well qualified to assist us with something involving a certain NATO partner."

The caller's manner of talking – clearly enunciated, but with accentuated vowels – was of a nature that Avery had come to identify with the beneficiaries of private educations; it was a verbal cue that always raised his guard.

The combination of the security bulletin on his desk and Morrison's reference to the military alliance of Western powers prompted a vision of unstable nuclear warheads. Paul had a vague premonition his life might be in for an unwanted course correction, perhaps one as painful as that experienced moments ago by the hapless bird.

"What is the nature of the assistance you require, Mr Morrison?" he heard himself asking in an affected tone that echoed that of the caller's.

"That is far too sensitive to divulge on this line. The important aspect for you to appreciate now is that this will take priority. Your current duties will have to be reallocated or postponed."

I've enough on my plate without another *admin bod throwing his weight around*, thought Paul as he absently patted the gloss-white helmet that, together with his leather gloves, still lay at the end of his desk. He considered telling Morrison to contact his department head, Fabian Gooch, but Gooch was not someone who reacted well to being handed organizational problems. Polite evasiveness was worth a shot: "A large number of people work on my project. It will be far from straightforward—"

Interrupting in a manner conveying steeliness and impatience, Morrison said, "Should your department head appear inclined to be unhelpful, emphasise that this pertains to a delicate and urgent matter having the highest level of secrecy. That's entirely all *he* needs to know. However, if he does feel compelled to speak to me, my direct extension is 93499."

"I see." Paul felt his throat tighten as he jotted down the extension number, and then he became aware of his heart beating rapidly. *Has it been pounding like this since that bird struck the window?*

"Our offices are undergoing refurbishment, so a special briefing venue has been arranged for you. It will be at the Tobe Institute, which is near Stoke Poges, at 2.00 p.m. tomorrow. The directions are being faxed over to you now."

Paul heard the nearby fax machine start its shrill whine. "Stoke Poges?" he said. He'd heard of the village but, as far as he could recall, not the institute. In any case it seemed inconceivable that his bumptious manager would allow him to attend the briefing, let alone permit him to drop his new responsibilities.

"The institute undertakes contract research for both private- and public-sector bodies. The Ministry of Defence is its chief source of funding. Many of its personnel therefore possess higher levels of clearance than you. However, no one from it will attend the briefing. It is simply providing a meeting facility where you'll be met by a junior colleague of mine – Patrick Maycross."

"Very well, Mr Morrison," Paul said, writing down the name of the person he would meet; unless it was bluster on the part of the caller, Paul's attending the briefing seemed to be a fait accompli.

"Patrick will be your Whitehall contact henceforth. It's unlikely we'll speak again."

"I understand," Paul said, understanding nothing.

It took a few seconds for Paul to realise Morrison – presumably impatient to disrupt someone else's day – had hung up. Further seconds passed before he placed the receiver down; he'd been replaying the brief exchange in his mind, trying to sieve out a clue as to what was required from him. What type of research did the Tobe Institute undertake for the MOD? Maybe finding out the answer to that would be a starting point.

He remembered the waiting fax.

***

Late the following morning, Paul Avery, wearing a dark-blue suit and the one tie made from silk that he owned – a birthday gift from Ann – set off eastwards from his workplace in a pool car. Reaching the village of Stoke Poges in Buckinghamshire involved a drive of about forty miles, half of this being on winding lanes and the remainder on a motorway.

He wasn't sure why he'd eschewed his usual sports jacket for today's curious meeting. Ann had probably been close to the mark: "If taking more pride in your appearance is a consequence of your promotion, I approve. You look hunky when you make an effort." Her compliment had been welcome because of the brooding tension between them during the last couple of days.

Nearing his destination, he stopped at a quiet country pub for lunch. He sat at a weathered trestle table in the garden, eating his Ploughman's lunch. A circling wasp, which was trying to settle on his slab of cheese, seemed to be channelling Fabian Gooch; the department manager had indeed reacted angrily yesterday to having a member of his staff approached without the observance of the usual Civil Service protocols.

Gooch, a thin, balding Yorkshireman with a penetrating gaze and an unconvincing comb-over, reprimanded Paul for agreeing to attend the meeting, but relented upon hearing the phrase "this pertains to a delicate and urgent matter having the highest level of secrecy". A wide-eyed expression, a look conveying both fear and shock, took over the middle-aged man's countenance. "Highest level... If *those* were his words, then that's bloody that then," he muttered.

After collecting his thoughts, Gooch said, "Assemble your team. Tell them something's come up which means you'll also have other duties, but you expect everyone to continue with their work plans. If anyone needs to get hold of you while you're away, they should leave a message for you with my secretary. I'll call Benedict in Paris myself and let him know. I'll try to convince him we can manage for the time being. He has enough on his plate without this distraction. It was he who advocated for your appointment, after all. In the event of something arising that needs an urgent decision, Andy or I'll step in on your behalf."

Gooch's response was as satisfactory as Paul could have hoped in the circumstances, in particular the gratifying information that Sykes had personally selected him for the promotion – Paul had never considered the prickly professor as being his champion. Nonetheless, Gooch's mentioning the well-connected Andrew Higstead – the Team Manager for "Vitrified Waste Storage" – was unwelcome.

Andy, known for arguing for the expansion of his responsibilities, always avoided directly confronting the more academically accomplished Sykes. But in the professor's absence, Higstead would frequently allude to similarities between the challenges associated with the storage of power station waste and the storage of the sludge that was formed as a by-product of plutonium creation for nuclear bombs. He would downplay the differing corrosion processes arising with these two types of high-level radioactive waste.

Paul's concern about a threat from "Ambitious Andy" to his promotion heightened when, as he moved to leave the department head's office, Gooch snapped, "No one's indispensable. Remember that!"

None of Paul's departmental colleagues had heard of the Tobe Institute either, but the senior librarian was able to retrieve a seven-year-old pamphlet outlining the services offered by the institute in the fields of microscopy, water filtration, building material development and wind power research. These subjects didn't seem to be likely candidates for funding by the MOD, as revealed by Morrison, so the choice of the institute as the meeting venue remained a mystery.

The Tobe Institute had been developed in and around a Victorian redbrick mansion house, which fronted on to a hedge-lined lane. There was a field with horses on the other side of the lane, completing the rural setting. The gravel drive from the gated entrance continued onwards past the house, to where a number of single- and double-storey modern buildings surrounded what was left of the original rear garden.

As Paul followed the signposts to Visitors Parking, he noticed five men in lab coats playing croquet on the raised lawn that protruded like a large green tongue from the back of the old house.

Perhaps low-paid, insecure, contract-based work was the future of his agency too, he fretted – a rumour was circulating that the RSMSDA, a non-departmental Government body that reported to the Nuclear Directorate of the Health and Safety Executive (another non-departmental Government body), was to be sold within a year or two as part of the Government's ongoing privatisation programme.

All of a sudden, Paul felt uneasy in these surroundings for an entirely different reason. The treed backdrop reminded him of Pendlefield Manor, the Suffolk home of his wife's parents, Bernard and Dorothy Reynolds, and this brought to mind again the personal matter that had been troubling him.

Ann had become discontent with their living near Wantage, the market town nine miles to the west of Paul's place of work. She'd unsuccessfully applied for a trainee position at a local auction house, and her enjoyment of voluntary work in a charity shop had waned because of recent personnel changes. Advertised local job vacancies – posted by engineering companies needing administrative support, or by estate agents, pubs and shops – didn't appeal to her.

Three years younger than he, and with a History of Art degree, her aim had been to find work as a junior curator at a gallery or museum, or perhaps as a research assistant within an academic publishing house. Had the couple settled in Oxford, as they'd once envisaged, such careers would have been more accessible, but house prices there had been too high. Commuting to Oxford from the Wantage area would necessitate a twenty-mile drive each way, with some of the journey being on icy, winding roads in winter. Ann wasn't a confident driver and Paul had worried about her breaking down in an isolated spot while he was away on one of his numerous business trips, so he'd felt relieved when she'd finally stopped applying for jobs in the city.

Although her being married to someone unable to talk openly about his work was not unique in the wider community – the area had other research establishments too, some having similar Government ties and others owned by multinational companies – this was little consolation; the arising social barriers contributed to her unhappiness.

Their recreational activities predominantly comprised occasional outings and meals with some of Paul's married colleagues and respective partners. However, most of Paul's contemporaries at work were single and male. These partook in a social scene centred round the sports and social club that stood within the grounds of the workplace. Whereas Ann wasn't sporty at all, Paul occasionally played squash at the club. Those matches nowadays left him feeling guilty because they were another manifestation of their living in his world, not hers.

Perhaps worst of all, the hilliness of the area induced in Ann a feeling she described as akin to claustrophobia. Homesick, she had come to yearn for the "large sky" uniting the flat landscape of East Anglia.

The day before yesterday, while they were watching a Sunday evening nature documentary, she silenced the television and broached their moving to north Suffolk.

"It's not that crazy. It needn't affect your precious work," she said, angrily crossing her arms after placing on the coffee table her most recent purchase of antique silver – a tiny pillbox with an enamelled lid.

"Well..." Paul couldn't bring himself to look at her; not into those accusing brown eyes. The muted scene on the screen – a lioness gently pawing its cubs – was more appealing than *this* topic and somehow more relatable.

"I'm sure I will get a good position in Norwich. We'll see each other at weekends, which is what we do most of the time anyway," she continued.

"That's an exaggeration, Ann. Half of the time, or maybe a little more than that," he countered, while her use of *will get*, as opposed to the conditional *would get*, seeded itself in his mind.

"A little more than half *is* most! And it's bound to get worse because of your promotion. We can sell this house, and you can rent a one-bedroom flat in Didcot. We'll be able to buy a house as good as this one, but close to my parents. I've checked with a few estate agents – property's cheaper there because it's further from London."

"I suppose... I suppose we could look into *all* the costs of moving. There's a lot to think about," he muttered, picking up the TV remote control and turning the sound back on.

This procrastinating gambit prompted Ann to get up and head towards the back garden. The French doors reverberated after she'd slammed them closed behind her. Despite being petite, at just over five feet, of the two she was always the noisiest mover about the house.

Paul could vaguely appreciate the emotional attraction of coastal settings, having, himself, been born in Durban. Nonetheless the prospect of four-hour drives on Friday and Sunday evenings – the much-loved motorcycle would surely have to be replaced by a second car – between north Suffolk and his office in Didcot didn't appeal. Would he have the stamina to do this week after week after week after week, with no relief in sight?

Yet he sensed he had no choice if he was to avoid their marriage becoming poisoned by bitterness. Ann had been unable to establish a satisfying career, and she was right about being left on her own a lot of the time. And then there was all the work he was bringing home, too.

Hearing her normalise their being together just at weekends would have been heartbreaking without his memory of Ann once remarking how much easier starting a family would be with the support of close relatives and friends. Yet there were numbing moments recently when he wondered if she'd really ever said it.

The only parking place was next to a birds' mess-splattered, green E-Type Jaguar coupé that trespassed into the available bay.

After a contorted manoeuvre to extricate himself from his vehicle, Paul allowed himself a few seconds to admire the sensuous lines of the sports car. The likelihood of his ever owning one was surely zero – more than half his take-home pay was needed to cover the mortgage on their semi-detached house, despite the ten thousand pounds borrowed from Ann's parents towards the deposit. And of course, if they were to relocate and...

Finding a better paid job, either locally or in East Anglia, would be difficult with his specialised degree. And the way the economy was – widespread company layoffs, high unemployment, increasingly impotent unions – this wasn't a good time to be taking risks. He reluctantly turned away from the distinctive car and proceeded to Reception, which was in a nearby single-storey prefab building. The receptionist had to break off from her typing to attend to him.

As he moved to sign the Visitors Book, the young woman leaned forward and snatched it from the counter. "That's not necessary," she said, curtly. "Mr Maycross is still in a meeting in the Main House, but I know he's expecting you." Her face was slightly flushed as she placed the book next to her typewriter.

Paul looked at his watch – he was ten minutes early – and then headed towards the nearby waiting area, which was a poorly lit space furnished with an old sofa and a matching easy chair.

All he'd brought in his briefcase was a notebook and a selection of brochures describing the activities of his organization. There was a chance, he hoped, that he was here because of a misapprehension about the type of work undertaken nowadays by the RSMSDA. If nuclear-missile protestors could get this wrong, perhaps distant colleagues in other ministries could too. To occupy himself Paul began flicking distractedly through these familiar brochures.

Forty minutes passed before Patrick Maycross, a tall, puffy-faced young man with reddened cheeks, caught the crown of his head as he came through the doorway. His grey suit was creased and the fronts of his black lace-up shoes were scuffed. The knot of his striped tie was loose, and the waywardness of his black hair conveyed the impression that a side-parting was work in progress. He was carrying a worn, brown, leather medical-style bag, which was secured by a single strap fitted with a brass lock. Around his neck hung a lanyard bearing a laminated visitor's pass.

"You're Avery, I take it?" the physically towering figure said, proffering his hand.

After their shaking hands, Maycross proceeded past the reception desk and walked towards the corridor that led into the depths of the seemingly unremarkable building. Still looking straight ahead, he called to the receptionist, "We mustn't be disturbed."

Paul picked up his briefcase and followed the man from Whitehall, who he estimated as being about thirty years old, three years or so older than himself. There was something about the much taller man's manner that suggested he was different from the usual highflyer; it seemed as though Maycross was someone whose middling rank belied his importance.

Maycross was clearly a "water carrier" for Auberon Morrison, who Paul had ascertained, through conversations with his department colleagues, was indeed a highly ranked civil servant. A few of his colleagues thought that Morrison was currently attached to the Cabinet Office, another that he had joined the Home Office from the Bank of England. The consensus was the mandarin had a reputation for aggressively driving projects that required interdepartmental cooperation.

At the end of the corridor, Paul came to a large hall in the centre of which was a suspended, windowless structure that had a plaque bearing the words: SECURE ROOM 2. "In here," he heard Maycross call out. Paul ascended the five wooden steps leading up to the open grey-painted, metal door. As Paul entered, Maycross was looking at his watch.

Morrison's assertion that the Ministry of Defence was the largest client of the institute began to make sense now. In the far corner of the room was a shelf filled with softly humming electronic equipment. One of these had a gauge with its quivering needle pointing to ZERO.

The floor was covered with red linoleum. The furniture comprised a veneered table and an assortment of chairs that wouldn't have looked out of place in a village hall. Maycross's bag, which had a Gladstone opening, was standing open on the table.

"First things first," Maycross said, moving to close the door of what Paul had surmised was a surveillance-proof chamber.

After taking documents out of his bag, he said, "I require your signatures on these before I'm permitted to brief you. I know it's all a terrible bore, but there you go."

"Is that really necessary?" Paul said, sitting down.

"I'm authorised to temporarily raise your clearance level once you sign them." Maycross placed the thin bundle of three forms on the table in front of Paul. "Think of it as a promotion," he said with a boyish smile, as though he'd imparted a witticism that only an imbecile could not appreciate.

"Actually I've just had a promotion."

"That's what drew you to our attention." After a pause, Maycross continued, "But this is a *special* sort of promotion."

There was something about that last comment and the way it was said. Paul deduced that the prior intimation of friendliness had at best been provisional.

He began reading the uppermost form. It bore the title: "Ministerial Level Clearance for NATO Category-X Programmes". Much of the densely written text seemed to mirror the Official Secrets Act he'd signed three years ago, but with emphases on inter-Ministry communications and working with "the following designated NATO powers". After the latter phrase, "USA" had been typed into the provided space.

"But I'm not in the Foreign Office," Paul said, his mind lingering on the reference to the United States.

"Nor am I, come to that. Your current agency affiliation won't matter, once you sign the form below that one."

Paul watched Maycross rearrange the order of the forms with hand movements that seemed to mime this unexpected fluidity of Civil Service appointments. Gooch would have been appalled all over again.

The second form was titled "Special Whitehall Appointments – Temporary". The name "Patrick Maycross" had been entered next to "Management Lead".

"This indicates I'll be working directly for you," Paul said. "I'm not sure what my department head will think."

"He permitted you to come to this briefing, didn't he? Secondment of experts is not unusual when needs arise."

"I suppose so."

Paul hesitantly signed the first two forms with his ballpoint pen and passed them to Maycross, who countersigned them using the fountain pen he took from the breast pocket of his jacket.

The last form, printed on grey paper, was titled "Grandee Paragraph 5 Order – Special Measures/Programme COLOURLESS".

Certain phrases stood out – "... maintenance of deniability for the Government of the United Kingdom"; "no disclosure of the directed activities to unapproved third parties under any circumstances"; and "no acknowledgement or support will be available whenever such provision would conflict with the national interest."

Did Gooch know it would be like this? No wonder he looked startled, Paul thought.

"What does that signify?" he asked, pointing at the letters "U.R." printed on the upper right-hand-corner of the form.

"Unacknowledged Registry," Maycross replied. "Neither of us has the clearance necessary to know where that's located. Auberon will pass the form on to wherever it needs to go."

Paul continued reading. "You can't expect me to sign this."

"Things are moving quickly. The maintenance of favoured Diplomatic relations with our key ally is at stake."

"No employment tribunal would accept a document like this as being binding."

"Employment tribunal! That's very quaint of you, Paul. Grandee Paragraph 5 Orders transcend the purview of the judiciary. It will never be presented in a courtroom. A Public Interest Immunity certificate will ensure that. Our intelligence services don't take their trousers down in public the way the Americans did in Washington a few years ago in front of the Church Committee."

Exasperated, Paul shook his head. He didn't know what happened in Washington in the Seventies, but the mention of intelligence services added a new dimension to his concerns. "Can't you at least provide me with a hint about what you want me to do? Surely that's reasonable."

Maycross sat down, taking the chair at the end of the conference table. He leaned back and folded his arms. "All I can say is your link to

South Africa is helpful."

"But I don't know anyone there. I was a young boy when I came to England with my parents."

Maycross unfolded his arms and held out his palms towards Paul. "You needn't be concerned about any of that. Your having been born there provides cover."

"Cover for what?" Paul said, persisting.

Maycross massaged his right earlobe between his thumb and forefinger. He started to squirm, seemingly unable to find a comfortable position for his long legs. "Assuming you perform successfully, there'll be a special bonus – three times the maximum ordinarily permissible at your grade."

Maycross's voice had deepened on the phrase "at your grade". The condescending tone landed like a hammer striking a cracked bell. Nonetheless, a bonus equal to 60 per cent of Paul's new annual salary was tempting. It would remove a financial obstacle – after the deduction of tax, the money would still be enough to cover the costs of a move to Suffolk, including those for carpeting and decorating a new home. But at what risk?

Temptation vanished as Paul read the last section of the form. "This is farcical!"

He held the grey form towards Maycross and pointed at the final paragraph. "I'm to *commit suicide* using a to-be-provided capsule if confronted with the likelihood of mission-endangering interrogation –" and picking up on Maycross's mentioning of the intelligence services "– so it reads like something intended for MI6 or whomever. Why aren't you approaching it?"

Raising his voice for the first time, Maycross said, "Officially MI6 doesn't exist. Anyway, who is saying it isn't involved?" Staring towards the offending document, he continued, but now adopting a more emollient tone, "That wording's a catch-all formality. It spares us from having a hundred different versions. You wouldn't have been chosen if we weren't confidant that you possess the necessary qualities and expertise. In any case, no one in the Secret Intelligence Service possesses your skillset."

The way the lioness had bared its teeth in the nature documentary came into Paul's mind. He put the grey form back on the table, leaned to his side and picked up his briefcase from the floor. "Perhaps I should be flattered, but I'm not signing that."

"You've no choice!" Maycross exclaimed, lurching forward on his chair. "Not unless you want to be deported."

"I'm a British citizen, working for the Civil Service, the same as you."

"We're hardly the same. It would take one call from me for your passport and citizenship to be revoked with immediate effect."

Paul looked towards the grey door, which now seemed to be far away while somehow the room itself was becoming smaller, drawing him closer to Maycross. "On what grounds?"

"Irregularities could be discovered in your and your parents' immigration files. Unless you do as we require, twenty-four hours from now you'll be staggering round the South African veldt without food, water and money. When you make your way to the embassy, you'll learn they can't find a record of you and your parents having left that country. Details of your years in England and academic qualifications will be sealed away, unobtainable, in effect non-existent, so when official enquiries are made on your behalf, they'll prove fruitless. You'll be reduced to begging for cash-in-hand jobs on street corners, and that will just be the beginning of your problems."

From where had these convoluted threats sprung? The briefcase handle began slipping in Paul's perspiring hand, but he managed to sufficiently tighten his grip, preventing the case from falling.

"Evidence will be produced showing Soviet sympathies run deep in your family and that you've personally raised funds for African Marxist terrorists, or something topically sensitive like that – something that would invoke national security, so we're regrettably unable to answer questions, even from your wife. Her telephone will be monitored, and she'll be questioned at a police station about your involvement with a proscribed organization."

The reference to his wife added anger to Paul's turmoil. Confronted with unintelligible accusations, Ann would become confused and scared. Would she believe their lies? She knew little enough about his work as it was.

"I'll report your threats to my department head. I'll contact my Member of Parliament, if need be. I'll go to the press."

"There will be layers of D-Notices banning publication. No news outlet will go near it. If those Defence Notices aren't enough to deter your M.P., there will be steps we can take to bring him into line. We know the peccadillos of all the lobby fodder. Backbenchers are two a penny.

"As for your superior, he of all people knows it would be foolhardy to obstruct top secret Government business." Maycross shrugged his broad shoulders. "Otherwise he'll come to discover that he is suffering from a severe psychiatric disorder, one affecting his judgement. A malignant brain tumour won't be hard to explain in view of the many years he's worked in the 'glow team'."

Brain tumour? How could they go about causing such a thing?

"I've heard enough," Paul said, finally standing up. Only people who'd worked in the RSMSDA had earned the right to deploy the nickname "glow team". Its coming from Maycross was somehow more egregious than the increasingly bizarre threats.

Paul proceeded to the door and grasped the handle.

"I didn't come here alone! You won't get as far as your car," Maycross shouted.

"How will carrying out your threats achieve anything?"

Maycross stood up and approached Paul. "We'll have to find someone else – someone who *understands* their duty. But as your new role gives you access to an international network concerned with the movements of radioactive materials and you're now aware of the links of our project to the USA and South Africa, you'll soon be able to glean enough to pose a security risk." Pointing at the unsigned form on the table, Maycross continued, "If you persist in refusing to cooperate, we *will* ensure you are out of the way and discredited. The inevitable consequences for your relatives' lives will be collateral damage for which you'll be entirely responsible."

Relatives... Apart from his wife, Paul had just one close relative.

Recollection of a scene Paul hadn't thought about since childhood raised the awful possibility that Maycross's use of the phrase "Soviet sympathies run deep in your family" hadn't been extemporised.

Barely a year after the family immigrated, Paul's parents joined a branch of the Labour Party in south-east London. Two tall men who said they were from the police visited their terraced home about that time. Paul was sent upstairs and the sitting room door closed. He overheard one of the plainclothes policemen repeatedly say the odd-sounding "communists" word. Paul's father, the next morning, told his son it had all been a misunderstanding.

Had entries in a police report detailing long-ago concerns about his father's connections with politically motivated dockside agitators surfaced when the only child was screened for an RSMSDA job eighteen years later? Paul's father was dead, beyond reach, but his mother wasn't.

Chapter 2

Once Paul had conceded and signed the third form, Patrick Maycross's demeanour shifted again. With the first part of the odious man's unsavoury objective for this afternoon accomplished, it seemed to Paul as if magnanimity had summersaulted into their presence. Maycross was beaming and offering refreshments, "... before we really get down to things".

Maycross left the security chamber for a minute or so to request the coffees. When he returned they sat down, directly across from each other.

Paul knew the threats would return, should he not continue to do what was required. His earlier feelings of confusion and anger had given way to powerlessness, but there was something else too, another sensation – perhaps of betrayal.

After the receptionist had brought them a tray holding two cups of coffee, a bowl of sugar cubes, and a plate of shortbread biscuits, Maycross took a colour photograph from his bag. It was of the outside of a dilapidated industrial building.

"The New Jersey factory of Altabrite Timepieces Corporation was closed in the mid-Sixties because of concern about the safety of its radioactive, luminous dials. By then the company was already entirely dependent on export business, such as to the UK," Maycross said as he added six cubes of sugar to his coffee, his hand moving like a metronome.

He placed more photographs on the table. "These are very rare interior views taken when the factory was still in operation. They are not publically available. There was a lot of secrecy for commercial reasons, so very few eyes will have seen them. Fortunately, there is little in the public record about what went on there."

One of the photographs showed opposing rows of seated women, hunched forward, applying paint to watch dials. A long windowed glove box, which had air-extraction ducting, lay on the bench between them. Pairs of elbow-length gloves, secured at intervals along each side, protruded into the box. With their arms inserted in the thin gloves, the workers used fine-tipped brushes to apply the luminous paint.

"In earlier times, their counterparts at other companies licked the brush tips to keep the hairs together," Maycross said, grimacing.

"They weren't told about the danger," Paul said. "Some died from cancer of the jaw. Radium, like calcium, is a 'bone seeker' element." He'd studied the radium watch scandal as an undergraduate.

"It doesn't bear thinking about," Maycross said. "Anyway, production at Altabrite didn't commence until the demand for luminous watches surged during the Second World War. This demand declined after the war ended, and then, once safer coatings became available, the company couldn't compete because it had invested heavily to do things in this way. Altabrite ceased trading and the factory was abandoned."

There was something that didn't seem quite right to Paul in Maycross's account of the reason for the business collapse, but precisely what this was eluded him. Instead he asked a more pressing question: "Has the site been decontaminated?"

"The Environmental Protection Agency was looking into including the place on its new 'National Priorities List'. Such a listing would have put the site in investigative and consultative limbo for years, and led to negative publicity concerning a potentially valuable piece of land, which lies in the outskirts of New Jersey's now thriving Atlantic City. However, as there's apparently a long list of more problematic sites in need of Government-funded remediation and because this one has become commercially viable – a casino and hotel complex is to be developed – another clean-up route has been pursued. The work's well advanced, I gather. 'Everyone's a winner', as the saying goes, including the American taxpayer."

"I see, but why does any of that matter to us?"

Maycross paused for a few seconds with his lips pursed before saying, "It's only the 'what', not the 'why', with which you will need to concern yourself. Believe me, it's vital you remember that, Paul."

He gathered the photographs together and returned them to his bag before continuing. "You'll know more than me about what happened four years ago at the Three Mile Island nuclear power station in Pennsylvania. Well, four years *before* that, a similar event almost occurred at the Hartling Springs power station, which conveniently for us is also in the state of New Jersey."

The name Three Mile Island was infamous in Paul's profession.

One of the two reactor cores partially melted down because of a combination of equipment and procedural failings. The incident had made the nuclear power industry's assertions about the robustness of its safety procedures look hollow. The subsequent political repercussions hadn't been limited to America. Protests against every proposal for a new nuclear power station in the UK had become energized too. It had even made Paul question his career choice. At times he felt he was working in a doomed industry. Perhaps that was why he'd pushed hard for his promotion – an opportunity to finally resolve the waste storage issue, a matter often cited by "anti-nuclear" campaigners, and which was as much about public perception as it was about the science.

"I've attended presentations about Three Mile Island. Nothing was said about Hartling Springs," Paul said, concluding that if Maycross was mistaken about a matter as significant as this, his other information might be flawed too.

"I said it *almost* happened there. But there was no fallout from Hartling Springs. *Fallout?* Isn't that the word for the escape of radioactive muck?" Maycross rolled his eyes. "Scientific jargon's your bailiwick. In any event, apparently things didn't get out of control to the same extent."

"Do you want me to look into what happened and compile a report?"

Maycross chuckled before responding: "Heaven forbid. The growth plans of the USA nuclear power sector were already difficult to justify because of concern about potential overcapacity. The Hartling Springs episode was kept quiet to protect the image of the industry.

"Of course, that aim's been well and truly undermined by what has since occurred. Worse still, one of the new regulations following the Three Mile Island inquiry requires *independent* monitoring to be implemented at every American nuclear power station. Unless steps are taken before that monitoring's rolled out, the physical evidence still being concealed at Hartling Springs will come to light and precipitate an even more damaging public enquiry. Questions will be asked as to why there had been no issuing of safety bulletins, ones that perhaps could have prevented the incident at Three Mile Island. And of course, what's left of public trust in the integrity of the industry will totally evaporate during the ensuing scandal. Even the future of the remaining reactor at Three Mile Island still hangs in the balance, you know."

Paul knew Maycross was correct. A scandal of that nature would surely put an end to the viability of the industry in the West for at least a generation. With little enthusiasm, he said, "But public safety must always override everything else. Why didn't the power station report the incident to the Nuclear Regulatory Commission?"

"You're not about to become sanctimonious, I hope. What precisely was reported to the NRC is not our business. Doubtless, Hartling Springs supplied some kind of incident report or commercial argument to account for why the affected reactor was taken out of service," Maycross said dismissively. "This is realpolitik – things are done in the interest of the bigger picture." He smiled momentarily, savouring his own insightfulness. "As I was about to explain, unless certain measures are taken reputational damage will not be confined to the power company that owns Hartling Springs, which incidentally is also a campaign donor to important-to-us politicians. Worst of all, confidence in Her Majesty's Government will be trashed."

Maycross stared for several seconds at the rim of his coffee cup, as if waiting for it to give him a signal. His gaze eventually returned to Avery. "In early nineteen seventy-seven, while the nascent American Department of Energy was emerging from the regulatory organizations that preceded it, our then Government secretly signed a contract to dispose of the unreported Hartling Springs radioactive waste. The intention was to simply dump it at one or more of the sites we've long used in the north-east Atlantic."

"How much damaged fuel are we talking about?" Paul asked, apprehensively.

"I'll come to those details in a moment. Unfortunately, the mopping up at Hartling Springs has continued for rather longer than was anticipated because of tedious difficulties of some kind or other. In the meantime, the UK has, as you know, committed itself to no further ocean dumping. Those treaties governing nuclear waste disposal have come into effect. There are international bodies and environmentalist groups tracking what each signatory does in practice. In our case, Radiation Watch, No to Nuclear and Greenfuture are sharing resources. They have the coordinates of our ocean sites. At any given time, one or other of their brightly coloured ships keeps the locations under surveillance.

"Personally, I would still take the risk, but Auberon is adamant. UK representatives must be confident that they can look the other nations in the eye, so to speak, without being undone by photographs taken from wretched spy ships." Maycross absently began rotating his cup back and forth on the centre of the saucer. After a few seconds, he took his hand from the cup and said, "It's probably for the best – we would also be vulnerable to exposure by whistle-blowers. Whitehall's riddled with them. Similarly, we can't risk importing the material to the reprocessing centre at Sellafield because that site is also under intense scrutiny from activists."

Paul was appalled by the casualness of Maycross's reference to the difficulties apparently encountered during the Hartling Springs reactor clear-up. And worse, how could the Government have signed such a compromising contract in the first place? Had someone, six years ago, in the RSMSDA agreed? And if so, could that someone have been Fabian Gooch? Or was that a suspicion too far – a gold-plated reason to justify his dislike of Gooch?

"Damage to the national interest if the disposal contract were to become public knowledge would be incalculable," Maycross continued. "And in the meantime, Diplomatic cogs that shouldn't be connected simply aren't turning any more. The negotiation to acquire the latest nuclear-missile system for our submarines is being stonewalled, and there's only one possible explanation – perceived reluctance to honour the Hartling Springs contract makes us look like an unreliable security partner who, to use the colloquialism, 'can't walk and chew gum at the same time'." Maycross grinned again, savouring the trite imagery he'd conjured.

Paul looked at his neglected cup of coffee. The beverage would be lukewarm now, but his throat had become dry. He took a sip. Anticipating what was required of him felt like waiting to be hit by a bus.

Maycross took a sip of his sweet coffee, too. He added yet another cube of sugar and began stirring slowly as he resumed his account of the situation. "President Reagan's recent call for a space-based missile-defence system has made everyone jittery about our being left behind completely, security-wise. This is the worst time for there to be political friction, particularly over a matter as tedious as the one with which you and I have been landed. The good news is that there *is* a solution open to us, one that's highly unconventional. It has the advantage of bypassing the leaky corridors of Whitehall completely. However, pursuing it necessitates the utmost care to avoid the undermining of yet another strategically important relationship."

Seemingly waiting for the man from the glow team to light up, Maycross put the teaspoon down and stared at Avery.

Paul rubbed his temples. He could barely bring himself to utter the words: "You don't mean we're going to ship this waste to South Africa?"

"The whole affair's similar to playing three-dimensional chess. I devise the strategy, and you'll be on the chessboard moving the pieces. You have nuclear waste-management expertise and a background that will mask the purpose of your presence in that country. You'll appear to be someone visiting the land of his birth after many years away, perhaps thinking about returning to live there. That'll go down well – new blood and highly educated. Just avoid talking about their politics."

Maycross relaxed back in his chair, seemingly satisfied with the way in which he'd brought Avery to this stage of enlightenment.

"To be clear, you want me to not only manage the shipping and burial of highly dangerous reactor debris from Hartling Springs, but to also incorporate contaminated material from the watch factory site?"

"Exactly, but you really must *suppress* all curiosity about the latter matter. Am I still making myself clear?"

"But we don't yet have a robust storage solution for high-level nuclear waste. That's what my team and our counterparts in other countries are trying to establish."

"You're not being ordered to set up an official facility with all the bells and whistles that you RSMS characters pontificate about. Regard this as a dump-and-go job."

Paul felt the earlier sensation of disorientation return, but now accompanied by rising nausea. His hands had become clammy again. The air seemed to be leaving the room.

"We have confidence in you. You'll do as good a job as can be done in the circumstances," Maycross continued. "You'll be doing a great service to the country."

After swallowing biscuit-laden bile that had suddenly risen to the back of his mouth, Paul said, "And how am I supposed to accomplish all this? You can't just move radioactive cargo round America and then ship it to South Africa without all manner of permits and checks from various agencies. Also, it's going to require a team. And as for preserving secrecy..."

"Sensible questions at last. I'll begin with the American end." Maycross removed a pink folder marked TOP SECRET from his bag and slid it across the table. "Names of your contacts at Hartling Springs are in there. Don't talk to anyone not on the list and always be circumspect during phone conversations on public networks. They'll help you achieve whatever you deem appropriate for the removal and transportation of their waste. The details of the waste is set out on the last page. They don't need to know its destination. Remind them of that, if necessary."

Paul turned the pages until he came to the table that detailed nearly ten tons of "Fuel Rod Materials" and various large items under "Miscellaneous Equipment Components". The weights and radioactivity levels of the individual items were tabulated. Although he'd feared much larger quantities, it was clear that whatever had taken place had been alarming to those present.

Nonetheless, compared to the thousands of tons of "spent" nuclear fuel that had accumulated during the last twenty-five years from all the commercial reactors in America, the quantities of materials listed were seemingly inconsequential. He was on the point of voicing this when the significance of the heading of the last column in the table struck him – Serial Numbers. Every item had an engraved serial number, from which the name of the manufacturer, date of manufacture, inspection report references, power company client and the destination nuclear reactor could be identified.

Any attempts, Paul understood, to "lose" these materials in one or more of the so-called long-term dry-storage casks that he knew were being constructed at certain American nuclear power stations would necessitate successive safety managers being brought into the cover-up. Getting the waste items out of that country was the "best" solution, but why someone close to the UK Government had agreed to undertake this was perplexing. Paul didn't want to hear any more about *realpolitik* and *the bigger picture*. "Desperation" would probably be more accurate – 1976, the year before the contract was signed, was the year the then Prime Minister resigned and, with the economy in a desperate state, the Government sought a loan from the International Monetary Fund. It had been a period of national humiliation, although Paul, at the time a second-year undergraduate, had been too preoccupied with his studies and student life to pay attention to such remote matters.

He closed the file and stared at Maycross, who embodied everything he detested concerning privilege and arrogance. However, the man opposite him combined these with a quality he hadn't been confronted with before – the belief in absolute power and untouchability.

"With regard to the Altabrite site, you'll liaise with this person," Maycross said, stretching to hand over a business card. "He's your primary contact, after me of course, until all stages of the work have been completed."

Printed on the card was the name Vernon Blackwood, followed by a telephone number. Underneath was: **Continental Investment Audits**.

Paul turned the card over, looking for more information. "What sort of company is this?"

"Consider its initials."

Paul read the name again. Why was a core agency of the USA security apparatus involved? Wasn't its purpose supposed to be the countering of foreign threats?

"Not subtle, are they?" Maycross said. "Being deported to South Africa would be the least you would have to worry about if you were to get on the wrong side of them. I'm not sure I'd survive, either, come to that, so don't make a hash of things. Nonetheless, all the internal regulatory permissions you need will be forthcoming via Blackwood. You'll have to sign a few forms, no doubt, but I'm giving you all the authority that you'll require. Your cover when you are in America, should anyone look into the matter, is that you are attached to the British Embassy in Washington while undertaking a survey of the US nuclear energy sector."

"This is getting better and better," Paul muttered.

Maycross lifted a green folder – also marked TOP SECRET – from his bag and pushed it across the table. "The location of the disposal site. Three members of the South African Government are aware of what we've planned. They are being *extremely* well paid for helping us to legitimize your cover story and for discouraging prying eyes, particularly from the South African Atomic Energy Corporation. You'll have to coordinate the labour you will need through the on-site management. As I said – this is three-dimensional chess."

Paul opened the folder. The first pages, photocopies of newspaper articles from the financial press, gave an overview of the owner of the site, Willingham Corporation, which was described as an up-and-coming Anglo-African company specialising in the clearance and repurposing of "end-of-life" assets across diverse industrial sectors.

The mine was part of the original goldfields in the Johannesburg region. It was now undergoing decommissioning. The last pages in the file outlined an economic analysis of why the mine was *"not commercially viable despite the hopes for a reprieve when the Gold Spot Price spiked at the dawn of this decade. The establishment of a permanent storage facility for imported nuclear waste is, however, currently being investigated. If successful, this will provide a further welcome stream of foreign currency for the economic sanction-affected country."*

Fading schematics – marked as the copyright of the former owner, the Randkop Mine Company – showing the extensive tunnel and shaft network were provided in an appendix.

"I don't understand. There's mention here of a storage facility for radioactive waste," Paul said. "That makes things a lot easier—"

"Don't get excited. It's a cover story that we planted to make it seem that the material you're going to take there is part of a trial being undertaken by Willingham. As far as the official situation's concerned, the material is very low-level waste being used to establish 'proof of principle'."

"And once the so-called trial's over?"

"The venture will be judged uneconomic – such are the vicissitudes of commerce – and Willingham will move on."

Avery's mind was fizzing with barely thinkable questions.

"Now what?" Maycross asked.

"I'll have to go there before I do anything else, and scope out what is technically possible. The railways in Africa have a different track gauge to ours and the Americans'. There's also weight limitations to consider – radiation-grade containers can weigh over a hundred tons – and then there's the matter of what dimensions of container can be physically accommodated."

"That's all very well, but right now it's more important you demonstrate to Blackwood that the ball's rolling. We need visibility. You'll be flying to America in the morning."

"In the morning!"

"On Concorde. Your ticket's booked."

The mention of Concorde stunned Paul momentarily. It took him several seconds to dispel hitherto unimagined thoughts of supersonic, luxury travel. "Th-The South African end of this is far too vague. I need information about the geological stability of both the mine and the wider area, including interactions with water courses, and will require assurances about security. It'll need continuous monitoring. No one will be able to disturb the waste for thousands of years."

Maycross straightened in his chair. With an alarmed expression, he said, "Examine a ton of rocks if it makes you happy, but don't be under the illusion that this location can be rejected. I thought I made it clear that the safety regulations we have in the UK won't apply. You can't leave behind flapping flags bearing the radiation symbol. Just tip the awful stuff deep underground in such a way that no one is bothered by it for, say, eighty years, by which time we'll both be dead, the Willingham Corporation will be a footnote in the history of ruthless capitalism, and it'll all be someone else's problem."

Avery used his handkerchief to wipe perspiration from his brow. Trying to reason with someone prepared to endanger public health on another continent seemed pointless. "I need to at least contact the mine's management. Have the shafts and the access points been modified? The arrangement of tunnels shown in these diagrams isn't going to be suitable."

"Preparatory work's been going on for several months," Maycross said. "As for your concern about weights and sizes, I have someone there, on the inside. I'll obtain the answers for you before you leave in the morning. The driver taking you to the airport will give you a letter containing the information."

"Thank you," Paul said, almost in shock. He felt defeated.

Protesting further now might ease his conscience, yet it would also risk his and Ann's lives being ripped apart. Was there a way past Maycross to Auberon Morrison? Or would that make the situation worse?

"Your contact... If he's already looked into the shipping side of things too, it would be helpful to know those details sooner rather than later," Paul said numbly as he closed the green folder and put it, together with the pink one for Hartling Springs, in his briefcase.

Waiting to be dismissed, the closed briefcase on his lap, he had a flashback to the day he'd attended the first of what would be a sequence of three interviews for employment in the RSMSDA. If only he'd known that three years later he would end up in this cell-like room...

He looked up and tried to hold Maycross's gaze, willing the man's awful smile to return and transform into laughter. This would all be revealed as some kind of loyalty test, surely. Or perhaps as being an assessment of how he'd function under pressure in his new research role? Would Gooch do that to him?

But Maycross's expression remained impassive. "Just remember what I said about the officials we've bribed. You will have allies in high places watching your back."

"Who owns Willingham?" Paul asked impulsively.

"Who do you think?" The awful smile finally returned.

Chapter 3

Paul Avery took his seat for the Wednesday, late-morning flight on Concorde from London Airport to New York's John F. Kennedy International Airport. Maycross had made it clear no expenditure was to be spared when time could be saved. Maycross had gone further, asserting that the *appearance* of being committed to fulfilling the Hartling Springs contract was of as much importance as making actual progress.

To this end, Maycross had provided him with a Government credit card having a credit limit of one hundred thousand pounds, so he could deal with "situations as they arise" – whatever that meant. The contrast with the miserly expenses permitted when he'd travelled abroad on routine RSMSDA business couldn't have been starker.

Seemingly regarding the compliant scientist as now having ascended to the right sort of collegiality, Maycross had confided, "Don't be afraid to treat yourself and your wife. Under the circumstances, no one will look closely. Ask salespeople to be creative with descriptions. Just keep things simple for the Treasury. It will defray your outgoings against the non-departmental allocation of your agency. And don't give a thought to old what's-his-name... Gooch. He's not in the loop. This is above his pay grade."

The driver who'd collected Paul from his house had handed him two envelopes. The one marked **Urgent** had contained a Diplomatic Passport in Paul's name and a form advising Customs officials of his Diplomatic Privilege, covering his carrying of instruments and papers for official government business. The second envelope was still unopened in Paul's inside jacket pocket. He would read it later, when his mind was properly awake.

Paul declined the offer of champagne from the female flight attendant. Sipping iced orange juice, he gazed at the field of clouds stretching out far below in all directions. Before returning to his worries, he touched the small oval windowpane and was surprised by the warmth of it.

Restricted by the Official Secrets Act and the documents he'd signed at the Tobe Institute, he'd told Ann the story that Maycross had contrived as a broader variation of the "energy sector analysis" cover being used for the trip to America – as part of an energy-related diplomacy programme, he told her, he would be ensuring conclusions from the enquiry into the Three Mile Island disaster informed the running of the power station that was approaching completion near Cape Town. The fact that nuclear power station design wasn't within his sphere of responsibility didn't come up – the extent of his technical ingenuity was never questioned by Ann.

It were as if he'd dipped his soul into Hell. If he ever were to tell her the truth she would despise him for not having confided in her from the beginning. "If you'd heard Maycross, you would have known there was no choice," he could imagine his future-self pleading. The possibility of her loathing him in the future was preferable to what could happen if their unsettled relationship was tested now.

Ann had quickly – too quickly – said she'd go to stay with her parents until he had finished the wretched task. He talked her out of the idea, although it would have made perfect sense. She'd be safer, surrounded by family and friends. "It's far too soon to think about doing that," he said. He should have encouraged her to go. But if she went, would she want to come back?

Scientists were supposed to discover answers to the most difficult of Life's mysteries. There was no mystery about Maycross; Maycross knew all the answers but none of the questions. There had to be someone... not Gooch, definitely not Gooch, someone he could turn to. But who could override a Grandee Paragraph 5 Order, seemingly an extrajudicial mechanism by which those truly controlling the State could pursue whatever they deemed necessary? Perhaps it derived from a Second World War emergency power, preserved because of the Cold War with the Soviet Union? Or perhaps it dated back much further than that, but under different guises? All he knew was that in practice the borderlands of national interest through which it slithered were as dark as the inside of a Gladstone bag.

Two digital displays, one to each side of the aisle, at the front of the cabin section clicked forward to Mach 2, eliciting excitement among the passengers. For Paul it signalled an unwanted fate was coming towards him at twice the speed of sound – faster than a rifle bullet. He had to use both hands to steady the glass of chilled juice.

***

Following an expedited passage through passport control at JFK, Paul proceeded to the baggage hall to await the appearance of his suitcase. He'd retained his briefcase as cabin baggage.

The handles of his luggage bore Diplomatic Privilege tags, also provided by Maycross, ensuring the items bypassed x-ray machines. The related credentials identifying him as a senior appointee to the British Embassy in Washington DC had enabled Paul to satisfy the check-in and border-security questions at London Heathrow with verbal assurances about the safety of the luggage contents.

His briefcase contained the confidential briefing documents and the details of his contacts. In his suitcase, padded by his clothes and other personal effects, was a delicate item he'd retrieved last evening from his office, after returning the pool car. It was a state-of-the-art energy-compensated radiation detector that had a composite plastic, steel and lead casing, a selection of "radiation-filter" discs, and a leather satchel containing the battery pack required to power the device. (Unlike a basic Geiger counter, the device was capable of displaying radiation dosage rates, taking into account the energies of the detected gamma rays.)

Laden with his briefcase and the retrieved suitcase, Paul walked through the Customs area and into the busy Arrivals Hall. Among the waiting greeters were people holding up cards. One of the cards had AVERY scrawled on it.

As Paul made his way through the crowd, he soon noted how the attractiveness of the individual holding the card was a perverse counterpoint to the ugliness of the plan that brought him here. First he saw her shoulder length, champagne-blonde hair, then her face with its pale-blue eyes and its fine nose, and then her thin lips bearing a pale-pink shade of lipstick. She was wearing a high-collared white blouse and a fitted beige trouser suit – attire suggestive of some kind of uniform – that suited her slim frame. Whoever she was, she clearly wasn't Vernon Blackwood and he was thankful for that. He didn't feel ready to meet Blackwood.

"I'm Paul Avery," he said, estimating the woman to be about the same age as himself.

“Mr Blackwood sends his greetings.”

“I’m due to meet with him this—” Paul stopped himself from completing the sentence. Maycross’s warning about the need to be careful about what he tells to whom came to mind.

“You’re staying at the Bennington, right?”

“Yes.”

“Okay, follow me, Dr Avery,” she said, turning towards the exit.

Once outside he paused for a moment to enjoy the cool early morning air. The local time was almost an hour earlier than his departure time from London Airport. Concorde was an aviation miracle, but even it couldn’t take him back twenty-four hours and reset his life to the way it was before the meeting at the Tobe Institute.

The young woman had parked her silver sedan at the end of a line of yellow taxi cabs. As Paul approached it, he noticed a card with the words “Priority Parking. New York Transit Authority” in green print, lying on top of the dashboard.

It beats displaying a notice saying CIA, Paul thought.

“The trunk release is under the chrome strip,” the woman said, getting into the driver’s seat.

The trunk lid had a boomerang-shaped aerial mounted on it. Paul felt around for the release button. He placed his two items of luggage in the trunk and closed it.

Settling into the front-passenger seat, he said, “It’s kind of you to collect me. I could have taken a taxi.”

“Cab drivers keep a lookout for Concorde clientele, hoping for large tips. The fewer people who notice your arrival the better.”

“Good thinking,” Paul said, nodding. “Maintain a low profile,” he added, remembering Maycross’s parting remark about not drawing attention to himself. Maycross had been correct in reminding him this was, after all, an existing requirement for his being an employee of the RSMSDA.

“I’m not telling you how to do your job,” she said, pushing the key into the ignition slot.

“All advice is welcome,” he responded, following this with a fleeting smile. “I should have asked your name.”

“Shannon Lennon,” she replied as she steered the car away from the kerb, making room for a returning cab.

His gaze was drawn to the object that was between the dashboard and the centre armrest. "I haven't seen a car telephone before – not in real life. Apart from radios in taxis, I mean."

"They're regular issue," she said. Apparently sensing her answer had fallen short, she added, "It's not always possible for me to get to a payphone."

Thirty minutes later, between mid- and up-town Manhattan, Lennon brought the car to a stop outside the twenty-storey Bennington Hotel on the east side of Lexington Avenue. Two grey-jacketed porters were already approaching as Paul and Shannon opened their doors.

Taking his luggage from the trunk, Paul said, "Thanks for the lift." He put his suitcase down and reached out his hand for her to shake.

Touching his palm in a perfunctory manner, she said, "I'll be joining you and Mr Blackwood this evening, Doctor."

"In that case, I'll see you then," Paul said, allowing his suitcase to be taken by the nearest porter while declining to release his hold on the briefcase. He'd heard of colleagues' careers being blighted through their losing of Government papers.

Without further pleasantries Lennon got into her car and pulled away, out of the shadow of the hotel and into the busy city traffic. A haze of exhaust fumes and tarmac dust hovered in the morning air. Car horns sounded as the traffic adjusted.

Paul gazed up in appreciation at the dark-grey façade of the Bennington Hotel with its countless windows. He forced himself to follow the porter who was now scurrying away with his suitcase.

***

From his tenth-floor room Paul telephoned Ann to tell her he'd arrived safely. She sounded more distant emotionally than she did physically – the connection was so clear, she could have been in the adjacent suite.

Ann had seemed sullen and suspicious during his departure – just as she was on the telephone moments ago – as if she believed he'd contrived this trip to avoid further discussion about them relocating to Suffolk. All of a sudden, moving far away from the RSMSDA headquarters struck him as being desirable and his concerns about it misguided. He resisted the impulse to call her back – "What changed your mind?" she would press, and in his anxious state he'd blurt out the truth.

Paul had only slept three hours last night before setting off for London Airport. Tiredness was finally overwhelming the adrenalin surge he'd been living on since leaving Stoke Poges yesterday. He forced himself to read the information in the second of the envelopes that had been passed to him by the chauffeur this morning.

The envelope contained a photocopy of a telexed message, which presumably had been transmitted securely overnight to Maycross by his contact in South Africa. The heading had been obscured with bands of black ink. The information, in block capitals for clarity, answered his questions about the sizes and weights of containers that could be accommodated. A smaller piece of paper provided a Washington DC telephone number that was "only to be used in an emergency". This inference that he was not entirely alone here brought a measure of comfort for the first time. (The telephone numbers that Maycross had dictated to Paul at the end of their meeting – a 24-hour Whitehall messaging service and his direct line – were seemingly for reporting, not for requesting assistance. "Leave messages whenever possible. It won't always be convenient for me to take calls from you," had been Maycross's instruction.)

However, the relief obtained from the promise of assistance through the DC telephone number shrivelled as he inspected the final item in the envelope – a small round-bottomed metal tube, similar to those used to hold replacement leads for propelling pencils. The top of the tube was sealed with a wax-like material.

Paul shook the tube close to his ear. The tinny rattle was suggestive of a glass capsule – presumably a cyanide capsule – bouncing against the inside of the tube. The suicide clause in the third form that he'd signed was evidently more than the formality Maycross had asserted. Paul folded the paper with the emergency DC telephone number and then rolled it around the metal tube and slid them into a compartment in his wallet.

He looked again at the telexed message. The last sentence stated that suggestions for shipping options would follow soon. The message ended, not in capitals, as: **Looking forwards to seeing you here soon, old boy. Love and Kisses, Tom**

Paul wondered if Maycross had coerced this *Tom* character too. Whoever Tom was, at least he was someone in the field, someone who was evidently connected to hard realities. He was also surprised that

Maycross had remembered his questions and took this as a warning that, despite the appearance of insouciance, the Whitehall man shouldn't be underestimated. With the new information and inferences rolling through his mind, Paul undressed and freshened up in the bathroom before trying to nap.

After a restless hour he got up and decided to go for a walk. It was the first time he'd been to New York. The reputation for crime was worrying. Pushing aside this concern – it was daytime after all and, anyway, being hospitalised by a mugger wouldn't be the worst thing that could happen if it were to halt his work here – he slipped on a pair of fawn, loose-fitting trousers, a black T-shirt and a lightweight, green windcheater. Before leaving, he transferred most of the cash from his wallet to the wall safe.

Sauntering in the downtown direction, he soon came across, on the other side of the street, an arcade-like corridor. Intrigued, he walked along the arched corridor until he reached what turned out to be the high-ceilinged interior of the Grand Central Terminal, a setting he remembered from numerous films.

The yellowish-brown stain, resulting from cigarette smoke, that covered the domed ceiling and the poor natural light throughout the huge space combined to produce an enveloping dinginess. Nonetheless, the architecture and layout of the marble-floored concourse remained imposing.

As the need to travel from the station could conceivably arise, he attempted to gather his bearings. In front of him, in the centre of the concourse, was the circular information kiosk. On the kiosk roof was its distinctive spherical clock with four faces. The large hands of this clock reminded him of the floor-indicator arm of the elevator in the Durban hotel where for about a year he'd stayed as a boy with his parents. And that brought to mind his father, who'd died from pancreatic cancer five years ago in northwest London – among his father's unfulfilled desires had been visiting Manhattan.

Paul hadn't telephoned his mother to tell her about this trip. Keeping her informed of his foreign travel was an expectation of hers. He'd found deceiving Ann enough of a strain without worrying his mother as well. Maycross's warning about his relatives becoming collateral damage unless he cooperated came back to him again, bringing with it a pressure in his gullet, as if he had a squash ball lodged there.

The truth was he didn't yet know how long this trip, the first of possibly several, would last. The meeting this evening with Mr Vernon Blackwood should bring the first step towards clarity.

Chapter 4

Paul, wearing a different navy-blue suit from that he'd worn during the flight from London, was sitting on a stool at the hotel bar, nursing his second tumbler of iced sparkling water, when a plump barman in a silver-and-black silk waistcoat approached.

"Your party of two's arrived, sir. They've gone through to the restaurant already."

After placing a ten-dollar bill under his tumbler, Paul straightened the knot of his red tie and headed in the direction of the "Explorers Room", the larger of the two restaurants in the hotel.

It was eight in the evening, but Paul's stomach was convinced it was 1.00 a.m. the next morning. He wasn't anticipating sympathy for his jet lag.

The dining room décor had a geometric, art deco-like theme with white and black as the dominant colours. It took only seconds for Paul's gaze to locate the almost luminous hair of Shannon Lennon. She was sitting at a corner table that was lit by a wall lamp, which had a multi-coloured glass shade evoking fanned peacock feathers. The man seated beside her was wearing a dark-grey suit. The way he was holding the menu card concealed his face.

Shannon noticed Paul approaching and stood to welcome him. Gesturing towards her companion, she said, "This is my chief – Vernon Blackwood."

Blackwood, a portly man of about fifty, put down the menu card. "Sit, pal," he said, ignoring Paul's attempt to shake hands.

Feeling slighted, Paul sat down opposite the couple. "It's nice to meet you, Mr Blackwood," he said, trying to remain in character as the dead-keen envoy from Britain, the awaited sanitiser of God-knows-what mess some over-reaching political faction had committed his nation to covering up.

Blackwood's sun-damaged complexion and the artificial blackness of his hair struck Paul as suggestive of someone who'd appeared in one too many Forties swashbucklers. But there was nothing theatrical about the yellowing, bagged eyes with heavy lids – Blackwood's gaze had a reptilian quality.

"How's Morrison?" Blackwood said, taking up the menu card again.

It took a few seconds for Paul to understand Blackwood was referring to the Whitehall mandarin whose telephone call had instigated his presence here. "He's fine."

"You don't seem so sure."

"Auberon works in a different ministry. At least he was, I mean, until my current secondment to his, er..." Nervousness was pushing words out of Paul's mouth before they'd been properly weighed.

"Next time you see him, tell him for me he's a goddamn prick."

Paul looked anxiously at Shannon Lennon, who remained expressionless.

"What's been the hold-up over there?" Blackwood continued.

From Paul's viewpoint everything, literally, had moved at supersonic speed. He wasn't responsible for any perceived delay but would have to accept the criticism nonetheless. Recalling Maycross's comment about the importance of appearing to be making progress, he said, "Temporary organizational issues – all now resolved."

"Organizational issues, my maiden aunt's ass. We get on with things, whereas your people wallow in moral indignation. You all have an insatiable need to be spanked by nanny for the transgressions of Empire. You're always overthinking things and looking centuries back for inspiration."

Anxious to change the subject, Paul signalled to a distant waiter. After turning back to his guests, he said in his politest manner, "Well, I'm pleased to be here now, Mr Blackwood."

"You goddamn should be. This'll be a cakewalk. You just have to stand around and sign forms on behalf of your little queenie. You don't look old enough to do jack, but you can manage that, right?"

"I do have a number of questions first," Paul said, suppressing anger at the continuing jibes, particularly that now they were directed at him instead of at his organizational masters.

The waiter, wearing a gaudy pea-green blazer, approached.

Paul and Shannon picked up their menus.

Blackwood said, "Fillet of beef – medium rare. Tell the chef to go easy on the potatoes. And I'll take the garden salad with French dressing."

Paul settled for a Caesar salad and Shannon opted for the fish.

"Not much appetite?" Blackwood said to Paul.

"My stomach's still on UK time."

"That'd be the Victorian era," Blackwood retorted drily.

Before Paul could put together a quip invoking Concorde, Blackwood said, "Okay, shoot. Your questions."

"Are we going to discuss this here? I mean it's very public."

"Lots of Brits stay at this place. You don't stand out. In any case, many of these people around us work for me."

Paul looked at the nearby tables. The couples occupying them appeared to be engaged with their own concerns. "What is the role of your company?" he asked.

"That of a facilitator. Next question."

"I've been provided with the names of the contacts at the power station, but as for the former watch factory site, I don't have one yet."

"She's sitting opposite you."

Paul hesitated, not sure what he'd assumed about Shannon. "Okay."

"Next question."

"Do I work from your offices, or do I set up my own?"

"We're not in the office rental business. Sort things out with Lennon here."

Paul nodded, wondering if he'd have to work from hotel rooms. "We'll need to obtain radiation-grade railway containers. I understand the contract with my government stipulates we cover such expenditures, but I'll require interstate transport licences and eventual export approvals. Will the Department of Energy provide these to me directly?"

Blackwood leaned forward, his brow furrowed. "Listen to me closely, my educated friend. You *do not* contact the fucking DOE. All documentation you need will be obtained via Lennon."

"So she'll coordinate with the DOE?" Paul said, his gaze flicking towards Shannon.

"She'll coordinate with *me*! Goddammit, who was the fool that briefed you?"

It was clear Blackwood was in charge of keeping everything "off the books". Given Paul's own government's role in the bribing of South African politicians, it shouldn't have come as a surprise that the American involvement was at least as shady. Paul felt as if he were swimming in the presence of sharks.

Avoiding mentioning the name of *the fool* in question, Paul said, "I was informed that the Environmental Protection Agency isn't involved. Also, it was made clear that I'm to take my lead from you, Mr Blackwood."

"Damn right you will," Blackwood said. "You remember that *one* thing and we'll get along," he added, seeming to relax at last.

Maycross had revealed his own fear about Blackwood's reach. Had the two met? Whether they had or not, Maycross was right to be scared. The man sitting opposite was unlike anyone Paul had previously encountered.

After taking a deep, steadying breath, Paul turned to Shannon, who'd hardly spoken. "It appears you'll have a lot of work to do, too."

The sommelier approached at this point, creating a welcome diversion. Blackwood perused the wine list before ordering a bottle of a fine Bordeaux red.

"Enough with the questions. Tell me about yourself, young man," Blackwood said as the sommelier moved away. "This is New York City. Did you look around already?"

Paul recounted his impressions of the architecture of Grand Central Terminal.

"Notice anything about the door to that information booth?"

"I can't say I did. I think I was too impressed with the clock to notice."

Blackwood sneered. "There *is* no door – not in the usual sense. Entry's via a staircase under the floor."

"Oh."

"Free advice – *always* look for the way out."

Again Paul glanced nervously at Shannon. She smiled awkwardly, seemingly equally uncomfortable.

From this point onwards the mood gradually eased as the food arrived and the wine flowed. More bottles were ordered. Paul felt the alcohol taking effect but welcomed the relief from tension this brought. The background babble grew as the restaurant filled. Blackwood seemed endlessly fascinated by the trivia of Paul's life, such as how a "science guy" ended up hitched to an "art lover" and collector of antique silver. He struck Paul as a practitioner of a sinister discipline in which he was the only master, equally distant from both the Sciences and the

Arts.

After coffee and dessert, Paul realised Blackwood had revealed nothing relatable about himself. He might just as well have been a hologram. As for Shannon, she'd been largely subdued throughout, only interjecting intermittently, seemingly in the manner of ventriloquist's dummy made of porcelain.

Just after eleven, the two from Continental Investment Audits departed, leaving Paul and his expense account to deal with the bill. The wine charge was nearly five hundred dollars for the three bottles they'd consumed.

Chapter 5

It was 8.45 a.m. on Thursday morning when Paul Avery, wearing the suit he'd travelled in yesterday, checked out of the Bennington. Slanting sunlight was throwing shadows on to the buildings across the road. A porter helped him lift his luggage into the trunk of Lennon's car. Paul handed over a five-dollar tip.

"Will you be staying here again, Dr Avery?" the porter asked.

A question Paul found difficult to answer. He'd fallen asleep quickly last night, but experienced an alcohol-induced rebound during the early hours. In the subsequent listless state, he wrestled with the shapeless unknowns of what lay ahead, and this left him with the headache that persisted still. "I'm not sure," he finally said.

"Well, have a nice day, sir."

"No time for a tour," Shannon said, driving southwards across the broad intersection with 42nd Street. Having placed the jacket of her black trouser suit on the back seat, Shannon looked more prepared than her passenger for the journey ahead of them. "We've a long drive and Times Square's a snarl-up according to traffic bulletins. At least we'll pass the Empire State."

That skyscraper landmark, one Paul's father had longed to see, came and went too quickly as they proceeded west along 34th Street. The truncated view out of the car window was neutralising the impact of the cityscape – the base of one tower could have been that of any other. Paul promised himself he would visit the iconic building one day and see it properly, as much for his father as for himself.

Will London look anything like this one day? A juxtaposition of multiple towers with the skyline of historical London seemed unimaginable.

After crossing the intersection with 9th Avenue, Shannon took a right turn, signposted Lincoln Tunnel Expressway, on to the snaking walled ramp that turned into an underpass before bringing them back to the surface at a point where the traffic was joined by that from other ramps. The westbound expressway gradually narrowed to two lanes as it dipped below street level and then below river level. The sky seemingly scrolled upwards as they approached the rectangular mouth of the Lincoln Tunnel's concrete-faced northern tube. With his thoughts of visiting the Empire State Building already fading, Paul sensed he was entering a tunnel with no end.

Within seconds they were travelling beneath the river towards New Jersey and a meeting with the project manager from the company, Banville Construction, hired to clear and develop the former site of Altabrite Timepieces Corporation.

***

Shannon was barely more disposed to engaging in small talk than her boss had been. Nonetheless, last evening Paul had heard her say she grew up in a small New England town, the name of which she omitted. She'd joined Continental Investment Audits upon graduating from college six years ago, having majored in American Literature. Paul, to his surprise, felt suspicious about the veracity of any of this; through playing squash he'd developed alertness to the ways opponents would try to feign where they would direct the ricocheting ball, but lies about someone's background had never occurred to him before.

She wasn't more forthcoming this morning, eventually confining her remarks to where they were headed – Atlantic City, situated in Atlantic County, on the Jersey Shore in the southern part of the "Garden State".

"Atlantic City's the only place in New Jersey where casinos are permitted," she said. "A state referendum was held a few years ago and the legislation was approved. Since then hotels have added casinos and new resorts have been built, with more on the way, like the one at our site."

It wasn't clear whether her use of "our site" was a manner of speaking about the job they were engaged in or something more literal. Pondering the implications of it proving to be the latter diverted Paul's attention from the passing scenery. He vaguely registered highways bisecting built up areas, their stopping at toll booths, and the navigation of intersections taking them from one freeway to another.

Maycross had mentioned Atlantic City during the briefing at the

Tobe Institute. Being named after an ocean made the place sound grandiose, although probably not to the snobbish Maycross. Probably to Maycross America was an ex-colony that had evolved into a heaving blob possessing a troublesome excess of power and wealth.

"We'll be there in less than an hour," Shannon said, "unless you want to stop here. You need the restroom?" They were approaching the service plaza on the Atlantic City Expressway, the road cutting a north to south diagonal across the heart of Atlantic County.

Paul looked at his watch. They'd been driving for more than two hours since leaving the hotel.

"There's restaurants too," Shannon said, pointing towards the low buildings lining the median of the expressway.

"I-I'm fine," Paul said absently. The summer of 1980, when he'd driven with Ann to the sweltering south of France, had come into his mind for no obvious reason.

"Okey-dokey," Shannon said, accelerating past the service plaza.

Soon they were slowing again, this time for a toll plaza.

Paul had by now realised what had reminded him of France – the seemingly endless French motorways, also driven on the disorienting right-hand side, had similar toll booths and service areas.

For miles thereafter the expressway was fringed by cedar trees and shrubs. The sun was high now and the narrow shadows beside nearby cars were deep black, like inked edgings. It was easy for Paul's mind to retreat to the honeymoon camping trip and making love to Ann on stony ground beneath a cheap tent to the nightly droning of cicadas.

As they slowed for yet another toll plaza, Paul forced his thoughts to leave the embrace of the past. If there were to be more such days, he would have to make sure that Maycross received only favourable reports.

Buildings started to appear ahead – a gas station and a store of some kind. Off to the right, he had a momentary view of the sea. "Is this Atlantic City?"

"Almost there. We're passing through Pleasantville."

Pleasantville? It sounded like the name of a place in a comic strip. He shook his head. Was he now a hapless character in such a comic? And if he were, who was holding the cartoonist's pen?

A roadside sign announced Atlantic City. A moment later an overpass cast a black gash across the expressway.

"See! That's how *our* casino will look," Shannon said, pointing at a set-back billboard that was covered with illustrations of the planned resort.

COMING SOON. THE MAYJAK RESORT – THE FUTURE OF OFF-BOARDWALK ENTERTAINMENT.

Paul quickly turned his head to scan the advertisement. It was Shannon's saying the "our" word again that formed the momentary soundtrack for the second it took them to pass the eighty feet long billboard.

A couple of miles later the expressway crossed an expanse of water. Taller buildings ahead were silhouetted against the blue of the ocean; they were entering the main part of Atlantic City.

Shannon turned off the expressway, looped back westwards on to Mayjak Drive and then entered the parking lot of a modern looking hotel that seemed more salubrious than its immediate low-rise surroundings. Paul noticed the name emblazoned atop the building – Banville Plaza.

"Banville owns hotels too?" Paul asked.

Shannon didn't respond as she looked for a parking spot.

"Will it run the casino, as well?" he persisted.

After turning off the engine, Shannon finally answered. "Not the casino, but the hotel operation will be Banville's."

"Who's putting up the money for the casino?"

"Why are you asking?" she said, looking at Paul.

"In case the name comes up during the meeting."

"Gilmeed. Heard of it?" she said, turning to retrieve her jacket from the back seat and shoulder bag from the rear footwell.

"I don't think so. Is it big?"

"Pretty. It's a Nevada-based outfit with a casino in Vegas."

"I see."

With the bag and jacket now on her lap, she said, "Stick to the technical stuff, Paul. No one here's going to expect you to be an expert on anything else."

Shannon Lennon had, albeit in a less terse way, reinforced Maycross's "It's only the 'what', not the 'why', with which you need to concern yourself."

"That suits me," he said.

She stared at him, holding his gaze. "We need to stay focussed when talking with these people."

They got out of the vehicle as it started to rain. Shannon quickly put on her jacket.

After checking in and leaving their luggage at the hotel front desk, they took an elevator to the top floor, the twelfth. Paul still had his briefcase.

The elevator opened on to a spacious lobby bounded by frosted glass partitions. **Banville Inc.** was stencilled in gold lettering on the glass. Beyond the partitions lay a brightly lit open-plan office suite. Distant voices could be heard over the hum of the air conditioning.

"How may I help you?" the young man seated at the reception desk said. He appeared to be barely out of his teens; his undersized suit looked as though it had been bought a couple of years ago for high school-prom night.

"Shannon Lennon and Paul Avery to see Mr Fransen," Shannon said.

"He might be at lunch. Are you expected?" the young man said, running his finger down a list of names. "I'm not finding you."

"I assure you he *will* want to see us," Shannon said.

The receptionist picked up the telephone receiver and pressed a sequence of four buttons on the telephone front panel. "Visitors for Mr Fransen – Shannon Lennon and Paul Avery. They're not on the list."

Following a terse exchange, presumably with Fransen's secretary, the receptionist told Shannon and Paul to proceed to Conference Room 3. He pointed to the room, which was located at the side of the lobby.

"There won't be a record of us coming here," Shannon muttered as they walked towards the designated room.

Paul recalled how the receptionist at the Tobe Institute snatched away the Visitors Book before he could sign it. There'd be no evidence of that meeting having taken place either.

He followed Lennon into the conference room. It was plusher than the unusual one at the Tobe Institute and free of shelves stacked with electronic jamming equipment. They sat down next to each other at the long conference table.

Several minutes passed before George Fransen, a lean man who was wearing a white shirt and a striped tie, but no jacket, joined them. He closed the door behind him. The company name was stitched on Fransen's tie and on the pocket of his shirt. Balding and with a moustache, he looked to be in his late fifties. His shirt sleeves were rolled halfway up his scrawny forearms. Nicotine had yellowed the fingers of his right hand and the side of his greying moustache.

"You two are gonna solve our little problem, I hope," Fransen said with a smile as Paul and Shannon rose to greet him. Fransen's height was closer to Shannon's than Paul's.

They sat down, with Fransen taking a seat opposite his visitors.

Addressing Paul, the Banville man said, "So you're the guy we've been waiting on. How soon can you get the stuff moved?"

"I don't know yet, sir. I gather the factory operated for more than twenty years. How much radioactive waste was found?"

"There are ten units, ready to go," Fransen replied, snapping the words out. He began drumming his palms on the table. "All of it collected from one area of the site."

"One area? So I'm clear, what units are you using?" Paul asked, wondering if Banville had developed its own way of quantifying radioactivity. As for "ready to go", Paul didn't know how to respond to that. Blackwood had told him that he "just had to stand around and sign forms on behalf of his little queenie." Dismissiveness was clearly a trait Blackwood and Maycross shared. Combining the watch factory waste with the nuclear plant waste would be a complex matter that seemingly he'd have to arrange by himself.

"I dunno what you Brits call them. Most of the guys just call them dumpsters. Strictly speaking, they're Champs. Fifteen feet long. You can see them filled with cardboard, food waste and so forth out back of this hotel. All our locations have them. They've multiple uses."

"But not for transporting radioactive material, of course," Paul said, hoping he was being teased. A nervous smile caused his lips to stretch and relax like a settling spring.

"Why not? They're strong and damn near rainproof!"

"I'm sorry, sir, but if you're being serious, it's... I-I mean it's highly unconventional," Paul said, struggling to contain himself. He began to wonder about the nature of the safety procedures that had been observed during the site clearance work.

"We're a can-do outfit, son. Champs are a standard inventory item. We order them five at a time."

"How secure are they against spillage?"

"Jeez," Fransen said. He smirked at Lennon, as though inviting her participation in putting the anxious egghead in his place. Looking again at Avery, he continued, "We're talking about teensy particles that were used in old dial paint" – he gestured with his right hand, the tips of the thumb and forefinger touching like a pincer – "mixed in with a whole mess of dirt, broke concrete, lumber and what-have-you." Fransen then pointed to his right wrist. "I've worn this Altabrite watch every day for thirty years. The numbers and the hands barely shine in the dark nowadays."

"That's because the light-emitting part of the pigment has degraded, but the dial remains almost as radioactive as when it was painted," Paul said, staring at the watch.

"You don't say?" Fransen said, bringing the watch close to his face as if expecting to see the radiation pouring from it.

Paul considered Fransen's routine wearing of the timepiece as unwise. The Linear No-Threshold model, which he'd been taught at university, asserts that exposure to ionising radiation is harmful, no matter how low the dose, and that the biological effects are proportional to the dose and accumulative – although the precise severity in any given instance will be subject to chance. Although this "LNT model" had critics because it ignored cellular healing, Paul still ascribed to the pragmatism of the theory.

Not wanting to further provoke Fransen, Paul returned to his line of questioning: "Have you found intact containers of the pigments?"

"Let me just check on that." Fransen stood up and walked towards the corner of the conference room where a waist-high chilled drinks cabinet stood with a telephone on top of it. He picked up the receiver.

"I've other questions too, Mr Fransen."

"José led the clean-up. You can talk to him yourself."

"Thank you," Paul said, standing up in anticipation of taking over the call.

Fransen began speaking in a Spanish dialect. After a minute or so, he handed the receiver to Paul. "His English is a little rough, but he's a good man."

Frustrating minutes passed as Paul tried to make himself understood. It wasn't clear whether José possessed radiation measurements, nor whether hazard suits were being worn on the site.

Paul turned to Fransen. "I'm not having any success. I need to visit the site anyway, ideally this afternoon. Please tell José that I want to meet him and take measurements of the radiation levels."

Fransen took the receiver from Paul and said something to José before ending the call.

"Let's not complicate things here. I need you to provide me with an address to transport the Champs to. You can do just whatever you please with them from then on."

"Mr Fransen, the radium in the paint emits alpha particles that will be absorbed by nearby body tissue. The emission of those alpha particles transforms the radium into atoms of radon. Radon's a radioactive gas that *also* emits alpha particles, but at a higher rate, so if it's breathed it poses an even greater risk to health. In fact, radon is probably leaking from that watch of yours."

Fransen threw up his arms. "I know all about radon! The land there's free from granite deposits. There's no damn radon problem. Don't go inventing one. I've worked construction long enough to experience the delay its presence causes."

"It's not seepage from rock that I'm talking about, sir. I need to evaluate what I'm going to be taking charge of, so I can work out how to manage any risks there may be to public safety. After I've done that, of course we'll discuss the next steps."

Fransen, his face reddening, said, "Your job's to free us to get on with what we do best – making money." Seemingly in need of a cigarette, Fransen fruitlessly patted his trouser pockets and then the pocket of his shirt.

"I only meant—"

Interrupting Paul, Fransen said, "I need to speak with Miss Lennon. You'll have to wait outside."

Paul looked at Shannon for support.

"We won't be long, Paul," she said in an even tone that sounded forced.

Paul picked up his briefcase and left the room, closing the door behind him. There was nowhere to sit in the lobby, so he meandered back towards the elevators. He could hear Fransen's voice, raised but rendered unintelligible by the dampening of the conference room wall. It felt like the worst possible beginning. Maycross would be furious...

What had he said that was so unreasonable? He'd tried not to appear condescending, but this was always a risk when talking to lay people. How could he be expected to take ownership of radioactive waste without being allowed to first inspect it?

Several minutes passed before Paul heard footsteps behind him. Turning, he saw the receptionist proffering a brochure.

"From Mr Fransen's secretary, sir."

"Thank you."

As the receptionist returned to his desk, Paul began turning the pages of the brochure for the "Waste Champion Series 7 Enclosed Receptacle". *Unbelievable*, was the only thought he could muster as he considered the accompanying diagrams. The container was indeed somewhat similar to the skips used for waste removal in the UK, but had an enclosed form.

It was fifteen feet in length, as Fransen had stated, six feet in width and six feet in height, and had a nominal capacity of fifteen cubic yards. Steel rings, secured by bolts to the corners of the container roof, permitted engagement with lifting hooks.

The walls at the ends of the container sloped outwards from the bottom before – at about four feet from the ground – sloping inwards to meet with the roof. The inward sloping part of each end-wall mainly comprised a hatchway, for the purpose of filling and emptying the container. Each hatch was closed by two mating, hinged doors.

When Shannon emerged from the conference room, her expression continued to give nothing away. She joined Paul by the elevators. "Wait till we're *outside*. We'll talk over lunch."

***

The rain that had greeted their arrival at the hotel had passed over, leaving a few puddles behind. Their lunch was to consist of hotdogs, bought from a mobile kiosk parked in a side street, fifty yards beyond the side entrance to the hotel parking lot. Most of the queuing customers wore the uniforms of hotel employees; others in oil-stained overalls had strolled over from a nearby car-repair workshop. The banter between the two groups of regulars was good-humoured.

Paul picked up one of the two greaseproof paper-wrapped hotdogs from the counter while Shannon paid the vendor.

"We can eat over there, where they won't be able to see us,"

Shannon said, nodding towards the low wall bordering the rear of the parking lot.

Paul considered the indicated position and then looked up at the top floor of the building. "Why would they watch us?"

"I can almost feel the scope sweeping my head."

"Scope? As on a rifle?"

"They're watching. That's all that matters."

"What if they are? They build and run hotels."

"They're also a front."

Avery's expression conveyed his confusion.

"Relax. They need us – at least for now," Shannon said, her voice sounding far from relaxed. She began walking.

"No one's going to take on *your* organization," Paul said, catching up with her.

With a barely suppressed smile, Shannon considered Paul's allusion to her employer's true identity. She said, "But these people are connected to a business with a much longer history of getting its way."

Questions jostled in Paul's mind as the couple reached the chosen spot. Paul put his briefcase down. They rested back awkwardly against the thigh-high wall.

"What happens next?" he said, frowning at the relish that had oozed on to his tie.

"Visit the factory. That's what you want, right? The place is just south of that hoarding we passed." Shannon manipulated her hotdog to avoid a similarly messy problem. She looked at her watch. "At three – sharp. We have around ninety minutes to kill first."

"How did you manage to persuade him?" Paul asked, still dabbing the tie with his handkerchief.

"There's conditions. One, you don't get to speak to José."

"But he's been overseeing the work."

"Two, you can't take any measurements until the containers have been removed from the site. Fransen won't have the workforce there spooked."

"It's as if... Don't they know what they've been handling?"

"My guess is not the specifics. Many could be illegals, so they won't be union."

Paul folded the greaseproof paper over what was left of his hotdog. "You mean there's no one to stand up for them. I don't know what to say, Shannon."

"The paint's not really as dangerous as you made it sound, is it?"

"You don't want it in your lungs or eyes, or on your clothes and shoes so that you take it home and expose your family to it."

Something in Paul's response made Shannon hesitate. It were as if she was seeing something in this new "colleague" she hadn't expected. "My guess is you don't know much about demolition." There was less assertiveness in her voice now.

"I've attended spillages of radioactive material, but it's true I haven't visited a demolition site. Have you?"

"It depends how you define 'demolition'." Shannon put the final piece of hotdog in her mouth and watched Paul as he considered her reply. Screwing up the paper wrapper, she said, "Look, many of the workers could be walking girders without harnesses on their next job. Danger's relative when a paycheck's at stake. Some will be in so much pain from old injuries they have to shoot up just to make it in each morning."

Paul took a deep breath and exhaled through pursed lips. The exploitative conditions Shannon had described led his thoughts back to the question Maycross wouldn't answer, but now from a different direction – why was Shannon's employer involved in the development of a casino complex? If it needed money, surely it just had to submit a compelling reason for a budget increase – something the pathetic board of the RSMSDA had notably failed to present to his own government.

"I have to find a shop where I can buy rolls of plastic film – the type decorators use to protect carpets when they're painting walls – and a lot of heavy-duty adhesive tape," he said. "Afterwards, I'll come back here and get changed before going to the site."

Shannon, frowning, stared at Paul. "I don't know if there are any stores like that around here. We can't ask the concierge. He'll be one of Fransen's informants. We could ask at that garage across the street." After a few seconds, she added, "What was that about us needing to change our clothes?"

"I didn't say *us*. I didn't mean..." He'd intended to ask someone manning the hotel front desk to arrange a hire car for him, so he could drive to the demolition site alone. Having Shannon beside him would, however, he accepted, reduce the risk of being refused entry. "I have disposable overalls, gloves and filtration masks in my suitcase. If you're coming, you must put them on, Shannon."

Shannon shook her head, clearly stunned. "Remember what you were worrying about a few minutes ago – about them shooting us?"

Paul suggested a circuitous route back to the main entrance of the hotel – one taking them through the fenced-off area at the rear of the building, where the waste was put out for collection. Dressed in smart attire, and with Paul's briefcase, they looked out of place as they approached the garbage containers.

"Great," Shannon said sarcastically, stepping round a greasy patch on the ground. "At least we can toss our hotdog wrappers."

Paul knelt and using his fingernail scratched rust from the side of one of the black containers. According to the brochure, the container body was fabricated from one eighth of an inch-thick steel plate and the hatch double doors, located around shoulder height at each end of the container, were from one sixteenth of an inch-thick steel plate. Such thicknesses could stop the passage of only a small fraction of the gamma radiation – a form of radiation similar in nature to high-energy x-rays, but arising from changes within atomic nuclei as opposed to changes within electron energy levels – that would also be emitted by the radium-containing pigment.

The hatch doors at one end of the container were open. When closed, these double doors could be secured together by a bolt. Although certainly sturdy – Paul estimated that each three feet wide door weighed about nineteen pounds – the lack of rubber seals along the door edges would enable leakage of hazardous radon gas.

"Fransen told us they're rainproof," he said, dropping the remnant of his hotdog on to the damp heap of cardboard boxes covering the bottom of the container.

Shannon did likewise with her scrunched wrapper. "Rain can get in if it's left open like this. Anyhow, as I remember it, he only said that they're 'damn near rainproof'."

"I didn't know 'damn near' meant 'not at all'. I'll add an American-to-English dictionary to my shopping list."

Shannon ignored the jibe and remained where she was as Paul headed round to the other side of the waste container.

When he returned, she asked, "What do you think?"

“I’m thinking I’ve a lot of shopping to do.”

Chapter 6

It was nearly 3.30 p.m. when Lennon's car came to a stop outside the chain-link double gates of the site that was formerly the home of Altabrite Timepieces Corporation. The tilted stance of the vehicle betrayed the weight of the newly bought items in the trunk.

During the short drive to this site in the western margin of Atlantic City, Shannon had described the surroundings as being the product of a pre-war attempt to create an industrial zone on drained, low-lying coastal land. It had been aimed at business ventures belonging to the "out-of-sight, out-of-mind category". The only active premises now comprised workshops, storage yards and a small strip mall – whose stores had grille-protected windows filled with sun-faded gadgets that featured years ago in cheaply made television advertisements. The signage on the solitary food store was in Italian.

The panel-board fence protecting the site had plywood patches where break-ins had occurred during the years since the closure of the watch factory. Absence of radiation-hazard signage didn't come as a surprise to Paul. Clearly the local population wasn't to be apprised of the site's past. There were, at least, KEEP OUT signs and warnings about the security patrols. There was no obvious reason for passers-by to loiter, and the closest stores were a few hundred yards away where exposure to wind-borne radioactive particles should be low.

Paul shook his head, demeaned by his having to accept such pitiful consolations. All he could do, he told himself, was avoid adding to the harm already caused by the mishandling of the radium residues. The effects of which might take decades to show up in the local cancer statistics. Any eventual attempt to prove a causal connection would no doubt be contested between Government and Banville lawyers before they agreed to blame the long-retired or deceased board members of Altabrite – who probably had been granted immunity anyway because their luminous timepieces supported the war effort.

They'd changed into casual attire at the hotel and donned the disposable, hooded overalls that Paul had insisted they wear.

Pinned to their clothes, beneath the left breasts of the flimsy, white overalls, each wore a badge containing pieces of film that recorded exposure to differing forms of radiation. Any positively-charged alpha radiation they encountered would be stopped by the material of the overalls and so couldn't be recorded by the badges. However, as alpha radiation was also strongly absorbed by intervening air, it would only be hazardous when its source was either close to their skin or airborne and breathed in. For now, it was gamma radiation that most concerned Paul. This highly penetrating form of radiation, plus any negatively-charged beta radiation (comprising high-energy electrons), would reach the badges by passing through the material of their overalls.

Concealing the badges was a compromise – it undermined their effectiveness, but would make it quicker to dispose of the overalls in an emergency and would be less confrontational for a workforce ignorant of the hazards to which it was being subjected.

"We're late," Shannon said, staring ahead.

"It took us longer to find the right shop than I'd hoped. There was no choice as we're clearly not going to get much help from the Banville people. I'll have to get very hands-on," Paul responded self-consciously. "I'm sorry."

"You apologise too readily," Shannon said, not moving her gaze from the entrance.

"No, I don't." That comment irked him, perhaps because he knew he had a mountain of apologising ahead of him.

"Maybe we *all* should apologise!" he snapped.

"Vernon won't like that attitude."

"Are you going to tell him?"

Shannon turned and looked at Paul. The splayed collar and shoulders of the oversized overalls bunched round her. "You're a real worry, Dr Avery."

"I am?"

A broad smile replaced her frown as she, seemingly enjoying his discomfort, threw her head back. "What with all your talk about you getting hands-on, I just don't know what to think."

Paul felt himself blushing. "Those overalls suit you."

She looked down, pushing her chin into the folds of the garment. "You think?"

"Your hood dropped back. You need to pull—"

A tapping sound came from the driver's window. A hefty, bearded man in a grey military-style jacket was crouched and staring in.

Shannon wound down the window, prompting the security guard to straighten up. "Shannon Lennon and Paul Avery. We're expected."

The man turned away and spoke into his walkie-talkie. After a few seconds the motorised gates began to slide open with a screeching sound.

"Go ahead," the guard said. "Park by that cabin," he added, pointing to a custard-coloured structure. "The foreman's in there."

Shannon engaged the automatic transmission and drove the vehicle forwards slowly. The gates started to close behind them. After advancing thirty yards, she stopped alongside the cabin identified by a sign as the Site Crew Office.

In front and to their right sprawled what was left of the watch factory. In places, only steel girders remained standing; in others, sections of walls still stood. Much of the roofing had been stripped, leaving the site open to the weather. Sounds of hammering and pneumatic drilling, and of men shouting came from the ruins.

Paul noted the absence of canopies or other temporary structures for containing the dust being disturbed by the clearance work.

"We must put these on," he said, holding up pairs of elasticated, sock-like shoe protectors.

"Are you serious?"

"Remember what I said about the workers taking traces of the radioactive paint home? I'm putting them on. You really should, too."

In addition to having changed their clothes, Paul and Shannon had also changed their footwear before leaving the hotel. She'd put on flat-soled shoes and he was now wearing work boots with metal toecaps.

Shannon reluctantly took the proffered shoe protectors that, like the overalls, were made from plastic-laminated paper. She had to slide her seat back before she was able to raise her feet sufficiently to pull the coverings over her shoes.

"Let me do all the talking," she said as she got out of the car.

They went up the steel steps to the cabin and opened the door. Inside, beyond a waist-high bookcase topped with wilting potted plants, five men – two wearing hard hats – were sitting round a desk. They were playing cards.

The creaking of the floor as the visitors entered attracted the men's attention. One of the men wearing hard hats stood up. He was on the far side of the desk, chewing gum, and seemed to be in charge. Like the others, he was in his late thirties or early forties.

"The aliens have landed," he said, scratching his stubbled chin. "Either that or you're Fransen's rocket scientists."

The man to his left chuckled but fell silent when his boss grasped his shoulder.

"I'm Shannon Lennon and this is my associate Paul Avery. He needs to inspect the garbage containers that Mr Fransen wants removed."

"Maybe that explains why he's dressed as the Easter Bunny, but what's your excuse, honey?" the foreman said.

"Miss Lennon's assisting me," Paul said.

"I bet she is, limey," said the man who'd laughed earlier.

The foreman picked up a rolled blueprint and thwacked his wisecracking workmate's head with it. "You give the tour, Herb. Take 'em down to the Red Zone."

Staring at Shannon, Herb said, "That suits me just fine, Marv." He slid his chair back and stood up. As he walked towards the visitors, the heels of his boots clomping noisily against the bare floor, he reached inside the front of his overalls and withdrew a comb from his shirt pocket. Combing his mussed, thinning hair back into place, he said to Shannon, "You're too cute to be staring at trash. Why don't you hang out here a while?"

"I need to talk to José too," Paul interjected.

The visitors' legs were concealed from the workmen by the bookcase. Paul felt Shannon's right sole pressing hard against the side of his left boot.

"Fransen said somethin' about you maybe wanting that," Marv, the foreman, responded, his mouth working his gum. "You'll make do with Herb."

Paul moved to protest, but refrained as the pressure from Shannon's foot increased.

"Keep your eyes on 'em, Herb" Marv said loudly. "We don't need civilians walking where they shouldn't when a wall comes down. Bring 'em back when they're done, so we can do the paperwork on those Champs."

“This ain’t no amusement park,” Herb muttered, walking past the visitors. He took his hard hat from a wall peg, opened the door, and proceeded down the steps.

Paul and Shannon followed their guide out of the cabin.

“Time’s money here. You start keeping that in mind,” Marv shouted.

Standing by the open trunk of Shannon’s car, Paul called out to their unenthusiastic escort, “Hold on a moment, Herb! We need to take these with us.”

The irritated demolition worker trudged back and considered the contents of the trunk – mainly comprising rolls of plastic film and boxes of gaffer tape. “You wanna toss those away?” He pointed towards the half-demolished factory building. “We got trash containers over there we can use.”

“These are for wrapping around the Champs that were filled with the... the special waste.”

“Why do you want to do that? They’re ready for taking away.”

“Uh... r-regulations.”

Herb shook his head and stared at Lennon.

“It’s what it is,” she said, shrugging. “Regs.”

“There’s no shortage of those, I guess,” Herb said. He took off his hard hat and scratched the back of his head. “Too far to carry and the suspension on this fancy sedan won’t make it over the ruts. I’ll tell one of the guys to bring it to you. Leave the trunk unlocked.” Pointing south, he continued, “In the meantime, keep walking in that direction. Stay close to the fence. Like Marv said, stuff’s coming down all the time. The Champs you want to see are at the far end.”

“Thank you, Herb, but I’ll take a couple of the things with me,” Paul said, reaching into the trunk.

“Your funeral, pal.”

When Paul straightened up, he was holding in his left hand an orange instrument, cylindrical in shape at one end and rectangular at the other. It was about the size of a large vase and had a hinged leather handle.

Shannon’s eyes widened with alarm.

“What’s that thing for?” Herb said.

Paul looked down at the weighty item, almost as if he were suddenly unsure what it was himself. "Well, uh... It's a—"

"Inventory recorder!" Shannon said, interrupting her companion. "Each container has to be assigned a shipment number, which we will generate with that."

Herb stared, his eyes narrowing, at her. "That doesn't make sense."

"Regs," Paul said, hoping the word would work its magic again.

"So *you* say, limey." Herb put his hard hat back on and started walking towards what was left of the factory. "Stay close to the damn fence!"

When Herb was out of hearing distance, Shannon said, "I didn't see you pack that. Is it what I think it is?"

"If you think it's a radiation detector, you're correct," Paul said, reaching again into the back of the trunk. This time he withdrew a leather satchel that had a long strap. He placed the strap over his right shoulder so that the satchel rested tautly against his hip. "This holds the power supply."

Shannon slammed the trunk closed. "Fransen insists that you wait for the containers to be moved first."

"You may have agreed to that, Shannon, but I didn't. I'm not going near containers filled with radioactive material without the means to take measurements."

Exasperated, Shannon said, "Let's get this over with. When we're challenged, I'll do the talking. There's a lot more for us to worry about than radiation." She started to turn towards the fence that protected the western boundary of the site.

"Wait, Shannon. Please hold this while I connect the power lead to it," Paul said, holding out the instrument for her to take. "It's heavier than it looks."

"You're not kidding," she said, taking the weight. "What's it made from? Solid lead?"

"A good guess. Some of its metal casing is lead."

Paul tugged the end of the battery lead out from a flap in the side of the leather satchel and pushed its connector into the mating socket on the radiation detector.

"Thanks," he said, taking the instrument back.

He slid off the metal cap covering the cylindrical probe end of the instrument and stowed it in a pocket inside the satchel. After he'd clicked the power switch to the ON position, the reading on the digital display shot up to a level about five times that expected for naturally occurring background gamma radiation. As Paul had feared, the site decontamination work hadn't been thorough.

As he followed Shannon, Paul monitored the fluctuating reading. The size of the site became apparent after they'd walked about a hundred yards; Maycross's old photographs hadn't conveyed the amount of land belonging to Altabrite. Only now could Paul visualise how the planned gambling resort, as illustrated on the billboard they'd passed this morning, could be accommodated.

To their left, the remains of the watch factory had given way to a swathe of weed-pocked asphalt and then to a rubble-covered region where a second building had evidently stood. This building, its outline revealed by the footings of the demolished external walls, had evidently been larger than the watch factory itself.

After looking round to check they weren't being watched, Paul strode across to where the half-buried concrete blocks denoted the destroyed building's western foundations. A weathered door lay among the rubble. The rusting enamelled plate that was screwed to the door bore the words:

DIAL PAINTING UNIT
OFF-LIMITS TO ASSEMBLY PERSONNEL

Paul considered the sprawling ruins again. In addition to remnants of internal walls and expanses of broken-up concrete, he could now distinguish machine parts jutting from the ground like broken teeth.

"We can't stop here," Shannon said in a harsh whisper, startling Paul.

"The company painted its own dials. It had to keep the timepiece making and the dial painting separate. But why didn't it simply buy in the luminescent dials from specialist producers?" This had been the nagging question that had eluded Paul during the briefing from Maycross.

Shannon considered the scene for a moment, seemingly trying to see what he was seeing. "It's obvious you didn't volunteer for this job. You're like a calf among coyotes, Paul. I *know* how it works. You were pressured by someone."

He stared at her, unsure whether to feel insulted or consoled.

She continued, "Look, as far as environmental officials are

concerned, there was *only* an assembly operation here, one using pre-painted dials. We can't let what we're doing raise questions about that. The EPA already has a major clear-up on its hands at a site that belonged to a producer of radium paint. That place also happens to be in New Jersey, the northern part – in Essex County."

"Raise questions!" Paul exclaimed. He shook his head in frustration. "I need a couple of minutes," he said, stepping over the line of concrete blocks and on to ground that was once inside the former dial painting unit.

"Don't act crazy! Come back."

Moving the radiation detector from side to side, he advanced cautiously. The gamma radiation level increased to thirty times the normal background level. When Fransen said the waste containers had been filled with rubble from one area of the site, he must have been referring to around here. Before the demolition work began, someone must have been brought in to pinpoint the spots with the highest levels of contamination.

Paul turned a knob on the instrument to change the display format from "Radiation Dose" to "Counts per second". He removed a metal radiation-filter cap from the end of the probe, knelt and held the instrument close to the ground. The reading shot up to several thousand counts per second as alpha particles, which would otherwise have been absorbed as they passed through even a few inches of air, entered the probe. With his fears confirmed, and taking care not to kick up dust, he slowly walked back to Shannon.

"The controls Altabrite had in place must have lapsed when the business closed. No one should be working here without protective clothing and breathing apparatus. The site should have been marked out as a grid and cleared one square at a time. Millions of dollars need to be spent on topsoil and debris removal. Ten waste skips are nowhere near enough for this. Three hundred radiation-grade containers would be nearer the mark."

"There's not going to be millions of dollars, Paul. There was just José's crew, and their work's finished. The big bucks will be for construction."

Paul stared at Shannon. It were as if Vernon Blackwood had just spoken through her.

"The more you see, the less you're going to like it," she said, turning away.

Paul reinstated the metal cap on the end of the probe before disconsolately following. The instrument reading, only applying to detected gamma radiation again, returned to the earlier level.

Catching up to Shannon, he asked, "What did you mean when you said I was like a calf among coyotes?"

Shannon took a moment before answering. She seemed reluctant. "You remember Vernon's advice – after you talked about the information booth at Grand Central?"

"He said something about always looking for the way out."

"Altabrite was bankrolled by a crime family that still had a mountain of cash from the liquor operation it ran during Prohibition. That money had to be laundered through legitimate enterprises having the potential for high returns. One of the investments that went sour was this one. The management tried to diversify into outdoor equipment such as luminous compasses and pocketknives, but the marketplace had moved on."

"*That's* who you were alluding to back at the hotel – a crime family!"

Lennon nodded. "For the family, time often provides a way out. Its bosses sooner or later die, usually violently, but they are replaced by the most ruthless of the next generation. There's more permanence in the governance of crime families than you'll find at any Federal institution. A gambling resort here will bring much more money than was lost."

Paul stopped walking and looked again towards the remains of the flattened buildings. The land not to be given over to a parking lot would be covered by tons of marble floor, rows of flickering slot machines and plush gaming tables, conference suites, a chandeliered hotel lobby, bars, shops, themed restaurants, entertainment lounges, and hundreds of guest rooms.

Money, he now understood, was expected to gush geyser-like for an *alliance* of organized crime with a faction of a major USA intelligence agency. In return for his help in removing the crudely collected radioactive debris, Blackwood and Lennon would somehow provide the documentation required for the passage of the hushed-up Hartling Springs' waste out of the country. These were the sordid details Maycross had kept from him.

"What is it?" Shannon said, unease in her voice. "Have I really shocked you?"

"You mentioned 'permanence'." Paul pressed a switch on the side of the radiation detector, rendering its readings audible. Instead of counting gamma rays silently, the device made a tearing crackle. "Radioactivity will persist here for more than ten thousand years. Make sure they don't stint on concrete for the new foundations. It's a good absorber."

Shannon took on a pensive look.

Paul continued, "Better still. Your military has places for this type of radioactive waste. I recall reading about a storage facility near Niagara Falls."

"Military?" Shannon shook her head. "Layers of paperwork. A different command structure. That would take too long and be out of our control. We're not supposed to operate in the field on American soil. The operation would become public, defeating what we're trying to accomplish."

Layers of paperwork... Paul had been worrying about this. Maycross had said something about giving him all the authority he needed to sign "clearance forms". Blackwood had said, "You just have to stand around and sign forms on behalf of your little queenie." Even the foreman here had referred to the paperwork on the Champs needing to be done. The Department of Energy would expect to receive an international transfer record for contaminated waste being shipped to the UK, a modest amount of radioactivity commensurate with the clearance of an out-of-the-way site that was formerly used for "timepiece assembly". And a site-reinstatement document would have to be conjured up, verifying everything was in order for construction to proceed. Officials looking too closely into the provenance of these documents would end up floating in a river. Blackwood would make sure of that.

Two days ago, during the meeting with Maycross, he'd been pathetically naïve. Not any more... Paul pressed the radiation detector switch again, and the instrument fell silent.

Chapter 7

In a row at the south end of the site stood Fransen's "Champs" – ten Waste Champion Series 7 enclosed receptacles. A wooden spike, painted red and hammered into the ground, stood sole sentry duty, distinguishing them from identical containers used elsewhere on the site.

As Paul and Shannon approached what the foreman had referred to as the Red Zone, they observed a black pickup truck entering through the rear gate, in the eastern section of the fence, across from them.

The noise from the truck engine and the smoking exhaust disturbed a large, dark-plumed bird that had been hopping between the tops of the containers. Its reddish-orange beak speared the air as it took to the sky, revealing a white underside and trailing pink legs.

"What kind of bird was that?" Paul asked.

"An oyster catcher, a wading bird," Shannon replied. "You can see a lot of them near here. I'll take you—"

"But it shouldn't be *here*," Paul snapped angrily

"O...kay," Shannon said, stretching the word as if to say, *Don't blame me.*

With the pickup approaching them, Paul's concern about encroaching wildlife spreading radioactive dust far and wide had to be put aside. He concealed the radiation detector, holding it awkwardly behind his back.

The brakes of the dented pickup squealed as it came to a stop twenty yards from the row of containers. The driver's door opened. A middle-aged man with black hair and a thick moustache lowered himself from the cabin. With his left leg seemingly locked at the knee, he limped to the rear of the pickup and unbolted the tailgate. Pointing at the flatbed, he shouted, "You want? Okay. Come."

Without waiting for a response, the driver returned to the front of his truck, but this time to the passenger-side of the cabin. He took a cigarette carton and a book of matches from his shirt breast pocket. After removing a cigarette, he tore off a match and struck it against the heel of his right boot. He took a deep draw on the cigarette and leaned back against the truck door.

Shannon started to move towards the pickup. "You were correct about us not getting much help."

"It's interesting he's chosen *that* spot to wait," Paul said. "It's as though he wants to have the truck between himself and the Champs."

Shannon stared at the driver for a moment, considering Paul's remark. "The workers may be desperate, but that doesn't mean they don't do what they can to protect themselves."

"I hope you're right, Shannon."

Avery and Lennon pulled themselves on to the back of the pickup and began to push the rolls of plastic film and the boxes of gaffer tape off the flatbed. The items thudded to the ground.

After they'd got down, Paul called to the driver. "Thank you."

"Sí," the driver said, tossing away the butt of his cigarette. He limped round to the driver's side of the cabin and clambered in.

Shannon and Paul watched the pickup depart; the still-open tailgate clattered against the rear of the truck.

"He couldn't get away fast enough," Shannon said.

"I wonder if that was José. I should have tried to strike up a conversation."

"You don't speak Spanish. Anyhow, I doubt that was him."

Once the pickup had turned left on to the road running alongside the eastern perimeter, Paul said, "Before we do anything here, we must put on the rest of our protective kit."

He disconnected the power cord from the radiation detector and rested the instrument on top of one of the boxes containing the gaffer tape. From the deep pockets of his overalls, he withdrew goggles, vinyl gloves and a dust mask. Shannon watched him put the items on. She hesitated before doing likewise.

After checking that Shannon had correctly tightened her hood and mask, he said, "These masks won't stop us breathing radon, but they'll filter out harmful dust." He pulled up his hood, picked up the radiation detector and reconnected the power cord. "Wait here while I collect the readings."

Working his way along the row of containers, starting from the end closest to the rear gate, he secured those hatch bolts that had been left in the open position. Satisfied that the hatches were bolted, he turned to Shannon. "It'll take a while for me to collect adequate readings. Watch out for that Herb character."

"You're going to rile Fransen," Shannon said, her words muffled by the dust mask. "Be quick!"

Paul heard the warning but was too focussed on his work to reply. He tapped the menu keys on the radiation detector to initiate the saving of the readings.

Collecting the readings took him nearly forty-five minutes. In order to differentiate between beta rays, gamma rays, and alpha rays, Paul collected readings first with a plastic disc and then with a more highly absorbing aluminium disc covering the delicate mica "window" in the end of the probe. The last readings, for alpha rays, were taken without any shielding disc.

Gamma radiation levels varied from fifteen to fifty times that of the typical background value.

High counts-per-second of alpha particles were obtained when the unshielded probe was held next to the patches of earth adhering to the edges of the hatches and the lower parts of the container walls. The instrument wasn't able to quantify the amount of radon leaking from the hatches because most of the alpha particles emitted by this gas were absorbed by the surrounding air.

Paul returned to Shannon's side, unplugged the radiation detector and rested it on the box he'd used for this purpose earlier. From the battery-pack satchel at his waist, he removed a cylindrical, steel canister that was about the size of a roll of photographic film. He unscrewed its cap, from which jutted an integrated fork-like scraper.

"It's nearly five already," Shannon said anxiously. "The foreman won't go home while we're here. He'll want to know what we've been doing all this time. Let me help you."

"After I've collected a sample, we can start wrapping the containers."

Paul filled the small canister with light-coloured soil that he scraped from the hatch doors of the waste container giving the highest radiation readings. After tightly screwing closed the canister, he slid it back into its lead-lined storage pocket in the satchel. He intended to eventually take other samples from inside the waste containers, but not until they'd been transferred to a location where he could work wearing a respirator.

The last occasion he'd used such a sample canister was shortly after his joining the RSMSDA. He'd been part of an environmental audit unit despatched to collect sand samples from the beach near the Sellafield – then called Windscale – power station in Cumbria. His boss at the time had been Andrew Higstead, the person who was probably now manoeuvring to take over Paul's project team. *It's a straightforward dereliction of the responsibilities he has here,* seemed a likely opener for Higstead to make to Gooch. Everything was "straightforward" to Andy.

"What's the problem now?" Shannon said.

Her mask and goggles made it impossible to see her expression. From her narrowed eyes and her tone of voice, Paul assumed it was one of exasperation.

"Er... Nothing. I was distracted. Stupid office politics." After easing its strap from his shoulder, he put the battery-pack satchel down beside the radiation detector. "Okay, we can start wrapping the containers."

Nearly two hours passed as Paul and Shannon, applying a succession of unspooling rolls of the clear plastic film, walked in opposite directions round each of the black waste containers. In this way, they double "spiral-wrapped" the containers. They tore off pieces of gaffer tape to stick down the ends of the film. The resulting taut plastic glistened under the lowering sun.

"Will this block all the radiation?" Shannon asked as they stepped back from the containers to look for any dangling, loose ends of film.

"Only alpha radiation coming from the soil that's adhering to the outsides," Paul replied. "I hope it'll discourage people from interfering with the containers and trap leaking soil when they're hoisted on and off the transporters."

"It will be torn easily. It won't look like this for long."

"Should we make Mr Fransen agree to my Plan A then?" Paul said defensively. "Do the decontamination work again, with a budget of millions of dollars."

After an awkward silence, Shannon pointed to the container farthest away from the rear gate. "We didn't cover one of the hatches on that last Champ?"

"I'll do that after we've left our protective clothing in it."

"I can't wait to take this crap off," Shannon said. Tugging back the sleeve of her overalls to see her watch, she added, "It's seven already.

They must be working a twelve-hour shift."

Paul shrugged, wearily. "We're not quite finished yet. I need to attach numbered labels, so that after they've been moved I will still know which was which."

Shannon watched as Paul tore ten pieces of cardboard from the emptied gaffer tape boxes. Using a marker pen, he wrote a number on each piece. He went from container to container, sliding the labels between the overlapping layers of film.

Once he'd finished, Paul said, "All done. We can dispose of our protective gear."

They pushed back their hoods, removed their masks and goggles, and began to unfasten the buttons of their overalls.

"Did you hear that?" Shannon said, turning to look back along the row of containers.

Paul stood still too, listening. After several seconds had passed, he said, "It's like a knocking sound." Had something clockwork, something unwinding, been tossed into one of the containers? Or had that large bird come back to peck at the shiny plastic?

They moved from container to container until they came to the first one they'd wrapped, the one closest to the rear gate.

"Someone's inside!" Shannon shouted. She started to tear away the plastic film.

"Stop!" Paul shouted, grabbing her wrist. "Put your goggles and mask back on. This container gave the highest readings."

She stared at him fiercely, not complying until he began putting his mask on.

With his mask and goggles back on and his hood pulled up, Paul wrenched loose the film from around the hatch. Shannon joined in, helping him to strip yards of the film from the upper part of the container.

The noise was becoming louder. Paul felt his heart beating faster. *What sort of maniacal place is this?* He disengaged the bolt locking the doors of the hatch.

As Shannon gripped one of the door handles, he grabbed her round the waist and propelled her sideways. "Stay back!" he shouted as she reeled away, struggling to keep her footing. "Dust's going to billow out."

Holding his breath, Paul grasped the handle of the right-hand-side door. As he lifted the hinged door, an arm, covered in soil, shot out like a mutant tentacle. It grabbed Paul's free arm and pulled him tightly against the end of the container, as if to drag him inside. He pushed aside the steel door so that it wouldn't fall back against his head. The protruding handle narrowly missed Shannon's face. The door swung outwards until it came to a clattering and jutting stop against the side of the hatch frame. From the swirling dust inside the container stared a pair of blinking eyes.

With his and Paul's arms entwined, the trapped man frantically began to pull himself free. Once the slithering man's knees cleared the hatchway, his weight caused him and Paul to collapse to the ground.

The freed man lay coughing on his back. His ripped clothes – grey trousers, check sports jacket, red tie and white shirt – set him apart from the work crew. He'd lost his shoes, presumably inside the waste container. Blood trickled from a gash on his right temple.

The man's face and hands had reddened with what Paul took to be radiation burns. His body was likely to be in a similar condition – the clothes would have provided protection from the alpha particles coming from adhering soil but no protection against gamma rays and little against beta rays. More concerning still was the quantity of radon the man could have breathed. Inhaled radon would have been firing alpha particles directly into his trachea and lungs, in so doing depositing a hazardous isotope of polonium that through radioactive decay would change into a radioactive isotope of lead, which in turn would lead on to yet further radioactive isotopes.

Suddenly aware again of the danger he'd placed himself in, Paul got to his feet and heaved closed the hatch door. Approaching Shannon, he pulled down his mask so he could talk unhindered. "He needs medical treatment. It's urgent Shannon."

She shuffled backwards, seemingly less anxious to become involved. Eventually she said, "I'll call Blackwood from my car."

"But in the meantime, he needs to be hosed down," Paul said, looking from side to side at the dusty handprints that now covered the sleeves of his overalls. "And when you get hold of Blackwood, tell him we require a hazard response unit, not a regular ambulance."

Shannon swept back her hood and shook free her hair. She took off her goggles and mask and threw them on the ground.

"Keep your shoe protectors on," Paul said as she knelt to remove them.

The clothes she'd changed into at the hotel – blue jeans, a grey T-shirt and a black windcheater-style jacket – were revealed as Shannon peeled off the overalls. Pinned to the left breast of the jacket was the dosimeter badge Paul had provided. She stripped off her vinyl gloves and dropped them next to the discarded overalls.

"In case of trouble," she said, lifting the side of her jacket to expose the gun holstered on her hip. She turned and started to run back the way they'd come.

Paul's shock at seeing the firearm was interrupted by an alarming realisation. "Don't run, Shannon!" She either didn't hear his cry or chose to ignore it. If she tripped and cut herself, isotopes in the soil would enter her bloodstream.

Shannon's remark about the plastic film that they'd laboriously applied not lasting long still troubled him. It undermined his confidence in his ability to improvise. Radiation workers weren't supposed to improvise. When radiation workers deviate from protocols, they become outlaws. And that's what Maycross had reduced him to – the scientist-equivalent of a surgeon patching the wounds of criminals. Which begged the question: What would he say to the medics if and when they arrived?

The murmurings of the man on the ground began to become intelligible, although the tip of his tongue was swollen. "Sirsty. Sirsty. Water. Whath happ... Whath happennn."

Paul knelt beside the man. "Don't try to talk, sir. We're getting help for you."

The man's features were so discoloured by dirt and the effects of radiation it was not easy to visualise his normal appearance. His brown hair was thinning and there seemed to be a couple of days' stubble on his cheeks and chin. There were no glasses, but those could have fallen off inside the waste container, along with the missing shoes. He was a little overweight, suggestive of someone with a sedentary occupation.

Paul stood up and went across to where he'd left the radiation detector. He reconnected the battery and placed the detector close to the man's torso. The instrument's response to impinging alpha radiation was the most dramatic he'd ever seen. After returning the instrument to its resting place, he said to the man, "Your clothes are covered in radioactive soil. We need to take them off. Help me as much as you can."

Paul undid the man's tie and slowly slid it free. He hurled the tie away; it landed coiled, ten feet distant. The man screamed as Paul attempted to ease an arm from the sleeve of the sports jacket. It was impossible to discern whether the pain arose from other injuries or from the burns.

"I have to turn you a little so I can free your other arm. I... I'm sorry," Paul said, imagining Shannon mocking him again for apologising.

Each movement provoked another scream. It took several minutes to remove the jacket. With that task achieved, Paul started to remove the man's socks.

The noise of a vehicle engine and the thuds of tyres bouncing against the rutted terrain caused Paul to look up. The pickup had returned. *What now?* he thought.

The truck came to a stop twenty feet away, throwing up yet more of the dreaded fine dust. The passenger door of the pickup opened. Shannon clambered out, using the running board as a step. The same driver as before got out his side, but remained by the vehicle, seemingly reluctant to approach Paul and the man.

"Help me, Miguel," Shannon shouted as she headed to the back of the pickup.

The driver cast a fearful look at the injured man before limping after her.

Not knowing what was happening, Paul continued gently removing the man's socks. He heard Shannon shouting but couldn't make out what she was saying. All became clear when he next looked. She was standing beside him, holding the nozzle of a hosepipe.

Paul stood up and took the nozzle from her. "I hope you didn't have to shoot anyone."

"The foreman told me drunks break in here all the time. A store on the next block sells cheap liquor. This isn't the first one that's been found in a garbage container. The security guys handle things without involving the cops." She turned and shouted, "Okay, Miguel."

The drone of a compressor unit came from the bed of the truck It powered a pump connected to a water drum. Within seconds, water began gushing from the nozzle.

Paul swept the jet over the man's face and hair. The man mouthed the falling water; unable to swallow, he began coughing.

"Don't let the run-off get on your shoes, Shannon."

She stepped back as Paul proceeded to hose the man's body, but the slope of the ground proved sufficient to cause the run-off water to drain away from them.

After a few minutes the flow slowed to a trickle. Shannon looked towards Miguel, who was waving. "Should I send him back to collect more water? He can help us for as long as we need him. Apart from that, the foreman doesn't want to get involved."

"But he's in charge of this site."

"And *now* he's aware of who I work for. Neither of us want to involve the police."

The reason for this was obvious. Their involving the police would be as likely as armed robbers aborting a bank heist when one of the tellers had a heart attack. "What about the medical assistance?" Paul asked, beginning to doubt there would be any such help.

"It's on its way."

"It can't get here soon enough."

"There it is!" Shannon shouted, putting her hand up to shield her eyes from the low sun.

"Where?" Paul said, looking towards the rear gate.

Pointing up at a dark speck approaching from the south, Shannon said, "There!"

"A helicopter?" Paul said. Once the surprise had faded, he began waving his arms, gesturing towards the rear entrance to the site. "It mustn't land here. The downdraught will fill the air with dust."

The helicopter tilted as it slowed, and then it veered away. It hovered above the road outside the gateway as the pilot manoeuvred the craft in readiness for landing.

Looking down at the soaked man, Shannon asked, "Is it safe for us to lift him on to the pickup?"

"You'll have to rinse your clothes under the hotel shower before having them laundered."

"So, not safe at all," she said, leaning down to take one of the man's arms.

The limpness and slipperiness of the man made it too difficult for them to carry him more than a few feet. Paul tied Shannon's discarded overalls round the groaning man's feet to protect them from the rough ground. With the man's arms across their shoulders, they began dragging him the rest of the way to the pickup.

Once they'd lifted him on to the bed of the pickup, Shannon went to the driver's cabin. When she re-joined Paul on the back of the truck, she said, "I told Miguel to drive us to the gate slowly."

A moment later the pickup shot forward. The rear fishtailed as Miguel swung the vehicle round and accelerated towards the gate. His passengers, including the afflicted man, who'd seemingly passed out, rocked and bounced on the hard bed of the pickup. Paul reached to take hold of the bed side panel. "You call this *slowly*!"

"I guess my Spanish isn't good either," Shannon shouted back.

Miguel brought the vehicle to a stop on the paved area by the rear gate. The helicopter – which was matt-grey in colour and bore no markings – began its descent.

"Only talk to these guys if they address you directly," Shannon said, before jumping down.

Paul watched her crouch-walk towards the idling helicopter, whose rotors were still spinning slowly. Looking again at the injured man, he noticed a wallet had been shaken loose. He examined the contents. A press card for Peter F. Wilson of the *Atlantic Daily Herald* was visible through the misted plastic window of one of the compartments; the card included a photograph of a smiling Wilson. After closing the wallet, Paul eased it back into the trouser pocket from which it had fallen. All of a sudden, Paul's wrist was grabbed by the awoken journalist.

"Tell D-Dooley," Wilson mumbled, his distended tongue pushing against his teeth.

"Who's Dooley, Peter?" Paul asked, bending over to hear. But instead of the man's frail words, above the swishing of the helicopter rotors Paul heard approaching voices. One was Lennon's. The others were male and had a military-like curtness. Instinctively he began to stand, tugging his wrist from Wilson's grip.

Chapter 8

For several minutes Paul stood dazed in the vestibule of his hotel room. His mood had darkened with the progress of evening, yet the rectangle of daylight that filled the floor-to-ceiling window opposite him remained stubbornly bright.

His thoughts were a repeating cycle of self-incrimination infused with a sense of useless pity for the journalist. Eventually another image broke through – it was of Ann laughing at something he'd done a couple of years ago. He'd wrapped the scissors that he'd used to cut the gift paper in with their Christmas present for her mother. "What are you trying to tell her?" Ann said. That absent-minded moment – that chink in his "usual perfection" – brought her delight, which nothing he did could accomplish recently. And now he really was letting her down, even as he was attempting to protect her. Like the skin of a snake, the sheen of perfection was being shed.

Should he tell Maycross? Or contact the DC number Maycross had provided? It wasn't really an emergency; at least it wasn't one that endangered him. And informing Maycross risked the setting off of a chain of unknowable events.

He shook his head to clear his mind. There was pressing work to do. Dosage conversion tables, based upon the radiation characteristics of the radium-226 isotope and its nuclear decay progeny, such as radon, were listed in the leaflet that he kept in the inner pocket of his notebook cover. With this information he could use the detector readings to estimate their exposure today, including worst-case allowances for ingested radon. Eventual analysis of his and Shannon's radiation badges by the Environmental Monitoring Unit at his workplace would provide more reliable estimates.

But first he needed to do what he'd insisted Shannon do: shower thoroughly. Perhaps if he showered long enough, the memory of Peter Wilson emerging from the waste container could be washed away too, along with the traces of radioactive dust. He took the radiation badge from his jeans pocket and placed it on the table that was beside the window.

He began his shower fully dressed. Afterwards, he left his sodden clothing lying on the bottom of the cubicle. Last thing tonight, after wringing the clothes out and checking the radiation reading, he would put them in the room laundry bag and place that in the corridor for collection.

After putting on one of the provided white terry cloth bathrobes, Paul sat on the double bed and turned to the telephone on the bedside table. He asked the front desk to connect him with the number for the Whitehall messaging service that Maycross preferred him to use – "Keep reports to the point. No unnecessary details or names."

Talking to a 24-hour recording machine was an uncomfortable experience: "I'm in Atlantic City, at the Banville Plaza. I have a chaperon. We went to the demolition site this afternoon. I intend to visit the other place tomorrow. Thank you for the details in the letter the chauffeur passed on to me. I look forward to receiving the rest of the information as soon as possible."

Before he could focus upon his calculations, he needed to reflect upon all that had transpired at the demolition site. Having a detail-seeking mind was his strength, whereas Maycross disdained practical matters. Maycross's strength seemingly lay in the politics of perception.

Paul lay down and screened his eyes with his forearm. He visualised the matt-grey helicopter lifting off with the stretchered-away journalist. As instructed by Shannon, he hadn't asked questions. Nor had the helicopter occupants asked him anything. Their protective clothing and sensing devices showed they were well prepared. The aircraft had an isolation chamber for infectious or contaminated patients. If Blackwood could provide such a hazard response unit within minutes, what could he accomplish with a few hours' notice?

The only exchange that had occurred was with the medic who retrieved the clothes Paul had removed from the victim. "Dr Avery," the returning man said, handing Paul his radiation detector and its battery pack. Not waiting to be thanked, the helmeted medic headed back towards the helicopter. Nothing else was said. Of course, Shannon might have told them his name, but Paul suspected Blackwood had already taken care of that. The passage of events subsequent to the departure of the helicopter were, by comparison, predictable.

***

Passing the radiation detector and battery pack to Shannon, he said, "Please put these in your car while I dispose of our protective kit. I recommend going round the outside to avoid further dust exposure." In truth, he wanted to be alone with his thoughts, if only for a few minutes.

After re-taping the plastic film over the hatch of the container from which they'd rescued Wilson, Paul stripped off his overalls and picked up Shannon's discarded things. He tossed both garments, together with their gloves, dust masks and goggles into the container at the other end of the row, the one having the hatch he'd left uncovered for that purpose.

He gathered up the empty cardboard packaging and the leftover rolls of gaffer tape, and threw these into the container too. After closing and bolting the hatch, he taped the end of the plastic film over it.

Dressed in jeans and a maroon polo shirt, but still wearing the shoe protectors over his work boots, he walked out the rear gate and round the large site until he arrived back at the main entrance. It was there he remembered to take off the radiation badge and put it in his pocket.

"I've been working here this afternoon, at the south end of the site," he said to the security guard, who was different from the one on duty earlier. This guard's face had stubble that unnervingly reminded Paul of Wilson's.

"Name?" the guard said.

"Avery." As the guard raised his walkie-talkie, Paul pointed at Shannon, who was leaning back against the trunk of her car, which was still where they'd parked it in front of the Site Crew Office. "I'm with her."

"I have to check anyway," the guard said.

"By the way, no one's minding the rear gate. It's open."

"I'll take that under advisement." The guard spoke into his walkie-talkie. Seconds later, the main gate began to slide open.

"Your contraption's safe," Shannon said tetchily as she and Paul ascended the cabin stairs. "I pulled a muscle carrying the thing."

"Take your badge off, Shannon."

Stopping on the stairs, she said, "I forgot I had that on. The foreman must have seen it already, but at the time he was distracted by what I was telling him about the man we found." She unclipped the badge and put it in her windcheater pocket.

Marv, sitting at the table, alone in the cabin, looked up from the paperwork he was doing. His weary gaze met Shannon's but he didn't ask for an update on the rescue episode. He was only interested in the clearing of the Red Zone.

Looking at Paul, he said, "All fuckin' afternoon. Whadda you mean you don't know where they can be moved? They're a motherfuckin' nuisance."

Paul told Marv that he'd notify Fransen as soon as he could finalise the matter.

"What's the holdup?"

Unable to divulge the linkage to waste removal from the Hartling Springs nuclear plant, Paul responded, "Now that I've seen the Champs, I know what I'll be dealing with. I'm just not at liberty to say more for the moment." Nodding towards Shannon, he added cryptically, "Her boss has got things in play."

Marv looked at Shannon, who put her hand on her hip. The foreman's gaze darted to the now visible gun. "I guess that's the way it'll be then."

***

Paul looked at the digits on the bedside clock. In less than ten minutes, at 7.30 p.m., Reception should connect him with the arranged transatlantic call to Ann. It would be half past midnight in England, the time they'd agreed he would telephone each night, enabling her to get enough sleep and him to become free to make the call.

For how long could he withhold the truth? Ann was bound to detect something was wrong soon; her irritation would give way to fear. Could he cope with the strain of pretending everything was okay, evening after evening? The clock displayed 7.25 p.m. Just five minutes to go. Paul swung his legs round, fumbled with his feet for his slippers and stood up. He headed to the bathroom to finish drying his hair and to splash cold water on his face.

The telephone call proved even more troubling than he'd anticipated. There were clicks on the line, which he initially dismissed as an artefact of the transatlantic connection. But when Ann said she had the feeling that she's being watched, he concluded Maycross had her under surveillance. Everything they said had an audience.

"A black van with dark windows was parked for an hour across the road this morning. I didn't see anyone getting in or out."

"It must have been a tradesman taking a tea break," Paul responded, inwardly cursing Maycross's lack of subtlety. Ann was used to being on her own. She wasn't prone to paranoia.

"I think the van came back tonight. I heard an engine running. It's hard to tell. There's no moon."

"Probably a taxi, collecting one of our neighbours. Try not to worry, Ann. You've turned on the burglar alarm, haven't you?"

Much of the remainder of the call comprised his increasingly desperate attempts to put her mind at rest about the van. If only he could have told her a precise date for his return to England. "Open-ended" was not the sort of adjective he should have used to describe his situation; that was the sort of adjective that required a comforting smile and an extravagant shrug of shoulders. He suspected that at the receiving end of a three-thousand mile call on a clicking telephone line, the term was as comforting as a bucket of icy water. Paul tried to console himself with the inverted reasoning that her being observed meant Ann was safe, perhaps safer than she'd ever been, from actual burglars.

Although he had yet to begin his radiation exposure calculations, Paul decided to keep his appointment to dine with Lennon. He needed to retain her cooperation, regardless of his concerns about Blackwood's activities. At 8.20 p.m., wearing a fawn sports jacket, open-necked cream shirt and black trousers, he emerged from the elevator into the brightly lit hotel lobby.

He stopped and considered the four men in business suits waiting by Reception. Perhaps they were hotel- or casino-décor reps looking for business opportunities. They certainly weren't holidaymakers – the Banville Plaza didn't seem to be a holiday destination as far as he could tell. He presumed the most popular hotels were near the seafront. Perhaps things would change when the Mayjak "off-Boardwalk" casino became a reality. The sooner he was far away from New Jersey the better, but would it ever be far enough? At least the men by the front desk weren't comporting themselves like the mobsters he'd seen portrayed in films; Shannon's account of the crime family owning the

Altabrite site was making him look for mobsters everywhere.

He turned away from the front desk and walked across the hotel lobby with the sensation of teetering on a slick tightrope in thick fog. To his right, sagging purple ropes, strung between waist-high metal pillars, formed the boundary of the “Hurricane’s Rest”. Unlike the restaurant last night, this place didn’t look as though it served wine costing a hundred and seventy dollars a bottle.

Why had he begun to regard Shannon as someone she wasn’t? During their wait to enter the demolition site, there was that teasing moment between them when he could have believed she was someone he could confide in. But no... She was every bit as implicated in all this – whatever *this* type of sanctioned illegality could be called – as Blackwood and Maycross. What had she called him? A calf among coyotes. Yet she was part of the pack of coyotes herself and he mustn’t forget that.

The menu was clipped to a board by the restaurant entrance. While he was perusing it, he was startled by Shannon.

“Punctuality says a lot about a person,” she said, speaking softly by his ear. She was so close, her breath tickled his neck.

Whatever his expectations, it didn’t match what he saw when he turned. He found it hard to reconcile this smiling young woman in a short, low-cut, black sleeveless dress with the person with whom he’d spent an appalling afternoon. How could she conceal the gun beneath this figure-hugging frock?

Shannon had clipped back her hair. The short pearl necklace seemed for her an oddly delicate adornment. But perhaps the most disconcerting thing was the transformation in her height, which had been boosted by stiletto-heeled black shoes. The alluring fragrance enveloping her was unfamiliar to Paul; it was very different from Ann’s favourite scents. He wanted to know what it was called and almost asked... until he recalled his misgivings of moments ago.

“I-I didn’t think to put on a suit,” he said, tugging self-consciously at the sleeve of his sports jacket. “I thought it was an informal restaurant.”

“Silly,” Shannon said, placing her palm lightly against his chest. “You look most handsome.” She opened her clutch bag and took out the radiation badge. “What are you going to do with this?”

“I’ll have them analysed when I get back to the office,” he said, slipping the badge in his jacket pocket.

"Promise you'll let me know if I have anything to worry about."

Before he could reply, Shannon threaded her arm under his. "Shall we go in?"

The maître d', a stout man dressed in an ill-fitting tuxedo, appeared and led them to a secluded booth that had bench seats. They sat down opposite each other.

"Your waitress will be right with you," the maître d' said before leaving them.

"Dinner's on me tonight," Shannon announced, picking up one of the menu cards.

Remembering Maycross's concern for "appearances", Paul said, "You bought lunch. Her Majesty's Government should pay again."

Shannon smiled. It was a smile that seemed to be a laugh. Paul, despite his distrust, found it captivating.

"I didn't mean to sound ungrateful," he said.

"You're not going to start apologising again?"

"Er... probably. In fact, while I'm at it I should apologise for manhandling you this afternoon."

"You took control. I admired that."

"Okay, thank you. Apologies over. I've used up today's ration."

"We'll go Dutch. Fair enough?" she said. "After saving that man's life, you've earned a good meal. If you hadn't insisted upon checking the segregated trash, he might have died in there."

"I suppose so, but..."

"But what, Paul?" she said, putting her hand on his.

Her touch was so distracting he momentarily forgot what he'd been about to say. "I don't know how long he was in there. If it was many hours, it's possible he still won't survive. And even if he does, the prognosis for his health will be uncertain."

"It's sad, but vagrants usually lead short lives. If it's not one thing, it's another."

"He wasn't dressed like a tramp."

"His clothes were filthy, Paul."

"He'd been flailing about in the dark on a mound of earth."

Shannon withdrew her hand. "You make my point. Homeless people oftentimes climb into garbage containers, thinking they'll be safe. You must have noticed the repairs to the fence around there.

People have been breaking in for years, looking for somewhere to shelter."

Paul shook his head. "Tramps don't wear ties, Shannon."

Shannon pouted. "I don't recall a necktie."

"I took it off when I was trying to undress him. No, he was *definitely* no tram—"

She put her hand on Paul's again, pressing firmly this time. "Have you chosen already?"

"I, er..." Paul followed Shannon's gaze.

The waitress was standing beside them. "Is everyone ready to order?" she said, turning over a page in her notepad.

They agreed to pass on entrees. Shannon ordered the "marinated chicken and saffron rice" and Paul hurriedly chose something from the pasta selection. They settled on a bottle of the "house white".

Paul looked around as the waitress left them. Like the other waitresses, theirs was dressed in black jeans and a white blouse. He observed that most customers were dressed as he – "smart-casual". Otherwise, there was a sprinkling of suited businessmen, dining alone, taking refuge behind newspapers and sneaking looks in Shannon's direction. None of the other female diners were attired as glamorously as his companion.

He couldn't remember the last time he'd been conscious of other men's envious glances. But whose fault was that? When had he and Ann started taking each other for granted? Incremental corrosion was something that he monitored in his laboratory, but when it came to their marriage, pinning down subtle weakening of the bonds between them had eluded him.

"Is something wrong, Paul?" Shannon asked. "You're quiet. Are you still thinking about that guy?"

"Uh..." Paul didn't want to disclose his marital concerns. "This trip was at short notice. That's not great for married life."

"Was Vernon right about you being poorly briefed?"

"I don't want to criticize anyone, Shannon. It's more a case of my not knowing what others have been told. I assume Fransen doesn't know about Hartling Springs, for example."

"And that's a safe assumption. See – a problem shared is a problem halved. Anything else on your mind?"

"I'll let you know when I think of something," Paul said, relieved that an awkward silence had turned into an informative moment.

While they waited for the food, Shannon broached the schedule for the next day. "Talking about Hartling Springs, I'm not going there with you tomorrow. Vernon wants to debrief me about today. I've asked the front desk to organize a rental for you. You'll have to take care of the charges when you pick it up."

"I hope I haven't made trouble for you," Paul said, fearing it would be he and Ann in trouble if Blackwood were to complain. Perhaps he should have reported the matter in the recorded message for Maycross, after all.

"Vernon doesn't like surprises or loose ends. The trash guy's both."

"Will you be able to find out which hospital they took him to?"

"I can't ask about that, Paul. Vernon would want to know what my interest is in the matter. I don't have an interest in the matter and nor should you."

"I see."

"Do you, Paul? Have any interest in the matter, I mean?"

"His medical condition is not exactly a common one. There are specialised medicines that can mop up ingested radionuclides. It would be good to know that he's in a hospital that can provide suitable palliative treatment. If he's suffered as much radiation damage as I fear, he might only have months to live."

"I can put your mind at rest then. He'll be in a top-notch medical facility, getting all the appropriate attention. When he's well enough, he'll be questioned."

"Why question a *down-and-out*?" Paul said, pointedly.

"Loose ends have to be inspected."

Paul looked away. There was something else that happened to loose ends – they were snipped off.

"Don't get side-tracked by this, Paul. We trust your technical expertise, but this isn't your comfort zone, is it?"

He looked again towards Shannon.

She smiled, seemingly sympathetically.

"You were right when you said I didn't volunteer for this. You also said you know what it's like to be pressured by someone. Is someone pressuring you, Shannon? Isn't there a boyfriend worrying about what might happen to you?"

"Actually girlfriend – my partner of the moment."

"I-I didn't realise."

Shannon leaned forward with both elbows on the table. The hunching of her shoulders caused the front of her dress to dip revealingly. "Why should you? Anyhow, I'm bi."

"Buy what?"

"No, not b-u-y. I'm b-i," she said, speaking the letters. With a broad grin, she added, "Sometimes I like the rough, sometimes the smooth, that's all."

Paul considered her remark for a few seconds. "Oh!"

"There you go, Doctor," she said, lifting a strand of hair back into place behind her ear.

Ann wore her brunette hair shorter these days, almost boyishly. It was thick too, like his. Paul couldn't remember her arranging her hair without a brush. This struck him now as a pity, a lost opportunity to project a delicacy that had nothing to do with antique silver curios.

His thoughts were interrupted by the arrival of the wine waiter. Paul fulfilled the tasting ritual. "That'll be fine," he told the sommelier before truly registering the unremarkable flavour.

Once the wine waiter had departed, Paul raised his glass. "To trash man," he said.

Shannon raised her glass. "No, to us."

"To us and to my wife, Ann, and to your *partner of the moment*."

"Rachel."

"To Rachel," Paul said, raising his glass again.

"You said you don't have children," Shannon said, referring to Blackwood's questioning of Paul last night.

"That's right."

"Do you want to start a family?"

"When the time's right. We want to build up our savings first."

Paul was becoming uncomfortable again – not only were the facts of his private life private, he wasn't even sure they were facts. It was his fault, he knew, for asking about Shannon's personal life. Why'd he done that? And what had he learned? Nothing about the pressure *she* was under. Nothing about her being coerced. And he was also more aware than ever how attractive she looked.

Smooth-jazz guitar music emerged from nearby speakers. The Latin-influenced melody heightened the intimate atmosphere. Their gazes hesitantly flickered together. Alarmed by his feelings, he turned away, hoping to see the waitress bringing their meals.

"Paul..."

"Hmmm?" he murmured, turning back.

"What did he *say* to you?"

Chapter 9

The car – a light-blue sedan with whitewall tyres and 223 miles on the odometer – the hotel had obtained for Paul from a local rental company was larger than he was used to driving. Also unfamiliar was the steering column location of the lever for the automatic drive.

With the rental agreement, insurance paperwork, credit card receipt and an unfolded map of New Jersey on the seat beside him, he manoeuvred the vehicle from the hotel parking lot out on to Mayjak Drive and across to the westbound carriageway. It was 9.00 a.m. and the Friday morning rush-hour traffic had already ebbed.

He'd slept poorly, if at all. If only he was a better liar... Courses in deception, or even Maycross-like "constructive ambiguity", had not featured in his management training to date. Shannon's question last evening, while they were waiting for their meals, had caught him by surprise. His subsequent denying that "trash man" had said anything was *stupid, stupid, stupid...* It soon became clear that she had seen them talking.

"Tell Dooley," was what the man had said, or something like that. Paul's instinct was to keep this to himself; it could be something he wasn't supposed to hear.

"You can't hold anything back. I can't protect you if you do," Shannon said.

The threat explicit in her choice of words crowded out the piped jazz music, rendering it an unlistenable cacophony.

"There's nothing to hold back! The man was hallucinating. Perhaps he needed a drink. That's what drunks always need, isn't it?" Paul picked up his glass and took a gulp of the wine, wishing it was water.

"Yes, Paul, that's what *drunks* want. It's good you're accepting that at last. But what made you think he was hallucinating?"

"He had a wide-eyed look, as though he was seeing something that wasn't there," Paul lied, his voice faltering.

Shannon pouted thoughtfully as once more she pushed back the errant strand of her hair.

There'd been enough time before they dined for Blackwood and her to have talked by telephone. Had she been pretending not to have been informed about the journalist's identity? Mercifully, she let the subject drop once the food arrived.

***

A terrible thought struck him now – had she also observed him looking through Wilson's wallet? Paul stamped on the brake pedal, realising he'd been about to drive through a crossroads against a red light. The car rocked on its suspension after coming to a screeching stop.

The traffic lights were strung high on overhead cables crossing the multi-lane junction, an arrangement not usually found in the UK. Although he'd driven in America before – while attending a conference – there'd been three of them then to look out for signs and traffic signals. "Focus, you idiot!" he said aloud. "There's no point in killing myself before they do it." He glanced at the map. Hartling was perhaps two hours away, if he didn't encounter hold-ups and the traffic flow through toll plazas was smooth.

The roadside sign informing him he was entering Hartling featured a babbling brook and a hooked fish, at the end of a taut line, thrashing the air with its tail. Paul felt that there was something foreboding about that snagged fish as he drove past the fading sign. The air inside the car began to feel stale. He turned up the blower on the air conditioning.

According to the information in the pink folder given to him by Maycross, this town in the southwestern part of the state had a population of about twenty-two thousand, of whom a significant percentage possessed Polish heritage. The impression he soon formed was that of a prosperous community. The detached houses seemed well-maintained. Front lawns were neatly trimmed.

He came to a T-junction, signposted "Riverside" to the right and "Shopping Center" to the left. There were no signs referring to the nuclear power station, but then he hadn't expected there to be any. He chose the right turn, assuming it would bring him to the Hartling River.

To his left, a domed stadium was set back from the road with an empty parking lot surrounding it. A sign announced: **Sharp Stadium, the new home of the Hartling Heroes**. A little farther on, on the other side of the road, was a vast construction site fronted by a wire fence. The fence sign, seemingly optimistically, declared: **Sharp Riverside Mall. Opening Next Summer**.

It wasn't until he reached the Hartling River, a meandering tributary of the Delaware, that he could see the grey rectangle of the nuclear power plant downstream to the west. He judged it as standing about five miles away. Behind the distant building were four chimney-like, fawn-coloured cooling towers, which were wider at the bottom than at the top; no clouds of condensing water were billowing from them to whiten the sky. A line of transmission towers carrying overhead power cables towards the horizon completed the scene.

Paul had visited several nuclear power stations in the UK and across Europe. He knew that, in this case, the simple geometry of the massive building was concealing the presence of two reactor containment halls, although perhaps only one of the reactors had been operational since the incident in nineteen seventy-five. Nuclear power stations always made him feel queasy. It was the sheer magnitude of the power being controlled. Knowing something truly dangerous had occurred at this one heightened the sensation.

It had been his father, then an engineer in a National Health Service hospital, who'd inspired Paul's early interest: "Nuclear power is nearer to magic than anything you'll see on television. Vast amounts of energy are obtained from tiny pieces of ore. It's as if thousands of rabbits are being taken out of an empty hat," he'd told his marvelling eleven-year-old son. Uncertain as to what the visit here today would bring, that clichéd reference to a conjuring trick seemed apposite for a wholly different reason – his and Ann's future needed to be extracted deftly from Maycross's unethical plan.

Fifteen minutes later, having negotiating a zig-zagging road that cut across fallow farmland, Paul stopped beside a wooden gatehouse displaying the name **Hartling Springs Nuclear Generation**. The entrance to the plant was still some distance away and was protected by a cantilevered pole that blocked the road and, beyond that, motorised steel posts that stuck up out of the ground. Elsewhere, glinting chain-link fencing, topped with razor wire, protected the facility. The scene was dominated by the two-hundred feet high power station facade and the half-hidden, five-hundred feet high cooling towers.

An unarmed, bespectacled man having a weathered complexion and looking to be in his mid-seventies moseyed from the gatehouse. Sewn on the left breast of his blue jumper were the words ***Sharp Power*** in gold thread.

Paul wound down his window and immediately felt the westerly breeze that was coming across the Delaware. The yawning river seemed to be reminding him that it was here long before the impertinent creation of mankind squatting on its bank.

"Nice car you got here," the elderly man said. "You lost, son? This ain't no place for tourists."

"I have an appointment with the plant manager – Mr Cantrell."

"You do, huh? You Australian?"

"British."

"Pretty much same thing, ain't it?"

"Well, I suppo—"

"You got some kind of I.D.?"

Paul withdrew his wallet from his suit jacket inside pocket. He removed his business card and handed it to the gatekeeper.

"What's this say now? Dr Paul Avery, Radioactive Substances Monitoring, Storage and Disposal Agency, Didcot, Oxfordshire, United Kingdom. That's some fancy mouthful, ain't it?"

"Afraid it is," Paul said, reflecting on how a more engaging name might improve his organization's prospect of remaining within the public sector. The way the man had laboured over each syllable had been disheartening.

Peering at the card again, the elderly man said, "You must be a real important person. I'll give the signal so you can drive on up to the Security building. They'll tell you where you need to go."

"Don't you work for Security?"

"It's my job to move along the lookie-loos, while being all friendly like about it. But I sure appreciate the question. How about you telling those guys to give me a pay rise?"

The man turned and looked up towards a security camera. He gave the thumbs-up sign. Handing the business card back to Paul, he said, "When the barriers permit, you drive on through. Security's on the left, around the corner. Stop and park up there. You have a nice day now."

The Security building dwarfed the modest gatehouse. Its thick concrete walls conveyed the impression of a nuclear bunker. Perhaps, Paul speculated, it would function as that – perhaps it had already functioned that way – in the event of an imminent reactor explosion. The occupants were uniformed and had the pallor of prisoners incarcerated without outdoor-exercise privileges. Communication was only possible through a plate-glass screen fitted with an intercom.

"I have an appointment with the plant manager," Paul said, holding his business card against the glass for the guard to read.

"I'll need to see more than that. Do you have your passport?"

Paul took his passport from his jacket inside pocket and placed it into the tray beneath the glass screen.

After the guard had returned the passport, he said, "Follow the path to your right. Someone will let you in when you reach the building."

As Paul turned to leave, he heard the guard shout, "Stay inside the lines!"

To each side of the tarmac path, more of the same black tarmac stretched into the distance. The white lines denoting the path seemed to have more to do with the stifling exercise of authority than they had with the guiding of visitors.

Paul assumed that on the far side of the huge structure ahead there must be a large parking area for the staff. Power stations, regardless of type, were as extensive as major airport terminals and could be just as sprawling. As he approached the grey facade, an unmarked door swung open. Two men, both wearing caps and dressed in sharply pressed navy-blue trousers and short-sleeved shirts, came out. Lightning-flash insignias with the name HARKNET were attached to their sleeves.

Paul noticed the large holsters on their hips. "Here we go," he said under his breath. It was always fascinating to see the way a nuclear power station was secured. Apart from their guns, these men looked like the security officers guarding large commercial and government premises in England.

"This way, Dr Avery," one of the men said before stepping back into the building. After looking from side to side, the other guard waved at the men in the gatehouse and then followed Paul and his colleague. The two guards set a crisp pace along a harshly lit corridor until they entered the Visitor Reception Suite. Paul was instructed to place his briefcase on the counter, unlock it, open it, and step back.

He was patted down, presumably for concealed weapons.

"What's that thing clipped to your shirt?" the lead guard said.

"It monitors my exposure to radiation."

"It's not one of ours. Why do you need it?" The suspicious guard's eyes narrowed.

"I provide advice about the handling of radioactive materials."

"Uh-huh. That doesn't answer my question."

"Then I suggest you speak to Mr Cantrell."

From his silence it became clear the lead guard wasn't going to disturb the plant manager. Instead, he pointed to the chair facing a tripod-mounted camera. "Sit down there and look at the camera. I need three clear close-ups. Remain still till I tell you I'm done." The guard's abruptness suggested irritation; perhaps Paul's radiation badge had triggered unease about his place of work.

As Paul stared into the lens, he heard the contents of his briefcase being rummaged through by the other guard. After one of the three Polaroids had been laminated on to a badge for Paul to pin to his jacket, he was shown to a seat in the nearby waiting room. "An electronic device is in your briefcase. What's it for?" the lead guard said before leaving Paul.

"It measures radiation."

The man's brow furrowed again. "You can keep your badge, but the device will stay here. You'll get it back when you leave."

Paul didn't argue. The radiation detector would be useless without the battery pack that he'd forgotten to take from his car. He would rely on his hosts to provide a similar instrument.

While Paul waited for his briefcase to be returned to him, he thought he heard the squealing whine of a fax machine. Was his image being faxed to someone for verification? Who'd be at the other end? Blackwood? Perhaps Fabian Gooch? No, not Gooch. Gooch would probably be kept out of the loop completely. As for Maycross, who could know the whereabouts of that type of man?

Maybe the fax had nothing to do with him at all. He looked at his palms, which prickled with perspiration. The atmosphere was oppressive; there wasn't a window in the Reception Suite to the outside. But it wasn't as oppressive as it would have been inside the waste container for...

The reporter from the *Atlantic Daily Herald* must have been caught snooping, attacked and left to die inside the garbage container. What other explanation was possible? Did the foreman know more than he claimed? Had Peter Wilson been looking beyond the marketing hype that surrounded the future gambling resort? Perhaps he was going to peel off the civic scab covering the time when an earlier version of a hoped-for prosperous future had turned into a luminous nightmare. When he struggled to say "Tell Dooley", was Wilson really trying to say "Tell Julie"? Maybe his wife's name? Would she be waiting at her wits' end for her husband to come home? That could be Ann's fate too soon – Paul could be made to disappear inside this power station, if not today then during a subsequent visit.

Quelling an impulse to leave, Paul turned his fevered thoughts to the job he'd been sent to do. Maycross's future being dependent upon what he achieved was the only consolation. If Paul Avery were to fail, he should do it royally and bring the whole mess down on that arrogant bastard.

Chapter 10

The plant manager's office was on the top floor. This location conveyed, if nothing else, a sense of confidence in the operation of the surviving reactor. The office had a lounge area near the door, which was furnished with three ageing, cream leather sofas. Absence of daylight was compensated by four feet square, frosted glass ceiling panels concealing fluorescent tubes. The light pouring from these imitation skylights made Paul squint as he was shown in by Cantrell's secretary, Margot Lewandowski.

"Make yourself comfortable, Dr Avery. Mr Cantrell will be with you momentarily," the heavily set, fifty-something woman said before leaving.

The only sound was the soft hum of air conditioning. Few pictures and photographs hung on the oak-panelled walls. The bookcase was barely a third full, and the pile of the purple carpet had been compressed along a path connecting the door to the desk at the far end.

Paul recalled from the information in the pink folder that the power station had been opened in 1965, eighteen years ago, as part of the nation-wide modernisation of the American energy sector. The facility's first reactor became fully operational in 1969. By this time the plant had established itself at the economic heart of the Hartling community, providing shift-based employment for more than a thousand people, and with the promise of further jobs once the second reactor was running.

Paul sat down on one of the sofas. With the briefcase on his lap he removed the pink folder and wondered what the guard who'd searched the case had thought upon seeing the "TOP SECRET and UK Eyes Only" stamp marks. If the guard had looked inside the folder, he wouldn't have seen anything that compromised the UK Government or this power station. There were no references to the reactor incident. The page with the table of radioactive waste had no title, and the serial numbers alongside the listed items of nuclear fuel and damaged equipment would not mean anything to an uninformed reader.

He studied again the Contacts list comprising seven names,

including the plant manager's, together with the respective job titles. The chime of the elevator in the lobby made him look up. Men engaged in a heated conversation were approaching. Paul put back the folder and closed the briefcase.

As he was standing up, the door opened. Two men, both looking to be of an age similar to Lewandowski's, entered. Their thinning hair was in disarray. They were wearing blue boiler suits and carrying white helmets. The sound from the men's safety boot heels was quietened by the carpet.

The fairer-haired man in front had a quizzical expression as he put out his hand. "Pleased to see you, Dr Avery. I'm Gavin Cantrell, plant manager." Indicating towards his much taller colleague, Cantrell added, "This is Hank Barnaby, my chief engineer."

Paul remembered Barnaby's name from the Contacts list as he shook the engineer's hand.

"We're sure relieved to see you," Barnaby said.

"Hank'll give you the tour," Cantrell said. "I'll catch up with you afterward. I've a pressing call to make. In the meantime, you can leave your things with Margot."

After leaving his suit jacket and locked briefcase in the care of Mrs Lewandowski, Paul followed Barnaby along a tiled corridor leading to the heart of the facility. Before beginning this tour, he'd hoped to have a discussion about the reactor incident – the only positive aspect of his coming here was the opportunity to learn what had brought a modern Pressurised Water Reactor to the brink of a meltdown. Had a malfunctioning pressure relief valve been involved, as at Three Mile Island more recently?

Such reactors didn't exist in the UK yet – although one was planned for the Sizewell power station on the East Anglian coast, within fifty miles of Ann's parents' home. The UK had until now favoured Advanced Gas-cooled Reactors, which used graphite bricks instead of pressurised water to slow down neutrons to the speeds required for fission chain reactions. This approach was thought to enable generation of the cheapest electricity. However, it was not proving to be problem-free.

Paul had also hoped for an early opportunity to gauge the openness of the people with whom he would be dealing. The perplexed look on Cantrell's face when they'd shaken hands hadn't been reassuring.

After walking fifty yards, the two men passed through a fire door and then turned left into another corridor. They proceeded to the end of this corridor, passed through another fire door and entered the control room of the operational reactor – designated as HS-1.

Six men, sitting at work stations, turned to see who'd entered. Upon recognising Barnaby they returned their attention to the control panels and gauges in front of them.

"HS-1 is undergoing refuelling," Barnaby said. "We do that every eighteen months. At the same time, we carry out safety checks and undertake non-routine maintenance on the steam turbine generators and the cooling systems."

There was something comforting to Paul about this control room environment. It was as though he were among innocent colleagues engaged in a familiar form of endeavour. But then he had the thought: *Do these workers know what happened to the other reactor?*

"Through here, Paul," Barnaby said, opening the door at the rear of the control room.

Paul followed the chief engineer into what seemed to be a combination of a lounge and a team briefing area. A bespectacled man with red hair sat eating his packed lunch at one of the metal tables. Crumbs speckled the table and the man's newspaper, which was open at the Sports pages.

"Jeez, Sam!" Barnaby grumbled.

"Oh... hi, Hank," grunted the middle-aged man before taking another bite of his egg sandwich.

Barnaby proceeded to the long counter that ran along a wall. "These show the plant layout." He pointed at the upper half of the first of the two blueprints lying on the counter. "We're here by one of the control rooms, both of which are located in the northern part of the facility." Moving his finger to the centre of the diagram, he continued, "The interior comprises the two reactor containment halls. They're separated by a hundred feet thick lead- and concrete-lined barrier extending the height of the building. Within that are two elevators and three armoured stairwells, each providing direct access to the lower basement and the first, third and fifth levels of each hall." He then pointed to the lines denoting the exterior of the building. "The power company had to prettify the plant to secure approval from the county. The coated-steel cladding gives the impression of a single structure. The idea was to resemble a paper mill or sugar refinery – anything but what it is. Back in the fifties, many dismissed nuclear power as space-age nonsense or were terrified we would make atom bombs."

It occurred to Paul that the façade surrounding the two containment halls would have played a role in covering up the reactor incident – workers' movements to and from the affected reactor being easier to conceal. "That's interesting. In fact, nuclear power *still* has its critics in Europe. There's even resistance to the addressing of the waste issue from pressure groups who don't want the technology to become widely seen as acceptable."

"Damn communists everywhere, I guess."

"How long have you worked here, Hank?"

A distant look spread across Barnaby's face. After taking a deep breath, he said, "Oh, pretty much from the start. I was working as a senior electrical engineer at the Ohio plant when I was deployed here to oversee installation of the steam generator control equipment. I was asked to stay on through the commissioning of the first reactor and one promotion led to another and another... and, well, here I still am."

"So your background wasn't in nuclear physics?"

The sounds of Sam coughing and the feet of his chair scraping the floor made them turn round. Leaving the newspaper and crumbs from his lunch on the table, the worker headed towards the control room.

Barnaby's expression betrayed annoyance, seemingly prompted by the interruption. After regaining his concentration, he moved to the second blueprint. With a terser tone, he said, "This shows the whole site. The rail track runs from our depot here to the switching yard over at Maizetown. You'll need to visit there."

"I assume this is the spent fuel holding unit?" Paul said, pointing at a rectangle labelled as 'Reactor Products Storage'. Its orientation ran north-south, parallel to that of the nearby steam turbine hall.

"That should be obvious to an *expert* like you." Barnaby looked about them, as if checking that they were still alone. Satisfied, he continued, "The storage hall had to be extended to receive the damaged materials from the HS-2 containment building. It has six holding ponds now."

"Is there anything left to be transferred?"

"Feel free to step inside the containment building yourself and educate us. Otherwise I don't need another armchair critic."

"I-I don't think that's what I'm supposed to be here for."

"Then don't go asking after my qualifications!"

Paul's stray question about Barnaby's background had struck a nerve. The presence of the eavesdropping Sam had made matters worse – maintaining authority was essential in this environment.

"I didn't mean to... I was just making conversation."

"Another thing you're not here for, son."

"Understood," Paul said, feeling chastened. At least he'd learned something about Barnaby's defensiveness.

"To answer your question, once we brought the reactor back under control, we had to remove and isolate some 10 per cent of the fuel rods. The pressure relief tank, the pressuriser, the control valves and rest of the primary cooling system all got contaminated. We dismantled each of those and replaced parts that we couldn't quickly decontaminate. An improvised cooling circuit, using spares shipped from our sister plants, is keeping the reactor core under control."

"It's hard to imagine the conditions you've been working under, Hank."

"We were luckier than Three Mile Island. We were able to prevent radioactive water from getting into the concrete floor."

"Is HS-2 operable?"

"Not yet."

Paul decided not to press for further information. Instead, he nodded supportively and waited for the engineer to continue the tour.

"Not much more we can do until the damaged material is out of here. I'll take you to the storage hall, so you can get a feel for things." He pointed to a red door bearing the words STORAGE PONDS. ACCREDITED PERSONNEL ONLY in white paint. "There's a changing area through there. We'll have to put on protective suits."

As Paul moved to follow Barnaby, his gaze fell upon the creased newspaper Sam had left. The front page headline was irresistible.

Barnaby turned back and looked over Paul's shoulder. "What have you got there? Oh... the *Atlantic Daily Herald*. Sam commutes from Pleasantville."

Paul barely registered Barnaby's hovering presence; the headline conveyed as much as his mind could process: REPORTER'S HOME

DESTROYED IN BLAZE. NO SURVIVORS.

Chapter 11

"Did Hank show you everything?" The plant manager stared, eyebrows raised, as Paul stirred his coffee. They were in Cantrell's office, sitting on opposing sofas with the coffee table between them. Cantrell's forehead glistened under the harsh ceiling lights. Barnaby had left to attend to another matter.

After the discomfort of the hazard suit, Avery had initially found the room temperature refreshing, but now it felt cold. "Yes, thank you. And I've provided him with a list of the information I need."

"How do we contact you? Through Vernon?"

Hearing Blackwood's forename made Paul inwardly shudder. Establishing who knew whom and who knew what was essential to his survival. Two pieces of the covert jigsaw had just interlocked. "I'm staying at the Banville Plaza in Atlantic City. You can telephone my room or leave messages with Reception."

Cantrell thought for a moment before saying, "Do you know anyone called Wilkinson?"

"No, I don't."

"In that case, if you're contacted by a Mr Wilkinson, it'll be Hank or me."

"Understood."

"All in all, it's probably better you remain in Atlantic City. Moving to Hartling could invite questions. We don't get many Brits around here."

Nor many Australians, Paul thought, recalling the remark made by the elderly gatekeeper.

Cantrell looked at his watch. "It's nearly three. I assume you ate lunch already."

"I'll get something on the way back to the hotel."

"Margot can order up something from the cafeteria."

"I'm keen to get back before rush hour and reflect on the next steps while everything's fresh in my mind."

"Hank said you made some sketches."

"Just the arrangement of the cooling ponds and how the different items are distributed among them, and the intended path to your rail depot here. Mr Barnaby said it's a routine procedure for him to lay down a temporary track."

"Hank and the guys do whatever it takes. The track is removed when it's not being used. It just gets in the way."

"He's arranged for me to meet a freight contact at Maizetown tomorrow morning."

"Is Hank going with you?"

"We're meeting there."

Cantrell nodded distractedly before staring fixedly at his visitor. "Don't get me wrong here, but you seem pretty young to be doing all this. Your British properness is all very well, but this is one hell of a responsibility you're taking on."

"I thought you seemed surprised when we met, Mr Cantrell. I've been provided with an excellent cover for my presence here – one that makes me affiliated to our Diplomatic Service. I'm visiting America as part of a cultural exchange study into the future of the nuclear energy sector, you see."

Cantrell took his handkerchief from his trouser pocket and dabbed his forehead. "I like that. It's good, very good. And you come across as credible, I must admit. But have you been made aware of what's at stake *for us*, specifically?"

"Not in detail, but I appreciate the compromising nature—"

"The thing is," Cantrell said, interrupting, "Sharp Power had plans for two new plants to add to the four it has. Those plans had to be shelved because of Three Mile Island, but we can't let them stay that way much longer. A competitor is already circling the locations we invested a lot of time and research effort in. We're in danger of losing first-mover advantage once the investment climate becomes favourable again."

"I don't need to know about that, Gavin."

"I believe it's essential that you do. We must borrow hundreds of millions of dollars to construct those plants. Our investors will disappear if they learn about the situation here and the creative accounting that's concealing the costs of dealing with the HS-2 reactor. On top of that, we've invested millions in Hartling on sports and retail facilities to maintain community goodwill and distract from the fact that 40 per cent of the jobs we promised years ago haven't been delivered.

All in all, there's a hell of a lot riding on your young shoulders."

Paul felt a twinge of sympathy. He could imagine how some of the money for a stadium and a shopping mall could have been misappropriated for, say, a new cooling pond or two. However, the sums for constructing two new power stations were too enormous to relate to. They belonged to an abstract economic realm. In his world, twenty thousand pounds would be life changing.

"Message understood, Gavin, but perhaps you can clarify a matter. Surely the removal of the quarantined equipment and fuel rods will constitute inconsistencies with your plant inventories. Isn't that a permanent auditing risk?"

"The serial numbers of those items have been purged from our records, and the additional low-level waste from the clean-up of HS-2 was recorded as HS-1 maintenance waste. Fortunately HS-1 was closed down for refuelling when the problem happened, so we inflated the waste figures for it."

Cantrell had answered a question that Paul hadn't thought to ask: Why was the material he was shipping to South Africa limited to the high- and intermediate-level waste categories? However, the plant manager hadn't fully answered the question that Paul *had* asked. Paul tried again: "But can't an auditor could go to the suppliers and—"

"Demand lists of the serial numbers for all the items they've ever supplied to us," Cantrell interrupted excitedly. He shook his head and, in a calmer tone, continued, "Then compare the serial numbers to those of the equipment and fuel to be found in this plant. That's what you're suggesting, isn't it? Physically dismantle everything, department by department, highly radioactive or not, to check that all the serial numbers are accounted for. It would be a mind-blowingly expensive and time-consuming undertaking that would take this plant offline. It won't happen. It would be like a detective looking for evidence of a crime he has no reason to suspect has taken place. No reason to suspect, unless you don't do your job, that is."

"Of course. Thanks for dotting the 'i's for me, Gavin."

"Do you have any other matters requiring clarification?"

"No, not at this time."

"Good. Then you also need to know you're going to be watched closely. It won't be just Vernon's people. We have our own."

More pressure. Not helpful. Hoping to appeal to the financial mindset of his host, Paul said, "That would be an unnecessary use of your resources. We've got the same objectives."

"But we've just met each other and everyone has to protect himself." Cantrell smiled for the first time. "Think of it as your backup."

***

Returning to Atlantic City, Paul took a detour to the strip mall near the site of the former watch factory. As he'd hoped, he found a newspaper vending stand. After slotting three quarters he opened the reinforced-glass case and took out the last copy of the *Atlantic Daily Herald.*

He folded the newspaper and tucked it under his arm. The parking lot was sparsely occupied, so a vehicle that hadn't been there when he'd pulled in moments ago stood out. The vehicle was a new-looking grey sedan with closed tinted windows. It was parked near the edge of the parking lot, well away from other cars. None of the elderly people near him, who were meandering from store to store, looked as though they'd just arrived.

Paul returned to his car and got in. After placing the newspaper on the front-passenger seat, he started the engine and drove towards the exit. He turned right, re-joining the traffic heading east. Moments later, in his rear-view mirror, he observed the grey sedan, sunlight glinting from its roof, easing on to the road.

He moved across into the left lane, marked for "City Center". The left-turn traffic signal was on red. When he came to a stop, the grey sedan was directly behind him, its left indicators flashing. The driver and the front passenger looked to be male, wearing suit jackets and ties. Were they Cantrell's people? Or Blackwood's? Or mobsters linked to Banville? Or were these distinctions without a difference?

The sedan followed Paul's looping route to the main entrance of the Banville Plaza. As he turned in to the parking lot, the grey sedan slowed before continuing westwards, away from the city.

***

Carrying his briefcase, the satchel containing the radiation detector battery, and the copy of the *Atlantic Daily Herald*, Paul entered his fourth-floor hotel room.

A bedside lamp was on. He didn't think he'd left it that way. Of course, by now a cleaner had come to service the room – the double bed was neatly made, the waste basket emptied, and fresh soap and towels had been left in the bathroom – and might have turned on that lamp, but had someone else been here too? Was it another sign that his movements were being monitored?

He placed his things on the table that was next to the window. It was 5.15 p.m. and still sunny outside. He drew the curtains closed and turned on more lights. After taking off and hanging his suit in the wardrobe, Paul checked the contents of the wall safe. The rest of his travel money was still there.

If concealed microphones had been installed, how could he find them? And should he even try? And what about a camera? Perhaps there was one behind an air vent? Absently fingering the radiation badge that was still pinned to the breast pocket of his shirt, he decided to seek privacy elsewhere in the hotel. Paul removed the badge and put it in his briefcase. He took out his notebook and a ballpoint pen and then placed the locked case upright in the bottom of the wardrobe.

He slid his dark-blue corduroy trousers from a hanger and put them on. For footwear, he selected khaki desert boots. After taking off his shirt and tie, he eased a royal-blue polo shirt over his head. It had a brass zipper at the neck, which he left undone. Paul put on his fawn sports jacket and dropped his wallet into the inside pocket. He took the newspaper, notebook and pen from the table and headed to the door, leaving the light on. The room would be left to the real or imagined surveillance detail.

In the otherwise empty elevator, he pressed the button for the lower basement; the words "Swimming Pool" were also next to the button. There were no interruptions to his descent. The steel door opened on to a quiet corridor. Paul went in search of a nook where he wouldn't be seen. Along the corridor leading to the swimming pool was an unmarked swing door on the right. Paul eased open the door, just enough to see inside. The lit room seemed to be a storage area – there were columns of stacked chairs, folded tables resting against the walls and two large boxes containing conference paraphernalia such as flipcharts.

He went inside and placed the newspaper and notebook on the floor beside the door. This freed his hands to lift down one of the chairs. Once seated, he picked up the newspaper and began reading the front page:

"Fire Department, police and medical first-responders attended a house fire at the *Fir Trees* estate in Pleasantville last night. Flames had already done too much damage for the single-story property to be saved.

The charred bodies of two people and a dog were found at the scene. Formal identifications have yet to be completed. The police have confirmed the destroyed home as being that of *Atlantic Daily Herald* investigative reporter Peter Wilson and his wife, Julia. The couple did not have children.

Pete worked at the *Herald* for almost nineteen years and will be deeply missed by his colleagues.

According to Fire Chief Art Daintith, it may be weeks before the investigation into the cause of the fire is concluded.

This story continues on Page 7."

Paul's concern about the fate of Peter Wilson had been vindicated, although in a manner he hadn't foreseen. The urge to confront Shannon propelled him to his feet but dissipated just as quickly. Doing that could make him a target for similar treatment.

He turned to page 7. The rest of the article included photographs of a more youthful Peter Wilson and his wife. If there had been any room for doubt – perhaps the man in the waste container had stolen or found Wilson's wallet – it was gone now.

Providing Shannon *hadn't* seen him looking through Wilson's wallet, she wouldn't conceive that he was capable of connecting the deaths from a suburban house fire with the person they'd rescued. Of course, if she *had* seen... And what about the men in the grey car? They might have observed him buying the local newspaper. Did they know about Wilson's murder?

The afternoon was ending with the same note of anxiety that had caused him to nearly drive through a stop-light this morning. Perhaps if he'd known then what he knew now, he wouldn't have registered the red traffic light at all. With that chilling thought, he slid the folded newspaper into the horizontal gap between the seats of two stacked chairs, picked up his notebook from the floor and left the room.

Chapter 12

Paul Avery stopped at the front desk to check for messages. He was informed a Miss Lennon had left one for him to call her on room extension 618. He thanked the young man and headed to the red-and-white-striped "Good Vibrations Diner" that occupied part of the hotel frontage.

The informal eatery was busy. Paul found a seat at a table for two, situated by the door to the washrooms. He asked a passing waitress for coffee and a slice of apple pie.

None of the other customers paid attention to him – he hoped he looked as though he might have spent the day on the slots in a Boardwalk casino – and in return he welcomed the feeling of being in the company of people with relatable concerns. It was a young clientele, one that Paul discerned from overheard exchanges included "locals" as well as hotel guests. Excitement prompted by today's being the end of the working week blended with talk about plans for the coming weekend.

Four days ago, like them, he was preoccupied with normal enthusiasms and concerns. If only he hadn't been at his desk to take the call from Morrison... Selective ignorance was Maycross's protective shell – that and compartmentalisation. Don't question the inclusion of the demolition site. Hard to do when you were in the field, dragging bodies out of skips. For now Paul was a valuable piece in his controller's three-dimensional game of high-stakes chess, but at some point he could be sacrificed in a defensive or offensive manoeuvre. Would succeeding in his tasks truly guarantee his and his wife's safety? The promise of a bonus somehow made things worse.

He opened his notebook and wrote the heading: "First Visit to Hartling Springs Power Station, New Jersey, on Friday 22 July 1983". The professional part of his mind began to function again as he noted down the key points from his conversations with Barnaby and Cantrell. Below the notes he sketched the layout of the Reactor Products Storage Hall. He hadn't anticipated the cathedral-like hugeness of the hall.

After they'd donned hazard suits, the tour began with a walk along the elevated passage that was separated from the storage area itself by a concrete wall. Small lead-glass windows, which reminded Paul of the windows in the Concorde fuselage, looked down on to the round cooling ponds. From this vantage position, Barnaby pointed to the hoist mechanism fitted to the overhead gantry that ran the length of the hall, and went on to describe the conditions of the fuel rods and the equipment that had been retrieved from the HS-2 containment building. All of these items had been transferred to the two most recently added storage ponds, within which recirculating cooling water absorbed the neutrons emitted by the damaged fuel pellets. Barnaby said that the damaged fuel rods had cooled sufficiently for their removal from the ponds. He reluctantly agreed to Paul's insistence upon receiving comprehensive temperature measurements, but not without another display of being affronted.

The reactor hall clean-up work had been undertaken by alternating teams brought in from Sharp's other three nuclear power stations. These men were Sharp Power "lifers", the "best of the best" according to Barnaby, who was clearly a lifer himself. "They got bigger paychecks than I ever have," he added for emphasis, "although I oversaw the work."

At no point did Barnaby divulge the cause of the reactor incident. And because of the manner in which the clean-up work had been sequenced, it seemed feasible to Paul that few, if any, of the specialist workers would have gained a full understanding of what had occurred. Given the chief engineer's sensitivity, Paul kept his curiosity to himself.

The waitress brought the slice of apple pie and topped up Paul's coffee. He told her he wouldn't be ordering anything else and for the charge to be put against his room account. The pie was sweet and moist, but it gradually seemed to dry in his mouth. An image of the Wilsons, burned beyond recognition, lying in the ruins of their home, had come to him. There would be no telling Julie, this women he'd never met, anything now. He wondered if her death was quick or if she'd been left alive to suffer the flames. Could he have prevented her murder?

Revived by the strong coffee, Paul left the diner and used a lobby phone to call Shannon Lennon's room. She told him to come up. Her voice seemed strained. Still clutching his notebook, Paul took the elevator to the sixth floor and knocked on the door of room 618.

Opening the door to the limit of the safety catch, Shannon peered out. Seeing Paul, she released the catch and opened the door. The sound of a whooping and hollering TV game-show audience burst into the corridor. She was wearing a white cardigan and a plain blue dress, which was gathered at the waist by a chain-belt. "Thanks for coming," she said as he entered. "Did you have a productive day?" She closed the door.

Paul registered the unease in Shannon's demeanour and noticed she looked pale. "I met the principal contacts and have seen the materials that have to be removed," he said loudly to defeat the din of the television.

"What's the next step?" she said, using the remote control to quieten the television.

"I'm meeting someone in the morning. An expert on railroad wagons – boxcars I think you call them. I need the weight restrictions for the routes connecting to the nearest ports."

"Can he be trusted?" she said distractedly, not looking at him.

"He's their coordinator for fuel shipments. I won't reveal anything that's compromising," Paul replied. Any connection with Shannon that Paul had sensed last evening had seemingly evaporated. What had happened to her today with Blackwood?

"You won't mind if I come along?"

"On the contrary, Shannon. I'm relying on you to produce the shipping paperwork. You need to know all the transport details."

"Sure, sure, that's me. Why not?" she said, still unsettled.

"If you recall, Vernon said I mustn't contact the Department of Energ—"

Shannon had used the remote to suddenly turn up the TV volume again. She grabbed Paul by the shoulder and pulled him close. "The room's bugged," she whispered, staring into his eyes.

Paul was stunned. Why was *her* room bugged? And if it was, why had she told him?

Shannon turned away, seemingly stressed. After a moment of indecision, she turned the television off and retrieved her shoulder bag from the bed. Moving towards the room door, she beckoned for Paul to follow. Staring up at the ceiling-mounted smoke detector, she said, "I need to visit a store. After that we'll eat and you can describe the paperwork we need."

On the way down to the hotel lobby, they said nothing in the elevator to each other or to the elderly couple dressed in evening attire. Life as a comfortable retiree struck Paul as a future that would never apply to him; it seemed as unimaginable as his affording a restored classic sports car, such as the one he'd parked next to at the Tobe Institute.

As he and Shannon approached the hotel main entrance, she said, "Stay here for exactly one minute, then come out and watch who leaves after me. I'm going to a nearby drugstore to pick up a few things. When I'm back, we'll find a diner some place."

"A grey car *followed me* this afternoon, Shannon," Paul said excitedly. "Two men. They wanted me to see them."

Following a few seconds of reflection, she responded, "We'll talk about that later. One thing at a time."

He watched Shannon depart through the revolving door into the glare of the summer evening. After counting to sixty, he did likewise. Shannon's reaction to his news about being followed hadn't given anything away. Had she known or not?" Standing under the forecourt canopy, he monitored the exit of the parking lot. When a cab stopped next to him to drop off guests, he moved to an unshaded area from where he observed Shannon's silver sedan moving between the outermost rows of parked cars.

While Shannon was waiting for a gap in the city-bound traffic, a white sports car pulled up behind her. When the traffic abated, Shannon turned right. The sports car followed as if attached by a rope, but it immediately moved into another lane and accelerated past, a loud crackling coming from its exhaust.

Moments later, a dark-blue station wagon with wood-panelling on its doors and rear flanks sped towards the parking lot exit. Provoking horn blasts, its driver steered the vehicle out into the stream of traffic. Paul found the idea of Shannon's being followed even more chilling than its happening to him. The churning sensation he'd experienced upon learning her room was bugged returned. Speculation about her was useless. She was a blank slate again.

The next vehicle to leave the parking lot was the cab that had caused him to move away from the front of the hotel. In the absence of other vehicles arriving or leaving. Paul ambled back to the hotel entrance and waited in the shadow of the canopy again. Nearly twenty-five minutes passed before Shannon's car pulled up beside him.

"Did anyone follow me?" she asked as he got in.

"A white two-seater, but I don't think—"

"That was an asshole showing off," she said impatiently. "No one else?"

"A dark-blue estate car with wood-panel sides. It was definitely in a hurry."

"You mean a station wagon?"

"Yes."

"One like that was parked across from the drug store when I came out."

"What does it mean, Shannon?"

"Let's go eat. I'll tell you what I know."

***

They travelled west for six miles, the low sun flaring across the windscreen, until they came to one of the out-of-town restaurants they'd passed during their drive to Atlantic City two eventful days ago. This time the neon-pink rooftop sign for ***Sandy's*** was lit.

The parking lot was crowded with sedans, station wagons and pickups; Shannon found a space at the end of a row. "Lots of folks out early on a Friday night," she said.

"Safety in crowds for us though," Paul said.

Shannon turned off the engine. "Vernon's furious with me because I allowed you to spend time around the garbage containers. A walk-by was all you needed, he said."

"A what? Anyway, I didn't give you a choi—"

Cutting him off, she said, "That's not the way Vernon sees things. I told you that we're not officially allowed to work in the field inside the country. Finding that man and then calling for a hazard response unit... I'm meant to be a background facilitator, not a crazy, flashing beacon."

"He'd never have got out without help, Shannon. Another day breathing alpha particles would have finished him. Anyway, I would have come across his body later."

"That happening anyplace else, particularly without me there, wouldn't have mattered nearly as much."

"Why did Vernon send the helicopter if he felt that way about things? Why didn't he order you to just leave the situation to me?"

"I can't say that to him. He was looking to blame someone, and he's unnerved by you because he needs you. So he unloaded on me.

"He's getting heat from his partners. The site's holy ground to the family, so it's pissed. Its goons are on the Banville payroll, not just at that place but at other sites too. It's a way of receiving income that can be declared to the Inland Revenue. Whatever you're seen doing is Vernon's fault as far as its concerned. Because you're his ticket to the whole game, he has to deal with it."

It was a lot for Paul to take in. *Does she know what's happened to that reporter and his wife?* There didn't seem to be anything he could say that would help the situation. *If Blackwood's unhappy, Maycross will be unhappy*. That insight should have been enough for him to worry about. He'd disregarded Fransen's clear instructions.

"He reads people, Paul. It's like he can get inside my head. He told me he doubts my *suitability*, my reliability." Shannon grasped Paul's forearm, causing him to turn towards her. "If whoever's tailing you makes it that obvious, then they're doing it to keep you in line. If I'm being followed, it's different. I won't be given a second chance.

"That's why I wanted to know if Vernon has begun having *me* watched. The only way to find out was by provoking them to show themselves, but I needed an extra pair of eyes. That's why I asked you to come to my room. Like I said, it's bugged. There's a wired room on each floor of the hotel. We made sure you got one too, so our conversations and your phone calls can be recorded."

His suspicion about his room – the bedside lamp left on – hadn't been misplaced. Hearing her confess affected him more than he'd anticipated. The difference between suspecting and knowing was profound. "How sure are you that you're being followed?" he said.

Looking into the rear-view mirror, she replied, "Well now I'm *certain* of it. The blue station wagon's driven past us for the third time. The driver's acting like he's looking for a parking place."

"Can't you get away from Blackwood, Shannon? Just leave?"

"Just leave!" Shannon pulled back her hair and turned her head away. "If I did, I wouldn't survive, not without a plan."

Despite the shadow inside the car, Paul could discern a raised welt on the pale skin close to the back of her neck.

"Vernon's cigar did that two weeks ago," she said. "That was when he *trusted* me, calling me his latest protégé. It was his way of showing me that leaving Continental will never be an option. He's got a liaison job lined up for me in South America. Something much, much bigger than this."

Paul reached across and took her hand. "I thought I was the one with everything to lose – deportation, a lifetime of financial ruin..."

She wrapped her hands tightly round his. With a trembling smile, she said, "Then see... your life isn't so bad. Blackwood's branded me, but that's not enough. Now I know he's sent someone to kill me if I make another misstep."

"Isn't there anyone who can help you?"

Shannon shook her head. "Using the Agency whistle-blower programme would be suicide because Vernon's untouchable. Even this project has some cover if it's exposed. Security laws set up for the wartime atom-bomb project can still be invoked to shield covert missions that are in one way or another radiation-related."

Security laws... Paul felt a sudden desire to kiss her. The universe inside this car, thousands of miles from his home, surrounded by strangers, had its own laws, too, governing the passage of time – a moment of neon-lit sanctuary for two hijacked lives.

The thudding of a car door shattered the stillness.

Paul eased his hand from hers and moved away. There was still a crinkle of orange along the western horizon – it gave colour to his guilt. Since meeting Maycross, he barely knew himself any more. He couldn't remember ever having felt so exhausted, so confused.

They watched the car next to theirs reverse out from its parking bay.

"We must go inside and order some food," Shannon said, her voice a distant monotone. "The station wagon's back."

Chapter 13

Maizetown, a railroad yard overlooked by a hotchpotch of dwellings on treeless slopes, was well signposted, unlike the power station at Hartling Springs. Paul drove and Shannon navigated. There was an awkwardness between them this morning, but each having a task brought a welcome formality to their few exchanges. She was in her beige, no-nonsense "government-worker uniform" – as Paul had come to think of it. Being hungover, he welcomed this too, needing to keep his mind on the road.

He'd sat up late, drinking miniatures of Scotch from the room minibar. Eventually he fell asleep in front of the television, waking at one point from a bizarre nightmare in which there were trapped victims in all ten of the waste containers, all screaming in high-pitched voices as if the breathed radon was having the falsetto-inducing effect of helium gas.

His evening call to Ann had given him a lot to fret about, priming him for the restless night. Shannon's revealing that there was a microphone in his room had added to the stress. This, combined with Maycross's likely tapping of his home telephone, meant every sigh, every inflection in his tone could be captured and analysed on both sides of the ocean by those seeking to control him.

Shannon and he hadn't arrived back from ***Sandy's*** until past eight, so the later-than-agreed call woke Ann. She wasn't interested in his excuse – slow waiter service at a packed New Jersey restaurant sounded exotic, not like something worthy of sympathy, but it did prompt questions such as "Why didn't you eat at the hotel?" and "Who did you go there with?" His weary dissembling soon evolved into expansive lying – mumbling something about being with "Government officials representing the energy sector" and sprinkling the descriptions of these imaginary characters with adjectives such as "tiresome", "demanding" and "humourless".

Ann had perturbing news of her own she wanted to share. She'd had a visitor. A tall man in an "obviously expensive suit" had brought "an enormous bouquet of the most gorgeous flowers". He'd driven from London to apologise in person for having taken her husband away "on a matter of national importance". Ann had found Patrick Maycross to be charming. Moreover, he'd shown "a genuine fascination" with her corner-cabinet display of silver curios, something Paul had never managed to convincingly feign. "He's extremely cultivated and much better company than the people I've met from your office," she said. "He knew all about hallmarks, too. I'm very impressed."

"Okay, that's interesting. Look, I've been thinking, Ann... You *should* go to your parents' after all," he said, troubled by the notion of Maycross visiting her again.

"You told me there's no need, Paul."

"I know but actually being here now, I see that the times I will get at home must be brief – days at the most, now and then, because of the deadlines. It won't be fair on you."

***

An expanse of crisscrossing tracks, looking like endless glinting runs of steel ladders resting on blackened timbers, lay ahead as they descended the eastern slope of the valley. The distant view of the Delaware disappeared when the horizon was replaced by the valley's western slope.

"These homes remind me of the one I grew up in," Shannon said.

Paul glanced a couple of times at the houses they were passing; with the hairpin bends, keeping the car on the correct side of the winding road required concentration. "Okay," he said, unsure what she meant – no two houses seemed to have anything in common, excluding possession of the same sad view.

"I liked the sweet-potato fries we had last night. We should go there again," he said, feeling obliged to say something positive.

"You want to see that pretty waitress," Shannon said. "I saw the way she let her hand linger on your back."

"You're kidding. When I asked for a cold beer, she asked me how old I am."

"She'd get in serious trouble if she served alcohol to a minor."

"I'm nearer to thirty than I am to eighteen."

"You have to be twenty-one to buy alcohol in America. Don't forget that, young man."

"Young man!"

"How do you think she made me feel? Like I'm your mom!"

Grinning, he snatched a look at his passenger. He was relieved to see Shannon was smiling too. That broad smile... If she truly didn't know about the reporter's fate, she wasn't an accomplice to murder; there'd be only one of those in the car.

"I loved the *fixin's* too," he said. "Did I mention those?"

"You just like saying that word over and over. You think we're all hillbillies."

"I plead the, er, the Fifth Amendment."

A gravelled area outside the chain-link fence protecting the rail yard served as its parking lot. Paul added his car to the row of vehicles, many of which were rusting and dented. He wondered if the spotless white sedan he'd parked next to belonged to Hank Barnaby. They'd agreed to meet at ten and it was now a quarter past.

"This time, I suggest that I should take the lead," Paul said, getting out. He opened a rear-passenger door, lifted his briefcase out from the footwell and took his navy-blue suit jacket from the rear seat.

Shannon got out but seemed distracted. She was staring at the valley slope they'd driven down.

"Because they're only expecting me to come," Paul added.

"It doesn't look like we were followed."

Paul glanced at the eastern slope before saying, "Maybe we're both becoming paranoid." He started walking towards the nearby single-storey building that fronted the yard. There was a taste of grit in the air.

A film of dust clung to the building's aluminium siding. A sign hung from the ceiling of the through-porch dividing the building into two wings:

MAIZETOWN RAIL YARD.

PRIVATE PROPERTY.

After advancing a few feet, Paul wheeled round. "I'm sorry, Shannon. God knows, you've more than enough reason to... you know, be on your guard."

"Where's your guy?" Shannon said, catching up to him.

Paul considered the plaques on the doors facing each other across the porch. Choosing STAFF OFFICES instead of SUPPLIES AND CANTEEN, he headed towards the door to their left. "In here, I gue—"

"Over here!"

The distant voice was Barnaby's. Dressed in a grey suit, he was standing in the rail yard with his foot resting on the high step of a diesel shunting engine. Beside him was a short, plump and nearly bald man, whose surviving hair comprised a ginger "band" around the back of his head. This man's choice of suit – a light-brown check pattern – and his yellow bowtie produced a clownish look.

"Good morning, Hank!" Paul called out as he and Shannon made their way towards the two men, stepping over the rails of the tracks. Because of her narrow heels, the stony ground made progress difficult for Shannon.

"Shannon will assist with the paperwork side of things," Paul said, gesturing back towards his companion. Hank's features took on a severe look, one Paul had learned to be wary of. "She works for Vernon Blackwood, if that means anything to you."

The Barnaby frown darkened further. "Then I'll be leaving you both in the hands of this gentleman, Paul," Hank said as Shannon reached them. "Art can answer all your questions."

"You're not staying, Hank?" Paul asked, surprised.

"I've got to get back to the plant. Just because it's a Saturday, it doesn't mean they don't need me." Hank turned away to commence his walk back to the entrance.

"I thought we were coming here to make decisions, not for a survival course," Shannon said, staring down at the fresh scuffs on the sides of her shoes.

"Art Richards. Pleased to meet you folks," the short man with a round face interjected, extending his hand to Shannon, then Paul.

After shaking hands, Paul said, "What's your line of work, Mr. Richards?"

"You're standing on it – *tracks*, that is. Getting things from place to place throughout the good ol' US of A on tracks. From here to anywhere, always in the most suitable way."

"Why are we meeting here?" Shannon asked.

"Hank got in touch yesterday. Said there'll be a load leaving the power plant sometime soon. Told me I must meet with a British Government contact of his to—."

"No, I mean why *here*?" Shannon interrupted.

"They don't like visitors at the plant, which suits me just fine. Hank always meets me here."

"I gather the lines to and from the power plant come through this yard," Paul said, staring southwards, trying to discern which tracks extended in the direction of Hartling Springs.

"There's just the one track, Paul. Always has been. It suffices for the plant's needs. One of their sister plants sends or picks up nuclear fuel using a transfer train. We undertake the car switching to or from Hank's smaller engine.

"Such shipments are few and far between, but we're glad of the work. Providing the switching service to the plant is pretty much all this yard's used for nowadays." Richards reached up and patted the door of the shunting engine. "Not a whole bunch of jobs for this big fellow to do any more, ever since the yard outside Philly took on pretty much everything else."

"Philadelphia," Shannon clarified for Paul's benefit.

"So, normally it's quiet here?" Paul said.

"Quiet? Oh, I get you. Yes, as a graveyard. But there's one thing we're the masters at. Minding our beeswax. Discretion's the name of the game." Richards put his forefinger to his pouting lips.

Paul turned to Shannon. Holding her gaze, he said, "Well, discretion *is* what we need."

Pointing at the slope they'd descended, she asked, "What about those houses? They can see everything that goes on down here."

"The ones that aren't empty belong to the maintenance crew or their old folk. They're all appreciative of the work that comes this yard's way. It's a fine life, all in all, being paid for doing next to nothing most of the time."

"I see," Paul said, nodding. "I know power stations have all sorts of costly overheads that the average person would never imagine. This yard is just one of those. I take it you're in charge here, Art."

"Pretty much, except the paychecks. They're taken care of by Hank, who" – Richards looked towards the parking area – "for some reason's skedaddled."

Following Richards' gaze, Paul noticed that the white sedan had gone. Barnaby had seemingly been unsettled by Shannon's connection to Vernon Blackwood.

Art continued, "He also provides the armed security team for the switching procedure. Road blocks, watch points. Anyone who doesn't belong is detained or sent on their way." Nodding towards the entrance, he said, "There's an office here we can use. How about we make ourselves comfortable, and you tell me precisely what this is all about?"

"I'd like to look round first?" Paul said.

Richards waved his arms theatrically. "Well, there's just a whole lot of tracks and switching points. Nothing to see."

"Is there a siding with a loading area that is accessible from the road?"

"There is." Looking at Shannon's shoes, Richards continued, "If the young lady's coming too, we should take my car."

Shannon gave Paul a look that conveyed: *Don't even think about leaving me out of this.*

About ninety minutes later, just after noon, Paul and Shannon returned to his car for their drive back to Atlantic City. As they approached the gravelled parking area, a grey sedan with tinted windows was reversing out. It took the road ascending the western slope of the valley.

"I'm sure that's the car that followed me yesterday," Paul said. "They must have been sent to confirm I was where I told the power station manager I'd be this morning."

"I'm hardly the right person to complain to."

"It's strange that they didn't just wait to check with Hank Barnaby."

"You told me that they *want* you to see them. That's the point."

"Yeah. Or perhaps they don't like talking to Hank about certain things. He's a prickly character."

"And perhaps you're more suited to this type of work than I thought, Paul."

"I hope not," Paul said, grimacing. He returned his briefcase to the rear footwell of the sedan. As they got into the car, he asked, "Anyway, what did you mean?"

"It doesn't matter," Shannon said, closing her door.

"Fine! I'm not going to apologise any more either."

"Now, that *is* a pity. It's a strength of yours – getting under people's guard."

"Fabian Gooch – he's my department head – said something to that effect during my last appraisal."

"I hope he's a better boss than Vernon."

"Gooch has gone up in my estimation a lot since I met Blackwood."

Paul turned the ignition key. In that moment, it struck him that the men in the grey car could have wired a bomb to the ignition system. He froze mid-breath. All he heard was his own heart thumping.

"Are you okay, Paul?" Shannon said after several seconds had passed. "I didn't mean to offend you. When I said you're suited to this type of work, I just meant you can size people up."

He breathed out slowly. "It wasn't what you said. I-I had a stupid thought. We'll stop somewhere for coffee and something to eat. My blood sugar feels low."

"You've earned it. That was a good meeting," Shannon said, settling back in her seat.

He nodded, still coming to terms with their not having been blown to pieces in a searing flash. She was correct about the meeting though; it had been as fruitful as Paul had dared to hope, despite Hank's abrupt departure.

Art Richards had provided Paul with diagrams of the radiation-grade casks used for transporting fuel shipments to and from the plant. Paul, in turn, had indicated it was possible that the upcoming shipment would require at least two, maybe three, such casks.

"They're not cheap and they're damn heavy. You buying or hiring?"

"Buying. They won't be returned," Paul replied.

"I hope you've got deep pockets. Hank can advise on how to get them. Best to speak to him. I just move them from A to B."

"I also need ten twenty-foot shipping containers, which have to be brought to that loading area you showed us, plus matching flatbed rail cars. And, of course, the necessary lifting equipment if you haven't got that here already."

"Ten shipping containers, you say?" Art's gaze darted from Paul to Shannon and back to Paul. Shrugging, he said, "I won't ask what for."

"Smart move, Art," Shannon said, with a knowing stare at Paul.

"The containers must be in excellent condition and be ventilated to avoid condensation under climatic variation. They will have to be lined internally with lead strips that I will obtain. Perhaps your crew can help with that work?"

"No problem. My guys do all types of fabrication."

To date, Richards' experience with nuclear loads had comprised movements between power plants within the USA. In the case of his work for Sharp Power, the company's Ohio plant had always been the provider of fresh radioactive fuel and was usually the receiver of the spent fuel too. He asked Paul which port his shipment was to be taken to.

"At the moment, it could be any port in this region of the US. The decision will depend on a number of factors," Paul replied. "I need from you an analysis of rail network loading constraints, covering bridges and anything else that will restrict the options available."

"You're making a lot of extra work for me. There's at least four ports right off the bat to consider. Portside cargo handling could be an issue too." Art absently stroked his bald crown as if taming hair that was no longer there.

"I'll cover your consultancy costs. Just let Hank know how much."

"Where will the ship take the cargo?"

"That will have to remain confidential," Paul responded, glancing towards Shannon. Turning back to Art, he continued, "I have a lot of homework to do too. After four or five more meetings like this one, we'll be in a position to agree the route." Paul didn't reveal he was waiting for provisional shipping details to be provided by Maycross's contact, Tom, in South Africa.

"Four or five meetings... What's the timing for your shipment?" Richards asked.

"Well, no sooner than two months, I would say. Probably nearer four. Could be six."

"Is there nothing more you can share with me?"

"Not at the moment. As I said, I have homework to do on the loads. If you give me your phone number, Art, I will provide you with more information as soon as I have it," Paul said.

Art hesitated before handing over his business card. "How can I contact you?"

"That shouldn't be necessary. I will be pressing you for updates. If for any reason something comes up, leave a message with Hank."

***

"You really handled Art well," Shannon said as they left Maizetown and its unappealing valley behind. The distant Delaware reappeared, but now framed in the rear-view mirror for only Paul to see.

"You'll tell that to Blackwood, I suppose." Paul hoped Shannon would indeed report favourably to Blackwood, and that Blackwood would report favourably to Maycross.

"I'll omit the 'could be six months' part."

"That length of time wouldn't apply to how long the waste containers will have to stay at the demolition site."

"You'll have Fransen and his foreman to contend with if it does."

"I know. I'll have those moved to Maizetown sooner than that."

"The *ten* shipping containers are for those, right?" Shannon said after a pause.

"How did you work that out?" Paul said.

"I'm psychic."

"By the way, paperwork will be needed, declaring the watch factory material as industrial, low-level nuclear waste. I assume Blackwood can come up with a company's details for us to put down as the shipper. Their customer is the Willingham Corporation."

"With his connections, Vernon can do anything."

As Paul drove, he reflected on Shannon's praise. He *had* handled things well. Perhaps he and Ann would survive. One day at a time, and today was "in the bank". After yesterday's shocking news about the reporter and his wife, this fact alone seemed a miracle.

"Why are you smiling?" Shannon asked.

Why? He hadn't realised he was smiling. An answer, perhaps the truth, came to him: "Maybe you don't look like my mom, after all. Art called you 'young lady'."

His right bicep absorbed the sting of her punch. "Ouch!"

Even if trusting her was a mistake, it was beyond him to do otherwise. Shannon's presence altered everything, turning a terrifying state of affairs into an exhilarating one.

Chapter 14

The roadside diner they stopped at for lunch had a more homely atmosphere – there were rocking chairs for sale on the white wooden porch – than that of the pub-like ***Sandy's***. The blue station wagon of yesterday hadn't followed them, but Shannon remained anxious.

"The people Vernon uses for this type of work aren't amateurs," she said, convinced Blackwood had put her on a short leash. "They must have changed their vehicle, so I have to assume it could be anyone."

By the time they reached the Banville Plaza, the city traffic was building for the rush hour. They said goodbye to each other in the hotel lobby. Paul explained he was going to the hotel store to buy something for Ann. Afterwards, he would catch up with his calculations and order a sandwich from room service.

"Let's meet in the hotel bar at ten," he suggested. "I assume it's free from Blackwood's microphones."

"As long as no one comes in wearing one."

With a twitch of a smile just moving the side of his mouth, Paul said, "In that case, we'll avoid anyone wearing a trilby and a trench coat."

"They won't look like that," she said angrily.

"I know," Paul said, but she was already turning away. He watched for a moment as she walked towards the elevators. There wasn't anyone following her. After checking at the front desk for messages – there were none – Paul headed to the gift store, which was located beside the elevators.

The windows bracketing the doorway of *AC Fine Arts* displayed colourful Italian "art glass" pieces and a selection of German and British ceramics – figurines, vases and decorative tableware. Paul's attention, however, was soon taken by the silver objects that were arranged over the bottom of the right-hand-side window display. One of the objects, a hinged box, had *All the Luck of Atlantic City* and a horseshoe symbol engraved on its lid.

"Is that box in your window display solid silver?" he asked the store assistant, a middle-aged woman with permed black hair.

"Yes, it's silver, sir. That one's the last we have. They're very popular with our guests." She walked to the back of the window display, knelt and retrieved the item. Holding it up for Paul to see, she continued, "It's for a pack of playing cards."

Paul took hold of the small box and examined it, turning it over.

"It says 'STERLING' right here, next to the maker's name," the assistant said, pointing with a red-varnished fingernail at the embossing on the base.

"I'll take it. Thank you."

"That'll be sixty-five dollars, sir."

It was only after he'd handed over his credit card that he realised it was the one Maycross had provided. He'd become accustomed to using the Government credit card to pay for meals and accommodation and without thinking had taken it from his wallet.

"Please put 'small metal box'," he said as the assistant was writing the item's description on the credit card slip.

"Small metal... I can do that, sir." She crossed out the words "Ornamental silv" and wrote "Small metal box".

The store assistant moved the slider of the printing device over the filled-in slip that now was lying face down, together with its backing duplicate sheet, on top of the face of the credit card.

Why hadn't he asked for the card back and handed over his personal one? This was an act of fraud, albeit encouraged by Maycross, the "extremely cultivated" man who'd made a favourable impression on Ann. As Paul gathered up the bagged gift, the credit card, the store receipt and the copy of the payment transaction, he felt disconnected from himself.

***

The softly lit Lucky Lou Bar, with its glossy black-themed décor, had few customers, even though it was a little after ten. Five people– two young couples and a lone middle-aged woman – occupied three of the round tables. Keyboard-based cool-jazz music, almost too quiet to be audible, contributed to the trying-to-be-sophisticated ambience. Business clientele had checked out yesterday and most of the vacationers were out enjoying gaming tables and cabarets at the Boardwalk casinos.

Paul, seated on a stool at the bar, was sipping his second cold beer when Shannon entered. They were both dressed casually but smartly – he in his fawn sports jacket, a white shirt unbuttoned at the collar and black trousers, and she in a tope summer frock with a white cardigan.

His right hand was resting next to his condensation-jewelled glass. Also on the counter was the paper bag used for wrapping the silver box. The top half of the bag – bearing the logo: *AC Fine Arts* – was folded over and trapped beneath the square bottom of the bag.

"Hi," Shannon said, lightly sweeping her fingertips over the back of his hand.

"What would you like?" Paul asked, gesturing to the barman as Shannon raised herself on to the stool next to him.

"That looks good."

"Another beer," he said to the barman.

"Did you finish your calculations, Doctor?" Shannon said as the barman moved to the row of beer pumps at the far end of the counter.

Paul turned to face her. "They're never really ever finished. There's always mo—"

She put her finger to his lips, cutting him off.

"You did ask," Paul said, gently moving her hand from his mouth. He noticed she was wearing a different perfume this evening. "I take things literally. Ann finds it irritating too."

"I didn't say I find it irritating," she said, leaning closer.

The barman placed Shannon's beer on the counter.

Nodding towards a corner table, Paul said to the barman, "We'll take these over there." He picked up his glass and the paper bag, which, containing something heavy, he rested against his hip. "After you," he said to Shannon.

Seated beside each other, they would be able to see anyone entering from the hotel lobby. Paul put the bag on the seat of the empty chair that was on the other side of him.

"Cheers," he said, taking another sip of beer.

"What's the plan for tomorrow?"

Paul put his drink down. "Who's asking? You or Blackwood?"

"Blackwood, of course. I have to call him, even if it's at midnight. He wants me to report everything."

"I'm going to church. Isn't that what people round here do on a Sunday?"

"Hardly. Anyway, I thought all you Brits were heathens."

"Charming."

"I'm sorry. I'm just a little surprised..."

"I'm joking, Shannon. I'm an atheist." He shook his head. "You're *always* apologising. Did you know that?"

Grinning, she said, "*I* am? So we're even. But if not church, then I repeat – what's the plan?"

"Seriously?"

"Yes!"

"I'll call the power station in the morning. Hopefully, Hank Barnaby will be there. He gave me the impression the place is his second home.

"I've calculated the quantities of lead shielding that need to be fitted inside the shipping containers. I'm hoping Hank can supply it. If not, he should know where I can buy it from."

"Sounds good. Any step toward removing those trash containers will make Vernon happy – which is what we both want."

Paul cleared his throat. He was about to say something that would lead on to a proposition that terrified him. It was related to a decision that had been on his mind since he'd telephoned Ann. While they were talking about her day, the ordinariness of it, he decided suddenly that participating in international crime to avoid deportation and separation from her wouldn't lead to a tolerable life for either of them. He would come to hate himself and she would be affected by the change in him. Stunned by this sudden clarity, he made an excuse to end the call, blaming crackling on his end of the line.

"I'm going to South Africa soon, Shannon. I managed to speak to my... my 'handler' an hour ago and, in principle, he's agreed. I'll meet him next Friday in England to finalise the arrangements."

"That's interesting, but what about your work here?" Shannon said.

Paul raised his eyebrows, as if inviting her to guess the answer.

After a moment's reflection, she said, "Is that the destination?"

"Where?" he said, disingenuously.

"South Africa?"

"How did you know that?"

"I told you this afternoon that I'm psychic."

"You'd need to know soon anyway, in order to prepare the paperwork."

"That's true," she said, looking round to see if anyone was eavesdropping. Shannon's gaze lingered on the lone woman, who, based on the empty glasses in front of her, was consuming her fourth cocktail.

Paul's throat tensed again as he said, "Shannon, you told me you'd need a plan to get away from Blackwood. Well, South Africa's a long way away, and Africa's a huge continent to get lost in. The borders between its countries are not exactly secure. You should think about making a new life there. A way to start would be to meet with me in Johannesburg, in a couple of weeks or so."

"Meet you in... Vernon won't agree to it. I'm not involved with that end of things."

"And you're not supposed to be working in the field on American soil either. If Blackwood needs persuasion, I've thought about that too."

"I've got Rachel to think about."

"Is the Rachel thing serious?"

Shannon hesitated, trying to clear her thoughts. "Maybe it's not, but I don't want her *killed* when they come looking for me."

"You'll have to split up with her or take her with you. What other choices do you have?"

Frowning, she took his hand. "Paul, you're not thinking that you and I..."

It took him a moment to comprehend, and another moment to quell the exciting notion. "I'm married. Things are strained, but no, I'm not thinking *that*, Shannon. I'm simply trying to help you."

Shannon became quiet, seemingly overwhelmed.

Paul continued, "What if an anonymous message concerning two missing people, people last seen breaking into the old watch factory site, was received by the local police... They would follow it up, wouldn't they? They'd go to the site and ask questions."

Horrified, Shannon exclaimed, "That could blow everything apart! You're not serious, are you?"

He took an envelope from his jacket pocket and removed a sheet of paper. "Read this. If the tone isn't American enough, tweak it yourself. I've addressed the envelope to the 'Missing Persons Unit' at the Atlantic City Police Department, whose details I got from the phone book in my room."

Paul had written the message in block capital letters:

MY TWO DRINKING BUDDIES SHANE AND ALICE SNUCK INTO THE OLD ALTABRITE WATCH PLACE IN MAYJAK TWO DAYS AGO TO LOOK AROUND. I HAVEN'T SEEN THEM SINCE. I BELIEVE THEY GOT TRAPPED IN THE DEMOLITION RUBBLE. SOME SAY THAT PLACE IS FULL OF THAT ATOMIC SHIT USED FOR MAKING WATCHES GLOW IN THE DARK. PLEASE GET MY PALS OUT BEFORE IT'S TOO LATE.

THANKS

A WORRIED FRIEND.

After reading the note, Shannon said, "Vernon. The family. Fransen. They'll form a line to kill you if you send this."

"No one will have any reason to think the message came from me. In fact, it won't have because *you* will post it. Just make sure you don't do it until after I've left for London.

"If the police do make enquiries at the site, Fransen and Blackwood will become anxious about publicity that they can't control. That'll be the opportunity to recommend your going to South Africa to ensure I'm doing everything I can to speed the shipment process up. Your itinerary will have to be established with my handler, Patrick Maycross, although Blackwood will want to deal with Maycross's boss, Auberon Morrison. That's unlikely to be possible though." Paul took a slip of paper from his trouser pocket. "Here's Maycross's direct number in London."

Paul could see that Shannon was struggling to come to terms with his idea. "Even tramps have friends who worry about them. The message refers to *two* missing people, a man and a woman, which is different to the rescue we were involved in. And the inferred timing of this fake incident is more recent," he said.

Shannon shook her head. "It's still crazy."

"Tomorrow's meant to be a day of rest, Shannon. Use it to think about my plan."

"If I *were* to vanish in Africa, Paul, your safety when you return will be compromised. Vernon will interrogate you about what you know. He won't be gentle. And whoever he replaces me with won't let you out of their sight for a second."

"He needs me in one piece. I'll survive. I wouldn't be able to deal with officials if I'm covered in cigar burns and bruises," Paul said. These statements were easy to make because he had resolved neither to return to New Jersey nor meet with Blackwood again.

Shannon took his face with both hands and kissed him hard on the mouth. Drawing back, she said, "I *will* think about it. It terrifies me, but I will think about it. I promise."

"Th-There's something else," he said, entranced anew. Picking up the bag from the chair next to him, he said, "This contains a miniature whisky bottle that I emptied. I've rolled a strip of lead round it, which is why the bag's heavy. There's a note explaining everything. It's your insurance policy. Don't look at the instructions unless Blackwood threatens you again. Given what you said about him being able to read people, you're better off not knowing for now. In the meantime, I recommend you keep the bottle under water in a bucket or bath. Water's an effective absorber of radiation."

PART TWO

Chapter 15

After a flight of nearly twelve hours, the passenger jet from London Airport descended towards the single runway of the Louis Botha International Airport. Paul reset his watch to Durban local time – just one hour ahead of the UK at this time of year. It was nearly eight in the morning of what looked to be the start of a cool, overcast Tuesday. According to the pilot's landing announcement over the intercom, rain was forecast.

One of the blue-uniformed cabin crew, a woman of an age suggesting she'd served many years in the job, had twice found cause to ask if he's feeling all right. Unlike the other passengers, he hadn't slept during the flight. Heart-squeezing anxiety wouldn't allow consciousness to slide away. He felt ill and knew he looked it too. Blue-black crescents had formed under his eyes during the last few days.

He could empathise with the stunt coordinator of the action film that had been shown on the cabin screens, not that he'd been able to concentrate on its plot. So many explosions timed to go off at the right instant and in the intended sequence – had these been fractions of a second too early or too late, the people doing the stunts would have been injured by blasts or flying debris. Everything meticulously planned: dummy cartridges in guns; fake glass instead of the real thing; and triggered poles fitted to the undersides of cars to propel the speeding vehicles into the air. But naturally the stunt coordinator had a team of experienced people and relied on proven protocols.

Whereas what Paul had set in train had nothing more than desperate hope behind it. He was relying on people, particularly those closest to him, doing life-changing things on his say-so. Unlike in a film, there could be no retakes. Everyone would live with the consequences.

It seemed as though an eternity instead of nine and a half days had passed since his conversation with Shannon in the quiet bar at the Banville Plaza. Would she post the message he'd prepared? Any number of outcomes could result. Perhaps he should have been open with her about the murdered reporter's identity. Who had he really been trying to protect?

The terminal, a short walk from the parked plane, was tiny compared to the one he'd departed from at Heathrow. The passengers' luggage was already appearing on the carousel as Paul entered the building.

For this trip, he was simply a tourist arriving wearing navy-blue corduroy trousers, a grey sports jacket and a blue shirt. His cabin luggage was a holdall instead of a briefcase.

"I'm home," he said to the passport control officer, who was thus prompted to take another look at Paul's British passport. He'd long had ambivalent feelings about his birthplace and the life he might have lived if his parents had made different choices. The surreal thought that he might be detained and conscripted into the military flashed through his mind. With a sense of relief he put the returned passport into the inside pocket of his jacket.

A scruffy man with wavy, dark-brown hair and several days' worth of stubble was standing near the terminal exit. Clamped between his lips was a half-smoked cigar. He was wearing dirty plimsolls, blue denim jeans and a creased, cream, linen sports jacket over a grey T-shirt. He smelled of whisky too. The sheet of white cardboard he was holding had PAUL scrawled on it.

"Tom?" Paul said apprehensively, estimating the man as being in his mid-thirties. "I'm Paul Avery."

Maycross's man lowered the sign and took the cigar from his mouth. "Course you are. Recognised you from the photo Head Office faxed to me, old fruit," he said, breathing out smoke.

"Don't any other Pauls come to South Africa?" Paul said, nodding at the sign.

"Do you know, there was one, an old boy who came out before you. I told him I was waiting for a bloke with fair hair. Took it well." Grasping Paul's hand and shaking it firmly, Tom continued, "Not a worrier, are you, sweetie?"

"Well, I..."

"Oh shit. We'll have to do something about that." Tom reached for the shoulder strap of Paul's holdall. "Give me that thing."

Paul, carrying his suitcase, followed Tom out through the swing doors. They headed to the front of the short queue of waiting taxis. "The James," Tom said to the moustachioed driver who had got out to stow their luggage.

The taxi ride had an element of time-travel to it. Paul was five years old when he was last in the country, so his recollections were fragmented and more weighted with emotions than with reliable details. The concrete freeways and flyovers were additions of the last twenty-two years and even if it were otherwise they would have had no part in his early life – his family and their trunks of possessions had left Durban on a passenger-and-mail steam ship, not on an aeroplane.

Paul was in the back of the taxi, with his new colleague sitting next to the driver. The vehicle was right-hand drive, as in the UK, for driving on the left side of the road. When the cityscape hove into view, Paul leaned forward. "Can we go via the Victoria Embankment, please?"

The driver glanced at his watch before saying in a deep Afrikaans accent, "Victoria Embankment it is."

Forty minutes later, Paul was able to glimpse the port. The Bay of Natal was to their right. His view was initially interrupted by the walls of the elevated Southern Freeway and then by vehicles going in the other direction as they descended on to the Victoria Embankment. In his mind's eye, Paul could see a seaplane, probably carrying mail, landing on the flat water, it having flown from his memory. He turned quickly to his left, hoping to see the block of flats his family had lived in.

All too soon, the driver was obliged by the road layout to turn left, away from the bay and into the grid-like heart of the city. They headed northwards before turning east again, on to a road leading to the coast. They emerged by the beaches, and turned north towards North Beach. The Indian Ocean was throwing up foam-flecked waves, as if it were trying to tell him that this was all a dreadful mistake and, no, he wasn't home.

Chapter 16

The taxi stopped outside the columned entrance to The James. Located on a corner and set back from the promenade, the six-storey Edwardian hotel, despite its grandness, was dwarfed by the towering newer hotels standing farther along.

Paul recognised The James – or, rather, the imposing whiteness of it. His father had been an acquaintance of the hotel's then manager, someone who, after the passage of more than twenty years, must have been long retired now. As a child Paul had play-visits with that manager's son. Being served hard-boiled eggs with toast sliced into "soldiers" remained a vivid memory.

The accommodation arrangements for this trip had been left to Tom to organize, so since hearing their destination Paul had looked forward to finally being a paying guest at The James. Carrying his suitcase and holdall, he started eagerly towards the hotel entrance while Tom was paying the driver.

"Easy there, sweetie," he heard Tom call out as the taxi drove away.

Paul turned round.

Tom grasped the strap of Paul's holdall. "We're not staying in there. Counter-surveillance lesson one, old fruit."

"Brilliant," Paul said under his breath as Tom set off down the side street. Looking dejectedly at the hotel, he wondered how far he would have to lug his suitcase. With a force like that of the crashing ocean waves, fatigue washed over him, displacing the adrenaline that had been keeping him awake.

A block of flats bearing the name Cornish Mansions overlooked the park behind The James. This ten-storey building ran the length of the side street, to the next crossroads, where Tom waited for Paul outside the entrance. The entranceway incorporated a gated ramp down to the basement garage.

Using his key, Tom opened the glass door to the lobby. "Not exactly The James here, Paulie-boy, but it's more private."

The novelty of Tom's ways of addressing him had quickly faded. Paul's nerves were frazzled, but he didn't trust himself to find the right tone for complaining. It was essential to cultivate the man's cooperation, not alienate him.

They got out of the elevator on the fifth floor. The flats were arranged along linked walkways that together formed a square looking down on to the courtyard that was open to the sky.

"This is us," Tom said, using a different key to open the door to his flat.

The inner hallway ran the width of the flat, connecting all the rooms. The lounge had a balcony overlooking the park and the back of The James.

"No TV. Never here long enough to need one. Anyway, how many American films can one watch and remain compos?" Tom said, walking over to the old radio that was on the sideboard. He turned the radio on and twiddled its tuning dial. Sombre music emanated from the speaker grille. "Ah... Do you like Mahler?" he asked. "Very moving."

"I'll take your word for it," Paul said, putting his suitcase down.

"Classical music helps me to adjust," Tom said, with his palms covering his eyes as if he were struggling with something – perhaps alcohol withdrawal, perhaps the humidity. Lowering his arms, he said, "I'll show you to your room and where the facilities are, Paul." Handing Paul the holdall, he added "You'll find the shower's pretty fierce, so be careful."

"Thanks for the warning," Paul said, welcoming the slang-free use of his name. "I *would* like to freshen up."

"You can have a drink to take with you. There's Scotch in the kitchen. Or is it too early? There's orange juice, if you prefer."

Paul looked at his watch. *Early!* It was a little after 9.30 a.m. Still, if Tom was desperate for a drink... "Hell, I think I will. Scotch might revive me."

"Right you are then," Tom said, moving towards the hallway.

Paul put his luggage down and followed Tom into the kitchen, where weak daylight came through the frosted glass window that looked on to the walkway. Tom turned on the light and took a half-full bottle of Scotch from one of the below-counter cabinets. After taking a tumbler from another cabinet, he proceeded to pour Paul's drink.

"Aren't you joining me?"

"Never drink the stuff," Tom said, handing the tumbler to Paul.

"I see," Paul said, incredulous. Up close, his host still smelled like a distillery.

"The bathroom's at the other end of the corridor. You'll find your bedroom next to it. You should be comfortable. The neighbours are quiet."

"Right. Thank you, Tom."

"After you've finished in the bathroom, I'll brew some tea."

Paul was dumbfounded. His host's manner of speaking had become courteous and formal, as if the man possessed a split-personality.

"Sounds good," Paul responded, trying to sound at ease.

Paul returned to the lounge with his drink, collected his holdall and suitcase and went in search of his room. It occurred to him that, unlike its tenant, the flat was free from the lingering smell of tobacco.

The single window in the bedroom was a pane of glass above the door. As this looked on to the windowless inner hall, Paul had to turn on the light to see. The light-grey carpet in the room was a continuation of that in the hall. A single bed stood on the right-hand-side of the room. There was a chest of drawers against the far wall, and beside the door was a wardrobe. A poster of a leaping dolphin had been taped to the wall above the bed. Paul's verdict was that of tidy functionality. Only the dolphin conferred any personality. It was clearly a room in which no one stayed for long.

Paul put down his suitcase and swung the holdall on to the end of the bed. He sat on the bed and took a sip of the Scotch. The water from the shower, Tom had informed him, would be fierce. Well, *fierce* would also have been a good adjective to describe the taste of the whisky. He hadn't recognised the label on the bottle. Was it a cheap blend or an exclusive single malt? Based on his experience of salaries in the public sector, it seemed more likely to be the former. But more importantly, what should be made of Tom's assertion that he didn't drink the stuff? Did it matter if Tom was in denial about his vices? Perhaps such a proclivity could be a vulnerability?

Look for the positive in everything was the mantra Paul's father had preached. But the trouble with this mantra was the thinking of it brought to mind the actions Paul had instigated, yet could do nothing from here to oversee. Worrying about what was happening with each of these lay behind his recent sleeplessness.

When these fears barraged him in unison, as frequently occurred when his mind wasn't distracted by life's necessities, he'd become prone to descending into a stultified state. To combat this he had been attempting to imagine each source of anxiety as an ornament – like one of Ann's silver curios – on a shelf. Being able to focus on just one anxiety at a time was his strategy for surviving the coming weeks. But the imagined ornaments all took the same form: that of the pitiful silver box he'd bought at the Banville Plaza hotel. The only difference was in the name he mentally emblazoned upon each.

With the Scotch burning his throat, he allowed the imaginary box marked "Mom" to open. (He'd always used Mom instead of Mum, a habit that he attributed to the conditioning from his Durban childhood.) Both she and Ann should have started house-hunting in Suffolk.

Whereas he'd continued to hide the truth from Ann, he'd found himself unable to lie to his fifty-nine-year-old mother, Beth. Within minutes of arriving at her ground-floor maisonette in Pinner, an affluent north-west suburb of London, he'd told her everything about the threats that had been made against him – threats that also extended to his relatives – and in doing so he'd violated his obligations under a NATO Category-X programme and its attached Grandee Paragraph 5 Order, and presumably broken the Official Secrets Act as well.

They were sitting next to each other on the sofa in the lounge, drinking tea. The nearby windows were being drummed by a summer shower. She was wearing a green-and-white check-patterned dress.

"I believed things like that were all in the past," she said, almost letting go of her cup.

He took the cup and saucer from her and set them down on the coffee table.

Beth said, "It feels the same as when we were forced to leave South Africa because we'd gone to meetings of the Liberal Party and helped to distribute its pamphlets. We had only wanted true democracy and to stop the forced movements of natives in Natal. The security police harassed your father's place of work. His boss had to fire him. It was made clear that he would never get another engineering job."

"You and Dad never said anything to me about that, Mom. I thought we came to England because of the better medical treatment available for Dad."

"You were too young. The years passed and then your father

died...”

“I remember when we were living in Woolwich, two detectives came to question Dad.”

There was a look of surprise in her grey eyes. “That was a frightening moment. We suspected that the South African police had contacted the police in London, telling them made-up things – that we were communists who needed to be watched. After that day, we stayed away from politics, not even voting.”

Beth agreed that Paul shouldn’t carry out Maycross’s scheme, no matter the consequences. If resigning from the RSMSDA and seeking employment in or around Norwich was what was necessary, then so be it. Most importantly, she also agreed to move to north Suffolk too. Living near the sea, close to her son and his wife and in-laws would be, despite the described circumstances, a comfort, she said, particularly with retirement from her clerical job at a greetings card company imminent. She would focus on the positive, “as your father always did.”

“I don’t know how quickly I’ll be able to find a new job, Mom. I’ll be willing to do anything, but the thing is, we will probably need some help financially for a few months and to cover the costs of the move. I don’t want to ask Ann’s parents. We already owe money to them.”

“This maisonette must be worth a lot more than we bought it for. I’ll do what I can, Paul. But you must tell Ann the truth as soon as it’s safe. Perhaps after we’ve all settled in...”

She stood up and went into the hall to retrieve an address book from the window ledge on which the phone sat. Returning to the lounge, she showed him the addresses and telephone numbers of three friends in Durban with whom she still corresponded. “If you *are* deported to South Africa, you must go to these people for help,” she insisted. “They will take you in.”

Whether in practice he would be prevented from receiving such help was unclear. Nonetheless, Paul gratefully wrote down the names and contact details. “Mom, don’t imagine you would be able to join me there,” he said, reaching for her hand. “It wouldn’t be allowed. They’d cancel your passport to stop you. Anyway, I’d be depending on you to keep Ann from going to the police or to the press. Otherwise she’d be arrested for interfering with national security.”

***

After showering and putting on jeans and a T-shirt, Paul went in search of his host. He found Tom sitting in an easy chair in the lounge, listening to the radio. Mahler had given way to Tchaikovsky. Tom had combed his hair and changed his clothes too; he was wearing a green polo shirt and khaki casual trousers. Although still unshaven, he smelled of cheap cologne.

"Feeling better?" Tom said.

"I see what you meant about the water pressure."

Tom stood up and turned off the radio. "Let's have that tea, shall we?"

They went into the kitchen. On the counter were two cups and saucers; a teaspoon, spotted with tea leaves, was next to the open teapot.

"Take a seat, old chap," Tom said, turning on the electric hob element under the kettle. "The water won't take long to boil again."

Paul sat down at the kitchen table, which was next to a wall.

"Good old British digestives," Tom said, pointing at the plate in the centre of the table. Next to the plate of biscuits was a small jug of milk and a bowl of granulated sugar.

Paul considered the biscuits.

"Plain, I'm afraid. No chocolate," Tom said.

"They're fine," Paul said, taking one of the digestives and putting it on the side plate Tom had set out for him. "It's just that I'm confused."

"About the biscuits?" Tom said, glancing at the kettle again.

"I mean about you, Tom."

Tom turned to focus on Paul. "How so?"

"Since we entered this flat, you've changed. More than just your clothes."

Tom walked across to the table and sat down. "Go on," he said, his face expressionless. "I'm all ears."

"Your mannerisms... the way you talk—"

A piercing whistling was coming from the kettle.

Tom looked back at the stove. He grinned and patted Paul's arm. "Hold that thought," he said, standing up.

After turning off the hob and filling the teapot with the boiled water, Tom sat down again. "Do you recall what I said to you after the taxi had dropped us outside The James – about counter-surveillance lesson one?"

"Vaguely, Tom. I wasn't really..."

"Lesson one's about concealing your movements. And lesson two is what you've just picked up on – the impression you leave on people. Both lessons put friction into the ether, so that you don't make life easy for the other side."

"Friction?"

"If anyone should ask that taxi driver where we're staying, he'll say The James."

"I see." It seemed to Paul that not drawing attention to himself was no longer enough. Now he was supposed to employ diversionary tactics.

"And in the Arrivals Hall at the airport, if the other Paul – that bow-legged old fellow who came through Customs before you – were to be asked to provide a description of me, he'd recall some scruffy blighter who seemed a bit blotto."

"Why should either of them be asked anything about us?"

"Well not *now*, but in the future who knows what sorts of investigations might be instigated?"

"The future. Understood. Friction in the ether," Paul muttered, feeling far from reassured.

"Good chap. The tea should have brewed by now."

"The thing is," Paul said as Tom stood up, "is *this* the real you?"

"Hah! Now you're catching on. Always leave people wondering."

Tom poured two cups of tea through a strainer. He carried the cups to the table. "Help yourself to milk and sugar." After sitting down, he said, "You'll get the hang of it. Did you do Drama at school?"

"No," Paul said, adding milk to his tea.

"Oh well... No matter. That might be an advantage. One doesn't want to fall into the trap of hamming things up. The key's not to take things so far that you can't summon up the effect whenever you need it. That's why I rarely employ wigs and make-up."

"I wouldn't know where to start," Paul said, lifting the cup to his mouth.

"I'm positive you'll be better than that other fellow."

"There was another expert here?"

"He was hopeless at masking *his* personality – that of a mad professor tripping over his own brilliance."

"Professor?"

"Knows his stuff. Couldn't have got this far without his input."

"His name wasn't Benedict Sykes?"

Tom nodded. "Your boss, so I understand."

"You're well informed, Tom. Though he's usually away, travelling to somewhere or other..." As the words left Paul's mouth, he was struck by how little he knew about Sykes's movements.

"Good old B.S. was what I used to think whenever he was in full flow after a few drinks. Never would have dared to accuse him of bullshitting to his face though."

"He's just very enthusiastic."

Tom smiled. "Your file also states that you were born here in Durban. You must be keen to look round. We can take a walk when we've finished our tea."

"I'd like to do that."

"And at the same time, we can decide who I am."

"Do you mean, who you are in relation to me?"

"Indeed. Why are you staying here? Why will we be going to Jo'berg together?"

"I suppose you could be a friend of the son or daughter of one of my mother's old friends," Paul suggested, remembering his recent conversation with Beth.

"Hmmm... That could unravel."

"I certainly don't want them to get into any trouble."

"We need to come up with something else."

Paul fell silent. The "unravel" word had struck too many chords "So you've seen a file on me," he said. "I hope it's thin."

"Yours is larger than most because of where you work."

"Are there security files on *everyone*?"

"Everyone in the UK? No. Just on three million or so now, I believe."

Chapter 17

That's certainly changed, Paul thought, staring at the pinkish-red surface of the promenade. The promenade he remembered had looked like that of a typical British seaside resort – plain concrete, bordered by a walled embankment with steps down to the beach. It was vibrant now – an impression heightened by the sun, which had broken through the clouds – and suggestive of other modernising changes in this land.

With their windcheaters open they walked south, having joined the promenade near The James. None of what Paul saw ahead was familiar. The shark aquarium on their left was much more exotic than the bowling green and its tearoom that only existed in his memory now.

He lifted his camera and took several photographs, avoiding Tom. It was hard to appreciate that it was winter; the temperature was that of a late-summer day back home. He hadn't experienced truly cold weather until his family moved to England. Their ship had docked at Southampton in the middle of winter.

Somewhere along here, his mom and dad had played a trick upon him. His mother still had the framed result – a black-and-white photograph of him on his scooter. Camera-shyness had made the curly-haired little boy an evasive subject. The arm of his father, encouraging him forward, was in the photograph that was taken as the two returned to the spot where Beth had waited with the dreaded camera she'd kept out of sight until that moment.

That embarrassed five-year-old boy in a T-shirt, white shorts, white socks and black, laced shoes hadn't been conscious of apartheid and politics. Little changed in this regard as Paul grew up in England. Instead, he became fascinated with the natural world. His parents, probably because of the police harassment his mom had described, had never sought to influence him politically. The career path he chose was one his father had gently encouraged.

Looking about him now, the ethnic diversity of those strolling along the beachfront contrasted with the memories – although there'd been a friendly black houseboy – of his childhood. Apartheid-based rule still pertained, yet economics was seemingly trumping application of the race laws to foreign tourists whose money was so desperately needed.

Whatever the future of this uncertain country required, it wasn't the radioactive waste that he was supposed to bring. Throughout the last hundred years, South Africa had its share of incomers looking for "rich pickings", but Maycross was a new kind of chancer. He was not interested in what could be taken.

"I suggest we don't walk down there," Tom said as they approached the end of South Beach. Ahead was the less-developed area named "the Point", which projected across the mouth of the bay. "How 'bout a bite of nosh, eh?" Tom continued, suddenly adopting a vaguely cockney-sounding dialect. Perhaps he was trying something out.

Paul stifled the impulse to laugh as they turned round.

"If you could fancy a spicy Ruby Murray, I know a helluva good place along there." Tom pointed across the road to a street that led away from the beachfront.

The Indian restaurant was above two gift shops. From their table by a window, Paul could still see the ocean, where it lay like a metallic band strapped to the end of the street. Tom ordered curries and accompanying dishes without looking at the menu.

After the waiter had left them, Tom lowered his voice, "Once we've finished lunch, I'll go back and get my car, so I can take you to the port. I'll pick you up by the City Hall, which is about a mile from here. The walk there will give you an opportunity to do some more sightseeing."

"Sounds good to me."

There were other diners sitting near to them, so Paul refrained from asking questions about the conditions at the mine. He also avoided a question that he doubted he would ever get the truthful answer to: How did the Englishman opposite him become embroiled in Maycross's plot? Instead, he asked, "Did you bring Benedict here too?"

After a moment's reflection, Tom replied, "Now I think about it, the prof and I stayed in Jo'berg."

Paul nodded, hoping to learn something about Benedict's involvement. If Sykes's ego had rendered him susceptible to flattery, he could simply have swallowed the legitimacy of the Willingham Corporation's interest in repurposing an exhausted mine. But surely he must have come across as an inflexible oddball, someone unadaptable to Blackwood's "special" way of working. Perhaps Sykes had only been consulted about preparations for an "experimental" waste depository.

"Did Benedict mention bentonite?" Paul asked. He had to *act* the part that Maycross had given to him. Perhaps he had something in common with the theatrical Tom after all.

"I should say," Tom said, raising his eyebrows. "He kept banging on about it. Now I've got fifty metric tonnes of the stuff on pallets. I'm not sure what I'm supposed to do with it though."

"Being clay-like, it will absorb rock movements around the stored containers."

"That makes sense," Tom said. "Thanks."

Paul was astonished by the incuriosity that had just been revealed. It was an echo of much that he'd encountered since embarking on Maycross's plan. Hank didn't want to know about Shannon's role; Art Richards didn't want to know the purpose of the shipping containers; Fabian Gooch had instantly acquiesced to Paul's irregular secondment upon hearing the phrase "this pertains to a delicate and urgent matter having the highest level of secrecy"; Tom had procured fifty pallets of bentonite without knowing why; and then there was Shannon...

What was he to make of Shannon Lennon? Neither crude corruption nor a "fearing the truth" explanation felt right. How could she have allowed herself to become ensnared? Had there been some kind of grooming? Had she been lowered task-by-task into Blackwood's corner of the Underworld? With each task, the light of decency dimmed until the darkness was only broken by the glow from Vernon's cigar pressing into her flesh.

After lunch, Tom walked with Paul northwards along Point Road. At the corner with West Street, Tom said, gesturing westwards, "City Hall's down there, on this side. I'll meet you opposite it, by the public gardens."

The day had become warmer and clammier, adding to the effect of the large lunch, which Paul was regretting having eaten. Although some of the commercial premises he was walking past had canopies that projected over the pavement, these moments of shade provided little relief; the return of his earlier drowsiness became crushing.

Most of the people going about their business were black. Having been raised among white Europeans and because he'd travelled here distracted by fears, the demographic contrast felt irrationally surprising, as if he'd woken into a dream.

All of a sudden, a figure stepped from the shadow between two buildings. "Do you have a job, boss?" the middle-aged white man said. "I'm good with cars."

"No, I'm sorry," Paul answered without stopping. It were as though he'd come face to face with his future-self – the desolate one promised by Maycross if he didn't cooperate.

After walking for a few more minutes, he arrived by the grand City Hall. Baroque and anchored in a landscaped setting incorporating palm trees, the grey, stone Edwardian edifice was a building that his parents must have visited many times. Looking across the road, Paul saw the entrance to Medwood Gardens. He crossed to wait for Tom.

From this side of West Street, he could better appreciate the scale and the colonial architecture of the municipal building. He began taking photographs. For the moment he was just what he was pretending to be – a tourist returned to the city in which he was born. Durban, which had comprised a fading, glimmering bubble with his five-year-old self at its centre, was materialising around him.

Chapter 18

While Paul waited for Tom to collect him, his fears seized their opportunity. What advantaged a particular imaginary silver box at such moments was something he'd avoided reflecting upon – he had enough puzzles. All he knew was that one or other of the boxes of worry would assert itself like a nagging tooth. This time the box that came to the fore was marked *Hartling Springs*.

The morning following the evening he'd spent with Shannon in the Lucky Lou Bar, he phoned the power station from his hotel room and asked to be put through to Hank Barnaby. As he'd hoped, the chief engineer was at his desk. He agreed with Hank that they would meet that afternoon at Maizetown to discuss the next steps in their "project". Hank initially sounded reluctant until Paul assured him that this time it would just be the two of them.

"I need a large quantity of lead sheet material for a concurrent activity, Hank. I assume you keep such sheets for maintenance work and incidental shielding purposes."

"Tell me what you need, and I'll check."

Before he left for Maizetown that Sunday afternoon, Paul phoned Shannon's room to inform her of the meeting. This telephone conversation was actually for the benefit of those monitoring the listening devices in their rooms. He repeated exactly what he'd told the chief engineer, adding that Hank didn't seem to like an audience.

"You make him uncomfortable," he said to counter her protests about not being included. "I'm barely in his trusted circle myself, so I'm not in a position to insist on you coming. Of course, I'll let you know how I get on."

The meeting with Hank took place in the conference room at the rail yard. Hank had made himself busy by the time Paul arrived. He was collating the information Paul had asked for during his visit to the power station. They sat across the table from each other.

"This is the fuel-rod data," Hank said, sliding a number of colour-coded diagrams across the table.

Paul studied the "temperature maps" of the damaged fuel rods. "I agree, they seem to have stabilised," he eventually responded.

"It took five of my best guys two days to obtain those measurements."

"And I appreciate their efforts, Hank."

"I know what I'm doing, young man. Maybe you'll bear that in mind in future."

"We're both doing our jobs. Thank you again for the measurements, Hank. If I can move on now, what if three of your radiation-grade casks were required."

"Art told me you said as much, but I reckon we can manage with just two."

"Most of the space in the third one would be taken up by material associated with the concurrent activity that I alluded to this morning. I can't say more about it, beyond confirming it has no direct bearing on your power plant."

Paul's latest calculations had shown that one of the ten shipping containers that he'd ordered from Art needed to be replaced by a radiation-grade cask. This was because the intensity of the gamma radiation coming from one of the "Waste Champion Series 7 Enclosed Receptacle" containers – the one in which the reporter had been imprisoned – was too high for adequate containment by sheets of lead.

Hank frowned. "If it has anything to do with that young woman you brought here, and her *friends*, the less I know the better."

"Duly noted. In regard to the lead sheets, Art's crew will be doing work for me here. If I'm satisfied with their initial results, the rest of the sheets will be required. I'll telephone him tomorrow and tell him to liaise with you regarding collection."

"I'll wait for his call. More to the point, when will you need the three casks?"

"What's the usual lead-time, Hank?"

"Once I have your say-so, I can get them shipped here within a few days from the yard at our Ohio plant. It would take nine months minimum to get hold of new ones."

"Only a few days... That's excellent, but I still have checks to carry out at the destination before I'm able to confirm their suitability. I'm leaving in a couple of days to do that work. It will take me, say, four or five weeks before I can come back to you."

"You're *leaving*—" Hank started to say, clearly anxious to have the incriminating high-level waste removed. "Those casks will have to be paid for. They're damn expensive."

"I'm open to suggestions about the best way that such payments can be transferred without causing auditing problems."

Paul watched as Barnaby made a note of the matter.

***

The beep of a car horn snatched Paul's mind back from the conference room in Maizetown. A midsize brown Honda had parked by the kerb. It felt as if the lid of the silver box had been flipped shut before he'd finished with it. He'd wanted to recall the subsequent telephone discussion with Art and their agreeing the modification of one shipping container in readiness for his supposed return to New Jersey in about a month's time.

The car horn sounded again, but longer this time.

"Don't let me down, Art. Buy me time. Make it appear as though something's happening," Paul murmured to himself as he lowered his head to look into the car.

Tom beckoned to him from the driver's seat. "You're looking worried again."

Paul opened the front-passenger door and got in. "It's an occupational hazard."

"This came while we were having lunch," Tom said, passing to Paul a curled strip of telex printer paper.

"Where did you get this from?"

"I have a line in the flat. It was a hell of a job getting it installed without attracting awkward questions."

After engaging his seat belt, Paul began reading. Despite the brevity, the message oozed Maycross. He recognised the word COLOURLESS. It was the name of the specified special measures programme on the grey form that he'd been coerced to sign.

To: Tallyho Furnishings
Range: COLOURLESS
Urgent Instruction for PA.

SL to arrive Friday 5 August. Collect from Jan Smuts airport and provide all support required. Flight details to be advised. Be forewarned. Something has upset the client.
Kind regards, Head Office

Many seconds passed before Paul realised he needed to start breathing again. Shannon Lennon was coming and Blackwood was upset. She must have mailed the bogus "missing people" letter to the police. *Maycross must be frantic with worry. He doesn't know his three-dimensional chess game has another player – me.*

Shannon would arrive at the international airport in Johannesburg in three days' time. Elation at the thought of her presence heightened with each reading of the message.

"... park as close as I can get," someone was saying.

"What?" Paul forced himself to look to his right at whoever was speaking. Of course it was Tom.

They were driving along a wire fence-lined road that had industrial buildings on its left side and a flyover forming part of the freeway feeding traffic on to the Victoria Embankment on its right side. Paul had barely registered their leaving West Street. Being here now, close to the docks, felt like a miracle of teleportation.

"I hope you know who this SL chap is," Tom said, taking a left turn, in the direction of the quay. Windowless, warehouse-like premises belonging to marine service companies and importers lined the road.

"*She*, not he," Paul responded, resting the message on his lap. "And yes, I know her."

"Our plans have been decided for us. We'll have to leave for Jo'berg tomorrow," Tom said.

"Okay," Paul replied, still thinking about Shannon. Had Blackwood hurt her again? His hands formed tight fists, seemingly of their own volition. He pressed them, palms down, against his thighs.

The harbour opened up in front of them at the next T-junction. Tom turned right and drove along the quayside for a hundred yards. Coming to a stop, he said, "I can't go further than this." The quayside ahead was blocked by the gantry of a building used by a freight handling company.

Leaning across Paul, Tom pointed towards the container terminal on the other side of one of the manmade stretches of water dividing the port. A ship, massive and piled neatly with shipping containers, was berthed there. Overhanging cranes evoked feeding praying mantises. "Impressive, isn't it? But that dock won't be for us. According to the information I received from Head Office, you're proposing to send nine shipping containers and three radiation-grade casks. Special cargo like that will be unloaded along this quay, from a much smaller ship."

Maycross had forwarded Paul's provisional cargo details, including the dimensions and estimated weights of the containers, following their meeting last week. The meeting had taken place, just as their first meeting had, in the electronically shielded chamber at the Tobe Institute.

Tom continued, "There are rail yards behind that container terminal and the freeway connections are also good from here. My recommendation is that the cargo be moved to Jo'berg by road, although not as a single convoy. Just one or two lorries each day. It'll take a couple of weeks, but will avoid attention along the way."

"Either way, we'll need to establish that the weight and size of the radiation-proof casks doesn't cause problems," Paul said.

A watchful seagull took fright and flew away as Tom opened his door. "Come and meet Max, my shipping agent. You'll find there's little cargo-wise that phases Maximilian."

Paul folded the telexed message and put it in his windcheater inside pocket. He got out of the car wondering which version of Tom would introduce him to Max.

"A word to the wise, my love," Tom said. "Max bends maritime laws into pretzels, but he can't abide amateurs. Appear as confident as possible."

My love... Bloody hell, thought Paul.

He followed Tom across the quayside to a steel staircase. They went up three flights and then along a mesh walkway to a battered door. The sign said: "Manikin Import Services". As Tom reached for the handle, the door opened and out came a young black man wearing blue overalls and a woollen bobble hat. The lean man, clutching a fistful of Rand notes, walked past without saying anything.

"One of the onyathi," Tom said. "That's what the stevedores call themselves. It means buffaloes. He's probably got a sideline going with Max."

Tom led the way along the windowless, plank-floored corridor. A voice could be heard coming from behind the fire door in front of them.

"Yah, Max is here, all right," Tom said, turning the steel doorknob.

"Look what the cat's dragged in here now, Petra!" Max called out upon seeing Tom. "And who's that with you. Another of your poof friends?" His accent seemed to Paul to be a mix of German and Afrikaans.

"Don't pretend," Tom said, embracing Max. "You know you want to rag me all over this counter and leave me gagging for more."

"In your dreams, Thomas," Max said, slapping Tom's back.

Max, who Paul guessed to be fiftyish, had receding sandy-coloured, wavy hair. Heavily tanned and lined, his face had the look of someone who'd worked outdoors much of his life. He was wearing a fawn shirt, the sleeves rolled up, and grease-stained khaki trousers.

"This is *the* Doctor Paul Avery, who has come all the way from Her Majesty's England, just to see you," Tom said.

"Of course he has. Everyone does, sooner or later." Max turned to his assistant. "Put the kettle on, Petra. We have a doctor in the house. A clean mug with no chips or any of your lipstick smudges."

A small, elderly woman slowly got up from her desk at the other end of the narrow room, much of whose width was taken by a deep counter covered with open ledgers. "Coffee or tea, is it?" she asked. Petra's shoulder-length hair was straight and white. She was slightly hunched, as if defeated by the confines of the office.

Max stilled himself and, having now fixed Paul in his gaze, said, "Black tea with a slice of lemon for our very important visitor. Yes, Doctor?"

"Yes, thank you," Paul responded reluctantly. His mother sometimes drank her tea that way. He remembered it as being astringent.

"We have no lemons left," Petra cried out.

"Then run on those bandy legs down to Wharf 17 and bring back a score."

"How am I supposed to carry twenty lemons?"

"In a bucket on your head, of course."

"You just want me out of the way," the old woman said, easing past the men.

"I've been *trying* to achieve that for the last twenty-five years. Have you just noticed?"

"Then I *resign*," Petra said, departing through the fire door.

"I *fired* you ten years ago," Max shouted as the door slowly began to close. Petra's echoing grumbling was soon silenced.

"Ignore my cousin," Max said to Paul. "We don't need her here for Thomas's monkey business."

Max slid open a drawer in the work counter. He removed a pad and turned the pages. "Nine twenty-foot shipping containers and three radiation-containment casks. Yes?" he said.

"Provisionally," Paul said, "but there's still a few technical matters to be finalised."

Max turned towards Tom. "I need facts! I need a date too."

"You will have them, Maximilian. Very soon. That's right, isn't it, Paul?" Tom said, intently.

"Within a few weeks," Paul said, peering at the details in Max's pad. "However, it's unlikely things will change much from what you've got here. The shipping container gross weights might alter a little – plus or minus 10 per cent. All the external dimensions are fixed."

"That's better. I'll work with these, adding a 10 per cent allowance," Max said, closing the notepad.

Tom winked approvingly at Paul.

Max said, "We will move the load to Jo'burg by road, not rail. In this country, they would stand out if we use the railway. Three of the units – the casks – are damn heavy though. They will require special multi-axle trailers to spread the loads. We will move at most two units a day. I can arrange a quiet area for the rest to be stored out of the way until it's their turn. Are we agreed?"

Paul looked at Tom, who it seemed had passed off Max's plan as his own.

"W-What do you think, Paul?" Tom asked, hesitantly.

"I have no objections," Paul replied, perhaps a little too quickly. Was his not intending to actually go through with the shipment operation making him careless? *I must avoid that*, he resolved.

"Decided then," Max said. "Secondly, all hazard signs must be removed. Agreed?"

"In the case of the radiation-grade casks, that *can't* be done before they're loaded on to the ship," Paul said. "They're highly distinctive and will be travelling by rail to whichever American port we agree on. The nine shipping containers will also be travelling by rail, but I don't intend to put radiation stickers on them."

"Why aren't you moving everything by road at that end too?" Tom asked.

"Officials in American cities take a very close interest in nuclear loads that are being trucked through. Use of the railroad minimises that attention."

"Leave this to me," Max said, impatiently. "Hazard labels and signs will be removed or covered over before the containers are unloaded here. I have men on the inside who, for a few Rand, will do this. Agreed?"

Paul nodded in assent.

Taking a pile of large stickers from the counter draw, Max said, "These will be stuck on top of any signs that are too hard to remove." He passed one to Paul to inspect.

The white self-adhesive stickers were about eighteen inches square. TOWARDS A MODERN FUTURE and A WILLINGHAM CORPORATION INNOVATION VENTURE were printed with orange ink.

Paul recalled Maycross's claim: Preparatory work's been going on for several months. Handing the sticker back to Max, Paul said, "There is the matter of the bill of lading."

"That's how I *really* earn my corn, isn't it, Thomas? There will be two. One for USA declarations and one for importation."

"*You're* the man, Max," Tom said. "And it's a bloody lot of corn."

"I'm worth every Rand. An additional six hundred thousand for me. Don't forget that, Thomas. The chartered ship is registered under a Panama flag. Its master has carried out document switches before, in East Africa and the Middle East – crates of guns declared as farming machinery or irrigation parts. He will get four million. He has a number of people to pay," Max said. "The ship is on standby, which is costing the owner a lot of money in berthing charges and lost revenues."

Paul mentally converted the total sum to pounds sterling. 4.6 million Rand was the equivalent of about two hundred and thirty thousand pounds. He looked at Tom, who shrugged as if to say no problem. But why had Max used the adjective "additional"? Perhaps Tom paid him an ongoing retainer? How many loads were brought into or out of the African continent covertly to further his government's interests? And how many of them had involved Maycross?

A painfully loud ringing filled the confined space.

“Those fucking Japanese robot toys!” Max exclaimed. He glanced at his wristwatch. “I must go to Wharf 9. There’s ten thousand of the things. We’re done for now, yes?”

Tom and Paul looked at each other and nodded in agreement.

“Thank you for your time, Max,” Tom said loudly.

“It’s been good to meet you, Max,” Paul said, doubting he could be heard.

The noise of the alarm stopped abruptly, leaving a phantom of itself sounding in their ears.

“Get me that timing, Doctor,” Max said, shepherding them towards the fire door.

“You’re irresistible when you’re masterful, Max,” Tom said.

Chapter 19

It was 9.00 p.m. when Paul retired to the guest bedroom in Tom's flat. It had been a long day... or two... or had it been three? He hadn't slept properly the night before he set off for Heathrow and the three-hour post-check-in wait for what turned out to be a restless flight.

Tom had decided that they should depart for Johannesburg immediately after breakfast. In order to remain attentive during the long drive, Paul needed to catch up with his sleep. On the other hand, dozing in the car tomorrow would have the benefit of "removing" himself from Tom's mock-schizophrenic presence.

As soon as he put his head on the pillow, the same imaginary box he'd come to contemplate every night flashed into his mind. It always came to him with a blackish-blue hue, as if needing caresses by a soft cloth dampened with silver polish. This silver card box marked "Ann" looked unloved. Its physical counterpart, the real card box, certainly *was* unloved by her.

"*All the Luck of Atlantic City!*" she'd exclaimed upon reading the engraved lid.

"Don't you like it?" he responded, seeing she hated it.

"Who keeps playing cards inside a silver box? This ridiculous object tells me how much you really think of me? *All the luck...* What luck?"

Paul tried to comfort her, but she stepped away and turned her back to him.

He shouldn't have mentioned so soon that he would be going away again, this time to South Africa, in a few days' time. He could have waited another day to tell her. He hadn't even unpacked.

And yet Ann hadn't appeared upset initially, when he'd reminded her about his new responsibility for advising on nuclear power station design. In fact, he'd begun to wonder if Maycross's visit had made his absences appear noble, as the man from Whitehall had presumably intended. But once he'd given the silver box to her...

It seemed harder than ever to interpret her state of mind. The memory of feeling that he could read her thoughts was a mocking echo from a contented past.

Ann threw the box on to the sofa and headed for the stairs. With the thudding of her footsteps against the carpeted treads filling his ears, Paul retrieved the failure of a present from where it had wedged under a cushion. A bang came from the slammed bathroom door.

As he opened the glass display cabinet, he had a premonition that the rest of their lives would be owned by her unhappiness. Kneeling, he placed the small box at the back of the bottom shelf, where no one would notice it and the taunting inscription. Someone would have to make an effort to find it there, hidden behind an array of prized curios, each of which was adorned with intricacies that only a person who was "cultured" and "charming" could discern. Those adjectives, applied by Ann to his "handler", conjured everything that *All the Luck of Atlantic City* did not.

***

The sun was shining and Paul felt refreshed from last night's sleep and this morning's egg and bacon breakfast. Best of all, Tom was less garrulous than yesterday, as if he'd assimilated yet another personality during the night, or maybe he just had a headache. Whatever the reason for Tom's subdued state, two hours of near silence between them had passed since they'd set off from the garage beneath Cornish Mansions. They were dressed in the same casual attire that they'd worn yesterday afternoon.

According to Tom, the drive in a north-west direction, most of it along the N3 connecting Durban to Johannesburg, would take about nine hours, allowing for a couple of rest breaks. "We won't have time to make detours for sightseeing. You'll have to settle for what you see along the way."

"That's fine," Paul had replied, feeling cheated. It was like Manhattan all over again. He would have liked to stop in Pietermaritzburg – his mother had mentioned the place – but that town was already behind them. As for the mountains of the Drakensberg escarpment, these were still an unprepossessing bank of ridges a long way off to the west. Because their windows were half open, air was noisily whipping the interior of the car, discouraging conversation.

Tom wound up his window. "I've packed sandwiches and drinks. They're in the canvas bag on the back seat. It'll save time. Anyway, the tribal lands we'll pass have little in the way of *comfortable* service stations."

Paul took Tom's emphasis on "comfortable" as code for Whites Only. They were making good progress. Where the dual carriageway became a single lane, lorries struggling against the gradient could be easily overtaken on the straights. For the first time Paul could visualise a load from Hartling Springs one day travelling this way. If that happened, it would be without him. *Let Maycross deal with the consequences.*

Maycross... The imaginary silver box bearing that name was irresistible at moments like this. Paul felt his palms perspiring as they had last week when he'd started to walk from his car at the Tobe Institute. The green E-Type had been there again, but freshly polished this time. As on the last occasion, it had been parked antisocially across two bays.

The driver's door of the sports car swung open and, to Paul's amazement, out wriggled Maycross. "I see you looking. I'm too tall for this thing. My knees are almost under my chin," he called out. "And now the law says I have to put on the seat belt. I'm not a contortionist!" The awful man's good mood was as disturbing as his possession of the car.

Why hadn't Ann mentioned the gorgeous car? Of course, when Maycross had visited her, it had been during the late evening; the green colour would have been washed out by the gathering darkness. In any case, one car was the same as another to Ann. Maycross could have arrived in a Roman chariot for all it would have mattered. She was seemingly only attentive to loitering black vans.

Paul felt sickened that he'd smiled back at Maycross. His handler had to be made to believe that all was well, but what a price in pride to pay. Or had he for an unspeakable second succumbed to the oily charm that had so beguiled Ann.

During the harmonious meeting, Paul had described the work he intended to pursue in South Africa. He'd continued to withhold that he and Shannon Lennon had rescued someone at the Altabrite site. If

Maycross had been informed by Blackwood about the incident, he didn't raise it either. The concern about something having "upset the client" hadn't yet materialised.

The incline increased as the road approached the easterly sweep of the Drakensberg escarpment. Ridges filled the northern horizon, promising increasingly scenic views.

A sign for the turning to Howick Falls reminded Paul of another place that his mother had mentioned. The waterfall there, a tourist hotspot apparently, seemed to possess a special significance to Beth. She and his father must have visited there. Perhaps that's where he proposed to her? Paul wished he could have his father's advice, his father's approval of his intentions... On the other hand, it was a mercy that his father was not alive to learn of the son's problems.

"According to diagrams I've seen, the shafts in the Randkop Mine go to a depth of nearly two miles. Can we get the containers that far?" Paul said, turning his thoughts to the job he was supposed to be doing.

"We've aimed for half a mile."

"Why?"

"The upper workings to that depth had become very honeycombed. Blasting through and combining overlaying sections of tunnels was straightforward. It's avoided a huge amount of widening work. You'll see for yourself."

"So those parts are like caverns now?" Paul said, realising that the schematics he'd been given were so out of date as to be useless.

"Exactly. We've adapted a network of tunnels rather than excavating new ones."

"But only to a depth of half a mile?"

"Unless you get Head Office to come up with a lot more money."

"How much?" Paul asked.

"Hundreds of thousands of Rands. Millions. Tens of millions. How long's a piece of string? The costs and the time required will increase exponentially the deeper you want to go."

After reflecting for a moment, Paul said, "Based on how much Max and the captain are being paid, money doesn't seem to be a problem."

"It certainly isn't a problem for *me*," Tom said, chuckling. "As I said, you would have to persuade Head Office."

“Hmmm...” Paul looked out of the window, imagining such a conversation with Maycross. By resigning, he would spare himself that futile argument.

“By the way, it’s just called the Kop Mine now. Has been for several years, I believe,” Tom said, reopening his window.

***

It was dark by the time they arrived at the Hotel Willem, situated in the southern suburbs of Johannesburg. Paul had been at the wheel for the last three hours, taking navigation instructions from Tom. They felt the chill of the night air, around forty degrees Fahrenheit, as they stepped out from the warmth of the car.

The nearby section of ring road and its on- and off-ramps clearly post-dated the hotel, which was of a similar vintage to The James. Overlooked and bypassed by the new road, the Willem, had the appearance of a business eking out an existence while the world was being recast round it. The only outside light was from a lamp above the main entrance.

There were no leaflets advertising theatres, restaurants and “Places to See” on display in the cramped lobby. The brown used for both the exterior and the interior seemed a stubborn choice rather than a smart one. It were as if the hotel owner was too proud to make any effort to remodel, Paul concluded as they waited for someone to come to the front desk. Letting go of the past was, as for the management committee of the RSMSDA, hard sometimes.

Addressing Tom, he said, “Have you stayed here bef—”

A woman had come through the door behind the counter, causing Paul to abandon his question. She looked like a slightly younger and bespectacled version of Max’s cousin, the diminutive Petra; the two women had similarly sun-damaged skin and stooped postures.

“Yo, Mable,” Tom said. “I be here.”

“Ah, Mr Kernick,” she said. “I’d begun to think that you wouldn’t be coming.”

It was the first time Paul had heard Tom’s surname, but the legitimacy of this was undermined by his companion’s sudden adoption of a dialect suggestive of the West Country.

“Seems but foive minutes since I be last here, but I generally an’t one to forego the chance for a fun-packed time at Willem," Tom said, signing in as T. Kernick. "You won't be after proofs of my identity," he said, sliding the Guests Book along the counter to Paul.

"Still the joker, Trevor," Mable replied loudly; it were as if greeting the new arrivals was energising her. "I've put you in your usual room – the one with the hot and cold dancing girls." Turning to Paul, she said, "But I'll need to see something for your friend here. You're both booked in until Monday morning. Is that still correct?"

As Paul took his passport from his windcheater inside pocket, he considered the Tom-to-Trevor metamorphosis. *You could have tipped me off you were going to do that.*

Handing his passport to Mable, Paul was fleetingly tempted to try out a New Jersey accent, but wisely decided he didn't have it in him.

Chapter 20

Paul woke a countless number of times during the night. The strip of light entering beneath the door had, to his tired eyes, the intensity of a neon sign. He could not meditate on his mental array of silver boxes – the insistent voices inside those boxes were stifled by the nocturnal sounds of the Willem. The slamming of doors as fellow guests came and went wasn't the only noise. The plumbing was broadcasting a chaotic symphony comprising the rush of water, gurgling, creaks, and eerie knocks.

As Paul moved to sit on the edge of the bed, light fell across the face his watch – it was three minutes past six. There was no bedside clock in the sparsely furnished room to confirm the time. Perhaps such a clock had been stolen by a previous guest. Everything seemed both unlikely and likely to his groggy mind. If there were an automated calendar – one with a row of rotating digits in the room – he would not trust that either.

Yawning, he got to his feet, switched on the light and walked to the handbasin in the far corner of the room. Paul turned on the cold tap and joined the "Willem pipework orchestra". He splashed cold water on his face, grabbed the nearest towel and screamed into it, "I can get through this, Ann!" The exhortation was lost in the cacophony; he couldn't hear himself.

They would be going to the mine this morning, so Paul took a clean black T-shirt from his suitcase and put on his jeans and windcheater. As footwear, he chose the walking boots he'd lugged from England.

Downstairs, the cigarette smoke-filled dining room was already crowded with an entirely male clientele, all of whom were dressed in clothes similar to his. Three or four men sat at each table, but much of the badinage was between neighbouring groups. The spirited conversations quietened as Paul entered the room.

A blackboard showed the breakfast menu for today, Thursday, scribbled in chalk.

Shortage of sleep and a surfeit of unresolved emotions had left Paul hungry. He helped himself at the counter to a ladleful of runny scrambled eggs, and used the provided tongs to add sausages, bacon, and a mound of bubble and squeak to his plate. The conversations of the diners resumed as he looked round for somewhere to sit.

"Here, mate," someone shouted from a table halfway into the room, by the wall. "There's a free chair here. You can sit with us," the waving man wearing a red-and-green checked shirt said.

Paul weaved his way between the occupied tables. "Thanks, gentlemen," he said, arriving by the table with the spare chair. Three men were slouching there, their plates smeared with oily and burned residues. "It's crowded for so early in the morning, isn't it?" he said, sitting down.

After exchanging glances with his companions, the man in the checked shirt said, "This isn't early." He had thick, black hair and looked to be in his late thirties. After sliding a cigarette packet from his shirt pocket, he flipped it open and took out a cigarette. He tossed the open pack on the table for the others to help themselves. "You're not a miner," he said. "I was going to ask which crew you belong to." He offered the flame of his steel lighter to the man in a khaki shirt next to him.

"Just a tourist," Paul replied, reaching for the salt. "I take it you three *are* miners then."

"A tourist! Staying at this elephant's backside!" the man in the khaki shirt, who was opposite Paul, exclaimed in an Afrikaans accent. The scar on his left cheek disappeared into a hollow as he took a deep draw on his cigarette. After blowing a smoke ring into the air above the table, he said, "You're well and *truly* lost, *my friend*."

Silence ensued as the three men assessed Paul. The way the scarred one had said "my friend" seemed provocative to Paul. Perhaps these miners liked to start their days with a brawl to get their blood flowing...

"The only mining I'll be doing is into my family history. My grandfather *was* a miner around here. He died from silicosis long before I was born. His daughter, my mother, was born in Benoni."

"You don't sound South African," the scarred man said, pointing at Paul with his right hand.

Paul noticed that the tip of the confrontational man's right index finger was missing. Such injuries were probably not uncommon. Perhaps the men at this table were in charge of the setting of explosive charges, as his late grandfather had been. Cutting into a sausage, he explained, "That's because I was brought up in England. The only time my mother sounds South African now is when she's using her telephone voice."

The friendlier man in the checked shirt looked at his watch. "It's time, boys. Our lift should be here." He stood up and slapped Paul on the shoulder. "Enjoy your *sightseeing*."

"Thank you, and you all have a good day too," Paul said, flicking a smile at the three departing miners. There was something awkward about that turn of phrase. *Thank God I didn't attempt a New Jersey accent last night. I'd be struggling to keep it up.*

After finishing his breakfast, Paul went outside to get some air. It was still twilight, with sunrise minutes away. A yellow minivan, covered in dust and with a cracked windscreen, was moving away from the kerb. Several of the breakfast customers were crammed, shoulder-to-shoulder, in the back, their breaths fogging the windows. They weren't so animated now.

Paul speculated that the mineworkers might live at the Hotel Willem for weeks, if not months, at a time. The continuous comings and goings during the night could be the result of the men working at different mines, some taking longer to get to and from than others *Do any of them work at the Kop Mine?* More importantly, were any of them involved in the preparation of underground chambers for housing the radioactive waste that he was supposed to ship here.

The outrageous burial scheme was becoming less dreamlike. At some subconscious level, he'd still doubted Maycross's seriousness, despite all that had transpired in New Jersey. The desire to scream returned, but there was no towel at hand, just the empty parking lot and an elevated section of the ring road, along which solitary vehicles were seemingly pulled by their headlights.

Paul contemplated going for a walk, but the unlit road heading north towards the city looked desolate and ideal for muggers. As he stared in that direction, he distinguished from the haze a far-off figure dressed in white and carrying a jiggling torch. There was something about the way the track-suited person was moving that seemed familiar. Soon the jogger's flopping, dark-brown hair became recognisable. Paul decided to wait for Tom to reach him. It would be a good opportunity to finalise their arrangements for the day.

"Mornin'," Tom said, between gulps of breath.

"Is it safe to go running here?"

"Have to keep the fitnesses up," Tom said, still breathing heavily. Patting his tracksuit jacket pocket, he added, "Anyway, I have a gun."

"Course you do," Paul said, thinking about Shannon's gun.

"You 'ad breakfast?" Tom asked, turning off his torch.

"That was an interesting experience. There's a lot of miners staying here."

"So there be," Tom said, bent over with his hands on his knees.

"You're beginning to sound like a pirate, Tom."

"I an't Tom. I be Trevor when 'ere at Willem. I told you 'bout counter-surveillance lesson two."

"Friction in the ether," Paul said.

"Aye."

"What time do we leave to go to the mine?"

"Plenty o' time. Shower, dressed, breakfast," Tom said, looking at his watch. "Nine thirty'll be the boy."

***

The drive to the Kop Mine took about thirty-five minutes. The main roads on their route had tarmac surfaces but the links between these comprised dirt tracks within large areas of makeshift housing. Paul noticed several signs to mines, but none that referred to their destination.

The visitors' entrance was off a heavily used road bisecting the land belonging to the closed mine. Dilapidated fencing surrounded each of the two parts of the site. Three elevated bridge-like structures, which contained conveyor belts, spanned the road, visually stapling the two areas together.

Tom turned right, off the main road, and stopped by the gate. He sounded his horn. Minutes passed before someone came to let them in.

"The security team here's really on top form," Paul said acerbically.

"Now, now," Tom said. "We won't want a lot of interest being paid to your shipment."

Paul could concede the advantage of a loose regime for the "dumping" phase of Maycross's plan. But thereafter, little or no security would enable trespassers. Who could say what the future – the next ten thousand years – held for the land round here? It could all be swallowed up by the increasing city population. More people, more trespassers.

Tom parked by a two-storey brick building. The west-facing windows of the building front were covered in dust. Paul turned and looked in that direction. The dust on the building had probably been blown here from the hill of mined earth that stood a hundred yards away.

"Digging for decades will get you one of those," Tom said.

"I want to inspect it," Paul said, squinting. He thought he could see people moving about on the mound but, given the distance, couldn't tell whether this was just the dappling effect of the shadows being thrown by the thread-like clouds.

"Why?"

"Safety."

"Safety? Speak to the colonel," Tom said, getting out of the car.

"Who's the colonel?" Paul said, but Tom was already going through the front door of the building.

Clutching a blank notebook – he'd deliberately left the notebook that he'd used in New Jersey at home in England – Paul got out of the car and followed. There was one encouraging development, at least. His companion's dreadful West Country dialect was evidently being reserved for the unfortunate employees of the Hotel Willem.

The colonel turned out to be the Site Director, Stanley Evans, a retired British colonel from the Royal Engineers, who had lived in South Africa for the past twenty years. With Evans's pension at stake following the purchase of the Kop Mine by the Willingham Corporation, the offer to continue in a leadership position for an indefinite period must have been irresistible. Now in his early sixties and attired in a grey, double-breasted suit, Evans was still a striking looking man. His facial appearance, which included a well-trimmed moustache, struck Paul as that of an older but undebauched version of Vernon Blackwood.

The meeting was taking place in Evans's upstairs office. This corner office had windows facing south on to the main road and east on to ore-processing buildings and, beyond those, the compound filled with rows of now-deserted worker housing.

Present at the meeting was someone who was described by Evans as being his right-hand-man. Pieter Niemeyer, Dutch by birth as opposed to being of Afrikaner heritage, was in his mid-forties. He was wearing a dark-blue, single-breasted suit. Niemeyer had the watchful bearing of someone habituated to the dangers of working underground, reminding Paul of the pale men he'd encountered at breakfast.

A third person, also white, was sitting apart from them, in a corner. This bespectacled and overweight middle-aged man was wearing a light-brown mohair suit. With a broad smile that exposed a gold tooth, he said, "I represent the municipality, my friend. My name is totally not important. I will just be here, quiet as a church mouse. Take no notice of me, please."

"I see," Paul said, glancing at Tom. Presumably the "church mouse" was one of the government fixers mentioned by Maycross.

Evans seemed a little on edge. Paul wondered if the colonel was worrying about what was expected from his remaining workforce. It then struck him that his and Tom's casual attire might have caused offence. "I apologise for not wearing a suit and tie, Colonel," Paul said. "I dressed with a view to going into the mine."

"Don't mention it, Dr Avery," Evans said with a dismissive gesture. "But Pieter will provide you with highly effective apparel."

Paul couldn't stop himself from glancing at the watchful church mouse, who reacted by giving another flash of the gold tooth.

"While I think of it, Colonel, the hill of excavated earth... I could be mistaken, but there seems to be people clambering over it."

Evans frowned and shook his head. "Sometimes natives from the nearby townships scavenge for ore."

"That's what I'm worried about. Scavengers and radioactivity don't mix. If they were to get into the tunnels too..."

Evans gave Niemeyer a fierce stare. Looking again at Paul, he said, "We will take care of the matter."

"Thank you. I have a related concern too," Paul persisted. "The action of rainwater upon iron pyrite gives rise to ferric oxide and sulphuric acid. That acid will be dissolving the heavy elements in the mine tailings, such as uranium, cadmium, zinc, arsenic and so forth. The resulting contaminated water will be permeating into the ground water."

Niemeyer interjected, "This mine learned the hard way about acid drainage many decades ago. Rest assured, Doctor, the old tunnels over there will not be employed for the storage of your containers. They have mostly collapsed anyway."

Using all his will, Paul refrained from looking once again at the church mouse, who was clearly the most dangerous person in the room.

At this point, Tom stood up. "Now the introductions are over, gentlemen, I will leave you to it before things get too technical." Turning to Paul, he added, "I'll see you later."

Against the sound of Tom's retreating footsteps, Evans said to Paul, "And I will leave you in Pieter's hands. Afterwards, we will all have lunch here together, and you can apprise me of any *other* matters that require our attention."

"Thank you, Colonel Evans," Paul said, alarmed that he'd been deserted by Tom so soon.

"It's all yours now," he could imagine Tom saying. Perhaps that was a good thing, Paul then decided – the more the complexities of the waste burial operation were understood only by himself, the greater the likelihood of its abandonment following his resignation.

Chapter 21

The cage descended for two minutes before slowing to a stop. Niemeyer and Avery were wearing white overalls, reinforced boots and yellow helmets. Each helmet had a lamp fixed to it, but so far the lamps were not needed.

Niemeyer slid open the inner door of the cage and then pushed open the mesh safety door. They stepped out into a huge tunnel, which was lit by five strings of lights running along the roof, thirty feet above their heads. The harsh light, far-off voices, thrumming of generators, and gentle movement of air – the air felt several degrees warmer than that at ground level – were unconvincing evidence of the taming of this alien environment. This awareness caused Paul to wonder how many ghosts were watching them.

With his voice echoing, Niemeyer instructed, “Be careful as you step over those rails, Doctor.” He pointed to the track running down the centre of the tunnel floor.

“Thank you. I see them.”

“This way.” Niemeyer set off down the gentle slope of the cavernous tunnel.

“My colleague said that we can store the containers at a depth of half a mile,” Paul said, walking alongside his host.

“That’s correct. We’ve just descended eight hundred meters, or half a mile, if you prefer.”

“How can the casks and shipping containers be brought down here?” Paul stopped and stared at the railway track. It was clearly too puny for the massive casks from Hartling Springs.

“No, no, Doctor, the track is for rock removal. The wagons that run on it fit in special lifts. Your containers will simply be driven down.”

“Is the incline as gentle as this all the way down?”

“Indeed, Doctor. This mine started life on the other side of the road that brought you here.” Niemeyer pointed towards the top of the tunnel wall, as if to indicate a place far off. Moving his arm in an arc, he continued, “The old workings spiral as they become deeper. They run in that direction and then back and forth and back and so on.” By the time he'd finished explaining, Niemeyer had turned full circle twice.

Paul nodded in appreciation. The handling of the containers inside the mine had always seemed the greatest mechanical obstacle, yet the access issue had been addressed. How much of this was because of the involvement of Benedict Sykes? Had Sykes *chosen* the mine because of its layout?

"There is one part that requires more blasting work," Niemeyer added. "That won't be a problem, Doctor. Come, I have a lot to show you."

After walking for several minutes, they came to the source of the voices. Black workers carrying pickaxes were engaged in some kind of activity on the other side of the tunnel. Their overalls were blue and their helmets white. The beams of their lamps disappeared and returned as they went into and emerged from an otherwise unlit gash in the tunnel wall.

"Here, Doctor." Niemeyer said, starting to cross the tunnel.

Paul followed, remembering to step over the track rails. He clutched his notebook tighter.

"All good, boss," one of the workers said, upon seeing Niemeyer. "This one is almost ready now."

"I've brought our customer to see for himself, Thabo," Niemeyer said. "Take Doctor Avery inside. Show him."

"I will show him, boss." Looking nervously at Paul, Thabo said, "Come, you see."

Niemeyer grasped Paul's arm. "Turn on your lamp, Doctor, and mind your head in there."

With Niemeyer's assistance, Paul turned on his lamp before following Thabo into the passage, which branched at forty-five degrees from the main tunnel. The thuds of pick heads striking rock became louder with each step.

As Paul's eyes adjusted to the swirling beams of light ahead of him, he began to make out the hewn rock surfaces of the wall. Just in time, he ducked, avoiding a protrusion.

"Look out, boss!" he heard Thabo shout.

Thinking this warning pertained to the jutting rock he'd narrowly missed, he kept advancing. The side of his abdomen struck an unyielding, angular obstacle hiding in the darkness. "Argh! Damn!" he cried.

Looking down, the beam from his lamp revealed the corner of a steel wagon laden with rocks and earth – it was a visceral encounter with the manner in which the troubling mound above ground had been fed throughout the decades of the mine's operation.

"You okay, boss?" Thabo said, returning.

Paul waited for the searing pain to recede. Shielding his eyes from the glare of Thabo's lamp, he eventually managed to reply, "My fault, Thabo. I'm all right."

The sound of picks striking rock farther ahead had been replaced by laughter.

"The bunker is good, yes, boss?" Thabo asked.

As Paul sidestepped round the wagon, the significance of the "bunker" word dawned on him. *This isn't a branching tunnel. It's intended to be one of the storage chambers.*

Several minutes later, escorted by Thabo, Paul emerged from the bunker. Niemeyer, arms folded, was waiting. After gesturing for Thabo to go back and carry on with the work, Niemeyer said, "Did you find the bunker satisfactory, Doctor?"

"It's certainly large enough," Paul replied, wincing with pain. He opened his notebook, folded it back on to itself, and began to sketch what he'd just seen.

"Your lamp!" Niemeyer exclaimed.

Once Paul had turned off his lamp, Niemeyer continued, "After blasting, we finish each using manpower. That one will be complete today."

"Eleven more to go."

"We've achieved much more than that, Doctor. Come," Niemeyer said, setting off again down the main tunnel.

Paul, holding his side, limped after his enthusiastic host.

Fifty yards farther on, they came to a second opening, where the entrance to another chamber had been shaped to a neat rectangle. Reinforcement timbers had been inserted to prevent collapse. A white-and-orange metal sign reproducing the text of the stickers that Max had shown to Paul was riveted to the wall.

"And see, all along there," Niemeyer said, pointing to the other side of the tunnel.

From their vantage point, three more chamber openings, each adorned with the metal sign, could be seen. Beyond that the tunnel curved out of view.

"Do you want to inspect all of them, Doctor?" Niemeyer asked.

"Have you prepared all twelve?"

"Twelve!" Niemeyer exclaimed. "The one you went inside will be number thirty-four, and we're marking out locations for more, the next level down."

Paul was shocked. Why was so much work being done? The signage was a nice touch, but the number of chambers... It was surely far more than was necessary to convince any official bypassing the church mouse to inspect this supposed experimental storage facility.

***

"Help yourself, Dr Avery," Colonel Evans said, gesturing towards the food. Dishes of sandwiches, slabs of assorted cheeses, bowls containing bananas, apples, oranges and grapes, and two cake stands, one with a chocolate cake and one with an oozing Victoria Sponge, filled the trestle table that now occupied one side of the Site Director's office. A couple of flies buzzed around the food, spoiled for choice.

The church mouse, sitting in the corner again, had already helped himself. On his lap was a plate with a slice of each of the two cakes. Paul sensed the observer had become bored with the proceedings.

With their plates filled, Paul, Pieter Niemeyer and Colonel Evans sat down at a small table near a window. A jug of orange juice and a nested stack of plastic beakers was on the table.

"Are you quite all right, Doctor?" Evans asked. "I noticed you're walking with more difficulty than earlier."

"I managed to bash myself against an ore wagon."

Evans looked inquiringly at Niemeyer, who remarked, "Inside Bunker 34. I assumed the doctor would like to see one being excavated."

"Quite so, but we mustn't damage our invaluable expert."

"At least he's more agile than his predecessor," Niemeyer said, presumably alluding to Sykes.

Ever since Tom had revealed Sykes's involvement, Paul had wondered whether his workplace "champion" had deliberately placed him in Maycross's tactical cross hairs. It seemed unlikely that Paul's departmental rival, Andy Higstead, would have been suitable – Andy had once boasted about his brother working in the Cabinet Office, whereas Maycross had made it clear that the taint of a Grandee Paragraph 5 Order was kept away from the Prime Minister.

"We never did hear what happened to the professor, did we?" Evans said to Niemeyer. Turning to Paul, he added, "Indeed, you are a much younger replacement. Considerably younger than I expected. But I'm merely an old soldier, so this radioactivity business is something of a novelty."

Despite an unexpected frailty in Evans's voice, Paul concluded, *That remark would be worthy of Maycross.* This observation cautioned him to remain vigilant, particularly now that the church mouse had returned to the trestle table, seemingly for another slice of cake.

The sweet-toothed man turned sharply and smiled.

Paul nodded politely, and took his first bite of a quartered sandwich.

After a minute or so, Colonel Evans asked Paul, "So, Doctor, what are your conclusions about our humble efforts here?"

Paul had considered the answer to this question on his way back here with Niemeyer. His former self would have said, *You are participating in madness!* But as a piece on Maycross's chess board, positivity was the only option. "Very impressive. The access issue I was primarily concerned about seems to have been addressed," he said.

Evans gave Niemeyer an approving glance. Pieter seemed about to ask something, but remained silent when his boss made a subtle gesture – just a small hand movement. The Site Director looked again at Paul, this time with a kindly smile.

Paul took his cue to continue. "I want to get a better appreciation of the worst-case impact upon the water courses surrounding the mine. Pieter has been very helpful already in this regard, but prudence requires that I consult the library records to ensure nothing's been overlooked."

At this Niemeyer leaned forward to interject, but again Colonel Evans waved him away. "Off course, Doctor. We would expect nothing less than thoroughness. Are there any matters we can assist you with *now*?"

There it was – impatience. Paul knew he was straying into unwelcome territory. Maycross had told him the site couldn't be rejected. On the other hand, he had to appear to be taking the project seriously.

"Well, Colonel, apart from the matter of trespassers that I raised this morning, I have noted down a small number of safety recommendation, such as providing the workers with respirators and the availability of rudimentary Geiger counters." Paul removed a piece of paper from his shirt pocket and handed it to Evans.

Without looking at it, Evans passed the note to Pieter. "Consider your wise recommendations adopted forthwith." Evans then brought his hands together to form a steeple. "Are you able to indicate when we should be expecting your containers?"

"I'm hopeful that the transfer can take place within a few weeks," Paul said, trying not to choke on his words.

"That is most gratifying, Doctor," Evans said. At this point, he turned to Pieter and with a raised eyebrow invited him to comment.

"Your Trevor and you keep referring to twelve containers," Niemeyer said testily, his impatience unleashed. After glancing at his boss, he continued, "You've seen that we've prepared thirty-four bunkers already." His voice was becoming louder. "Our price is *per* container. Have we been grossly misled about the amount of money we are to receive?"

"I can help you there, Pieter," the hovering church mouse interjected, having quietly approached. His voice was gravelly, yet refined. "The good doctor is, I would dare to venture, not conversant with all matters. His is, naturally, a technical role. Our senior partner is sending someone better placed to reassure you."

"And *when* will that be?" Niemeyer asked.

"Her plane will arrive tomorrow, in point of fact." Flashing his gold-toothed smile at Paul, the church mouse continued, "I am informed that you know her, Doctor."

Paul felt the world dropping away – it were as if the entirety of the corrupted mine had split like a sinkhole.

***

It was mid-afternoon when the taxi from the Kop Mine dropped Paul Avery at the Hotel Willem. The taxi belonged to a local firm with whom the mine had an account, so there was no need for Paul to pay. He thanked the black driver and got out. Tom was waiting for him outside the hotel.

"Afternoon, my robin," Tom said as Paul, carrying his notebook, approached.

"Who do you think you're fooling?" Paul cried, lengthening his stride. He landed a punch on the side of Tom's jaw, knocking him to the ground.

Tom deftly rolled sideways to avoid a follow-up attack and sprung back to his feet. Holding out an open hand to maintain Paul at arm's length, Tom backed away. "I suggest we go for a drive and discuss your problem, whatever it is."

"Let's do that," Paul said, his anger subsiding. It was the first time he'd hit someone since a long-ago playground fight with a school bully. He wasn't sure why he'd punched Tom, but it had felt good. If only it had been Maycross...

They walked to where Tom had parked his Honda. Tom rubbed his jaw as he started the car. "You throw a good punch for a civilian," he said as he turned out of the parking lot.

In silence they drove two miles in the direction of the city before Tom took a left into the parking lot of an outdoors shopping centre comprising stores that sold large-box items such as refrigerators, lawnmowers and televisions. By this time Paul had calmed sufficiently to regret his loss of self-control.

Tom parked in a quiet corner facing on to the road they'd just turned off. Paul moved to open his door.

"Wait! Let's talk here. It'll be harder for you to hit me again, this way," Tom said.

Paul straightened up. "I'm sorry I did that."

"Okay, so what's your problem?"

Paul couldn't trust someone taking his orders from Maycross, particularly someone carrying a gun. In particular, he couldn't reveal how upset he was about the entire plan, yet he had to come up with a credible explanation for his behaviour.

"Niemeyer challenged me about the number of containers we're shipping. They've prepared thirty-four storage chambers, with more to come. What the hell's going on? I felt a fool in there."

"That's news to me too," Tom finally said

"They expect to be paid *per* container."

"Thirty-four, thirty-four," Tom repeated to himself, absently drumming the steering wheel with his palm. "Is that it, Paul?"

"Ye— No. That accent you've been using. It's a fucking insult. My mother's parents came from Cornwall. My gran lived with us until she died. She didn't sound anything like that. No one speaks like that. At least, not for the last two hundred years."

"Don't take it personally. There's a romantic affection for the Cornish in parts of Jo'berg, similar to the way there's a sentimental regard for the Irish in certain American cities. Young countries hanker for relatable roots. The people running our hotel haven't been to Cornwall or anywhere in Europe, come to that. For them I'm the personification of a Cornish Jack – the men who enabled the mining industry to take off."

"At least you have the sense not to speak that way at the mine."

"No point. We're in the same boat."

"Are we? I'm not sure that Niemeyer is impressed with either of us. And he referred to you as being *my* Trevor, as if you're answerable to me."

"Interesting."

"Don't take it personally."

Tom chuckled. "As long as you don't punch me again."

"No promises," Paul said, grinning.

"If that's really all of it, I'll buy you a coffee. There's a handy place nearby. Are you positive there's nothing else?"

Paul began to shake his head, then stopped. "There is something you should know, as you seem to have been left in the dark like me."

"I'm all ears."

"The man in the corner, the one who was at the meeting but not *in* the meeting... He said—" Paul stopped himself from mentioning the reference to Shannon. As betrayed as he felt about her seeming involvement in the wider plans for the mine, if there was any possibility of an innocent explanation, the less he said now the better.

"His name's Charlie Halliday, by the way," Tom said, filling the silence. "As long as we give him the money he needs, he won't let us down."

"Well, Halliday told Niemeyer not to ask me further questions about the need for additional storage chambers."

"He did? In that case, a message to Head Office would seem in order."

"If you say so," Paul mumbled. He stared out of the passenger window, contemplating Maycross's response.

How would Maycross react to his plan for the Hartling Springs radioactive waste being compromised? But hadn't that plan *already* been jeopardised by the inclusion of the Altabrite waste?

A distressing possibility struck Paul. What if the scale of the activity at the Kop Mine was already known to Maycross and he was concealing further work demands? If so, the sooner Paul made his move the better.

Chapter 22

Paul and Tom had ordered hamburgers and chips from the selection printed on the laminated menu cards. It was past 4.00 p.m. but still early for the serving of meals. None of the other customers were eating.

"They opened as a tea room. Because there wasn't enough demand around here for teas and fancy cakes they had to turn into a restaurant," Tom said. "They were trying to be too upmarket."

"Upmarket?" Paul said, taking in the grim ambience of Café Prima. The décor comprised a uniform shade of grey. "Given its location, I'm surprised anyone comes in here at all."

The young auburn waitress returned with their meals. "Enjoy," she said, transferring the heaped plates from her tray to the table. "Help yourself to the condiments."

The quality of the food was no better than that of the coffee, but the place had a particular attraction – one of the offices above it was another of Tom's communication hubs, the premises of a speciality-furniture distributor. The other two offices were vacant.

Paul picked up his hamburger and took a large bite.

"I came to my office after leaving you this morning. I found this – the flight details for S.L.," Tom said, placing the message on the table for Paul to read. "She's flying in via London Heathrow and will arrive at around seven-thirty in the morning."

Slowly chewing a gristly mouthful, Paul picked up the message that, like the one he'd read in Durban, was addressed to Tallyho Furnishings. *Heathrow... How long is the wait time there for the connecting-flight?* He guessed that, schedules permitting, Maycross would try to meet Shannon Lennon in the V.I.P. lounge, using his contacts. *He's bound to want to find out what's upset Blackwood.*

"As you two know each other, I suggest you collect her," Tom said. "Get the hotel to order a taxi for six tomorrow morning to take you to the airport." He took a business card for Tallyho Furnishings from his wallet and passed it to Paul. "Once you've collected her, call me on that number. I'll be working upstairs."

Absently flicking Tom's card, Paul said, "I doubt the Hotel Willem will be to her liking. It's more like a hostel than a hotel, and the men staying there ask a lot of questions."

"We've not been instructed to make a hotel reservation for her," Tom responded distractedly "She can stay wherever she wants."

Although he'd assumed Tom's attention was still upon him, when Paul looked up he saw that his companion had been scribbling on a paper napkin.

"This cover it?" Tom said, handing the napkin to Paul.

Questions raised about the number of items to be shipped. Expectations significantly exceed the quantity communicated by us. Any client update on this?

"It's succinct," Paul said, passing the napkin back to Tom.

Tom took a chip from the pile on his plate and stood up. "I won't be long," he said, heading towards the front door of the café. The external staircase leading to his office suite was around the corner.

***

When they pulled in to the parking lot of the Hotel Willem, Paul said he was going to speak to the front desk about ordering the taxi for the morning. He would also be placing a call to his wife. The bedroom telephones couldn't make international calls. After that, he would have an early night – one passing more peacefully, he hoped, than their first night.

"The Willem's not exactly a quiet place," Tom conceded. "It's a home from home for its guests. I like it. You shouldn't worry about the other guests being inquisitive. You just need a cover story for your being in Jo'berg."

"I told them about my grandfather. He worked in a gold mine, somewhere around here."

"Is that true?"

"You read my file."

Tom thought for a moment. "I can't remember. Anyway, use it, by all means. The point is, being a ghost is harder than people imagine. It's better to bore the locals into submission."

"I've a lot to learn about spy craft," Paul said, nodding. "Thanks by the way for giving me a break from your cod Cornish, Tom. I mean

Trevor."

"No problem, my robin. Proper job," Tom said, turning off the engine. "So you sure you an't be coming to bar for a few jugs?" Tom nodded towards the side of the hotel. "There be a handy way in 'long there what takes us straight to she."

"Don't push it," Paul said, shaking his head. "See you tomorrow sometime."

"By then we should have a reply from Head Office."

"Do you really have no idea where the extra containers they're expecting are coming from?"

Tom frowned. "I don't even know much about the containers you're sending. I'm fine with that. I'm just a good soldier."

"Just following orders," Paul said sarcastically. "Don't you have any curiosity about all this?"

"The procurement of a new nuclear-missile system is at stake. That's all I need to know."

Paul thought back to the first meeting with Maycross. The negotiations to acquire the latest nuclear-missile system for UK submarines were being stonewalled. Perhaps knowing that should be enough for him, too. "See you tomorrow, Tom," he said, getting out of the car.

He headed towards the main entrance. The closer he got, the lonelier he felt. His marriage surviving its fourth year felt improbable. It were as though unsaid things he'd never doubted – including their growing old together – had always been an illusion.

***

Ann had reacted to his suggestion about their moving to Suffolk with less enthusiasm than he'd anticipated. It had, after all, been her desire for them.

"That's what you want, isn't it?" he said.

He had raised the matter during breakfast, the Friday following his return from America. Later that day he would be driving to Stoke Poges to agree the arrangements for the South Africa trip with Maycross.

He'd buttered toast and poured mugs of tea. She was sitting at the kitchen table. Paul was leaning back against the sink counter.

"We've never talked about it properly. The only thing you've said up to now is that I should go to my parents' while you're tied up with your ever-so-important project."

"I did, but now I think we could relocate permanently."

"Why've you changed your mind?" she asked suspiciously.

"I haven't stopped thinking about it since you raised it – about how to make it work," he said. "My mother's retiring in a couple of months, and I'd worried about her becoming isolated. Now that she's agreed to move to Suffolk too, I feel better knowing she'll be close to us."

"When did you speak to her?"

"Well, I drove there yesterday, instead of going to the office." He'd anticipated the question and had to gamble that his answer would be sufficient. After clearing his throat, he continued, "I wanted to get all the ducks in a row before saying anything to you."

After a moment of reflection, Ann said, "But you'll be living in a flat in Didcot or somewhere else round here during the week. Or you'll be travelling. You won't be *near* her, Paul."

"And that applies to my being away from you too!" He looked at her pleadingly. "Unless I were to resign, I suppose, and get some kind of nine-to-five job in Suffolk."

"You expect me to look after her!" Ann exclaimed, discounting or not registering Paul's "resign" remark.

"She's not senile. You won't be living *with* her, just near her. I thought this would make you happy."

Ann picked up a knife and scraped some of the butter off her toast. She wiped the edge of the knife with a sheet of kitchen towel and then stared at the slices as if they were an irreparable mess. "But the thing is," Ann said as she cut one of the slices into two halves, "I'm not sure I want to do that any longer."

"I'll eat it then," Paul said, leaning forward to take her plate.

"I don't mean the toast. I mean live in Suffolk."

Jerking back as if struck by the high-voltage dart of a Taser gun, Paul stuttered, "You s-said you want to be c-close to your friends and family – your '*support network*'."

Looking up, Ann said, "It's never been solely about that. I don't feel fulfilled here."

"Exactly. You told me you'll be able to find a suitable job in Norwich. It's very arty in Norwich." He immediately wished he could take back the "arty" word. Ann never used it. It was a word one had to earn, he imagined. *His* saying it was like Maycross's dismissive reference to his agency as "the glow team".

Ann brought a piece of the offending toast to her lips before putting it back on the plate. "London's the centre of things," she said.

"London!" It were as if a second dart had struck him.

Ann's gaze remained fixed upon her plate, as if she couldn't look at him.

"Where's this come from?" he said. "We can't afford to live in Oxford, let alone London."

Only now did she look at him. "You'd made up your mind about taking the job here. I felt pressured."

"That's not fair. The job was... I mean *is* a good fit for me. Anyway, we agreed neither of us are city peop—" A dreadful answer to his question of a moment ago had occurred to him. He could almost hear that plummy voice dispensing poison.

"There's so many museums and galleries in London," Ann said, with a sudden air of enthusiasm.

London was chockful of arty institutions... It felt as if he'd glimpsed an unexpected part of the fabric of existence, as profound as the discovery of dark matter.

"Patrick has a contact at the V and A. He said he'll speak to someone there on my behalf."

And there it was – from her mouth, the worst words imaginable.

Those words hung over them all weekend. However, by the time he left for London Heathrow on Monday, Ann had seemingly reconnected with the idea – her idea – of their relocating to north Suffolk, although insisting "London is not off the table". Paul departed, trying to accept her tentative acquiescence as a victory. Nonetheless, anxiety ensured his sleeplessness during the long flight.

He'd asked Ann not to mention their relocating to anyone, apart from her parents. It would look bad for him if his superiors were to accidently hear. Because of the commuting distance, they would worry about his commitment, he'd explained. He would inform the RSMSDA in his own time, which would be after their finding a house.

They agreed that he wouldn't phone her from South Africa for a couple of days. This would give her time to settle in at her parents'. His mother, Beth, would join her in Suffolk in a fortnight's time, taking a few days off work as holiday. In the meantime, Ann would collate and circulate the property enquiries about houses for both Beth and themselves to estate agents in Suffolk and Norfolk.

***

Mable placed the call from the telephone in her cluttered office. The phone at the other end was ringing when she handed the receiver to Paul and left the room, closing the door.

He was too anxious to sit down.

"Hello," a man said, eventually answering the call. The sound of a television programme about antiques could be heard in the background. It was almost 5.00 p.m. in England.

Paul remembered that the telephone at Pendlefield Manor was in the lounge, the spacious front room with floral-patterned furnishings and wallpaper. Thoughts of their wedding reception, held in a marquee in the grounds of the house, intruded. That big day… Firm roots at last. Someone who adored him. "Bernard? It's Paul, calling from South Africa," he said, his eyes welling.

"Ah, Paul, how are you?" Before Paul could reply, Ann's father called out, "Dot, it's Paul! Calling from South Africa!"

After a few seconds, a woman's voice came on the line. "It's Dot here, Paul. She's not in at the moment."

He'd been so distracted, it hadn't occurred to Paul that Ann might be out. Perhaps he should have stuck to the half past midnight *her-time* arrangement adopted when he was in America. The one-hour-ahead time difference now instead of the previous five-hour-behind time difference had made that arrangement seem unnecessary.

"She's sightseeing. Took the train down to Kensington this morning. Visiting the museums and galleries. You know Ann."

Paul imagined Ann being interviewed by someone smarmy – a close friend of Maycross's. "Including the Victoria and Albert?" he asked.

"I would imagine so. That's her favourite. You can ask her all about it. She said she will be back around eleven, depending on the trains."

"How is she, Dot?"

After a hesitation, Ann's mother said, "She's a little agitated, Paul, to be honest, you know, with everything up in the air."

"You mean the house-hunting?"

"Well, there's that, of course, yes, and..."

The line went silent. "Are you there, Dot?"

"Yes, yes, dear, I'm still here."

"You were saying that Ann's agitated."

"Should I get her to call you? Or will you be in bed then? What's the time there?"

Paul swallowed the impulse to scream, *Of course! Get her to call me.* After taking a deep breath, he said, "It's only one hour ahead of you here, Dot. I'm in Johannesburg at the Hotel Willem, but I might be moving to another hotel tomorrow. Ann can call me tonight, no matter how late." Paul examined the letterhead on the stationery lying on Mable's desk. He told Dorothy the number. "Otherwise, I'll call her tomorrow at around this time."

"Oh, did you say Johannesburg, Paul? Ann said you were going to Cape Town. I'd love to see Table Mountain. Johannesburg's not as pretty, is it?"

"It's a long story, Dot. I'm not surprised Ann's confused. My work *is* connected to Cape Town, but my professional contacts are here."

"That's a shame. Perhaps there'll be another time. Perhaps you can take Ann there."

"We'll have to save up first."

"I'm sorry she's not in, dear."

"Give her my love, Dot."

Ann didn't call – Paul had asked Mable to let him know if his wife rang – and, of course, he didn't sleep. This time it was because of his wife's trip to London and Dot's circumspect use of the "agitated" word rather than the nightly din of the Hotel Willem. The imaginary silver box marked Ann would not close. Every triangulation of the emotional terrain of their marriage led to "ungrateful bitch", which he could not allow. His failings and the recent protective lies needed to be given more weight. He owed her that; he owed *them* that.

And yet it seemed as if they were breaking up without the words ever being said. Or perhaps he just hadn't noticed. Ann had a disconcerting way of making decisions without narrative preludes. It was a trait he suspected she'd inherited from her father, who'd spent many years in the military. She'd talk about the implications of a decision instead of explicitly saying what it was that she'd decided. It was, after all, how they came to be married. They hadn't discussed getting married before the day she described where they would honeymoon – "You won't be able to wear that in the south of France."

Chapter 23

With the sprawling city still asleep, the early-morning taxi ride from the Hotel Willem to the airport, situated on the eastern side of Johannesburg, had taken a little over an hour. Along the way, roadside signs bearing place names such as New Redruth and Kempton Park had reminded Paul of England. One of the signs near the airport pointed eastwards to Benoni, his mother's birthplace. Beth was always supportive of her only son, her only child. God knows what she would think of what he was doing here – of what was in his heart. Why hadn't Ann phoned last night?

The Arrivals Hall at the Jan Smuts International Airport was quiet. Paul studied the flights information board again. The expected landing time for Shannon's plane hadn't altered; it would be at least twenty minutes before she would appear, stepping from airside into his view as if through magic. The recalling of the moment when this situation had been reversed – when he'd seen the waiting Shannon at John F. Kennedy International Airport – still thrilled him. There'd been something of the Hollywood actress about her that had taken his breath way. Ann should have phoned; he wouldn't be having these thoughts if she'd phoned.

As he ambled across the tiled hall to a refreshments stand, Paul looked at his watch for what might have been the tenth time. He asked for a cup of coffee, his third this morning; he'd had two at the hotel, courtesy of the seemingly always-on-duty Mable.

After purchasing a croissant to eat with his coffee, Paul took a seat at one of the nearby tables. From here he could still watch the entrance from airside. Although it had been his audacious idea for Shannon to come here, an idea requiring her to mail his contrived letter to the Atlantic City Police Department, he hadn't truly expected her to go through with it. Her putting trust in him would be significant in so many ways, one of which he was fighting to deny. Yet there was an ominous counterbalance – Shannon's being the subject of the reply from the gold-toothed Charlie Halliday to Pieter Niemeyer. If she knew about the reason for the extra storage chambers, then her coming here could be nothing to do with the letter. Perhaps she hadn't sent it, after all. Paul used his handkerchief to dab his brow. *Too much caffeine*, he thought.

Fifteen minutes later and there she was – a slight figure in a fitted green trouser suit, hauling her luggage. She had a shoulder bag and was dragging a four-wheeled suitcase that had a handbag strapped on top of it. Other travellers, similarly encumbered, surrounded her. By this time the Arrivals Hall had filled with greeters.

Paul was front and centre of the eager throng, having abandoned Tom's spy-craft techniques and Maycross's caution about not drawing attention to himself. Although the sports jacket he was wearing was one that Shannon had seen before, he worried she wouldn't recognise him. If she didn't, that would put him in his place, rendering laughable the uncertain and complicating feelings he had.

She was lost from view when burly, high-spirited men crowded round three empty baggage carts. As Paul pushed forwards anxiously, she reappeared, sidestepping the men and their flailing luggage with the deftness of a rugby player evading a tackle.

Shannon Lennon smiled that photogenic smile in his direction and in that instant reaffirmed that he was still alive and actually here – about to share with her a square on Maycross's preposterous three-dimensional chessboard.

"Welcome to South Africa," he said, taking the handle of her suitcase.

She gripped his arm and, raising herself on to her toes, kissed him on the cheek. "It's good to see a friendly face after a long flight."

"It's good to see you too, Shannon," he said, noticing she was wearing a different perfume.

Squeezing his arm tighter, she said, "By the way, I'm using the name Sondra Lansing here."

"Same initials. That's nice," he said, looking about for anyone taking a close interest in them. He thought about Shannon's gun and whether she had got it through customs. "Where to?"

"I have a reservation at the Oceania International."

"Okay. Let's find a taxi, *Sondra.*"

***

Unlike the Hotel Willem, the Oceania International was a modern behemoth of luxurious accommodation for well-heeled travellers. Centrally located, it was a short walk from the most prestigious shops. The suite reserved for Sondra Lansing was on the sixth floor.

"Have you stayed here before?" Paul said to Shannon as he tipped the bellboy who'd helped with the luggage.

"You *know* I haven't been to Africa before."

After the bellboy had departed, Paul said, "Just checking."

Shannon, putting a strayed strand of hair behind her ear, said, half-smiling, "If we were in any other line, I'd be insulted..."

Paul took a long step forward and pushed her against the wall. "I'm a calf among coyotes, remember?" All of a sudden their brief history together outweighed three years of marriage.

"This room might be bugged," she whispered.

"Let's not say anything then."

His mouth found hers as he lifted her. She wrapped her legs tightly around him, and he carried her into the bedroom.

Chapter 24

Midmorning sunlight was rendering vivid the plush, corporately appointed furnishings. It felt to Paul like a room with nowhere for secrets to hide. Their nakedness added to that perception. He'd had enough of holding back, even if Blackwood's people *were* listening.

"Steady, cowboy," Shannon said, her hand pushing against Paul's shoulder. He was lying beside her, attempting to move closer again. "I didn't know there was so much life left in the British bulldog."

"Cowboy, bulldog... Make up your mind."

"I want both. American exceptionalism," she said, smirking.

"*You're* exceptional, it's true," Paul murmured. Who could weigh the guilt, the anger and the fear that had put him in this room, and condemn him for succumbing to temptation? Only one person, a stranger to his heart, thousands of miles away, waiting for the outcome of an interview at the V and A Museum.

"In that case, *you* have turned this exceptional girl's head."

"It's just the altitude," he said before planting a kiss on her temple. "Johannesburg is a thousand feet above sea level."

"I knew that," she said unconvincingly as she stroked his arm. "But now I really must have a shower and get dressed."

As Shannon moved to stand up, Paul grasped her wrist. He didn't want this moment between them to slide so quickly into the past, where it would have to be accounted for. "Are you positive you're bi?"

"Less certain by the second, Doctor, but let go. We have a lot to talk about, don't we?"

He reluctantly released her and fell back on to the pillows. "I'm worried I won't like what *Sondra* has to say," he said, watching her walking towards the bathroom.

***

An hour later Paul and Shannon were walking along a wide street that was lined with department stores. As in the centre of Durban, the pavements here were shaded by solid canopies. They were trying to affect the demeanour of window-shopping tourists. She was wearing a short, floral frock. Her white cardigan was worn cape-like, its arms loosely entwined under her chin. "I want to feel the cold," she'd said. "It will keep me alert."

"How about over there?" Paul said, looking across the road towards a large hedge-fringed square. In the centre of the square was a statue-topped fountain. Benches encircled the fountain. He took her hand.

As Shannon selected one of the benches, Paul studied the inscription beneath the life-size statue:

Stephanus Johannes Paulus Kruger
State President of the South African Republic from 1883 to 1902.

The name Paulus and the date 1883 – exactly one hundred years ago – felt like omens. He'd become susceptible to anything that felt as though it might offer answers. *I'm a step away from consulting a witchdoctor*, Paul thought as he sat down beside Shannon.

Perhaps the babbling of the fountain's leaping jets of water returning to the pool would render their speech garbled to eavesdropping, far-off dish-microphones – a possibility based on a film he'd watched nine years ago about a surveillance expert attempting to record a conversation between a couple in a public place.

"Who could have bugged your hotel room here?" he asked.

"Vernon can arrange such things, anywhere in the world. But there's others too – Intel services, including the local guys."

"At least the noise here, from the fountain, will make eavesdropping on us hard."

Shannon turned and glanced at the fountain. Laughing, she said, "So *that's* why you chose this spot. You're turning into quite the undercover operator."

"You're the expert. Can we talk freely or not?"

"There's no one else here, and there hasn't been enough time to stake out a long-range observation point, so, yes, we're safe."

"In that case, what happened after I left Atlantic City?"

"I sent the letter. Two officers visited the Altabrite site. Fransen's crew had to give them a tour. You can imagine – 'No radiation to worry about here, officer.' Denials of anyone having broken in, but the fence full of repairs.

"Of course, the family panicked when it heard about this. It immediately contacted Vernon, and he summoned me."

Paul was both enthralled and scared as he listened. "So it worked. You convinced him you had to come over here to ensure the fastest removal of the waste containers."

Shannon pouted for a moment before continuing, "Don't be so pleased with yourself, Paul. Vernon was angrier than I've seen him before, which is saying a lot. He blames your government for dragging its heels. It was terrifying, waiting for him to accuse me of being responsible for the cops' visit. Anyway, it's *you* that he wants me to keep an eye on."

"As long as he doesn't know I wrote the letter..." He took her hand. "Can't I be a little pleased with myself?"

"You've had your reward."

"Was that what it was?"

She pulled her hand free. Moving away windblown strands of hair, she said, "We both know what it was. There can never be an 'us'. I told you as much in that hotel bar."

He looked down at the ground, away from the mirror of her words. "Of course there can't be an 'us'."

"After I spoke to Vernon, I read the note you put with the miniature bottle," he heard her say.

"In that case, you now know who that man we found was." He turned to stare into her eyes. "Or did you already know who he was?"

"I told you, Paul, I thought he was a drunk. How did you find out he wasn't? How did you find out what happened to him?"

"There was a press card in his wallet. It had his name and that of the newspaper he worked for – the *Atlantic Daily Herald*. The next day, the front of that paper was covered with a report about his and his wife's remains being found among the ashes of their burned-down home." He turned away again before adding, his voice catching, "You promised me he would be given the best medical attention. What did—"

He stopped himself. Had Shannon known that the man they had rescued would be killed after questioning, regardless of his identity? And then there was the strange business with the gold-toothed man... It were as if he was in her power as profoundly as she was in Blackwood's.

"*What did* what?" she asked.

"It doesn't matter."

"I did as you suggested. I took the risk. I'm here, aren't I?"

Paul nodded and turned to face her again. "The rest of my note, the technical part, was clear too?" he asked, moving the conversation away from Blackwood.

"That *was* clever. The radiation from the dirt sample will match that from the ashes of the journalist. It would directly connect him to the Altabrite site. Threatening to send that sample to the police would have protected me from Vernon, at least for a while.

"Forensic analysis would lead to a homicide enquiry and the contamination at the site being featured on the news. The plan for the casino would have to be dropped, at best leaving the family swinging loose with a clean-up liability. But..." – Shannon paused as further events seemingly played out in her mind – "even Vernon's answerable to someone. It wouldn't have ended there for him. He'd have known that. I'm glad I didn't have to make that threat."

"I am too. Where's the bottle now, Shannon?"

"I hid—"

Cutting her off, Paul said, "The important things are that it's safe and that you or someone you trust can get to it. Unless you don't go back to America of course."

"Threatening Vernon would have been the last roll of the dice for both of us, even though you wrote down how I could get word to you to stay away."

The last paragraph in Paul's note had been intended to ensure that fear for his safety – as Blackwood would deduce who'd provided Shannon with the sample of radioactive soil – wouldn't have stopped her from threatening to send the sample to the police. In the event of her needing to threaten Blackwood in this way, she was to first contact Art Richards with the message: *"The shipping containers must have green crosses painted on the roofs."* Paul, by telephoning Richards, would be able to find out whether this curious instruction had been received. If so, he would know that it was dangerous to return to Atlantic City.

"All things considered, you're an extremely smart guy," Shannon said, taking hold of Paul's arm.

He deflected, "I'm hardly that. Ann..." Paul paused, wishing he hadn't mentioned his wife at this moment. "She doesn't think much of my choices in clothes."

Shannon leaned away to better take in his attire. "I meant you're clever-smart. Still, maybe you could update a little. Bright colours would look good on you."

"If you say so."

"Tell me, Doctor, do you do anything that doesn't involve scary radiation?"

"I play badminton once in a while, and I like working on my old motorcycle."

"I hadn't pegged you for a biker! *Now* we're getting to know each other."

"I'm not a biker. I am a motorcycle enthusiast," he quipped, stiltedly.

"My Hell's Angel." She kissed him fleetingly on the lips.

"Aren't you cold?" he asked.

"No. I'm from New England."

He took her by the waist, wanting to prolong the moment. There was something he needed to hear her declare. "Tell me that you won't be going back. Not to Blackwood."

"A new life, being alone... in an unfamiliar land. It's a frightening prospect too," she said hesitantly.

"You can't go back!"

"Don't press, Paul," she said before yielding to his embrace. "Allow me a little more time."

They kissed beneath the indifferent gaze of the statue of Stephanus Johannes Paulus Kruger.

Chapter 25

It was as they left the square that Shannon informed Paul that she was expected at a meeting. He wasn't invited. The meeting was to take place nearby in twenty minutes' time. She would ask him questions tomorrow about the progress being made at the mine and then decide whether to inspect it for herself. Blackwood wanted regular updates.

"How long have you known that we're using an old mine?" Paul asked.

"Blackwood told me when he agreed to me coming here." Shannon took her cardigan from her shoulders and began to put it on. "Tell me the name of your hotel," she said. "I'll call this evening – as Sondra Lansing, remember. Which reminds me, when I was checking out at the Banville Plaza, the desk clerk said a message had just come in for you to call a Mr Wilkinson. The clerk didn't have a contact number for you, so wondered if I could pass the message on."

"A call from someone of that name is the code for me to contact Hartling Springs. I told Hank I'd be going away for four or five weeks. He must have forgotten how soon I'd be leaving."

"Call him today."

"Maybe. I don't... I don't know," Paul responded distractedly, still wondering how Blackwood had found out about the mine in the first place. Based on Halliday's remark to Niemeyer concerning Shannon, Blackwood seemed to have more influence there than Maycross.

"It could be important, Paul."

"I don't care! I'm not going back to New Jersey, *ever*, Shannon."

"What do you mean?" she asked, taken aback.

"I decided before leaving Atlantic City. I didn't tell you so that you wouldn't be compromised in your dealings with Blackwood. No one knows apart from my mother, and now you. The only reason I haven't already resigned is to buy us time, so we can sort out our next moves."

"You shouldn't be so honest with me, Paul. I'm used to being around liars."

He put his hand on her shoulder. "It's a relief being open with you. Just don't go back to Blackwood. Please!"

"No, we can't do this now!" she exclaimed, squirming free. "The name of your hotel."

"It's the Hotel Willem." He reached for his wallet in his sports jacket inside pocket. "I've written the number..."

But she was already several feet away now, a white-backed figure merging into the midday crowd.

"You're meeting Charlie Halliday and Pieter Niemeyer, aren't you?" he said under his breath.

Frustrated, Paul stared absently at his wallet. He'd expected to spend more time with her, perhaps the whole day. They could have returned to her hotel room and...

The protruding edge of a green-bordered business card caught his eye – Tallyho Furnishings. Tom had told Paul to telephone him after he'd collected Shannon from the airport.

As Paul put his wallet away, he noticed an elderly passer-by staring in his direction. He realised he was smiling to himself. The old man must have thought the smile was for him.

***

After watching the taxi turn round and head back towards the city, Paul made his way up the external spiral staircase to the office of Tallyho Furnishings. Peering through the door glass, he saw Tom sitting at his desk. Beyond Tom, a teleprinter was on a stand beside a fax machine. Without knocking, Paul entered.

Tom rocked back. "What are you doing here?"

Paul sat down across from Tom. Having judged the décor as being as dull as that of the restaurant downstairs, he said, "This colour scheme doesn't feel very 'Tallyho' to me."

"You should have telephoned with news hours ago. I don't like random officers coming here, drawing attention."

Wary of this departure from Tom's usually agreeable mood, Paul said, "I told the taxi driver to take me to the Café Prima. I've learned from you how to conceal my movements."

"That's progress, I suppose," Tom retorted begrudgingly. "Anyway, as you're here, take a look at this." He passed a faxed message to Paul. "You've landed me in trouble with Head Office."

Paul considered the contents of the message.

To: Tallyho Furnishings
Range: COLOURLESS
Query is NOT to be repeated.
Kind Regards, Head Office

"He's not being very helpful," Paul said. "Anyway, why doesn't he put Top Secret on his faxes?"

"Insecurely transmitted communications like this one are phrased in accordance with my 'legend', my cover. The meaning's clear enough to us."

"Okay," Paul said, nodding. "We've no need to know, apparently."

"Exactly. So, how did it go with our American visitor this morning? Was she satisfied?"

Paul's thoughts returned again to the suite at the Oceania International. "Seemed to be."

"Where is she?"

"At a meeting, somewhere near the city centre. She wouldn't tell me where or with whom." Paul passed the fax back to Tom. "I assume the meeting has something to do with the matter behind our unwelcome query."

Tom took a lighter from his desk draw and set light to the message. He let the burning paper drop into his metal wastepaper bin.

"She'll phone me at the Willem this evening," Paul said, anticipating Tom's next question. "She wants to see me tomorrow, to get my views on the mine."

"Didn't you cover everything this morning?"

"Barely. We ran out of time."

Tom stared at Paul suspiciously.

"She wants to go into technical details. She has her own report to make," Paul added.

"I want to meet her. What name is she using?"

"Sondra Lansing. I'll pass on your request. By the way, you called me a random officer. Is that what I am?"

Tom thought for a moment. Grinning, he replied, "No, my lover. You be right special."

PART THREE

Chapter 26

It was Saturday, the morning after Shannon's arrival in Johannesburg. She and Paul were sitting in the packed restaurant at the rear of the second floor of Dryden's department store. Dressed in a pale-blue trouser suit, Shannon looked like a store executive taking a midmorning break from the back office. They were drinking coffee from cups embossed with the capital D. The menu on the table bore the slogan: *Dryden's - All Your Family's Needs in One Place*.

"I'd have been more than willing to come to your hotel again," Paul said, smiling.

"I think that my hunch was justified. I think I'm being watched there," Shannon replied. "They could be dangerous. I don't want you being seen."

"*My* people or *your* people?"

"Neither," Shannon murmured, eyeing Paul over the rim of her cup as she took another sip.

Paul stared in puzzlement.

"It's better that you don't know any more," she said as she placed her cup back on its saucer.

"If it's Charlie Halliday and his corrupt officials, you needn't worry about me," Paul said. "They're on my government's payroll."

"Don't say that name in here. But no, not him, although I will be seeing him this afternoon, together with the rest of the management from the mine."

"You've... you've not met with him yet?"

Shannon shook her head, almost imperceptibly.

"Why the intrigue? I've been open with you—"

At that instant, the table shook, interrupting Paul. A fair-haired boy had crashed into it, toppling their cups and spilling the remains of their coffee. The child had slipped while playing with a toy warplane, which was now lying upside down on the table.

"I'm awfully sorry," the boy's approaching mother cried out, clearly embarrassed. "I will pay for your drinks."

"That's not necessary," Paul said. "No harm been done, really."

“Are you sure? You’re very understanding.” The woman retrieved the plastic toy and pulled her child up from the floor.

Using their paper napkins, Paul began to soak up the spilled coffee as the woman and her child returned to their own table.

“Perhaps meeting here wasn’t the best idea,” Shannon said. “It’s more crowded than the hotel concierge led me to expect."

“I like crowds,” Paul said, trying to sound conciliatory. As he returned to wiping the table, he recalled he’d had a toy fighter plane, too, when he was small. Made of tin, it fired rice-sized pellets as it was cranked. Those green, plastic pellets were soon lost...

“Paul!” he heard Shannon exclaim.

He stared at her.

She looked about them before leaning forward to talk quietly. Using her hand, she teased into place the strand of hair the sudden movement had set free. “The man you mentioned. How did you know I will be seeing him?”

“He let it slip when one of the key people at the mine had a question I couldn’t answer. According to him, *you* have the answer.”

“Your boss will probably enlighten you when you get back to England, Paul.”

I doubt it,” Paul replied, thinking of Maycross’s dismissive fax to Tom.

“Is that because you don’t intend to see him again? That worries me, Paul.”

“Have you spoken to him yourself, by any chance?”

Shannon hesitated before answering. “Yes, I met him.”

“At Heathrow?”

Shannon nodded.

“I guessed he would ask to meet you. Was he ingratiating?”

“He probably thought he was being charming. It was obvious that he’s terrified.”

“He deserves to be. Tell me that he should be.”

“All right, he should.” Shannon gazed off to the middle distance before focussing again on Paul. “I passed on a message from Vernon. Now he knows that we’ve hijacked the operation at this end, but he’ll have to keep paying for it and fronting it to his people. I told him he should think of it as a sign of professional regard. Vernon is always looking for opportunities and realised there was a good one here. The government officials whom Maycross is paying are being paid by Vernon too."

"Hijacked? Is that all you can tell me? It feels as though you're trying to protect me the way I tried to protect you from Blackwood. What other poisonous stuff does he intend to dump here?"

"I am trying to protect you. There's nothing you or I can do," she said, her voice strained.

More mirrors and smokescreens, thought Paul. "And my boss is really going to accept this?"

"If your boss were to pull out, deals critical to the UK will collapse immediately, whereas by cooperating, he not only gets to stay alive, his post-government career will be a lucrative one."

Paul had no doubt about the choice Maycross would make. "By the way, his man here wants to meet you," Paul said.

Shannon thought for a moment. "Tell him to contact me. He can join me at my hotel for dinner tonight."

"I thought you didn't want me to go there."

"Just him, Paul. Tell him I'll meet with him alone. I don't mind *his* being seen. In fact, it might help me."

"Okay. He'll probably identify himself as *Trevor* when he calls."

"What's the nature of his cut-out operation?"

"His what?"

"The front he uses to evade the South African authorities."

Paul hadn't heard that term before. Of course, Tallyho Furnishings was to Tom what Continental Investment Audits was to Shannon – covers for their respective unsanctioned activities.

"It's a furniture business. You should know he carries a..." Paul patted his side, as if to indicate a holstered gun.

"I'll bear that in mind."

"Shannon, he can be an odd character, but..." Paul paused, wondering how to outline Tom's idiosyncrasies. He decided to allow her to discover them for herself.

"I can take care of myself," she said, calmly.

"God knows what'll happen when I resign and you disappear."

Frowning, Shannon said, "I admire your integrity, Paul, I really do, but you're underestimating the situation you are in."

Trying to sound confident, Paul said, "I'll get another job. It won't be easy because of the economy at the moment, and Ann won't be happy about our being poorer, but once I'm able to tell her the truth, she—"

"It's good that you haven't told her. Change your mind, Paul," Shannon said, cutting across Paul.

He shook his head. "I wouldn't be able to live with myself."

"Do you know Benedict Sykes?"

"Sykes?" Paul said, thrown by the question.

Shannon looked about them again before continuing. "We learned that he'd been the scientific consultant originally."

"I gathered that from Trevor." The Sykes connection still felt raw and laden with niggling questions. Perhaps the professor could somehow help Paul to extricate himself from Maycross's clutches without the need for resigning?

"Sykes's ability to remain silent was found wanting by one of our operatives –someone sent to befriend him. He was the worst kind of loose end."

Paul felt blood draining from his face. The restaurant seemed to tremble as if it were preparing to take off in pursuit of the boy's toy plane.

"He had a fatal accident, choking on a piece of meat at home."

"W-When?" Paul struggled to say.

Shannon looked at her watch. "Half an hour ago."

Half an hour...

Paul had fallen asleep last night after quietening his thoughts by visualising a silver box with *Shannon* engraved on the lid. He'd entered Dryden's thirty minutes ago, excited to see her again. Now he could hardly bring himself to look at her.

"Perhaps it's not too late to alert him," he said, snapping to his senses. "I've got to find a telephone."

Shannon grasped his forearm as he moved to stand up. "If you are detected attempting to interfere, we're as good as dead. Vernon's team knows how to find us, and they move *fast*."

She was right. Blackwood would have had a listening device planted in Sykes's telephone. "Couldn't *you* have done anything?" he said, sitting down.

Her strained reply was almost pleading. "Could I have warned him? Yes, but I want to live."

It was that simple. Given the choice between Sykes and Shannon, *this* – her sitting across the table from him – was the outcome he'd have chosen too.

With his elbows on the table and his head face down in his hands, he heard Shannon call out, "Waitress!" A moment later: "Another two coffees, please."

Her voice struck Paul as too calm. She'd probably even smiled at the waitress, as if the world was still a place of give and take between civilised people. Today was just another day. She was a natural at the game.

"Take a few deep breaths," she said.

"I'm all right," Paul said, using his handkerchief to dab his brow. But the image of Benedict writhing across a table made him touch his throat as if it were himself being choked. He didn't want to contemplate the mechanics of the murder – the likely use of forceps to push the lump of meat down into...

After a minute or two of silence between them, Shannon said, "Think about the mine. Are there problems we should know about?"

"We? Just say Blackwood for once." Paul reached into the inside pocket of his sports jacket and withdrew folded sheets of paper. Dropping them on the table, he said, "There's a summary."

"Don't be like this. We must remain totally professional until—"

The waitress had returned with the coffee and was setting down two cups and saucers. "Can I get you anything else?" she asked.

"No, thank you," Paul replied, wondering how much the waitress had overheard. "Until *what*?" he said to Shannon, once the waitress had moved away to take an order at a nearby table.

"I was going to say, until each of us is safe."

Safe... He recalled the phrase she'd used before telling him about Benedict – *"you're underestimating the situation you are in."* He'd been in denial. If Sykes could be murdered in bustling Paris, what hope would Paul have in a quiet market town in Suffolk, where the police were far more used to recording stolen bicycles than investigating suspicious deaths? And Blackwood didn't care about collateral damage during his tidying-up operations. Ann might be murdered too, just as the wife of the reporter was. "After what you've told me, that doesn't seem possible."

"Which is why you have to carry on with the operation. I don't see how you have a choice." She smiled, seemingly out of pity. "Just keep Blackwood happy. Once the work's over, don't give him cause to doubt your silence."

"What about you?" he asked, hoping for but not expecting an answer.

"I've initiated something." Shannon reflected for a few seconds before continuing, "I don't know how it'll work out."

"Does it have anything to do with those people you think are watching you at your hotel?"

Shannon nodded. "I'll miss you, Paul," she said softly.

The woman he'd slept with yesterday had materialised at last. He slid his hand across the table to hers. The commotion of the restaurant seemed to retreat.

Chapter 27

After telephoning Tom from the department store, conveying Sondra Lansing's invitation to dine with her this evening, Paul walked to the Johannesburg City Library in the business district. The front of the library looked on to a garden-like square crisscrossed with paths and had steps leading up to three huge double doors.

In the foyer, as Paul studied the layout – a staircase ahead of him led up to a gallery, and there were doorways to the left and right – someone approached. Her arms trapped a pile of books against her body. "You seem lost, sir. Can I help you?"

"Yes, please. I'm a tourist with an interest in the old mining community. In particular, I would like to read about the river systems and the aquifers that are close to the mined areas southwest of the city."

"I see, well the Reference Library's through there," the librarian said, looking towards the doorway to the right of the entrance, "but we're closing soon. One o'clock on Saturdays."

As the encumbered librarian moved away, a group of black children reached the bottom of the staircase. It could be their or their descendants' long-term health that was in Paul's hands. The knot that had tortured his stomach since the telephone call from Auberon Morrison twisted again. He'd allowed himself to believe he would never go back to the Hartling Springs power station and the Altabrite site. The demonstration of Blackwood's lethal reach had changed everything. Poor Benedict...

***

Frustrated, Paul sat on a bench in the landscaped square fronting the library. He tried to prepare himself for tonight's belated telephone call to Ann. He'd failed to call her last evening, as he'd promised Dot he would do. Being with Shannon had been too fresh, too unravelling. He hadn't been able to trust himself not to be overwhelmed with guilt and confess. There would have to be a reckoning, but not yet – he had to restore his balance first. Unleashed emotions would imperil their survival.

And there was the consolation that by continuing with Maycross's plan, his intentions were again aligned with what he'd so far told Ann. However, he would have to explain the situation to his mother. How much could he tell Beth about Sykes's fate without terrifying her? Yet, if he wasn't open about the tentacles of Blackwood's network, she would be ashamed of her son for complying with the waste dumping scheme It was important that she truly understood that his taking refuge at her ageing friends' homes in Durban was not a viable option; he would be tracked down and her friends would be killed too – all loose ends.

After spending the afternoon window shopping, Paul returned to the Hotel Willem. A young man was in Mable's place behind the reception desk. There seemed to be, disregarding a slight disfigurement – a faint scar left by the correction of a hare lip – a family resemblance.

"Good evening. May I have my room key?" Paul said.

"Of course, sir. Your name and the room number?"

"Dr Avery. Room 39." Paul noticed the receptionist's name badge said Henry.

Henry checked the hotel register before retrieving and handing over the key. "I see you're leaving us on Monday, Dr Avery."

"If I needed to stay longer, would that be possible?"

"Let me see." Henry opened the register again and turned the pages. "I could hold your room, sir. For how long would that be?"

"I need to talk to a colleague first."

"I understand. Be assured, we'll do our best to accommodate your requirements."

Henry's manner was beginning to undermine Paul's assumption that he was the cheeky Mable's son. "I take it Mable's not around. She lets me make international calls from the office."

"Do you want to make a call now, Dr Avery?"

Paul looked at his watch. "Actually, I do, and another one later, at about ten-thirty."

"Ten-thirty... I see. And what number do you want to call now?"

Paul handed to Henry a piece of paper with the work number for Hank Barnaby.

"America, sir?"

"New Jersey."

Henry looked at his watch. "Mightn't this person be having lunch, sir?"

"I'll take the chance," Paul said, half hoping that Barnaby wouldn't be available. Although it was Saturday, a logged call to the power station would at least show responsiveness to the weeks old message that had been left for him at the Banville Plaza – appearances were everything, according to Maycross.

The workhorse Barnaby wasn't at his desk this time. His weekend secretary – it wasn't Mrs Lewandowski – had to use the intercom to summon him. It took five minutes for the chief engineer to pick up the receiver. "Avery?"

"Yes, it's me, Hank."

"Where are you?" Barnaby sounded out of breath.

"Somewhere in Africa. I shouldn't be more specific on this line."

"Huh. Africa... I guess that explains the delay on the line."

"A message was left for me at the hotel. It would have been a couple of weeks ago, after I checked out."

"That was *me*," Barnaby snapped. "What's taken you so long?"

"I just found out from our mutual friend – the one you met at Maizetown. I told you I'd be away for four or five weeks, Hank," Paul said, trying to remain tactful. "Whenever something's urgent, Gavin knows a person who can get a message to me," he added, recalling that the power station manager was familiar with Vernon Blackwood.

"I talked to Gavin. He said to wait on you."

"Well, you've got my attention now, Hank."

"Art wanted me to warn you. He right away saw that the information he was collecting is extremely time sensitive. A lot of track maintenance work's scheduled, potentially involving rerouting. Anyway, he's since obtained everything you asked for. You're going to have to make a decision damn quickly or only one option will be possible without incurring months of delay."

Paul tried to gather his thoughts. Things he'd intended to abandon were requiring his detailed attention again. "It'll be another two or three weeks before I can sit down with Art, Hank."

Paul heard a deep sigh at the other end of the line.

"I thought you understood the urgency of our situation, *Doctor*," Hank shouted.

"I do, Hank."

A loud voice coming from the hotel lobby – a man telling obscene jokes, presumably to Henry – was making it hard for Paul to concentrate. The man's Afrikaans accent seemed familiar.

Pressing his palm against his free ear, trying to muffle the nearby banter, Paul said, "I do understand, Hank. That's why I flew here."

"Are you still there, Avery?"

"I'm here, Hank. I'm grateful to Art for putting the information together so quickly. Look, I'll organize a way that you can forward his report to me so that I can discuss it with my colleagues here."

"That's sounds a lot better. I'll let Art know. Now, what about the, er, the *packages* themselves. Have you verified their suitability?" Hank was clearly alluding to the radiation-grade casks.

"I haven't come up against an insurmountable problem, size- and weight-wise, so far."

"Maybe we're getting somewhere at last."

"Will you be in your office tomorrow afternoon? It's Sunday, but—"

"I'll be here, *waiting* to hear from you, young man," Barnaby interjected.

Taking Barnaby's change in tone as encouraging. Paul asked, "By the way, have you supplied Art with the material he needs?"

Hank had to think for a moment before understanding that the question pertained to the lead sheets he'd sent to Maizetown. "Over a week ago. He's got his guys doing as you asked."

When Paul returned to the hotel lobby, he was greeted with the cry: "It's the tourist!"

Recognising the man with the scarred cheek as the confrontational member of the group he'd met over breakfast during his first morning at the hotel, Paul forced a smile. "That's me. How are you?"

"I thought you'd buggered off back to Blighty."

"Not yet. No one can have too much of a good thing, I guess."

"Too much of a good thing! That's a good one, eh, Henry?" the scarred man said, playfully punching the receptionist's shoulder.

As the man's shoulders rolled in the course of unleashing this punch, Paul caught sight of the name HARKNET. It was written in yellow across the back of the man's windcheater.

"Thanks for your help," Paul said to the discomforted receptionist. "The line was clear."

"That's good to know. I'll expect you at half past ten then, sir?"

"Indeed, that's right."

"You two having a dodgy date?" the scarred man said, pouting affectedly. "It's like *that* is it?"

Ignoring the insinuation, Paul turned and headed towards the stairwell.

"Join me for a drink," the man called out.

You've had too much already, Paul thought as he turned back to face the man. "I've things to take care of. Thanks for the offer."

"See you in the bar later then."

"Maybe," Paul muttered as he opened the fire door. HARKNET, he'd just recalled, was the name on the insignias of the security guards at the Hartling Springs power plant. Given the circumstances, the coincidence was troubling. He would mention it to Tom.

From his room, Paul phoned Tom's. There was no answer. *He must have left for dinner with Sondra Lansing.*

A few minutes after 10.00 p.m., dressed in jeans and a T-shirt, Paul went back down to the lobby.

"Ah, Dr Avery. Are you having a good evening, sir?" Henry said, looking up from his newspaper.

"I listened to the radio – an episode from a science fiction serial."

"That one gives me the creeps, sir. The banging on the outside of the spacecraft..." Henry shuddered.

"Why aren't there TVs in the rooms?"

"Not much demand from our regular clientele, sir. Anyway, it would be expensive. Mr Deeckers, the proprietor, has talked about putting one in the bar."

Paul handed Henry a scrap of paper with the telephone number for Pendlefield Manor. "It's only the Eighties. You wouldn't want to rush things, I suppose," he said facetiously, thinking about Shannon's city-centre hotel. Her suite had two televisions, one in the lounge and another in the bedroom.

It was Dorothy Reynolds who answered this time. She sounded flustered. Paul had remembered that she and Bernard usually went to bed at around 9.30 p.m. and had hoped that they'd retired for the night, so that he would have Ann to himself.

"She's staying the night at a friend's house, Paul. Wendy, a friend from her schooldays, and her husband. They live near Beccles."

"Can I phone her there, Dot?"

There was a strained silence until Dot spoke again. "She doesn't want you to. You were supposed to call her last night. She's upset, Paul. What's going on between the two of you? Is there something we can do? You know that Bernard and I are very fond of you."

"I think we need to work it out for ourselves. I'll ring tomorrow. Perhaps she'll talk to me then, Dot."

Absently, Paul put the receiver back on its cradle. *What's going on between the two of you?* The answer was beyond him. "It's never just one thing," he recalled a worldlier colleague mutter over a drink a couple of years ago, following the man's then recent separation from his wife. Paul wished he'd pressed for deeper insights, but the sentiment resonated now nonetheless. At the time it hadn't – he'd assumed there was always a clear dividing line, a trigger point. He'd since accepted that emotions had shifting rules that were impossible to pin down in the columns of a spreadsheet.

***

Tom, gripping the steering wheel so tightly his knuckles whitened, was unable to conceal his displeasure as he and Paul set off from the Hotel Willem at ten in the morning. Going close to the townships surrounding the Kop Mine invited the risk of hijacking and worse. Being a Sunday – most inhabitants would be around, some hungover, others cheerful in their going-to-church attire – compounded his concern.

"Are you sure you need to do this? You look tired."

"I can't sleep well at the place," Paul said, looking out of the passenger-side window. They were on the elevated southern bypass, heading west. It seemed as though it would be another cloudy day.

"You should have had a nightcap or two. That's what I do. It blanks out the noise."

"I'll bear that in mind." The noises hadn't been the problem. He'd hardly noticed them. His sleep routine hadn't worked; all of the imagined silver boxes refused to open, as if soldered shut.

"The hotel's quiet this time of the morning. I could take you back, and you could catch up on your sleep."

Paul turned to look at Tom. "Thanks, but I need to get on with my research. Everyone's impatient for my blessing, not that I have a real veto. I can only try to influence things at the margins – limit the damage."

Tom glanced at Paul. "That's the nature of the operation. Don't beat yourself up."

Easier said than done, Paul thought, looking out of his window again.

"And don't say I haven't warned you about the dangers of going to these places," Tom said.

"I won't."

"Tensions have remained high since the decree that black children must be educated in Afrikaans instead of in English, and restrictions were placed on the subjects they're taught."

Paul looked at Tom again. "Was that what caused the 'Soweto uprising'?" He recalled a newspaper article he'd read years ago. It had been in the World Affairs section of a broadsheet Sunday newspaper, which his then student flatmate had bought.

"1976. The police fired live ammunition and used tear gas against the protestors."

"Brilliant," Paul muttered as he turned back to the window.

A few minutes passed before Tom spoke again, still seemingly hoping the trip could be abandoned, "I can't help thinking we're taking this risk for nothing. There's a major plan to construct dams and tunnels that will bring water from Lesotho to the river system feeding this part of the country."

"Lesotho?" Paul opened the map he'd brought with him. Lesotho was a landlocked, mountainous country. They'd passed within fifty miles of its north-eastern extremity during their drive from Durban four days ago. "That'll be a huge undertaking, won't it?"

"It'll take years, decades probably, and a vast amount of money. I won't be surprised if Halliday gets his hands on some of it."

"Bringing in fresh water should dilute any toxic contaminants that are being leached out of the ground. Nonetheless, I want to see the situation as it is now."

Tom grunted in frustration and gripped the steering wheel tightly again.

An hour later, they parked at the side of a dirt track on a rise overlooking one of the smaller townships – named "Saskia" after the daughter of a long-ago Boer landowner. Tom asked, "Do you know what necklacing is?"

Paul looked up from his scribbled-on map. "No."

Tom mimed the striking of a match. "Whoosh!" he exclaimed. "A petrol-filled tyre round your neck. Not a good way to go."

"You've got your gun."

"There'll be a firearms in there too. These places are tinderboxes. Crime's increasing in the city."

"Apartheid can't last much longer, given the level of international pressure and the trade boycotts."

"I'm not so sure about that. This system has worked out pretty well for Western corporations."

"Pass me your binoculars," Paul said, eschewing discussion of the injustices of the so-called separate-development approach to governing the country.

He adjusted the focus of Tom's field glasses as he moved his gaze around the township. Tightly packed huts in the centre remained an unresolvable smear of corrugated iron and painted wood. "How many people live here?"

"Nearly three thousand, I think. They'd be better off moving to Soweto, closer to the city where there's more access to jobs and better infrastructure."

Looking towards the northern fringe of the township, Paul changed the subject, "How did it go with Sondra?"

"Oh, she's an interesting woman. Pretty, too." After a moment of heavy silence, Tom continued, "But she's the usual American Intel agency type."

"Have you met many?"

"When I was living in Rhodesia with my then girlfriend, because of my former experience in the Security Service, MI5, I was approached to become an asset of the Secret Intelligence Service. I picked up and passed on sensitive files from a spy inside the government. Through my handler I met a few CIA agents socially."

Paul lowered the binoculars and stared at Tom, trying to encourage Maycross's man to reveal more about his interaction with Shannon. "And?"

Tom took the cue. "She and I did the usual pirouetting. All friends on the same side, except when we're not. I assured her we're doing everything that's necessary."

"So you're satisfied that she's not going to make problems for Head Office, report wise?" Paul asked.

"I didn't say that. You know her better than I do."

"Not a lot better," Paul lied. "But I thinks she's on board with our progress here."

As Paul resumed surveying the township, he heard Tom say something else but he was too distracted to register the comment. He'd been watching a distant woman, who'd been crouching for several minutes beside a pond. She'd just stood up and lifted a plastic container of water on to her cloth-wrapped head. *They don't have a communal piped water supply.*

After lowering the binoculars, Paul said, "I didn't catch the last thing you said, Tom. Just the word 'troubling'."

"I said there was one troubling thing."

"Which was?"

"She was being watched."

"Why do you think that?"

Tom absently moved his tongue against the inside of his cheek for a few seconds before saying, "Israelis, Egyptians, Jordanians, Saudis... Don't know which. Middle Eastern anyway."

"Couldn't you have been mistaken?"

"Perhaps. It might have been the French, I suppose," Tom said, shrugging. "Definitely not the South Africans. They would have arrested us all by now, if they had any idea of what we're up to. Anyway, Halliday and his friends are keeping those waters calm."

"I meant mistaken about the whole 'she was being watched' thing."

"During my Security Service days, I spent some time seconded to A Branch – the watchers. I still remember the observation techniques."

"Could it have been the Americans?" Paul said, thinking about the cautious Blackwood.

Tom shook his head. "Why would they monitor someone working on one of their special ops?"

"They could have been watching *you*."

Tom appeared momentarily thrown by this suggestion, but after reflecting he said, "The primary line of sight from the outset was wrong for that. No, it was definitely her they were interested in."

"Did you tell Sondra?"

"I considered it, but no. If she's any good, she would have known, and she didn't see fit to say anything to me."

Yes, she does know, Paul thought, remembering Shannon's warning at Dryden's.

"Can we go now?" Tom asked impatiently.

"I suppose so," Paul said, accepting that venturing into the settlement to collect a sample of the pond water wouldn't be wise.

"Thank God for that."

"There's another matter I need your help with, Tom."

"Tell me when we're driving." Tom started the car, undertook a three-point turn on the dirt track, and headed back the way they'd come.

***

Having listened to Paul's account of last evening's telephone conversation with Hank Barnaby, Tom drove them to his office.

Sitting at his desk, with Paul opposite, Tom explained, "This report you want them to send here, detailing train routes that connect the power station to the ports, is sensitive. Faxing it in its raw form via the public network would make it vulnerable to interception. We can't risk the South African security people becoming curious about my business cover.

"On the other hand, making the report appear compatible with the work of Tallyho Furnishings would be difficult. I would have to request that Head Office uses their US operative to either instruct the author or modify the report himself. Done in haste, it would have cock-up written all over it. The whole bloody operation, my role, your role, our government's role, Charlie Halliday, Max..." Tom threw his hands up. "Boom!"

"Is there a confidential mailing box address we could use? It could take days in the post, though, and time's—"

Cutting across Paul, Tom said, "No, no. Still risky and, as you were saying – slow." Tom rested back in his seat. He closed his eyes for a few seconds to concentrate. Finally, he said, "The report will have to be collected from Barnaby tomorrow morning and *flown* here by private jet. A Diplomatic bag marked for the embassy in Pretoria will be used. The SIS station inside the embassy will send me a signal when the parcel is ready for collection from my dead letter box."

Paul shook his head, amazed. "MI6 can arrange a jet?"

"Let's get things straight, Paul. You're obviously *not* in MI6, nor is Head Office, and I'm no longer an asset employed by it. This is *not* an MI6 operation. Got that?"

"Heaven forbid I should think that."

"This is a compartmentalised operation. I was headhunted for it three years ago. Acceptance was not a totally free choice. I had a lot of debts at the time."

"Not a free choice. That I can relate to," Paul said, remembering the threats he'd received from Maycross.

"Anyway, it will be for Head Office to approve and arrange the jet. They will use my opposite number, who works out of DC, to handle things.

"Tell Barnaby to be ready for handing over the report at, I suggest, ten a.m. local time. It must be done at a place that is away from the locations connected to your shipment operation."

Tom's use of the "your" word irritated Paul as he reflected on possible handover locations, dismissing one after another. "The power station's paying for a new shopping centre in the outskirts of Hartling Springs – the Sharp Riverside Mall. It's still a construction site. Hank could park opposite it for a few minutes, ostensibly checking on the progress being made."

"As long as he doesn't attract attention to himself."

"I'll warn him," Paul said, concerned at the prospect of saying anything to the touchy engineer that might come across as patronizing.

"After you've finalised the location and time with Barnaby, I'll put the details in an encrypted memo for the Pretoria Station to send to Head Office. In the meantime, I'll send a code word signal to the station that means I'll be placing an item in my dead letter box tonight."

“Will a jet be used to take the memorandum to England?”

“No. I’ll instruct the station to transmit the contents by radio relay to our listening post in Buckinghamshire, where it’ll be deciphered and securely telexed to Head Office, who will then contact the Washington Station, from where it will be passed to our man there.”

The Tobe Institute’s in south Buckinghamshire. That must be where the listening post is, Paul guessed. The institute was, after all, providing a surveillance-proof chamber for the meetings with Maycross. The old pamphlet unearthed by the RSMSDA senior librarian had evidently omitted the institute’s clandestine services.

“Any other questions?” Tom asked.

“I’m trying to come to terms with your ways of communicating – encrypted memos, dead letter boxes, and so on.”

“It’s not just about secrecy. Compartmentalisation insulates the local SIS station, which isn’t permitted to participate in operations that haven’t been agreed with the South African National Intelligence Service.

“The station doesn’t know anything about the true nature of Tallyho Furnishings. It treats me as just another Whitehall-authorised business operator conducting sensitive commercial activities that have significant UK trade benefits. It can’t even decipher the memorandum it will be transmitting to Head Office.”

At that point Tom stood up and started walking towards the rear of the office. As he approached the teleprinter, he turned back to face Paul. “It’ll take a few minutes to prepare and send the code word notification. I’ll meet you downstairs. Get yourself a coffee.”

“All right, but for the record this isn’t *my* shipment operation. I hate what I’m doing. It’s a Grandee Paragraph 5 Order, leaving me no choice.”

Tom seemed bemused. “A what?”

“Grandee Paragraph 5.”

Tom shrugged.

“They’re filed in the Unacknowledged Registry.” Paul felt for the first time an improbable sense of advantage, as if it were himself now who was closest to the inner workings of Head Office.

“There won’t be anything filed *anywhere*,” Tom said. “That Grandee Paragraph whatsit and the guff about an Unacknowledged Registry must have been made up to win your cooperation.” After an impatient glance over his shoulder at the teleprinter, he continued, "Go and get that coffee, Paul. I've already told you too much for my own good."

Removal of part of the veil surrounding Maycross had only exposed another layer of duplicity. "Compartmentalised also means 'off the books', right?" Paul asked, perhaps needing to hear something, anything, that he'd deduced confirmed.

Tom rubbed at the back of his neck as he said, haltingly, "It depends... on what you mean. Everything has to be paid for, including the work at the mine here and Max's activity at the docks. And then there's Charlie-boy and his cronies... All payments are handled by Head Office."

"Using some kind of *illegal-activity* budget?" Paul said, half-jokingly.

"Intel-service budget allocations were political bunfights for decades. That's why they're diluted across the spending ministries to prevent concerted interference. This operation, large and compartmentalised as it is, won't touch those budgets at all. Plausible costs will be buried under relevant headings, such as Defence Procurement and Trade. Other items not having natural homes will most likely be lost in the consolidated expenditure of non-departmental public bodies."

Paul nodded as he recalled that Maycross had told him that his expenses would be allocated to his agency, which was a non-departmental government organization.

Maycross's American counterpart was pursuing a freer approach, a virtual "Bank of Blackwood" – siphoned money bypassing bookkeeping eyes. Money to finance something in South America – where Shannon was to be sent. Truly off the books. No wonder Vernon had been able to move in when his impatience morphed into opportunism. Having levered Altabrite in with the Hartling Springs contract, he was now lining up other toxic sites for commercial exploitation too. Better to be an agile mover than a first mover.

Yet Tom had given no indication that he knew any of this. Perhaps he'd served too long – with confessed soldier-like loyalty. Paul winced at the notion of himself one day becoming enslaved to Head Office.

Tom hadn't finished though. "Nonetheless, it must take someone close to the heart of the Government to pull this off. Not so much a big hitter, more of a puppet master."

Puppet master... That description brought the enigmatic Auberon Morrison to Paul's mind. How would he react to Blackwood's takeover? Will Maycross inform him? If so, perhaps Morrison will retreat deeper into the bureaucratic undergrowth, where he'll be able to protect his back from more directions than anyone else knows exist.

"Talking only about the 'ends' and saying nothing about the 'means'," Tom said. "It's an art." He smiled awkwardly and took his hand from his neck. "You see, the grey suited committee men who think they are in charge, the Oxbridge elites with knighthoods, they have their hands full with Northern Ireland terrorism and combatting anti-nuclear missile sentiment. At all costs, they mustn't look bad in front of Uncle Sam again.

"The defections of Philby, Burgess, Maclean and their Soviet-sympathising ilk still rankle after decades. And then along comes a new generation of British traitor – Geoffrey Prime... Remember that case, Paul?"

Prime... Paul had watched the security-sanitised television coverage about the court case that was held last November. His mother had been more interested than he'd been. Prime was imprisoned for the selling of secrets to the Russians during his earlier employment as a linguistics specialist at the Government Communications Headquarters, GCHQ, near Cheltenham.

"He received a long sentence, didn't he?" Paul said.

"Thirty-five years, including three for indecently assaulting young girls," Tom replied. "Another blow to the standing of our intelligence services."

Tom's insights were becoming as unsettling as they were enlightening. Even a return of the linguistic charades that had distracted Paul from his soul-destroying obligations would have been welcome now.

Perhaps sensing Paul's discomfort, Tom said, "Take the faux-official waffle that was told to you as a compliment. Your recruitment was critical after the prof. moved on."

Of course, he doesn't know about Benedict being killed either. As Paul was thinking this, he realised that Tom, with his accumulation of experiences from working with the domestic and foreign intelligence services, must be older than he'd hitherto believed, certainly closer to forty than thirty.

"At the moment it's us who are centre stage, whether we like it or not. There's no one in the wings to feed us our lines or to rescue us if the audience turns nasty. I'm more used to wearing a costume mask than you are, but you're definitely the star," Tom said.

Chapter 28

When Tom joined Paul in the café below his office, they agreed to order a meal – a late lunch. There was a fresh nervousness between the two following the rush of admissions that Tom had made. It were as if their relationship had been recast; Paul's sheepdog status relative to Tom's shepherd role had shifted. They were both puppets of Head Office, both complying under duress with Programme COLOURLESS.

Paul felt a twinge of guilt that, of the two, perhaps it was only he who was withholding key information now. Yet, what did he really know about Tom? Nothing about his personal life. Nothing about the nature of the debts Tom had had in Rhodesia. Nothing about what had motivated the man to enter the Intel world in the first place, years ago. And with that thought, Paul felt his defences renew.

His suggestion that he make the telephone call to Barnaby from Tom's office was rejected.

Tom said without explanation, "Let's stay with what you've been doing so far, calling from the hotel. Once you've agreed the handover details, I'll come back here and prepare the memo for Head Office."

***

Tom reclined in Mable's chair while Paul stood speaking to Hank Barnaby. The office door was closed. It was a little after 10.15 a.m. on the US east coast. Paul remembered Tom's instruction not to say anything about the use of a jet. "Just assure him that the transfer will be expedited" was the way Tom had put it.

The handover arrangements were agreed. Tomorrow at 10.00 a.m., Barnaby would be parked across from the site that was to become the Sharp Riverside Mall. He would be in a white 1982-model Lincoln Continental. Paul recalled the long, boxy car that he'd parked next to when he'd first visited the railyard at Maizetown. A black car, make not known, would pull up behind Barnaby. Its driver, male, would get out, approach and say "I thank you". Hank, without speaking, was to hand over the report from Art and then drive away.

Being a Monday morning, a lot of traffic could be expected, but with the distractions of the working week ahead no one should register anything remarkable taking place. The event need take no more than, say, five minutes. By covering these aspects of the rendezvous, Paul skirted Tom's "don't attract attention" advice. Barnaby spoke in an even tone during the entire call. Gavin Cantrell may have been listening in, Paul suspected.

"What if your opposite number doesn't have a black car?" Paul asked Tom after the call had ended.

Tom laughed. "He'll *hire* one. If he can get hold of a jet, he can get hold of a black car."

Only now did the DC telephone number that Maycross had provided with the cyanide capsule and a copy of Tom's initial fax come to Paul's mind. Was that a number for the Washington Station or was it Maycross's man's direct number? It already seemed a lifetime ago that, in his Manhattan hotel room, he'd put the capsule and the piece of paper with the emergency number in his wallet.

Tom gave Mable's desk a double-slap, readying himself for action, and stood up. "Full speed ahead." Leaving the office as Trevor, Tom took the opportunity to speak to Mable about extending his and Paul's room reservations.

"Through to next Saturday," Mable said, repeating the request aloud as she wrote it down on a pad. "That's fine, Trevor. Dr Avery here spoke to my nephew yesterday about you two probably extending your stay."

"Ah, he be a good lad," Tom said, winking at Paul. With an exaggerated look at his watch, he added, "Now then, time waits for no man. See you two laters."

Paul watched his colleague stride towards the exit. Tom would be returning to his office to prepare the encrypted memorandum containing the report handover details.

"Doctor, there was a call for you. I forgot to mention it earlier." Mable moved along the counter, turning over pieces of paper and looking under the Guests Book. "I don't know whether I'm coming or going. A lot of guests checked in today, and I'm behind with my paperwork."

"Is this it!" Paul said, picking up a folded piece of paper from the floor. It had fluttered from the counter as Mable moved the Guests

Book.

"That's where it got to," Mable said, taking the note from him. She unfolded the piece of paper and strained to read her scribbled writing. "The caller had an American accent, I remember. Sandra someone... Lantern?"

"Sondra Lansing?"

"That must have been it, Doctor." Mable placed the note on the counter and used her palm to flatten out the creases. "Meet me at... She wants you to meet her by the... the fountain at six o'clock."

The fountain? It had to be the fountain with the statue. "This evening? Tomorrow morning?"

"I don't know," Mable said with a forlorn expression.

Paul looked at his watch. "Assuming it's this evening, I will need a taxi at a quarter past five."

"That's not long. I'll book it now," Mable said, heading towards her office. She turned in the doorway. "Where is the fountain, Doctor?"

"Tell the taxi firm that I want to go to the shopping district in the centre, where Dryden's is."

Because of the time of day, Paul was not surprised to find that the bathroom serving the six bedrooms in his corridor was vacant. After showering, he returned to his room and shaved for the second time today at the washbasin. He'd brought one bottle of cologne with him from England. He hesitated before dabbing it on – it had been a gift from Ann for his last birthday.

A look in the full-length mirror, which was fixed to the inside of the wardrobe door, made him concede that the clothes he'd just put on – black trousers, cream shirt, unbuttoned at the neck, red woollen V-neck jersey, and his green windcheater – were all badly in need of ironing.

The taxi pulled up in the parking lot moments after Paul came out of the hotel.

***

It was already dusk as they approached what the driver had told Paul was President Square. The surrounding shopping area was quiet – Sunday-quiet. Cloud that had lingered throughout the day had darkened since sunset but had gained a reddish tinge along the western horizon. It was five to six.

He should have told the driver "Drop me outside Dryden's department store" and walked from there. Such Tom-like evasions had disappeared from his mind when he'd got in the back of the taxi. But he was here now, with an irrepressible hope for a bliss-filled evening.

As the taxi departed, Paul remembered Tom's comment this morning about the increasing amounts of crime in the city. His concern increased as the level of darkness within the square ahead became evident. He decided that it was the wrong place to meet at this time of day. Shannon's immunity to jet lag was impressive, but perhaps she hadn't adjusted to the change of hemisphere.

His footsteps echoed as he walked through the paved opening separating two department stores. He stopped at the entrance to the square. From the silence he deduced that the fountain had been turned off for the night. It, together with the statue of President Kruger, stood somewhere off to his right. He stared in that direction, waiting for his eyes to adjust.

"Sondra!" he called out.

There was no reply.

Too late he heard footsteps behind him. Strong arms encircled him, shifting him off balance. A rough cloth hood was pulled over his head. His muffled cry of protest was interrupted by the pain of a needle puncturing the base of his neck. "Shannon!" he tried to shout.

His struggle lasted only seconds before the liquid darkness of unconsciousness surpassed even that of the hood.

Chapter 29

Paul began to come to, but the darkness persisted. He was on his back on some kind of hard bed or cot. As he tried to sit up, he realised his hands were strapped together at the wrists in front of him. The exertion made him cough.

"Welcome back, Dr Avery," a man said, his deep voice interrupting the silence. The accent was hard to place. His English sounded fluent but his words fell like treacle, somehow glued together, hiding their meaning. It were as if Paul was an infant again.

"Take things slowly. You will feel a little drowsy for another hour."

Drowsy... another hour...

Paul felt the man's hands on his back, raising him to a sitting position. Eventually, he was able to lower his legs from the bed and place his feet on the floor.

"Drink this."

Paul felt the hard rim of a glass pressing against his lower lip. He turned his head away.

"It's only water," the man said.

Paul took a sip, just enough to taste the liquid. Reassured, he took a larger sip.

"Good," the man said, removing the glass from Paul's mouth. "I'm going to take off the mask now."

Paul was now sufficiently awake to comprehend that the hood that had covered his whole head had been replaced with a mask. He squinted as this mask was removed, until his eyes had adjusted to the light from the naked bulb suspended from the ceiling.

It was the seemingly spinning, windowless room, not the man standing close to him that Paul first tried to take in. The room was about fifteen feet square and had plain yellow walls. Its floor comprised bare floorboards. Apart from the shelf-like bed, there was a wooden table surrounded by three chairs. On the table was a telephone, a jug of water and a half-filled glass. There was something else, too. Lumpish. Black. To his blurred vision, this shapeless thing might have been a squashed rat, or perhaps it was the coiled mask. Until...

He felt with his bound hands for his wallet – indeed it was missing from his windcheater inside pocket.

"That's better, isn't it? No one likes being blindfolded."

Only now did Paul look up to study his captor's face, but the man was turning away, taking hold of one of the wooden chairs. The sleeves of his grey shirt were rolled to the elbows, and his blue denim jeans were secured by a brown belt. He seemed a little overweight.

The man placed the chair in front of Paul and sat down. His thick, short hair was black and wavy, with no sign of grey. He had an olive complexion, a moustache and heavy stubble on his chin, cheeks and neck. The parted collar of his shirt exposed thick chest hair matching the hair on the back of his exposed forearms. Beneath his brown eyes, puffy, dark folds of skin gave the man a slightly unwell look.

Paul coughed to clear his throat. "Who are you? Where are we?"

"This is a safe house. It is a place where no one will be looking for you. You've been brought here to provide information."

"Information concerning what? I'm a tourist," Paul said, his gaze darting towards the door, which was only five feet away. Could he loop his bound arms over his captor's head and pull him face down on to his knee, rendering him unconscious, and then escape? But what if Paul was still too groggy to walk, let alone run? And what if he broke his knee in the manoeuvre? Anyway, the door was probably locked. "Safe house? Safe from what? You still haven't told me who you are."

"No, I haven't, but you can call me Sundial."

"And you can call me bloody Flower Pot."

"You are in no position to be awkward, Doctor Avery. You went to President Square this evening. You went there to meet someone."

I'll make you pay, if you've hurt her. Paul looked at his left wrist for his watch, but, like his wallet, it too had been taken from him. "How long was I unconscious?"

"Almost five hours. Cooperate with me, and you'll be back at the Hotel Willem before breakfast time. Although it would be unwise to eat there until the effects of the sedative have fully worn off."

"Why did you kidnap me if you know where I am staying and my movements? You could have left a message for me there."

"Left a message..." Sundial smiled at the suggestion. "How civilised that would have been, Doctor. The work you and we are engaged in precludes such politeness. We could not allow you to ignore us or give you the time to take countermeasures." Sundial leaned forward and placed a hand on Paul's shoulder. "This way your compatriots won't know you have talked to us... and they will never know, unless you reveal it to them. And if you were to do that, there would be negative consequences, particularly for the person you went to meet."

"Who is 'us'? I see only you."

Sundial removed his hand. "You will come to understand." Sundial looked at his watch. He stood up. "Be patient."

A moment later, the telephone started ringing. Sundial picked up the receiver. "Talk to him, convince him," he said to the caller as he carried the telephone towards Paul, its lead stretching after it. He placed the telephone on the chair he'd been using. "A friend for you, Doctor."

Cupping the receiver in his hands, Paul asked, "Who's there?"

Upon hearing her say his name, he exclaimed, "Shannon!" Gathering his thoughts, he stammered, "I-I m-mean Sond—"

She interrupted him. "I've told them my real name. It's okay."

"I-I went to the square. I was attacked and brought here."

"They're connected to MOSSAD, Paul, the Israeli foreign intelligence service."

"I've heard of them, I think." Paul looked towards his captor, as if to put a face on the organization. He was familiar with the name, perhaps from films or news bulletins. What interest could they have in him? He'd never been to the Middle East... Then Tom's words of this morning came back to him – *"Israelis, Egyptians, Jordanians, Saudis... Don't know which. Middle Eastern anyway."* That was the way Tom had referred to the people he'd spotted watching Shannon at her hotel. "The man imprisoning me said he wants information."

"Cooperate, Paul. They won't hurt you."

"I was injected with something to knock me out!"

The line went silent for a moment before Shannon said, "That wasn't part of the arrangement. Are you all right?"

"What arrangement? Did you set me up? Is that why you weren't at the square?"

"Did you resist?"

"They didn't give me much of a chance."

"I'm sorry, Paul."

"What's this all about, Shannon?"

"Remember at the department store yesterday... I told you I'd initiated something. They'll give me sanctuary in Israel, but only if they believe that I'm a worthwhile asset. You're the only person here who can authenticate my identity, my role with Vernon."

"Did you meet them that first afternoon, after we left the square?"

"Yes. I lied about having a meeting nearby. I took the train and went to their embassy. I can't survive alone in Africa, Paul. Vernon would find me within a couple of years, just as he can find you here or in England.

"While I was intimidating your boss in the lounge at Heathrow, it felt as if I were threatening myself too. I already knew what was going to happen to Sykes. After Maycross left me, I phoned the Israeli embassy in Pretoria and told them I was on my way to Johannesburg, and that I wanted to defect."

"This is a lot for me to take in. I want you to be safe."

"You must tell them everything. All about Hartling Springs, the casino, Vernon, your role... The plan involving the mine. The name of your handler in South Africa. Don't hold anything back."

"What will they do with that information?"

"They won't interfere, if that's what you mean. It's not their business. They are allies. They need to be sure about me. None of this changes anything for you, Paul. Carry on working for Blackwood and Maycross as if nothing has happened. Keep to the plan."

As Paul wrestled with the implications of what Shannon was asking of him, Sundial grabbed the receiver from his hands. "That's enough!" Sundial put the receiver back on its cradle and returned the telephone to the table. "You must tell us everything about your purpose here."

"She said you'll help her."

"We are *considering* providing her with a new life, but only if she has sufficient intelligence value."

"Aren't we on the same side? I don't understand how this..." Paul shook his head, but the giddiness wouldn't clear. "That drug you injected... The room's still spinning."

"We are allies, but allies have different priorities from time to time regarding military and security matters, or even energy policies. Inside-information provides... Let's say that it avoids misunderstandings. Doesn't your Secret Intelligence Service want to find out what its international partners really think and intend to do?"

"I'm not in it. I don't know what it wants."

"What are the two of you doing here in South Africa, Doctor?" Sundial opened his hand, revealing something small on his palm. "And why do you have this in your wallet? UK Government issue."

Paul stared at Sundial, trying to gauge what lay in store. He'd forgotten about the capsule, the physical embodiment of the Grandee Paragraph 5 Order, the order that Tom had dismissed as made up. Perhaps the capsule contained something innocuous instead of cyanide. The way his head hurt, a quick end was not without appeal.

"Do you prefer to make the ultimate sacrifice for your country, or will you help your beautiful lover to go to Israel?"

Beautiful lover... Her hotel bedroom *had* been bugged after all.

Sundial returned the glass capsule to its metal holder and then pushed the holder into the pocket inside Paul's wallet. Turning back to Paul, he said, "I wanted to be certain that I have your attention."

He certainly had Paul's attention. He also must have read the emergency Washington DC telephone number that had been wrapped around the capsule holder. Had he already established whose number it was?

***

Sundial pressed the STOP key on the cassette tape recorder and used the EJECT key to spring open the cassette compartment. He withdrew the cassette and placed it inside its plastic case. Almost sixty minutes of betrayal, preceded by thirty minutes of seemingly innocuous facts about Paul's childhood, education, marriage and career choice.

Once Paul had started to talk, compliance had become easier. His childhood in Durban had led on to the long boat trip to Southampton, then to his schooling in south London, and his father's death in a hospice. At times catharsis had threatened, but Sundial had hurried him past these moments with the ease of a master interrogator.

"You have done well, Doctor," Sundial said, passing the cassette case to his colleague, the one who'd brought them the recorder. The three of them had sat at the table throughout. The jug was empty. Disloyalty, even towards Maycross, had proved to be thirsty work.

PART FOUR

Chapter 30

The interrogator was true to his word. Paul was dropped off outside the Hotel Willem at a little after 6.00 a.m. He felt in a detached condition as he walked up to the entrance. He could see himself as if from a thousand feet – that blond man with the outreached arm down there was some kind of animatronic version of himself, a creature directed by a crossfire of electrical impulses.

As he pushed open the front door, three things attacked his senses: the cloying warmth of the lobby; the smell of early-breakfast bacon from the restaurant; and a shrill cry from Mable.

"Dr Avery! Are you all right, Doctor?"

Paul's eyes had barely brought her alarmed visage into focus when everything became too much. He wheeled round and charged back outside. After staggering six steps to the side of the entrance, he bent over and retched. Having not eaten for many hours, there was little undigested to vomit. The straining added abdominal pain to the palette of discomfort that he vaguely sensed would comprise his recollection of this moment. He straightened up and took deep breaths of cold air. At some point, Paul realised his hand was covering the place on his neck where the sedative had been injected. Was the drug still affecting him? He shook his head, hoping to free himself.

All of a sudden he sensed someone sneaking up. Crouching and twisting, Paul thrashed with his arms, fending away the hood that would be forced over his head. Yet the hands were still able to grab him. If only he could land one hard punch...

"Whoa, Paul. It's me – Trevor."

"Tre-vor?" Paul mumbled, ceasing struggling. He knew that name. It was interesting, a whooshing from the prehistoric past, like the double-tap of fossilised amber landing on the toe of a T. rex.

"Mable called me. I was getting ready for my morning run. Said you seemed to be in a state." Letting go of Paul, Maycross's man continued, "It looks like you've had a good night out on the tiles."

"Out on the tiles... Now that's *Tom* speaking. Where be Trevor?" Paul said, prodding Tom's shoulder with his forefinger. The smirk faded as his mouth formed a curious pout. "Oh," he said, collapsing.

***

Paul awoke midmorning with a headache, unable to recollect going up to his room. Looking towards his legs, he saw he was still dressed. It took a minute to shake off the delusion that he'd had a "night on the tiles", a phrase that had come into his mind, although those words were not ones he remembered ever using. Had he really been with Shannon? That's what he'd intended, hadn't he? Meet her in the square with the fountain... Why couldn't he remember being with her? And then it all returned, an unwinding dream with the whiskered face of Sundial at its focal point.

Paul sat up and reached for the telephone. There was no answer from Tom's room. He'd been listening to the ringing tone for nearly a minute when he came to his senses and slammed the receiver down. *Tom's the last person I should tell about Sundial.* Shannon had implored him to cooperate with the kidnapper, and knowing he was responsible for her being here in South Africa, he'd done so. This version of the truth was as much that, right now, he could face.

Paul looked at his watch. It was quarter past ten. It had been taken from him, yet it was back on his wrist. Panicking, he reached into his windcheater inside pocket. The wallet was there. He opened it. The cyanide capsule holder, once again wrapped in the piece of paper with the Washington DC emergency telephone number, was in its place too.

Paul could remember almost nothing of what had happened following the loud click of the EJECT key on the cassette tape recorder. Was the jug of water he'd been given drugged? A tasteless hypnotic compound to disinhibit him. He couldn't remember Sundial or his helper drinking.

Paul dialled 0 for an outside line and then the number for Tom's office.

A pre-recorded message, in an unfamiliar woman's voice, answered upon the third ring: "You've reached Tallyho Furnishings. Please leave your name and number, and someone will return your call shortly."

After hesitating, Paul said, "It's me. Thanks for getting me to my room this morning. I owe yo—"

There was a click and then Tom came on the line. "Don't mention it, old love."

"Too much vino. Perhaps that, combined with the altitude..."

"Everyone lets off steam once in a while. Why don't you have a quiet day?"

"Don't you need help with the... the delivery we're waiting for?"

"Your internal time clock must be out of whack. Think about it."

Hank wouldn't be handing over Art's report for nearly five hours. And then the package had to be flown to Jan Smuts International Airport and picked up by someone for the SIS Station that Tom said was located within the embassy in Pretoria. The package should be available for collection from Tom's dead letter box *tomorrow*.

"You're right. I had that sense of panic. You know, like thinking you've forgotten an exam. Stupid of me."

"Try to go back to sleep."

"No chance. I need to do some research at the City Library. I'll eat here before setting off."

"The library should be quiet enough, I suppose," Tom said. "I'll see you later. I'm spending the day here on company paperwork."

***

The taxi pulled in to the drop-off lane for the Oceania International. Paul paid the driver and got out. He was wearing one of his dark-blue suits, together with a white shirt and red tie, having given his crumpled clothes to Henry to take care of. The suits were all that he had left to wear now. At least he would look like someone who belonged at the Oceana.

"My name is Paul Avery. I'm a friend of one of your guests – a Miss Sondra Lansing. Please let her know I'm here," Paul said to the nearest of the maroon-uniformed receptionists behind the front counter.

"Yes, sir," the young woman said. "Do you know her suite number?"

"It's 627. I did ring about an hour ago, but there wasn't an answer from her suite. If she's still not answering, please page her. It occurred to me she could be using the pool or the gymnasium."

"Of course, no problem, sir," the receptionist said, looking down at the hotel register. After a few seconds, with a puzzled expression, she turned away and consulted one of her colleagues, an older woman.

Paul sensed he was going to be disappointed, but resolved to wait for Shannon to return from wherever she'd gone. The foyer had comfortable sofas and he could order coffee. He needed to... He didn't know what he needed. Express anger about the situation she'd placed him in? Tell her he didn't know whether he had said enough to convince Sundial of her value? Or just stare into those eyes?

He looked round for anyone watching. The dusky complexioned man sitting nearby with a newspaper? *Don't look for stereotypes*, he imagined Tom advising. Perhaps the arguing, middle-aged couple coming out of the elevator?

"Miss Lansing has checked out, Mr Avery. I gather it was around the time you called. She wasn't due to leave for a few days, so our records still have to be fully updated." The receptionist gave a wide and unfathomable smile, perhaps the product of her training for customer-facing roles.

"I see," he responded absently. If he hadn't had to sleep off the effects of Sundial's cocktail of drugs, he could have come here earlier. "Did she leave a message for me?"

Claire consulted her senior colleague again, who in turn asked someone else. Paul watched, with increasing hopelessness, the succession of head shakes.

"I'm afraid there's no message, Mr Avery."

"Thanks for your assistance, anyway."

"Of course, sir. Have a nice—"

"Don't say that!" he snapped, cutting her off.

Turning away, he regretted the rude outburst, but Shannon was gone. Probably boarding a flight to Tel Aviv at this moment. No final goodbye. Trite wishes for a nice day had no place in his life.

Chapter 31

Paul took a taxi for the five-minute drive from the Oceania International to the City Library. It was during this journey that he realised he'd failed again to keep his promise to telephone Ann. He wasn't even sure that he could blame Sundial. He'd set off last evening expecting to meet Shannon in the square, with the hope that he'd spend the night with her. Would he really have telephoned Ann from the Oceana? Calling a wife who didn't want to speak to him had slipped too easily from his mind.

He looked at his watch. Ann was probably out. She *should* be out, house-hunting. But she might be attending another Maycross-inspired interview in London. Commuting by rail from north Suffolk to work in central London would be feasible, but it would be expensive and add several hours to the working day. Or would she live in London during the week, in the same way that he would be living in a flat in Didcot? Who knows what Ann had in mind? It didn't seem a marriage-sustaining prospect. Flats in London would be much more expensive than flats in Didcot. She would have to *share...*

The taxi pulled up outside the library, and Paul was relieved to abandon the train of thoughts that had seemed to be transporting him to the end of a loveless line.

Two hours passed in notetaking – he'd had to first purchase a notebook from a stationer near the library – from hydrology, minerology and topography tomes. In these scholarly works the settlement of Saskia was only mentioned incidentally, although the terrain was described in considerable detail. Even the small pond he'd seen the woman take water from was described.

He then moved on to distilling the key points to be raised with the management of the Kop Mine. Unable to order the abandonment of the "storage project", he reduced his initial list of nine demands down to what he hoped would be accepted as two practicable recommendations. If these were adopted, he would be able to sleep a little easier and consider he'd fulfilled Maycross's only technical requirement – *"Just tip the awful stuff deep underground in such a way that no one is bothered by it for, say, eighty years, by which time we'll both be dead, the Willingham Corporation will be a footnote in the history of ruthless capitalism, and it'll all be someone else's problem."*

Paul doodled a box around the finalised recommendations. It was his way of signifying to himself acceptance of the conditions under which the unaccounted-for radioactive materials at both the Hartling Springs nuclear power station and the Altabrite site would experience the passage of millennia. Now he could allow his mind to return to the issues surrounding the transportation of those materials from New Jersey to their final resting place.

Assuming that Maycross hadn't baulked at the cost of implementing Tom's plan, Art Richards' report was about to be taken aboard a private jet. If so, it was another example of the mind-boggling expenditures incurred in the pursuance of the COLOURLESS programme. Paul could relate to only the cost side of the balance sheet. The geopolitical, military and strategic penalties of not succeeding were outside his competency. That was territory owned by out-of-sight facilitators, such as Morrison and Blackwood.

Paul shuddered as he looked up from his notepad. While he'd been working, many of the chairs close by had been taken, mostly by young people who looked like college students, but also by a few older individuals in business attire, perhaps pursuing part-time courses. It was approaching 5.00 p.m., weekday closing time. People were already readying themselves to leave.

Was he being observed here? How many tourists spend their precious holiday time reading obscure publications like those he'd consulted the library staff about? Not that he had anything to hide from Sundial, at least. That bridge had been crossed. According to Shannon, there would be no interference. Perhaps there wouldn't be now, but what if Sundial blackmailed his government in ten or twenty years' time? Once Paul had returned to his job in the laboratories of the RSMSDA, perhaps he at least would be able to resume a normal life, everything he'd done in this one forgotten. With that thought, he closed his notebook, stood up and joined the exodus of library users.

***

"You be lookin' better," Tom, as Trevor, said, joining Paul in the restaurant at the Hotel Willem. "Mable said meet you 'ere at eight o'clock. Didn't know you would be dressin' up though."

Paul had been lost in his thoughts – the telephone call to Ann this evening had been as unfruitful as his previous attempts – and hadn't noticed his colleague approaching. "Until my laundry comes back, this is all I have to wear. You're on time. When did you get back?"

"Oh, 'bout forty minute ago. Have you ordered?"

"Not yet. Any news on the parcel?"

Tom nodded. "Fetch it 'morrow, round midday."

"Should I meet you at your office?"

Shaking his head, Tom said, "Bring it back 'ere, I shall."

"You hungry?" Paul said, nodding towards the food counter.

The two men got up and ordered their meals. (Self-service was confined to breakfast time.) One of the two aproned women behind the counter also resembled Mable, Paul thought. *This place really is a family affair.* After collecting knives and forks from the provided racks, they returned to their table.

"Take a look at this." Paul handed Tom a piece of paper on which he'd transcribed his recommendations for the Kop Mine. "My work this afternoon."

Tom studied the recommendations. He frowned as he returned the piece of paper to Paul. "One be expensive. The other be time consuming."

"So?" Paul asked.

The woman who looked like she could be Mable's younger sister and, therefore, possibly Henry's mother arrived with the meals.

"Thank you," Paul said. He was surprised to see the woman wink at his companion. Tom's history at the Hotel Willem was probably something that was best left unexplored, he decided.

"We'll see what the colonel has to say about them," Tom, sounding momentarily more like himself than his Trevor guise, said after the beguiled waitress had left.

They ate mostly in silence. Paul was preoccupied with what Ann's father had said. "You've missed her again. She's in Norwich, spending the day with one of her old friends. Old boyfriend, isn't it, Dot?" At which point, Ann's mother, sounding flustered, had taken over the phone. "That was a long time ago, Paul. Bernard doesn't know what he's talking about." The telephone call deteriorated into polite evasiveness before he promised to try again tomorrow. "Don't promise to call, Paul, if you aren't going to keep to it," Dorothy responded with an uncustomary edge.

"Not hungry?" Tom asked, gesturing with his fork at Paul's meal.

"I thought I was," Paul said, putting his knife and fork down on his plate. "Must be the after-effects of last night," he lied.

Who was the old boyfriend his wife was spending time with? Yet the emptiness Paul felt at this moment, he knew, had as much to do with what had happened at the Oceania International this morning as it did with the growing distance between himself and Ann, whom he'd strived from the beginning to protect.

***

It was approaching 2.00 p.m. on Tuesday afternoon when Tom knocked on Paul's bedroom door.

"You've got it," Paul said, looking at the large brown envelope in Tom's hand.

"No suit today, I see."

Paul was wearing freshly ironed black jeans and a blue shirt, unbuttoned at the neck, over a black T-shirt. "Henry came through with the laundry," he said, pointing at the neat pile of ironed clothes on his bed.

Tom closed the door and walked across to the small table standing beside the sink. Paul moved aside his toiletries to make space for the parcel contents.

"You do the honours," Tom said, handing the package to Paul.

Within seconds the contents were sprawled across the table. A folded map showed the whole US eastern seaboard. A smaller map was centred on New Jersey, but took in the abutting parts of New York state to the north, Pennsylvania to the west, and Delaware and Maryland to the south. Both maps included the routes of rail lines. Ports had been ringed with a red marker pen. A handwritten table correlated the branching and interconnecting rail routes with the respective port connections. Timetable booklets had been provided for each of the six routes that connected most directly to the switching yard at Maizetown. Handwriting in the margins of these booklets detailed changes corresponding to the maintenance periods that had been slated since publication. Lastly, a hardback notebook contained Art's analysis of the applicable load restrictions, existing and during the maintenance periods, along each of the routes. At the back, Art had written his conclusions.

"What do you make of all this?" Tom asked, perusing the smaller of the two maps.

"What... What do you mean?" Paul responded distractedly as he re-read Art's conclusions.

"Does it cover everything?" Tom said impatiently, placing the small map back on the table.

"If it's correct, it's not exactly what I wanted to read."

"What's the problem? Something endangering the operation? Head Office won't—"

"I can see why Hank Barnaby was anxious," Paul snapped, interrupting Tom.

"Do *we* need to worry?"

"We'll have to consult Max. It will depend on what he says," Paul replied, trying to remain calm. "Anyway, it's me that will have to worry, not you. You don't have to deal with Sondra's boss."

Tom nodded as he considered Paul's reply. "I'll call Max and set up a meeting for Thursday. You'd better study this lot in the meantime. We'll leave in the morning."

Paul spent the rest of the day transcribing and cross-referencing Art's notes. Gradually the unfamiliar became familiar. He didn't find any inconsistencies, but the work left him with questions he hoped Max could answer. It also left him despondent. If there *was* a way through, he would have to coordinate the shipping arrangements very soon. All without Shannon, and with Blackwood's and Gavin Cantrell's heavies watching his every move. He despised afresh what he had become. Once again he didn't call Ann. She didn't deserve to hear the despair in his voice. Instead he remembered and acted on Tom's advice about having a nightcap or two.

Chapter 32

It was 11.15 a.m. Wednesday 10 August when Tom's car pulled out of the main gate at the Kop Mine. Tom and Paul had just had a difficult session with Colonel Stanley Evans and Pieter Niemeyer. This meeting had been arranged the previous morning by Tom, while he'd been waiting for the coded message telling him that the parcel from America was ready for collection from the dead letter box in Pretoria. The short notice of the meeting this morning had made it impossible for Charlie Halliday to attend.

Paul had put on a suit and tie for this visit to the mine, whereas Tom, maintaining his Trevor alias but without the theatrics, had kept to casual attire because of the long drive ahead of them today. They had already checked out of the Hotel Willem. Tomorrow, the two of them would visit Max at the port in Durban to discuss the report from Art Richards. There was no secure alternative to their meeting in person, Tom had informed Paul.

"Did you notice the company name on the jacket of the guard at the gate?" Paul asked, as they headed west on the road bisecting the mine. "It's different from last time."

"A change of contractor then. That's probably Halliday's doing."

It's more likely Blackwood's doing, Paul surmised. "I met someone wearing a jacket like that at the hotel."

"Did you? Normally the guards are locals, not brought in."

"It's the name of the company guarding the nuclear power station in Hartling Springs."

"What?" Tom said, momentarily braking as if readying himself for an evasive manoeuvre. "Shit!" He expelled a deep breath and, after looking into the rear-view mirror, accelerated back to their former speed. "That's worth reporting. Well spotted, Paul."

Tom fell silent, seemingly digesting the significance of the information as he continued driving towards the ring road that would take them to the turnoff for the route to Durban.

After a few minutes, Tom said, "Don't feel too bad about the meeting, Paul. It wasn't a definite 'no' to either of your recommendations. We'll have their final answers in a few days."

"It didn't sound as though there's going to be a 'yes'," Paul snapped.

Niemeyer in particular had been hostile to Paul's recommendations for the control of the groundwater in and around the mine. At Tom's insistence, these recommendations were made verbally only and no minutes were taken.

"Pieter said he would look into the practicalities," Tom said. "I think that's fair enough."

"That was just to get rid of me."

"Moving half of that waste mountain across the road to the other side of the site is quite a request, to put it mildly. It took more than a hundred years to produce it."

"Don't take their side, Tom. We must prevent acidic water from slowly finding ways to seep into the bunkers where our containers will be buried."

"Hmmm..." Tom hummed. "It's not only the work that would be involved. Head Office would have to cover the cost anyway. It's the *visibility*. Doing that will inevitably attract a lot of attention."

"You mean from the trespassers, the people who shouldn't be there in the first place."

"Well, yes, them, but also the remaining workers. Word travels fast inside and between townships. If Charlie-boy had been at the meeting, he probably would have had a fit."

"It can be carried out over several years. I made that clear, didn't I?"

"Once you've started, you can't disguise an activity like that, Paul. Look, your other recommendation – excavation of deep drainage channels to keep contamination from the containers away from the township. I think they might go for that. If they do, consider it a victory."

The satisfaction that Paul had felt at the City Library as he was drafting the two recommendations now felt like a dream from a different life. He released a grunt of frustration and then chuckled. The chuckle turned into a manic laughter.

"What?" Tom asked.

"I was imagining Pieter's reactions to the ideas that I held back."

"Doubtless all of them enormously expensive and labour

intensive."

"Except one. Ghosts aren't expensive, are they?"

"Ghosts!" It was Tom's turn to laugh. "Why ghosts?"

"To keep scavengers away. A lot, perhaps hundreds, of workers must have died in those tunnels. I almost felt their presence when I went down there. I read at the library that their ancestors mean a lot to tribespeople. Their connection is different from the one we have with our forebears. It's more like a living relationship than a historical record."

"Was it your intention to have the colonel running up and down in a white sheet and shouting BOO?"

"See... Ridicule. That's exactly why I dropped it."

"No, you could be on to something. I'll give it some serious thought, Paul."

"I'm sure you will," Paul said, closing his eyes to rest them. After a minute or so, perhaps longer, he heard Tom speaking.

"You should consider a career in counter-intelligence. Ghosts. Just brilliant."

They drove on for hours, taking turns at the wheel. During one of these switchovers, Tom said, "I tried to get hold of Sondra this morning, to inform her we were leaving for Durban today. She could have come along, or made her own arrangement to join us there by flying down. The hotel reception told me she checked out on Monday."

"She's left her hotel?" Paul said in an incredulous tone as he settled in the driver's seat.

"I expected her to stick around longer."

"I did too."

"So she gave you no indication of her plans?"

"No," Paul said, with a brief shake of his head. Manoeuvring back on to the road, he continued, "I assume I'll see her when I return to New Jersey."

"Hmmm... I don't like it," Tom murmured. "It seems sudden."

"Maybe Head Office will know what's going on. Anyway, now I think about it, why aren't *we* flying to Durban if that's an option?"

"I avoid appearing on flight passenger logs whenever possible."

"Of course. Friction in the ether," Paul said, sarcastically.

Shannon would be, he hoped, safe in Israel by now. Far from Blackwood's smouldering cigars. "Have you ever been to Howick Falls?" he asked his companion, attempting to change the subject.

***

Paul awoke in the gloom of the dimly lit garage beneath Cornish Mansions, disturbed by a hard nudge to his bicep.

"Wakey, wakey, sweetie. Home sweet home," Tom said.

Rubbing his eyes, Paul asked, "What time is it?"

Tom opened the door, activating the car interior light. Moving to get out he said, "Nearly nine, Paulie-boy."

"And normal service is resumed," Paul mumbled, reflecting on the glib, somewhat camp, manner Tom reserved for Durban.

As they walked up the ramp with their suitcases, Tom said, "No food in, old bean. There's a burger place across the road, at the other end of the block. Or we could go for an Indian."

"No thanks to both."

"We'll just drop off our cases firs— What?"

"I'm going for a stroll along the promenade to clear my head, and then to the restaurant in The James." Paul left unsaid his intention to telephone Ann. Perhaps the plush surroundings of the hotel and its childhood echoes would armour him, allow him to pretend to be a human being, if only for a few minutes.

"I don't know. After all we've been through together, you're dumping me," Tom said in a simpering tone as he used his key to open the door to the ground floor hallway.

"You'll get over it."

In the elevator, Tom said, "Promise me you won't get wrecked again tonight."

"Don't worry. I need to be on top form for Max in the morning."

"Max in the morning..." Tom crooned. "There's a tune in that somewhere," he said.

Having consumed two large gin and tonics and a prawn-and-chicken sandwich platter, Paul walked from the restaurant to the chandeliered lobby of The James. With the assistance of the concierge, who sold him a phone card, he used the public telephone near the entrance.

What time was it there? Paul looked at his watch. 10.17 p.m. minus one hour: 9.17 p.m. Who would answer this time?

"Hello," he heard a woman say. It didn't quite sound like Ann's mother. Had he been connected to the wrong line?

"Dot?"

"It's *Ann*, Paul."

"You sounded a little like your mom, but different."

"I only said one word."

"How are you?"

"Do you really care?"

"Of course! It's not easy here for me. I'm a little out of my depth, to be honest. So much money at stake. Anyway, I know you've been out and about a lot."

"I was in yesterday, waiting for your call."

"I just meant you've been out whenever I *have* called."

"Instead of waiting in all the time, waiting for you to remember me, you mean."

"That's not fair, Ann. My time isn't my own. I drove—" Paul covered the receiver momentarily as a chattering group of cheerful residents emerged from the nearby dining room, which overlooked the promenade. Once they'd passed, he continued, "I drove hundreds of miles today."

"Who's with you? She was laughing."

"I'm in a hotel lobby in Durban. There's people coming and going. I don't know them." The phone went quiet at the other end. Eventually Paul said, "How was your trip to London the other day? I've lost track of time. Your mother said you were going to visit the museums. Make a day of it."

"I told you about the V and A. I told you Patrick had a contact there."

Patrick... That name made him feel nauseous. "I remember clearly. Did you have an interview?"

A muffled, scuffing sound came from Ann's end.

"Are you still there?" Paul thought he could hear her crying.

In a forced tone, she said, "He was polite and interested in my background, but he said there isn't a suitable position for someone without practical curating experience."

"I'm sorry, Ann."

"It was too good to be true. I should have known."

"You've still got Norwich."

"Patrick said he will speak to the management of a couple of art galleries in London."

"So, you're still in contact with him?"

"He's called me a couple of times, asking how I'm getting on."

"Ann, this is important. Did you give him your parents' telephone number before you left Wantage?"

"Why's that important? I must have done. At least he's trying to help me."

At least he's trying to help me... Paul had to compose himself before speaking again. Had Maycross employed security resources to track down Ann in Suffolk? Knowing she was staying with her parents, he would have had to find out her maiden name, and then her parents' address. "Does he know you're house-hunting? We agreed my bosses shouldn't know about our plan to relocate until we're ready."

"I can't remember everything I've told Patrick. He's not your real boss, anyway. And if they're sending you all over the world, why will it matter where your home is?"

"Okay. Okay. I just wanted to..." Pursuing the point felt futile. Blackwood would be able to find them just as easily as Maycross had. He'd made the right choice in accepting Shannon's blunt analysis of his situation. "How's my mother? Have you seen her? Where is she staying?"

"Your mother's coming to Suffolk *next* week, Paul."

"Of course. Next week. I told you I'm losing track of time."

"Mum said she must stay with us."

There was certainly enough spare bedrooms at Pendlefield Manor, but Paul was worried about how Ann and Beth would get on, given the circumstances. "Have you told Mom she can stay? Otherwise, she'll be booking a hotel."

"I'll phone her tomorrow."

"Thank you, Ann."

"When are you coming back?"

This was the first question that buoyed him. "It will be sooner than I expected. Within days, even."

"I see," she said, too coolly, as if she had become hardened to his absences.

There were things he wanted to know, but this wasn't the opportunity to straighten misshapen longings. Never ask questions if you don't know how you'll react to the answers... Advice he gave himself now, knowing he'd rarely been able to follow it.

"I'll have to return to the States," he said softly, "within a few days of being back, though. Just so that you kno—" He thought he heard a click at the other end. "Ann, are you there?" Silence. Thousands of mile of it.

The breeze from the Indian Ocean had come through the nearby doorway as someone else had left the hotel. The momentary caress died away almost before he felt it.

He put the receiver back on its cradle. With a nod to the concierge he went out into the night air. Gulls were tussling over a morsel of food under the lights of the promenade. The victor took to the air, leaving the losers to their hunger. Worse than having lost Ann's trust was the sense that something had happened to *his* feelings for her.

Chapter 33

The premises of Manikin Import Services was more extensive than it had appeared to Paul during his first visit with Tom to the docks. He learned that there was another room, situated beyond the galley-like office that Max shared with his assistant. The connecting door was covered by the black curtain.

Inside this anteroom, three leather-upholstered club chairs, a coffee table and a drinks cabinet were to the right of the doorway, and a mahogany dining table, complete with six matching chairs, were to the left. Natural light entered through skylights. This morning thick cloud cover had made it necessary to turn on the wall lights. Arcs of metallic ink suggested leaves shimmering in the vicinity of the lights – the wallpaper had a gold-and-black leaf pattern.

Max gestured towards the club chairs.

“It’s certainly more comfortable in here,” Paul said, taking the nearest of the chairs.

“Ocean-damaged cargo that was *not* so damaged, as it turned out,” Max said, grinning.

“Maximilian likes a bargain,” Tom interjected. “He’d much rather get something for free than pay a single Rand.”

“So, what do you have for me?” Max said, ignoring the taunt. He sat down next to Paul, leaving Tom to take the remaining club chair.

Paul withdrew from a supermarket plastic bag the bulging envelope containing the items prepared by Art Richards. He emptied the contents on to the coffee table. As soon as he’d separated out the smaller of the two maps, the one centred on New Jersey, Max snatched it from him and began to examine it, mumbling, “Nein, nein, ja, wahrscheinlich...”

“Are you familiar with all of those ports?” Paul said.

Max looked up, his brow furrowed with concentration. Noticing the notebook that Paul had opened, he snapped his fingers. “Pass me that.”

After handing the notebook to Max, Paul explained, “It’s an analysis of the railway routes that lead to each of the ports shown on the maps. Unfortunately, because of coming track improvement and maintenance work, not all of the ports will be reachable during any given period. Also, it seems, some ports require more use of transfer vehicles to load the cargo than others do."

"What is this place – this Maizetown?" Max asked, pointing to the name on the map that had been ringed by the use of a black marker pen.

"It's the railyard that will be the starting point for the shipment."

Max put the map down on his lap and began turning the pages of the notebook. "Ja, Ja... This is good work, my English friend."

I'm glad you think so, Paul thought. He'd found that the complexities of moving rail freight in the USA, because of the numerous private rail companies involved, made the state-run British Rail service look to be a paragon of simplicity.

Clutching the small map and the notebook, Max stood up. "We will work at the table. Bring all those with you."

The three men settled around the dining table. Paul leaned across and spread out the large map of the USA. Using Art Richards' notebook and the accompanying timetable booklets, Max and Paul set about the task of identifying the best route for bringing the shipment of radioactive waste to South Africa. Tom sat quietly, unable to make an input at this stage. At one point, at Max's instruction, he went next door to request that refreshments be brought in by the fearsome Petra.

The three massively heavy radiation flasks were the primary source of difficulty. After nearly two hours of heated discussion they had produced on one sheet of paper an analysis, reconstructed from Art's notebook, setting out all the possible movement "time slots" for five shipping ports only, having dismissed one because of berthing restrictions. Max had spent much of the meeting consulting thick shipping manuals, which had also been brought in by Petra. These manuals detailed the berthing arrangements and the cargo storage, handling, security and customs procedures adopted at the respective ports.

Ports to the west and south of Maizetown, including the huge port at Baltimore, required the crossing of the Delaware River. Ports to the north, such as the combined Port of New York and New Jersey, avoided the Delaware River but had other issues. The captain of the ship that Max had lined up for the job had reported having arguments with the authorities in New York. He'd narrowly avoided arrest. In addition, the more Max described the layout of the various berths there, the more Paul became uneasy. If he were moving *only* the radiation flasks or *only* the shipping containers (containing the least dangerous of the waste from the Altabrite site), the cargo handling requirements would be less likely to attract inquiries.

The rail bridges crossing the Delaware River were all to the north of Maizetown – the farther north, the shorter the crossing distance for the narrowing estuary. According to Art's notebook, not all of these bridges were rated for wagons as heavy as those carrying the radiation casks. In addition, the timings for track maintenance and upgrading work determined the weight of the loads that could be carried over certain routes during the coming months.

Max used green and red marker pens to highlight "go" and "no-go" periods for each port and track combination. Most of the green marks corresponded with periods beginning in four months' time, when Christmas-related cargo would be approaching its peak. While such a timing might not concern the detail-free Maycross, Paul knew Gavin Cantrell and Hank Barnaby would not be so relaxed. As for Blackwood, the pressure caused by the letter stunt he'd undertaken with Shannon would only increase with her disappearance.

Only one green band addressed the urgency of the situation. It involved shipping the radioactive cargo in five weeks' time. The Delaware River would be crossed near Philadelphia. The train would skirt the city to the north and switch to a line that would take it southwest, across the Susquehanna River, and onwards to a switching yard feeding a satellite port, Sollers Head, in the south-east of Baltimore.

Paul and Max stared at each other. It were as if each was waiting for the other to announce the decision. Shannon's absence would require Blackwood to provide someone else to arrange the shipping paperwork. Paul hoped he could survive the inevitable interrogation about her whereabouts without betraying her. Finally, he said, "Sollers Head Port, it is, Max."

Max stood up and slapped Paul on the back. "The work begins, Doctor." Turning to Tom, who had a distracted look on his face, having been a confused spectator to the proceedings, Max said, "And *you* get the money ready, my friend."

"Tell me how you want it paid."

"Cash, U.S. dollars, for my captain. A cheque in Swiss francs for me. Direct to my account there, as usual."

“Which one of your accounts?” Tom asked, but Max had turned away to open the connecting door to his office.

“The brandy, Petra. Quickly. Bring a glass for yourself,” Max cried.

A couple of minutes later, the four were clinking cut-glass brandy glasses, which were probably more of Max’s ocean salvage.

“A huge step toward to my long and happy retirement,” Max said. “*Even* for you, too, Petra,” he added, grinning at his bemused assistant.

The dubious brandy burned Paul’s throat, but he took a larger mouthful, and then another. He emptied the glass and dropped his head in shame.

Paul and Max continued working at the dining table for a further three hours. Fortified by bananas, apples and pineapple juice, they compiled their respective lists of things to do, only rarely needing to consult each other. In the meantime, Tom had departed to book Paul’s flight to England and fax a cryptic progress report to Head Office.

PART FIVE

Chapter 34

The taxi arranged by Maycross pulled up outside Paul's semi-detached house near Wantage in Oxfordshire. It was nearly 10.30 p.m., Monday 15 August. The very last of the sun had hours ago slipped below the inky distant hills that Ann hated because they made her feel closed in. Weary after the long flight, Paul thanked the driver and with his holdall hanging from his left shoulder he carried his suitcase along the asphalt driveway to the front door. Two weeks had passed since they'd said an awkward goodbye. He opened the door and stepped inside.

There was no point in calling out Hello, but he did it anyway, his voice echoing in the small hallway. He did not turn on the light. Familiar possessions coming alive around him was not something he was ready for. The furnishings may not have changed, but he had. He wondered if he would be able to look at himself in the mirrors. More at home in Tom's fifth floor Durban flat, the creature he'd become didn't belong here. He was an interloper in his old life.

Leaving his suitcase in the hall, he felt his way up the stairs. Upon reaching the top landing he turned left, away from the bathroom and towards the box room at the front of the house. It was next to the master bedroom. The door and the curtains were open. The streetlamp opposite filled the space with yellow light and jagged shadows. He sat down on the single bed that he'd been banished to following the "silver box episode". Both Ann and he had needed space to marinade in their emotions; neither made an issue of the sleeping arrangement.

The tug of the holdall fell away as it came to rest beside him on the bed. He unzipped it and removed the paper bag containing the two gifts he'd bought in Durban over the weekend. Neither of these souvenirs was another contemptible silver offering. He'd learned his lesson. These were five-inch square wooden plaques featuring moulded metal representations of a leaping springbok and an elephant respectively. The stall at the indoor market near the City Hall had sold plaques featuring a lion, a rhino, a cheetah and a giraffe too, all in action poses. And there had been colourful stalls with racks of bead necklaces, animal-print scarves, T-shirts, and tribal-inspired imitation shields and spears. Why he'd chosen these plaques was unclear to him. Perhaps because they were not things that Ann, if she had been with him, would likely have chosen. Picking something intended to delight her would have raised the stakes too high again. Anyway, one of the plaques was intended for his mother, who would appreciate a reminder of "home".

Paul put the plaques down beside the holdall and considered turning the light on. He should telephone Ann and let her know that he was home. And yet, telephones, he'd come to understand, were dangerous portals. Ever since the call from Auberon Morrison that sunny July morning, four weeks ago, he'd not made nor received a call that hadn't diminished him.

When Max, at the end of their planning session at the docks last Thursday, had thrust at him a piece of paper with a telephone number, he'd sensed another pigeon-crashing moment. "Petra has reminded me," Max said, "that an American-sounding woman called yesterday. She said her name is Sondra and that she is a colleague of the colonel, who gave her my number as a possible way to reach you. This is the number she left for you. It has a Pretoria dialling code. Be careful unless you know who she is."

Paul went to The James that evening, ostensibly as a dining-room customer again, but really to use the lobby phone once more. He dialled the number Max had given him. Recalling the distress in Shannon's voice was enough to squash the current impulse to turn on the light.

When he eventually felt sufficiently composed to telephone Pendlefield Manor, to his surprise his mother answered.

"Yeees," Beth said in her telephone voice.

Although pleased to learn that she had arrived in Suffolk safely, what she went on to say was far from comforting. Ann and her parents had gone out, to a cinema in Norwich. They had invited Beth, but she had pleaded tiredness.

"I don't feel at all welcome. There is a lot of tension in the house. It is veeery embarrassing, Paul. As for the location, it makes me feel as if I'm trapped in the bundu."

"It's hardly the bundu, Mom. There's shops not far away. Ask Ann to show you." Pendlefield Manor was quite isolated, but not in a wilderness. "When they get home, tell them I'm coming to see you all tomorrow."

"Oh, that's a relief, Paul. I look forward to hearing you tell me all about Durban, but you must tell me *everything*, especially about those wicked peop—"

"Yes, of course, the *Fraziers* who moved into our old flat and were cruel to their pets," Paul said loudly, panicking. The line was probably bugged. "I-I can't talk now. I'll see you tomorrow, Mom," he added quickly before cutting off the call before the confused Beth could protest. The Fraziers didn't exist. The exchange consolidated his new belief that telephones opened up unforeseeable opportunities for downfall. Aliens in space films had the right idea with their silent use of telepathy.

The film that Ann and her parents had gone to see, Beth had told him, was "Gandhi". Its story was based on the life of Mahatma Gandhi, the globally-admired activist for Indian independence from the British Empire. Once she's seen the film, he would by comparison appear to be a coward who was too craven to prevent himself being imposed upon at work. "Gandhi was *assassinated*," he said to himself.

***

To Paul's surprise he'd found that their car wasn't in the garage. Unless it had been stolen, Ann must have driven to her parents'. He'd previously assumed that she had taken a taxi to the station in Oxford and travelled by train to London and on to Norwich, from where her father could have collected her.

Midmorning Tuesday, dressed in his motorcycle leathers and boots, it took him four attempts to kick-start his Triumph. The machine didn't take well to periods of not being used. The extra burden Paul was carrying as a result of last Thursday evening's call with Shannon made him fret about his power of concentration. Two wheels were more vulnerable than four to rutted or wet surfaces and to gusts of wind. He half-rode half-walked the rumbling motorcycle down the driveway from the garage to the kerb. Lowering the visor on his helmet, he told himself that his worries would swiftly be displaced by a life-or-death focus on the road ahead.

Paul reached Pendlefield Manor, three miles south of Ringsfield village, in under four hours despite pulling off the road twice because of concern about being followed. However, the cars that had suspiciously remained behind him for too long despite his slowing down didn't double back to find him.

Pendlefield Manor seemed smaller than he'd remembered. It was certainly smaller than the Main House at the Tobe Institute. Facing on to open farmland, even the treed backdrop seemed sparser. Perhaps Bernard had paid for some tree clearance work to prevent subsidence damage to the property. He would ask his father-in-law. It would be a harmless question with which to pass some awkward time. His mother's allusion to the bundu suddenly seemed apt now; the rural setting contrasted starkly with the suburban environment of her maisonette in Pinner.

Paul parked on the large gravel frontage, turned off the engine and dismounted, leaving the machine inclined on its stand. He took off his helmet and rested it on the ground. His mother's red Fiat, his and Ann's pale-orange Morris Marina, and Bernard's large white Rover were parked at random angles to one another. *Looks like a full house*, he thought, taking from one of the motorcycle panniers the bag with the souvenir plaques he'd bought in Durban. As he approached the front door, he wondered which version of Ann he would meet – the bubbly young woman he'd fallen for at university or the dissatisfied wife she'd gradually become.

The door swung open. Filling the doorway was the bespectacled Dot Reynolds, arms already open for a hug, and Beth, close behind her. The women were giggling and exchanging smiles like the best of friends. They were both around five feet in height, but his mother was the heavier set.

"I'd know the sound of that motorbike anywhere," Dot said.

"The thing terrifies me," Beth said.

"Let me just take off my dirty boots," Paul said as Dot tried to usher him into the large hallway that he'd admired since the first time he'd come here with Ann.

"Please hold this, Mom," he said, reaching out to pass the bag containing the souvenirs.

"Have you lost weight, Paul?" Beth asked after he had divested himself of the mud-spattered boots and stepped inside in his socks.

"Maybe a little." Paul kissed Dot on the cheek before hugging his mother. As he and Beth ended their embrace, Paul registered that her expression belied the cheerfulness she'd attempted to project.

"You must be thoroughly exhausted, dear," Dot said, leading the way past the oak staircase towards the rear sitting room. "Bernard can get us all a nice celebratory glass of—" she started to say. "*Where* is that man? Bernard!" Patting Paul on the arm, she said, "Excuse me a moment, dear. I'll just go and find him. No doubt he'll have his nose in his crossword puzzle."

After Dot had left them, Paul said to his mother, "Where's Ann?"

Beth hesitated before answering. With her free hand she took hold of his. "She's not here, Paul."

"Where's she gone, Mom? Our car's outside."

Before Beth could reply, Dot returned, accompanied by Bernard. Dot began plumping the cushions that festooned the sofa. "Let's all sit down and have a nice chat," she said.

"Right then. Sherry all round, is it?" Bernard said, rubbing his hands together.

Stunned by Beth's comment, it took several seconds for him to register Bernard's invitation. "Yes, a small sherry would be great. Thank you."

"Good egg," Bernard said, moving to the drinks cabinet. "And you, Beth?"

When Beth didn't respond, Paul gently squeezed her hand. "Mom, sherry?"

Beth took her hand away from his. Her lower lip was trembling as she took a tissue from her cardigan pocket. Paul eased the bag with the souvenirs from her other hand.

"Oh dear, it's going to be like that is it?" Bernard said, seeing Beth dabbing tears away. "I'll pour one for you anyway."

"Thank you, Bernard," Beth said weakly.

Dot, witnessing the exchange, fell back on to the sofa and began sobbing into the pillow she was holding. "I'm so, so, so, so sorry, Paul."

Chapter 35

Paul pushed open the freshly painted but now tightly fitting door to Stovepipe Books. The walls of the bookshop were lined with crammed bookcases It was an independent bookshop in a side street that was a few minutes' walk from the cathedral in the heart of Norwich. The humid warmth of the crowded interior prompted him to unzip his leather jacket.

Although his arrival had been announced by the bell attached to the top of the door, no one turned to look at him. The motorcycle helmet, which he'd carried since parking the Triumph in a kerbside bay, was a bulky impediment as he manoeuvred farther into the shop.

He guessed there were at least seventy people present, impressive for 6.45 p.m. on a workday. This was the time of day when cities have a lull before the evening crowds converge on the cinemas, theatres, pubs and restaurants. Everyone seemed to be looking expectantly towards a space at the end of the room that was occupied only by a chair and a small table. On the table stood three piles of what appeared to be the same slim book.

Paul noticed that some of the attendees were sipping from plastic beakers. He was looking around for the source of the complimentary drinks when the tapping of a gavel stilled the room.

A tall, grey-haired man in a brown corduroy jacket and with a yellow cravat tucked inside the spread collar of his shirt was standing beside the table now. After setting down the gavel, this middle-aged man said, "I see a lot of familiar faces. Thank you everyone for coming to this special literary event. For those who don't know me, my name is Lester Holleyman. As the owner of Stovepipe Books, it is my pleasure to introduce one of the finest young poets of his generation – Norwich's own Terence Merton. Terence will be reading from his latest and may I venture that it is a most timely anthology, *The Absent Soul of Mammon*."

The audience cheered and clapped as Holleyman looked to his right, presumably towards the waiting speaker, whom Paul still couldn't see. Holleyman then, as if through an afterthought, picked up a book from the top of the nearest of the three piles on the table. Holding up the hardcover book, he announced, "Terence will sign copies after his reading. Don't be shy to come forward and purchase a copy."

The crowd cheered again, not at the aloft book but at the advance of Terence Merton. Merton and Holleyman shook hands quickly, and the latter retreated to the side of the shop.

Paul recognised Merton from Bernard's description: about six feet tall; broad shoulders but a slovenly posture; long brown hair covering his ears and the back of his neck; and oval wire-framed spectacles that accentuated his blue eyes. "All in all, he's a scruffy blighter," was Bernard's summary. "If he'd been under my command, he'd have been in the glass house until he shaped up. I don't know what my daughter is thinking."

Merton was wearing a crisp turquoise polo shirt that had regular creases suggesting the garment had only recently been removed from its packaging. In contrast, his trousers were old khakis, the leg bottoms of which he'd tucked into his black, calf-length, laced boots.

Looking around for Ann, Paul heard Merton loudly say, "Coloured Jackets." The poet had located a poem about a third of the way into the anthology he was here to promote. He was going to begin his readings without any small talk.

"Yellow and red stripes, blue and white stripes;

"Screaming traders in the pit calling out their bids;

"Sell! Buy! Sell! Buy!

"The flailing arms of those coloured jackets blurring in the light of the market arena;

"Modern gladiators fighting for Mammon."

Okay, Paul thought, allowing his mind to drift back to his purpose. *I can't listen to this pretentious drivel. Is she here?* He looked again at the side from which the speaker had emerged. The combed-back hair of Holleyman was all he could make out above the heads of the enthralled crowd. Ann was not tall enough for him to see, even if she was standing there.

"More juice for you, Miss?" a woman said.

Paul looked round, surprised, and surprised that he was surprised to see her. Ann, dressed in a very short summer frock he hadn't seen her wear before, was easing her way through the crowd and refilling people's beakers from a bottle of apple juice. He reached out his hand to touch her shoulder.

“Juice for you, si—” Shocked at seeing Paul, Ann involuntarily let go of the glass bottle; it shattered on the floor with a loud retort and the juice splashed in all directions. Everyone turned to look at them. The closest began frantically wiping their clothes. In his own world, Merton, eyes still locked on the page, kept chiding Mammon, but few were listening to him now.

***

Having been shepherded out from the bookshop by its irritated owner Paul and Ann stood facing each other on the pavement. It was still light, but also chilly in the shadow of the shop.

“Why did you come here?” Ann said, indignantly.

“*Why did I come?* Who is he to you, Ann?”

She folded her arms against the cold. Her expression seemed to be one of confusion, more than it was of guilt or humiliation.

“Aren’t you going to say anything?” Paul pressed.

“He’s a poet!” she exclaimed.

“That’s a matter of opinion,” Paul responded bitterly.

“He sees me! He’s always understood me. Ever since school.”

“School? I see you too.”

“You don’t.”

The bookshop door jerked open and out came a quartet of disgruntled poetry-reading attendees. “You ruined my new slacks,” one of the two men in the group said to Ann as they headed towards the turning to the cathedral.

“I’m sorry,” she said despondently, but they had no more time for her than they evidently had for the poet.

“Put this on,” Paul said, taking off his leather jacket.

She pushed his arm away. “I don’t want it.”

“Perhaps I don’t show it enough, Ann, but you’re always in my thoughts,” Paul said, persevering. “You’re cold, aren’t you?”

She relented and allowed him to place the coat round her shoulders. “It’s heavy,” she said.

Movements caught Paul’s peripheral vision. Turning, he could see through the glass pane in the bookshop door that more members of the audience were about to come out. Resisting the temptation to make another jibe at Merton’s expense, he said, “Can we go somewhere, find a quiet pub where we can talk?"

Ann was hesitant in responding. The rubbing sound of the door being pulled opened once again, accompanied by its bell tinkling, seemed to panic her into saying, "Okay."

"Is there a pub that you prefer? This is your city."

"I don't care."

"Let's try that place then." Paul pointed towards a white-walled public house at the end of the road.

"That's the Queens Head," Ann said, as if to confirm her familiarity with the ancient city.

They crossed the road and walked slowly westwards towards the hostelry, whose old walls had bowed. Paul wanted to put his arm round her waist, to claim her, to comfort her, but feared that she would flee back to the embrace of the bookshop. The last woman he'd held was someone else. He'd never been tempted to be unfaithful before then. Perhaps the ending of their marriage would be the best thing for both of them, but right now that prospect felt like a catastrophe to be regretted for the rest of his life.

***

Lying alone, exhausted, in his and Ann's bed – back at their home in Oxfordshire – during the early hours of Wednesday morning, he reasoned he must have died. A muntjac deer had leapt from the dark bushes into the beam of his headlight as he was tearing down a country lane. How had he managed to avoid the startled creature? Or had he hit it, which seemed more likely? That would have been fatal for both of them. Not everything in life is reversible. There are things that can't be undone.

His mother had pleaded with him not to ride back. They were alone in the hallway at Pendlefield Manor. Bernard and Dot had gone unhappily to bed.

"Wait until tomorrow, Paul. It's too late now, and you must be completely drained from the long journey here, and then going to Norwich."

"I'm expected in the office in the morning, Mom," he replied, understanding she was really thinking about the toll of his returning from Norwich without Ann. He leaned and kissed her cheek. "It's over for us, Mom. You don't need to buy a house here. Keep your maisonette for now, but leave it on the market for a while, just in case..."

"It's over... Your marriage? Don't be silly. You must fight for her!"

"That would be the worst thing I could do," he said, staring absently over his mother's shoulder at the featureless salmon-coloured carpet. Focussing again, finding Beth's gaze, he continued, "I'm compromised by the work I told you about. There's things I have to do that might lead to a way of surviving, but I won't take Ann on that journey. She'll be happier and safer without me."

"Go to my friends in Durban. They'll look after *both* of you."

Paul hugged Beth. "I can't ask her to live as a fugitive in South Africa. Anyway, your friends would have to be multimillionaires with a fortress and a private army to be able to protect us."

It was Beth's turn to tighten their hug. Her voice was breaking as she said, "I know, like your father, you'll always do the right thing."

Do the right thing...

Those four words had replayed in his mind during the motorcycle ride back from Suffolk to Wantage. Those four words, and the image of Ann sitting opposite him in a warm wooden-beamed alcove at the Queens Head. She had a glass of white wine, which she barely touched, and he had a soft drink. Ann had taken off his leather jacket, and it was hanging from the back of his chair.

"You've done something to your hair," he said.

"I've had it lightened."

"It suits you."

"I've worn it like this *before*."

After reflecting he said, humbled, "Of course. I forgot. That was a couple of years ago, wasn't it?"

She shook her head. "You don't notice me, Paul."

"But the poet does?"

Instead of answering, she sipped her wine for the first and only time.

"Have you been in here before?" he asked, looking about them. It was very much a "locals" drinking hole. Loud, good-humoured teasing could be heard coming from the young men playing darts in the main bar area.

"You mean with Terry?" she said.

"No, I meant with anyone."

"If you don't want to ask me about him, what do you want to talk about?"

"Okay. Fine. Let's talk about Terry. You've known him from school, you said?"

She nodded. "We used to go out."

"He was your boyfriend?"

She nodded again.

"Is this the way we're going to do this? I ask you 'yes' and 'no' questions, as if we're in a game show?"

"You don't have to do anything."

Paul took a sip of his iced drink and waited for his composure to return. Eventually, he asked, "So, how did the two of you meet up again?"

"That was *your* doing. You told me I should go to my parents'."

"Yes, to make things easier for you while I was away, and so you could start house-hunting." His response sounded distant to him, as if it belonged to someone who'd relinquished his life. He took a couple of deep breaths to ground himself. "According to your mother, Terence Merton no longer lives around here, so I'm none the wiser, Ann."

"But his parents still live near Mum and Dad. Terry lives in Durham. That's where he studied English at university. He has settled there. He's here as part of his publicity tour."

Paul decided not to ask more questions about how his wife had come to be with the poet. He preferred simple inferences. That way would be less painful than hearing a full account of love lost and re-found.

"Durham's a long way from here. It's *very hilly* there, Ann."

"What's that supposed to mean?"

"Just an observation, to bear in mind."

"You can keep your observations."

At least he's better than Maycross, Paul thought. "I mean, is it serious?"

"I feel as if I'm alive around Terry. I like helping him – like tonight."

"Until I burst in and ruined everything!"

"I suppose Mum and Dad told you how to find me."

Paul nodded. "When is Terry... When is he leaving?" He'd nearly said *Terry the Poet*, but that would have sent her running.

"At the end of the week. He's giving readings at bookshops

throughout Norfolk and Suffolk."

"Bernard said you're staying at his hotel."

His saying that seemed to make her uncomfortable, which is what he'd wanted. She cleared her throat. "Yes."

Paul noticed Ann's eyes had become tear-filled. His had too. The resentment he was feeling, he reminded himself, was hypocritical; he'd lost any right to judge her. "Is your wine all right?"

"It's fine."

He wanted to ask how much poets earn. He wanted her to be safe. That hadn't changed. "Where will he be going to, when he leaves Norwich?"

"It's a *substantial* tour," she said, emphasising the word substantial. Using a forefinger, she moved a drinks coaster back and forth on the table. "If you really want to know, the next venue will be in Cambridge, then to London, Oxford, Reading, Bristol, Exeter, Swansea, Stratford-upon-Avon, York, and finally back to Durham."

Paul nodded as he digested the detailed reply. He wondered if she would be accompanying Merton to all those places that she'd so diligently remembered. Another question that was best not voiced. The answers were not his business any more.

He walked her back to the bookshop. The reading from *The Absent Soul of Mammon* was still underway. As the door closed behind Ann, a notion occurred to Paul, one that had he said out loud earlier would have been too much to take on any given night. Had they "settled", fallen into marriage? Thinking back to the excitement of the wedding, perhaps the taking of that step was too convenient and comforting, rather than predestined or against the odds. Paul watched Ann being welcomed by Lester Holleyman. Then the tall man looked past Ann and stared in Paul's direction as if sensing his disruptive presence outside in the darkness.

Paul turned away and began walking eastwards, towards where he'd left his motorcycle. "I feel as if I'm alive around Terry," Ann had said. Focussing on protecting and providing for his young wife had had the effect of smothering her ambition. It was painful to acknowledge that he'd committed such an unthinkable burial.

Chapter 36

It felt unreal to be sitting at his desk, if only momentarily. It was midmorning on Wednesday. Paul had come to the office to photocopy the status report he'd prepared for Maycross and to collect a pool car for the drive to the Tobe Institute. He'd requested the meeting via Tom's cryptically worded fax to Head Office last Thursday, following the planning session with Max at the docks.

Absently taking in the open-plan surroundings, he registered that the oily imprint of the pigeon was gone; the windows had been cleaned in his absence. Other things had happened too, he noted as he flicked through the August edition of the staff newsletter.

Concern about the spreading of protests by the anti-Cruise missile movement had eased. An editorial article conveyed the appreciation of the Head of Site Administration for the cooperation of the staff during the "recent period of heightened risk to the site." Meanwhile in West Germany, the campaign against the nuclear power industry had intensified. A grainy, black-and-white photograph on page 3 showed hundreds of placard-waving people blockading the entrance to a nuclear power station. A second photograph showed a close up of two of the people who'd addressed the protestors. Paul thought he recognised one of these faces. His guess was confirmed by the description accompanying the photograph: "Stewart Burnham, the new leader of Radiation Watch, joined local campaign organizer Eckhart Müller on the improvised stage."

The photograph was not in colour, but the suntanned and broad-chested Englishman still made the pallid, shabbily dressed German beside him look like someone who'd spent the last six months eating rice cakes in a cave. The article went on to comment upon the recent claims of fund-raising success made by Radiation Watch – "... claims consistent with the global profile of this radical anti-nuclear organization that is prepared to tests the limits of the law on both land and sea."

Paul closed and folded the newsletter. He slipped it into the side pocket of his suit jacket for finishing later. Because of his recent promotion, he no longer needed someone senior to him to countersign his car-request form. Nonetheless, before departing, out of courtesy he stopped by Gooch's office.

"Hello, stranger," the department secretary, Allison, said, looking up from her typewriter. Her desk was in the outer office that surrounded Gooch's. She was about Paul's age, very slim with short, spiked blonde hair. A tiny pit at the side of her nose suggested that at one time she'd worn a jewellery stud. "If you want Fabian, he's not in. He phoned this morning to say he's feeling unwell."

"Okay. It wasn't anything important."

"I can't believe that," she said, smiling. "You're quite the man of mystery around here now."

"How do you mean?"

Allison huffed before attempting to respond. "Since Professor Sykes's death, everything's been... I don't know."

If there was one person Paul didn't want reminding of before meeting Maycross again, it was Benedict Sykes. He was also uncertain how to react as he hadn't been officially informed about the man's death; until now, he'd only had Shannon's frightening account.

His pensive expression prompted Allison to exclaim, "Didn't you know? I assumed you would have heard. He was your new boss, wasn't he?"

"That's okay. Thank you for telling me."

"You sure? Fabian didn't take the news well, if you ask me. He and the prof. must have known each other for a long time. They were about the same age, I mean." Allison began sharpening a pencil into the wastepaper basket by her desk. "Perhaps Fabian's human after all," she said, turning the pencil in the unicorn-shaped sharpener. "He was even moodier than usual last week."

Office gossip was something that Paul missed, and he had always enjoyed Allison's take on things. She was, in his view, one of those non-career minded people whose effectiveness made them indispensable, no matter how much irreverence they displayed.

"Did Fabian look as though he was coming down with something yesterday?" he asked, his curiosity provoked.

Allison had put down the sharpener and was testing the pencil tip on a scrap of paper. She stopped and looked up, gazing absently, trying to recollect. "Coming down with something? Not that I noticed. This week, he actually seemed back to his *cheerful* self." She made wiggling two-finger quotation-mark gestures as she said the word cheerful. "Yesterday morning, around eleven, he came out of his office with an urgent admin memo. *All* Fabian's memos have to be typed immediately. I mentioned that you'd phoned to ask me to reserve a car for tomorrow morning. He grunted, returned to his office and closed the door. He didn't come out again all day, as far as I can remember."

Paul frowned. After looking at his watch, he said, "I must go. I've a long drive ahead of me. Thanks for the news about Professor Sykes, Allison."

As he turned to leave, Allison said, "You're looking knackered, Paul. And you look thinner too. You've got to take care of yourself. No job's worth an early grave."

"I'll try to remember that," he said, smiling weakly. His mother had commented on his appearance too. Ann hadn't said anything. Perhaps she could be as guilty as he when it came to "not seeing".

Paul left with the suspicion that the chatty secretary was formulating a fresh line of gossip, one with him instead of Gooch at its centre this time. If only she knew even half of the truth...

***

Paul watched Maycross read the status report and its recommendations. The man from Whitehall sipped his heavily sugared coffee as he studied the seven-page document, which had been compiled and honed last Friday at the kitchen table in Tom's Durban flat. Tom's favourite Mahler symphony, wafting in from the lounge, had provided a sombre mood to the work.

Pages 5 and 6 were filled with diagrams of a "Waste Champion Series 7 Enclosed Receptacle" and a twenty feet long shipping container that was double-lined with ductile strips of one-fifth of an inch thick lead sheet. (The lead sheets were shown screwed to the back and front surfaces of large plywood panels.) Page 7 showed crude schematics of the bunker excavations at the Kop Mine.

After fifteen minutes had elapsed, Maycross pushed the document away, seemingly bored. "People don't understand that when a company's share price increases by two pounds, that doesn't mean anything." He was looking as if he was under more pressure than any human being could be expected to withstand. "It's the percentage change that counts."

"Quite so. The percentage," Paul mumbled, thrown by the change of subject. Then Paul remembered that when he had entered the surveillance-proof chamber, twenty minutes ago, Maycross was reading the Financial Times.

"You must explain that to my wife. She wants me to sell my shares and buy her a new car. I want to invest in an American company that has applied for a secondary listing in the UK. Gilmeed. Entertainments sector. A hot tip for you. A chance to get in on the ground floor for someone with available funds."

"That wouldn't be me then," Paul said, trying to recall when he'd heard the name of that company before.

Maycross leaned forward to retrieve the report. "Never mind, Paul. This is good work, at least. It makes a lot more sense than Tom's fax did. Well done."

"So I've your approval to go ahead?"

"God, yes. Of course. Tout suite!"

Paul withdrew the card for Continental Investment Audits from his wallet and absently tapped its edge on the table. "I need to make three or four telephone calls to get the ball rolling."

"I have the use of an office here. You can use its telephone," Maycross said. "But that business card reminds me that our friend from the other side of the pond contacted me yesterday. He's looking into the whereabouts of Shannon Lennon. You must have been one of the last to see her."

"She checked out of her Johannesburg hotel on Monday morning, last week. She was using the name Sondra Lansing. I assumed she was back in America by now."

Maycross shook his head. "Blackwood's concerned, to put it mildly. You were supposed to be looking after her, Paul. I have a bad feeling about this."

"Tom wanted to invite her to the planning meeting with Max." Paul shrugged. "That wasn't possible. In fact, if she's really *missing*... that could delay things. In particular, I will need help to put together the shipping documents. Mr Blackwood will have to replace her quickly."

"So she hasn't seen this?" Maycross said, holding aloft Paul's report.

"No, as I said, Tom tried to get hold of her."

"But according to Blackwood, Colonel Evans gave her a telephone number to reach you in Durban. You should have consulted with her then."

"I wasn't at the docks the day she phoned there, which was last Wednesday. She did leave a number for me to contact her, which Max gave to me the next day, at the end of our session. I tried to call her that evening. The line was dead, as if disconnected or non-existent. I wondered if Max's assistant had made a mistake when she wrote the number down." Paul's throat had tightened as he'd lied. He simply hadn't considered that Blackwood might consult the colonel about Shannon's movements.

Maycross let the report drop to the table as if he was suddenly appalled by it. "That means Blackwood doesn't know about these recommendations either."

"Now I have your approval, I can inform him."

Maycross put his elbows on the table and rested his forehead on his fingertips. "I really don't like this. You are making it sound as though I've delayed things."

"You couldn't have done more, Patrick. Tom's fax was necessarily brief, so that its contents looked to be compatible with his legend as a furniture importer. In fact, he didn't have the full details when he sent the fax because Max and I were still working them out. Arranging my flight and this meeting were the essential actions for you, and here we are. Neither of us are responsible for Shannon."

"Make sure Blackwood knows all of that." Maycross straightened up; he put his palms down flat against the table top. With a relieved grin, he said, "Tom's legend! Putting aside his eccentricities, he must be a good teacher. You've mastered the jargon already. Perhaps your talents were wasted in the 'glow team'."

Maycross's expression became stern once more as something else occurred to him. "We must get the story about Lennon absolutely straight before we talk to Vernon." He stood up and began pacing back and forth. "According to you, she phoned the port in Durban on Wednesday, having first contacted Colonel Evans. That was two days *after* she had checked out of her hotel." He ceased pacing and wheeled round to look at Paul. "Where did she go in the meantime? I'll remind you once again that *you* were supposed to be looking after her," he bellowed.

"Shannon didn't want me to look after her. She had at least one meeting with Evans without me, in fact. She seems to know things about the Kop Mine that neither Tom nor I know."

"What things?"

"Tom sent a message to you, you will recall, querying the disparity between the number of containers we're sending and the number expected at the mine."

"Oh, I see," Maycross said, his face flushed with either anger or embarrassment, or perhaps with fear. He fell quiet for a moment, seemingly lost in further thoughts concerning the "Lennon story". He took his fountain pen from his suit breast pocket and returned to the table. "What was the telephone number you tried to call?" he asked, holding his pen at the ready for jotting the number down on the back of Paul's report.

Paul took his wallet from his jacket inside pocket and fumbled with the compartments as if searching for something. The number was there, on the scrap of paper Max had passed to him, but he didn't want Maycross to know. Maycross would tell Blackwood, who would try to trace the number's address. "I must have left it at Tom's place."

"Is that where you made the call from?" Maycross asked, raising his pen.

"No. I called from the lobby of a nearby hotel. I didn't want to use Tom's line. He said it's not secure."

Maycross screwed the cap back on his pen. "*Tell* me you didn't leave a sensitive contact number on a shelf next to a public telephone."

Paul stared at the table, grasping for a decisive lie. "No, no, I recall now. I didn't want to risk being questioned at the airport check-in desk. My notes, everything I couldn't explain carrying as a tourist, I destroyed. Including phone numbers. Only my handwritten report was left, taped to my back under my shirt, the way Tom suggested."

Maycross took the cap off his pen and wrote down "SL's number was destroyed". He put down the pen and resumed pacing back and forth. "You have to remember that number, Avery. Otherwise, I wouldn't want to be in your shoes."

"Max told me it was a Pretoria dialling code. Beyond that... it's a blur, I'm afraid," Paul said, suspecting Maycross's concern was really for himself. He imagined this was the way Maycross had looked when

Shannon informed him that Vernon had taken over the South Africa operation.

Maycross returned to the table, picked up his fountain pen again and scribbled down the word Pretoria. "What was the name of the hotel that you called from?"

"The James."

"The date and time?"

"Last Thursday, as I said. That would have been, er... the eleventh of August. At around eight forty-five in the evening."

Having written these details, Maycross sat down and slumped back in the chair. The block of scrawled text in front of him was better than having nothing to report to his new – although unofficial – boss.

Maycross re-read Paul's report, this time thoroughly. He asked technical questions about the effectiveness of the lead shielding in the shipping containers and probed the reasons for the selection of Sollers Head as the shipment port.

He and Paul then argued about the sequence of the telephone calls to be made. Maycross wanted to call Blackwood first, but Paul maintained that this would lead to disappointment if Hank Barnaby and Art Richards subsequently said that they couldn't meet the proposed shipping schedule.

"Then they'll be to blame, not us!" Maycross protested. Blame and the avoiding of it had become the focus in Maycross's world; the appearance of progress had slipped in his order of priorities.

"We need them, Patrick. They're essential. If they can identify genuine issues, we must know what those are before we raise Mr Blackwood's expectations," Paul persisted.

This immersion in details was a relief to Paul. It was preferable to the shadow of the "bigger picture". He knew Maycross wasn't competent to critique the scientific particulars, but the tedium of repeating the explanations in increasingly basic terminology was a small price to pay if it were to keep threats at bay... Unfortunately, it didn't for long.

As the two walked to the Main House to make the telephone calls the Whitehall man said, "I still have a bad feeling about the Lennon business. Don't forget that your delightful wife and your mother remain under surveillance, Avery. If things go awry in any way affecting my career or investments, I will make you all suffer."

Perhaps it took the combination of Shannon's surname and the "investments" word to remind Paul of the moment he first heard the name Gilmeed. "It's a Nevada-based outfit with a casino in Vegas," Shannon had told him when he'd asked who would run the casino at the Altabrite site. A financial interest in Gilmeed was Blackwood's way of bribing Maycross.

Chapter 37

Paul had reached the M40 and was driving west in the direction of Oxford when the aftermath of the meeting at the Tobe Institute became too much. He pulled into the breakdown lane, got out of the car and vomited on the gravel by the metal crash barrier. Afterwards, he leaned back against the side of the car and wiped his mouth with his handkerchief. Maycross's threat was all he could think about: "If things go awry in any way affecting my career or investments, I will make you all suffer."

The calls to Hank Barnaby and Art Richards from what was more a telecommunications hub than it was an office were as positive as he could have hoped. Although initially Hank had sounded daunted by a four-week deadline for removing from his plant the radioactive waste that had burdened him for the last eight years. Sometimes getting what you desperately want after struggling for a long time can have that effect, Paul concluded. Art, the apparently incurious contractor, by contrast, was raring to go and delighted that the research he'd undertaken for Paul had been so helpful. He endorsed the decision to use Sollers Head Port. Paul told him to instruct his men to fit lead-lined plywood panels to all nine shipping containers, rather than wait for him to get there to inspect the first one.

But the subsequent telephone call, jointly made with Maycross, using speaker-phone on a scrambled line, to Vernon Blackwood had been alarming, perhaps less for the content than for the fact of it. As for Hank, proximity overcame anticipation. In Paul's case, it was the dissolving of the bravado with which he'd handled Shannon's warning about this eventuality that undid him. But that night in the small bar at the Banville Plaza, when Paul had countered her warning with, "He needs me in one piece. I wouldn't be able to deal with officials if I'm covered in cigar burns and bruises," his mind had just become set against returning to New Jersey. His plan had reversed since Benedict's murder. Suddenly hearing the slayer's voice again, his amplified breathing, transmitted from some corner of hell... It had felt as though concrete was hardening in Paul's arteries.

Maycross's pleasantries were dismissed by Blackwood's curt "Cut to the chase". The "Lennon story" was indeed Blackwood's priority. "I'm recording this call. I'll be able to determine whether either of you are lying." Blackwood remained quiet until Paul had finished his selective account of Shannon's movements in Johannesburg.

"I want that goddamn number, one way or another. We have a drug that will empty your mind as easily as squeezing a wet sponge."

Paul assumed that Blackwood's drugs would be more powerful than Sundial's, and induce worse, perhaps permanent, after-effects. The expression on Maycross's face suggested that the Whitehall man was imagining himself in Paul's position one day.

"I want you here, son, by the end of the week. No excuses."

At that point, Paul offered to outline the shipment plan that he and Max had put together, but clues concerning Shannon's whereabouts were all Blackwood would countenance listening to. No gratitude was expressed for the progress they were making.

"Transmit the details through the usual channel. We'll discuss it when you get here."

"I'll have the report sent to you immediately, Vernon," Maycross interjected.

"Here, by the end of the week, son," Blackwood repeated, as if only he and Paul were participating in the call. Then there was a click, followed by a soft hum.

***

Back in his car, Paul turned off the M40 at the elevated junction for High Wycombe, instead of proceeding to his intended turnoff for the taking of country lanes all the way back to Wantage. He drove around the large roundabout that spanned both carriageways and took the exit back on to the motorway, now heading eastwards.

It was rush hour, but most of the traffic was heading west, away from London and towards Oxford. He was finally taking an irreversible action. It had been Maycross's resurrected threat against his wife and mother rather than the thought of being interrogated by Blackwood that, he convinced himself, had been the decisive factor. As for an avalanche, what would follow would be unstoppable. However, unlike the chaotic paths taken by falling rocks, his path during the coming hours would receive meticulous steering. Maycross, anxious to comply with Blackwood, had insisted that Paul fly to New York on Friday morning – if not sooner.

Paul left the motorway about twenty minutes later at the Hillingdon junction and headed north towards Ickenham. He was familiar with these outer-London roads because of the numerous trips he'd made over the years to visit his mother. He had taken Beth for Sunday lunches at some of the pubs he would soon pass.

He drove through Ickenham and then past West Ruislip Underground Station as he headed towards Ruislip Manor. The traffic slowed and bunched at junction pinch points but these delays gave him time to relax. Paul began to feel calmer than he knew he ought to feel. He just had to keep breathing and one by one complete the tasks that would upend Maycross's chess game.

At the junction with Ruislip Manor's high street, Victoria Road, he turned right and descended the hill. Paul passed under the grey railway bridge that carried trains to and from the Underground Station. Cars were parked along both sides of the shop-lined street, leaving just enough space for traffic to flow in each direction.

He took the first turning on the right and immediately began looking for the two landmarks that Shannon had described to him during the telephone call that he'd made from the lobby of The James– a synagogue on the left and a park entrance on the right.

Chapter 38

The landmarks were directly opposite each other, just as Shannon had described. On the left side of the road was the single-storey, white synagogue with its flat roof and surrounding low brick wall. On the other side of the road was the asphalted entrance to a park. Inside the park, brightly painted swings, climbing frames and roundabouts were being enjoyed by screaming toddlers, their watchful mothers in attendance.

In search of a parking space, Paul turned left into the first street running parallel to the high street. Most of the houses had driveways, so the residents parked their cars off the road. Having parked by the kerb next to the side of the synagogue, he got out and, carrying his briefcase, walked back towards the park entrance.

"When are you flying back to England?" Shannon had asked.

"Monday, I think," he'd replied, not yet having the airline-booking confirmation from Head Office.

"Then, you have until..." Shannon had gone quiet for a moment, as if listening to someone in the room with her. "They'll give you six days upon your return to make your decision. You have until... you will have until 8.00 p.m. on Sunday the twenty-second. If you don't appear before then, they'll take your decision as no."

"They'll be waiting in the park until then? Day after day, waiting just for me."

"They will be waiting for *us*."

... *for us.* After last night's scene with Ann, the "us" word had seemingly been scratched out of existence.

Earlier in the telephone call, Shannon had, her voice choking with emotion, informed Paul that the Israeli agents had explained that her sanctuary in Israel would depend upon Paul Avery going too. "They have a shortage of nuclear scientists with your international background." Initially, for a year or two, he could teach, she told him. Later, he would be expected to help with the country's nuclear weapon programmes. "It's you they want, much more than they want me. They said hiding me might give rise to more political trouble than I'm worth.

But if I can persuade you to go too, they promise to protect us. Otherwise, they'll cut me loose and alert the South African National Intelligence Service to my presence as an undeclared foreign agent. That will go bad for me quickly, Paul. Halliday will have me killed to protect himself and his government co-conspirators."

The contact instructions she'd subsequently laid out seemed more suited to a TV prank than international espionage. Having reached the end of the path, with the children's play apparatus to his right, he found himself entering the body of the park. The whole park was enclosed by single rows of tall trees. To his left was a playing field ringed by an asphalt footpath. At the far end of the field was a second, a smaller, gated access point to the park. He was supposed to leave that way. "Find the third bench from the main park entrance," Shannon had said.

It was nearly 6.00 p.m. The briefcase and business suit made him feel out of place as he headed towards the oval footpath. But who would see him, apart from a distant dog walker and the nearby young mothers watching over their small children?

Having sat down on the appointed bench, which faced on to the centre of the field, he leaned back. Despite Shannon's insistence, it seemed unlikely that a protracted surveillance exercise would be conducted in the hope of his accepting the terms of the deal. Nonetheless, if no one were to approach him now, he would come back tomorrow.

After a few minutes, the dog walker, a small, elderly woman with a black Scottish terrier on a lead, passed slowly in front of him from right to left. The woman's grey coat looked as though it would be too warm for the time of year. Only her small dog looked round, its erect pointed ears listening for the slightest sound.

Paul watched them walking away and then leave the park through the gate at the end. Another dog walker, a man wearing a denim jacket, blue jeans, black beret and sunglasses, had waited for the woman and her dog to come out before he entered with his excited fox terrier. Unlike the woman, the stocky newcomer took the fork for a counter-clockwise circuit of the field. When he reached Paul, it would be from the left.

The man stopped about thirty feet away, bent over and disconnected the lead from his pet's collar. "Fetch, Ralph," he shouted as he threw a yellow tennis ball. The black and white terrier took off across the field, seemingly flying more than running.

Ralph quickly returned and dropped the ball at its owner's feet. Sideways jumping in tight circles, the smiling terrier was anticipating another throw. However, the man just picked up the ball and recommenced walking. Ralph pranced by his side, eager for further play.

Approaching Paul, the dog walker said, "Have you any idea who lived nearby here, sir?"

Paul was supposed to reply "You will need to give me a clue", but instead he said, "Hello, Sundial." That was a name he had neither expected nor wanted to ever say again.

The man smiled and removed his sunglasses and beret before sitting down beside Paul. He held up the tennis ball. "Here, Doctor."

Paul threw the ball as far as he could. Ralph charged after it.

"It was the Krogers. Helen and Peter. Not their real names of course. The famous people who lived nearby."

"Soviet spies, weren't they?"

"Yes. American communists. Arrested in 1961 for their part in providing the Soviet Union with classified naval research documents. Sentenced to twenty years in prison, but released in 1969 as part of a prisoner exchange."

Ralph had returned with the ball and was nuzzling Paul's knee. Paul obliged, sending the terrier chasing after the ball again.

"That was all a long time ago," Paul said.

"And yet here we are. Different teams but also players in the great game. Your defection... Is that not why you have come?"

"I'm trying not to think of it that way," Paul said. "More as friends helping each other."

"You've certainly made a new friend here, Doctor," Sundial said, leaning forward to clip the lead back on to the collar of the panting Ralph. He patted the dog and eased him away from Paul.

"How is Sondra?"

"You mean Shannon Lennon. I hoped we were past such evasions."

"How is she?"

"Living quite well at our expense in that safe house you were taken to. She will be thrilled when I report back this evening. Within the next twenty-four hours, she'll be put on a plane to Tel Aviv."

Paul explained the difficult situation he faced. If he was to evade

Blackwood, he had to leave for Israel from London Heathrow on Friday morning. His flight to New York – not on Concorde this time – had been booked by Maycross for then. If the anxious Maycross had had his way, Paul would have been flying to America tomorrow. "I have family matters to attend to, Patrick. If you want me to function effectively, be reasonable," Paul had successfully pleaded.

Sundial took something dark in colour and rectangular from his jacket pocket and discretely handed it to Paul. "Friday is no problem. Here is your passport. It is an Israeli one under the name Michael Benton. You'll be given another in Israel after you've changed your appearance."

Paul was going to open the fake passport to inspect it when Sundial raised his hand to deter him. "This is a public place. The upper floors of some the houses opposite can see us through the trees."

Paul put the passport in his jacket inside pocket. "How will I get the ticket for the flight?"

"Go to the El Al reservations desk. It will be there."

"Thank you."

"Welcome to Israel, Michael."

Sundial put his beret back on and was about to stand up when Paul said, "There's something else. My mother and my wife – one of them might need to join me soon."

Paul told Sundial about Maycross's threat. "Once I fail to board the New York flight, he will have them detained and questioned about my whereabouts. They'll be threatened with charges alleging they're accomplices to my involvement in bogus communist plots. He will do that to put pressure on me to return from wherever I've gone, with the intention of forcing me to carry on with his mad scheme."

"And what do these women actually know?"

"Ann, my wife, doesn't know anything about my recent activities. I lied to her. My mother knows enough about the South Africa end of things – the planned radioactive waste burial at an old disused mine. She doesn't know about your helping me to escape."

"You said only one of them might need to join you."

"Ann won't be prepared to leave the country, certainly not for my sake. She seems to be very involved with someone else."

"I see."

"Is there anything your compatriots could do? I mean blackmail

Maycross to leave my family alone? I've told you what he's up to."

Sundial hesitated, seemingly unsure how to respond.

Paul knew what he was asking would require the Israelis to expose their involvement. In harbouring Shannon and Paul, they would already be taking a calculated risk.

"I'll see what can be done. In the meantime, we will watch these women," Sundial said.

"I appreciate that. By the way Maycross takes his orders from someone named Auberon Morrison. Your knowing that is likely to frighten Maycross."

Sundial wrote down Morrison's name and the addresses and telephone numbers for Beth Avery and for Ann's parents. "Before I leave, is there *anything* else you want to tell me?"

Paul was about to shake his head when his curiosity returned. "How many times have you and Ralph walked round this park?"

Sundial considered the question for several seconds and then laughed. "You believe that we have been walking around and around for days. That would have been extremely conspicuous, don't you think?" Sundial patted Paul's arm. "No, we have been watching the main entrance, passing our time in comfort. I knew that you would come."

Chapter 39

Paul waited until a few minutes had passed after Sundial left with the well-behaved fox terrier. Sundial had departed by the main park entrance, but Paul, as instructed, took the side entrance, which brought him out at the end of a cul-de-sac lined with bungalows. To his immediate left was a narrow alley that took him back to the road fronting the park. Within four minutes he was back in his car. The magnitude of what he'd just done left his heart pounding. This surprised him as he'd believed he'd come to terms with the decision two hours ago, when he'd turned his car round on the M40 near High Wycombe. Combing his fingers through his short hair, trying to reconnect with himself, he contemplated the actions that still lay ahead of him. It was only through visualising his being with Shannon soon that he could make sense of his life.

Paul consulted the map book he'd brought with him to decide the best route home. The M4 route would be shorter in distance, but this would require him to first head towards the surroundings of Heathrow Airport and risk encountering heavy traffic. No, he would retrace his journey here and head back to the M40.

As he drove he thought about how Maycross had been at today's meeting – initially relaxed, then erratic and finally panicky. That was the effect Blackwood probably had on most people. Following their call to Blackwood, Maycross insisted that he and Paul meet early on Friday morning, just hours before the departure of the hastily booked flight for Paul's return to America.

"Nothing can be overlooked. We'll go through the shipment plan one more time. And perhaps you'll have remembered that blasted telephone number by then." The latter notion had brought a wistful look to Maycross's face. It would be good news with which to ingratiate himself with Vernon. "And, of course, I still need all your receipts from South Africa. I've complained to Auberon about the tedious bean counters. Unfortunately he's got more pressing matters on his hands, deal-making in the aerospace sector. If you think you are under pressure, Avery, try being in his shoes. You don't speak Arabic, by any chance?"

Maycross had seemed almost apologetic when he raised the expenses matter. "Tom, Max and the colonel are booked as service contractors, but because you are a Government employee, the Treasury has to balance the itemised charges you incur."

Contemplation of the likely course of the Friday meeting with Maycross caused Paul to reproach himself for not having had the presence of mind to ask Sundial about the Pretoria telephone number that Shannon had used. Would it be traceable and, if so, would that link Shannon to her Israeli helpers? But he hadn't envisioned that the person meeting him at the park would be Sundial. This had thrown him – as they'd talked, his mind had kept drifting back to the hazy interrogation session in the room with yellow walls and bare floorboards.

It was hard to think of the interrogator Sundial as his saviour. But Paul had to trust that was the case. He still hadn't properly examined the fake passport, but *believed* it would be flawless. The prospect of living as a lecturer in nuclear physics would be enough of a mindbender to prevent him from sleeping tonight. He'd have to visualise a new silver card box with *Michael Benton* engraved on its lid and start filling it with answers to the backstory questions that using a false identity would raise.

Despite Sundial's seeming helpfulness – for which Paul and Shannon would have to repay in ways still unclear, and perhaps not even possible, over the coming years – there was still one sickening vulnerability: Maycross carrying out his threats against Ann and Beth.

Sundial had been less than convincing in his response to Paul's appeal for Maycross to be warned off from harassing Ann and Beth. Maybe Sundial *would* act to protect them, but the thought of leaving this matter in the hands of coldly calculating foreign intelligence agents made Paul perspire. Something had to be done to change the power balance. He had always sensed this would be necessary, but the time had finally come for vague thoughts to be crystallised into the worst single act he'd ever conceived.

When he parked on his driveway, Paul accepted that he was too tired to carry out what was required. Nonetheless he couldn't resist going into the darkening back garden. He looked down at the seven feet long, plastic-lined pond he'd installed during the late spring. There still weren't any fish in it, just tufts of rushes and a filigree of waterlilies to provide shelter and oxygen and, submerged below the still surface for the last three weeks, a lidded glass marmalade jar containing the stainless-steel canister he'd used at the Altabrite site. Asserting Diplomatic Privilege, he'd brought the sample of radioactive soil back from America in his briefcase, wrapped in folds of lead sheet. The canister was only half full as he'd given – in the bar at the Banville Plaza – the other half of its contents to Shannon.

***

Paul rose promptly on Thursday as if it was any other workday. Sitting at the kitchen table he considered how to extract the radioactive dial pigment from the meagre soil sample. Ideally, he needed to create a clear radium-rich solution, but the paint's constituents (radioactive radium sulphate blended with the light-emitting agent, zinc sulphide, which by now had lost much of its phosphoresce after decades of bombardment by alpha particles) were insoluble in water. Similarly, he didn't have a laboratory centrifuge to separate the fine white pigment crystals from the soil. All he could think of doing was repeatedly adding water, stirring, allowing the solids to settle and then decanting off whatever soluble organic matter was present in the soil. In this way he could minimise the impact upon the taste of Maycross's coffee. Fortunately, Maycross drank coffee that was strong and very sweet. The brownish colour of the final slurry would not be very different from that of the coffee. By the addition of dissolved sugar and instant coffee granules, the taste and appearance of the final soil and pigment mixture could be further masked.

Paul set to work in the only part of the garden that wasn't overlooked – between the conservatory and the side fence. Disposable gloves protected his hands from alpha particles. A collar around the small canister, fashioned from curved lead strips, provided a measure of protection from gamma rays during the post-rinse, settling periods. He collected the rinse water – in total, amounting to only a few table-spoonfuls – in the glass jar that had been employed to protect the canister while it was in the pond.

The washed slurry, mainly comprising gritty soil, left in the steel canister had a volume of about two-thirds of a table-spoon. With the probe of the radiation detector against the underneath of the canister, the instrument display indicated a gamma radiation dose level that the RSMSDA calibration tables equated to about seventy-five micrograms of the radioactive isotope radium-226. This quantity – many trillions of atoms – was sufficient for painting about two hundred and fifty to five hundred watch dials. Based upon historical accounts of radium paint formulations used for commercial (as opposed to military) applications, the soil residue in the canister contained about one gram of pigment material– just a smear – most of which was zinc sulphide.

If gamma rays had been the only form of radiation, the indicated dosage level would be insufficiently harmful, particularly as much of the slurry would pass through Maycross's digestive system within hours. But it *wasn't* the only radiation. The accompanying level of alpha radiation, now being contained by the steel walls of the canister, was high enough to be damaging to the mouth, oesophagus, lungs, stomach and gut. Within a couple of hours of consuming the pigment Maycross would receive a non-fatal dose sufficient to induce radiation sickness with associated nausea and lowering of his white blood cell count. He would go on to experience what Peter Wilson had endured. Would that be poetic justice? Paul wondered. If so, perhaps even Terence Merton would approve.

Paul had dismissed the simpler approach of administering the contents of the cyanide capsule – assuming the capsule was genuine, as Sundial had declared it to be. Cyanide would take effect quickly and would be fatal. Becoming a murderer was not necessary. Whereas by using the radioactive slurry, Maycross would become incapacitated gradually. Oesophageal burning would take place slowly. Maycross would then become sufficiently ill over the following hours to render him incapable of orchestrating the persecution of Ann and Beth. The Whitehall man's three-dimensional chess game would be interrupted for a long time.

To complete the poison, Paul added a table-spoonful of sweetened coffee, almost filling the canister. The resulting potion would have to be shaken, tipped into Maycross's drink and then stirred just before it was consumed, so that the toxic crystals didn't have time to completely settle out. This would not be straightforward to achieve. Also, the grittiness of the beverage would need an explanation. Distractions would be essential. The first step in devising these required a call to Directory Enquiries.

***

After lunch, Paul set about the most emotionally taxing part of his plan. Back at his kitchen table, he wrote and rewrote letters to Ann and Beth. He would post these in the morning, to ensure they would not be delivered until after his arrival in Tel Aviv.

The letters were vaguer than he would have liked because of his fear that they might be intercepted and read by people working for Maycross.

To Beth, he simply wrote:

I have gone away, Mom. I don't know what the future will bring, but I will be able to sleep again. I truly believe that we will all be safe because of the steps I have been forced to take.

All my Love
Paul

To Ann, he wrote:

Seeing you in Norwich with Terence Merton made things clear to me. I let you down by not recognising all of your needs and accept that it is too late for us. I have gone abroad to take up a new job.

After you have sold the house and settled the mortgage, you should have a few thousand pounds of profit to put towards a new beginning.

Someone recently asked me how a "science guy" ended up hitched to an "art lover" and collector of antique silver. I had never thought about us in those terms. I never questioned our marriage. I still don't. Whatever happens, I hope that you will have a wonderful life.

Try to think of me kindly,
Love,
Paul

After sealing and addressing the envelopes – Ann's letter was addressed to her parents' – Paul put them in his briefcase, where in the morning they would be joined by the canister of radioactive soil.

Paul placed the radiation detector, the glass marmalade jar, his helmet and his folded motorcycle leathers on the floor in the back of the pool car that was still on his driveway from last evening. It was already 3.00 p.m. when he reversed the car on to the road, but gruelling hours still stretched ahead of him.

He returned the car to the motor pool supervisor at his workplace, put the radiation detector on his desk, and retrieving his Triumph motorcycle from the employee parking lot. Within a few minutes he left the RSMSDA site for the last time, setting off for Stoke Poges in order to carry out the final preparations for tomorrow's escape. After riding for a mile, he stopped beside a farmer's field where the land drained into a brook. He trickled the small quantity of radioactive rinse water out of the glass jar on to the grass, leaving it to be slowly washed away by runoff rainwater from the field.

It was a time of goodbyes. As he got back on the motorcycle, he reflected on all the hours he had spent restoring the machine. It had never let him down. He would be returning home tonight by public transport, a slow and tedious journey that he knew would involve three or four changes of bus.

Chapter 40

Paul waved from his front door to the driver of the black Mercedes limousine that had moments ago pulled up at the kerb to take him to the Tobe Institute. In view of the hour, the uniformed driver had switched off the engine and left only the sidelights on. Despite it being just 4.15 a.m., Paul had been awake for the last ninety minutes. He'd showered and put on one of his navy-blue suits. Today was definitely one to look professional, as someone to be trusted completely.

After locking the front door, he walked down the driveway, carrying his briefcase and suitcase. This time he'd packed not for working under Blackwood's direction in New Jersey, nor for a new life he could barely begin to imagine. The suitcase was filled with old camping gear that for several months he'd been meaning to get rid of. Maycross would expect him to bring luggage.

"Good morning, sir," the alert driver said, getting out to assist Paul with the cases. He was the same man that had taken Paul to the airport to catch his Concorde flight a few weeks ago. Perhaps Maycross always asked for the same driver.

Paul sat in the front-passenger seat this time. In his hands were the letters to Ann and his mother. The opportunity to engage with small talk, even if it was only about the weather, would keep him from replaying in his mind what he was going to do in the cell-like chamber at the institute. He was going to disable his malevolent "controller", but his intention could not be sanitised by that use of language. No, he was going to poison Maycross. *Maycross*. It was personal.

"Do you know the way," Paul asked the driver.

"Yes, sir. I've been there before. We should make good time at this hour."

As they passed through the empty market square in Wantage, Paul asked the driver to stop by a pillar box. Once he'd posted his two letters, they continued towards Harwell. They joined the northbound carriageway of the A34, heading towards Oxford. Upon reaching the northern bypass they headed east to the still quiet M40 motorway. They came off the M40 near Beaconsfield. It was dawn as they passed through the open gates of the institute at just after 5.30 a.m. There was silence apart from the whinnying of the horse in the field opposite.

The chauffeur drove the limousine towards the rear of the site and stopped outside the Reception building. "Here we are, sir."

They both got out of the car and retrieved Paul's suitcase and briefcase.

"I haven't been given instructions to collect you, sir."

"My colleague will be taking me to the airport."

"Very good, sir. I hope that you have a good flight."

I do too, Paul thought as he watched the car move away. He regretted that he hadn't asked the driver his name. They'd spent most of the journey talking about the impressive engineering of the Thames flood barrier that had been operational since last year. The driver had taken his children to see it. Paul wondered if he would ever see it. Could he ever return to the UK?

The glass door to the Reception building was locked; the waiting area inside was in darkness. The meeting wasn't scheduled to begin for another thirty minutes, so Paul sat on his suitcase to wait for Maycross. It struck him that unless the receptionist came soon too, there would be no refreshments. They were supposed to finish by 8.00 a.m., in time for Maycross to drive through rush-hour traffic to Heathrow Airport. He'd lost touch with normality; hardly any sane employees worked the hours he'd been working. He'd become so lost in details, he missed the obvious. No coffee, no opportunity to poison Maycross.

A few minutes later, Maycross's E-Type Jaguar sped by, heading towards Visitors Parking. Paul thought he saw Maycross raise a hand in a desultory greeting. For a moment he almost forgot his loathing for the man. It would be a relief to abandon the plan, to not become a monster. But that would leave imperilled his mother and Ann. That, or return to Blackwood, luggage or no luggage. He had to go through with it... somehow.

The distant clunk of Maycross's car door closing had the effect of a starting pistol. Paul's jaw clenched as he stood up.

Maycross approached, looking characteristically dishevelled. He was holding the handle of his Gladstone-type bag with one hand and trying to lasso the lanyard attached to his visitor's pass over his head with the other. Arriving at the Reception building, Maycross did the last thing Paul wanted him to do: he smiled.

"No rest for us workers, Avery," Maycross said, infusing humility with pomposity.

There's the real you, Paul thought, regaining his resolve. "And there will be no coffee for the workers either," he said. "No one is in Reception yet."

"I'll see about that," Maycross said as he leaned to touch his pass against the sensor plate to release the electronic lock.

Maycross pushed open the unlocked door and went inside. Paul followed awkwardly, carrying his suitcase and briefcase as the self-closing door pressed against him.

"Turn the lights on," Maycross snapped as he advanced towards the unoccupied counter.

Paul lowered the suitcase to the floor and looked about in the darkness for the switch.

"There, there! To your right," Paul heard Maycross bark.

Paul pressed the switch. Fluorescent tubes flickered into life above their heads. The waiting area and the length of the corridor leading to the hall that housed the surveillance-proof chamber lit up.

Maycross put down his bag and reached over to lift the telephone up from its place behind the raised front of the counter. He picked up the receiver, pressed a button on the front of the telephone, waited for the connection to be made and then said in a monotone voice, "Customer code Vanquish. Coffee for two. Milk. Sugar. Biscuits. Immediately." After replacing the telephone, Maycross turned to Paul. "See how I look after you?" Then he picked up his bag and began walking along the corridor.

You don't know how much you've helped. With his heart pounding, Paul followed his prey. Just taking the briefcase, he left his suitcase of worthless things by the Reception counter.

Five minutes later the two of them were sitting opposite each other in the surveillance-proof chamber.

"The first order of business. That telephone number... Tell me that you have remembered it, Avery."

"As a matter of fact," Paul said, reaching into his jacket inside pocket, "it came to me during the drive here. I wrote it down."

Maycross's eyes widened with pleasure as he took the scribbled note from Paul. "That's a relief. More so for you than me, I dare say." After looking at the number, Maycross consulted his watch. "It'll be five past seven in South Africa. Let's see who answers."

"That's still early. Why don't we wait until we've had our coffee and have got my expenses out of the way?" Paul lifted his briefcase on to the meeting room table.

"Yes, not everyone is up at the crack of dawn. The coffee should be here any moment."

"Who's bringing it?"

"The Security Centre in the Main House has its own catering facilities to cover out-of-hours requests."

"You mean they have a kettle and two chipped mugs," Paul quipped.

Maycross laughed. "They need my generous patronage too much for that."

"I imagine they do," Paul responded, removing the set of South African receipts from his briefcase. He immediately closed the case again to keep the lead-wrapped canister concealed. Handing the receipts to Maycross, Paul said, "The largest sum relates to the settled invoice from the Hotel Willem in Johannesburg. I've also attached credit card receipts for two meals I had at The James in Durban and a number of cash-payment receipts for taxis and for other meals, such as those I had with Tom."

The longer it took to deal with this trivia, the greater the chance of Maycross losing his alertness. A jaded Maycross would be easier to fool with sleight of hand than a watchful one.

As Maycross perused the receipts, Paul opened his briefcase again to remove a packet of cookies. He tore open the brightly printed wrapper and slid out the contained plastic tray. Pushing the tray of stacked peanut cookies to the centre of the table, he said, "Unless you're allergic to peanuts, Patrick, help yourself."

Maycross peered at the offering, hesitantly.

"It was too early to have breakfast before I left home, and I'm not a great fan of airline food. These are a favourite of Ann's," Paul said, amiably. Ann rarely ate biscuits, and she detested peanuts. He'd come across and purchased the cookies at a small independent supermarket in

Stoke Poges yesterday, just before it closed for the day at 6.00 p.m.

Maycross reached out and using his long thumb and forefinger took one of the cookies. “Ann likes these?”

“They’re very hard to get apparently. Nearly always sold out.” Paul picked up a cookie and took a large bite, hoping to convey that these were a treat to be relished. The peanut pieces and the glaze holding them in place conferred a crunchy texture. The glaze was too sweet for his palate. Paul had to force himself to swallow.

After taking a cautious nibble, Maycross took a larger bite and began to munch enthusiastically. “Extremely good,” he said, returning his attention to the pile of receipts. “I can’t see anything questionable here. Not this time, eh, Avery?” Crumbs dropped from his lips. “That’s a pity.”

Maycross was alluding to the receipt for the “small metal box” that had been reluctantly included among Paul’s previous receipts for the days spent in America. The vendor name, *AC Fine Arts*, *Atlantic City*, on that receipt had stood out. “Something for Ann?” Maycross had remarked. “Good man.” Paul had asked Maycross to tell the Treasury to debit his salary for this payment, but Maycross wouldn’t hear of it. “I am certainly not giving them an excuse to do other than rubber stamp our submissions. Don’t worry yourself about it.” Paul was left wondering whether Maycross’s generosity was really a way of accruing evidence that could be used to discredit him.

“No, I paid cash for all my personal items, from my pock—”

A thumping sound interrupted Paul. He stood up and opened the door. A short uniformed security guard was on the top step, holding a tray.

“Coffee as ordered,” the man said.

The tray held a small cafetière, two cups and saucers, a bowl of sugar cubes, spoons, a jug of milk, paper napkins and an assortment of individually wrapped shortbread, caramel wafer and digestive biscuits.

After carrying the tray to the table, Paul closed the door. As he turned back to face Maycross, he said, “I was about to say, Patrick, that I paid for souvenirs with my own cash, as I’d intended to do in America too.”

“You disappoint me.” Maycross shrugged and gathered up the receipts. He then leaned sideways to put them in his bag, which was on the floor beside his chair.

"They've provided us with a cafetière. While I dispense the coffee, you could try that number, Patrick."

Maycross looked about him for the piece of paper with the telephone number. Picking it up, he said, "Don't you want to listen in?"

"I can contain my curiosity for a while longer," Paul said drily, hoping to build on the sense of tedium.

Several seconds passed as Maycross considered the situation. Eventually, he said, "I suppose so." Just before he left the chamber, he looked at Paul. "A cafetière is not *difficult* to operate. Are you up to something, Avery?"

Paul was in the process of transferring the cups and saucers from the tray to the table. He felt his hand shaking as he put the second cup down. "I'm trying to save time. If you prefer, I'll make the call and leave you to pour the coffee."

Maycross opened the door. With a frown, he said, "Don't put any sugar in mine. I like to do that myself."

Paul took a couple of deep breaths as he watched the door close behind Maycross. Recommencing the unloading of the tray, he nearly spilt the jug of milk. How long would he have? If Maycross used the secure telephone in the Main House, he would be gone for at least ten to fifteen minutes. Plenty of time to...

Perspiration prickled Paul's brow. He would never get away with it. Maycross was already suspicious. *Stop. Just stop now. Pour the coffee and sit down.* But his hands kept moving. A small, self-sealing plastic pouch of sand was the next item in his armoury. He took it from behind the divider flap that was secured to the inside of the briefcase lid. *Do it*, he told himself. *It's just harmless sand.* The fine white sand was from a glass Isle of Wight souvenir lighthouse ornament that he'd had to sacrifice.

Paul tipped the sugar cubes from the bowl on to a paper napkin. With his fingertips, he dusted some of the fine sand from his palm into the bowl, where the deposited grains looked like a sprinkling of pepper. *Blame the caterers*, he thought, rehearsing the conversation to come. He placed eight sugar cubes in the bowl and rolled them in the sand. On top of these he tipped pristine cubes. Having accomplished this step, he glanced at the door. The room was so highly soundproofed he would get little warning.

Returning to the task, he repeatedly struck the wrapped biscuits with the side of his hand. He felt the biscuits shattering into chunks. Maycross would be obliged to select another peanut cookie. His confidence grew as he pressed steadily on the plunger of the cafetière, pushing the coffee grounds to the bottom. To save time, he didn't wait for any escaped fine grounds to settle out before pouring the coffee for Maycross.

The next step was the defining one. Paul reached into his briefcase and withdrew the canister from the enclosure comprising two folded and interlocking pliable sheets of lead. He unscrewed the lid and inverted the canister over Maycross's cup, forgetting to first shake the mixture. Only the separated watery layer trickled out, leaving behind the viscous radium-rich sediment.

A faint scuffing noise came from the door. *He must have made the call from Reception.* Employing the lid's integral scraper, Paul frantically scooped the sediment into Maycross's coffee. The door handle was turning as Paul screwed the lid back on the emptied canister. Without looking round, he picked up the cafetière with his free hand as he plunged the canister into the side pocket of his jacket.

He sensed the door was fully open now. The room was filled with the sort of silence that only occurs between frozen breaths. How much had Maycross seen?

"What are you playing at, Avery?"

Looking round at Maycross, who was standing in the open doorway, Paul replied, "Pouring our coffee."

"Don't say anything until I close this." Once the metal door was shut, restoring the immunity to electronic eavesdropping, Maycross continued, "That number you gave me is useless."

Paul recommenced filling his cup. His heart was beating the way it had following the pigeon's collision with the window near his desk. "Really? I told you there was no ringing tone when I called it," he said with a sense of relief. The challenge about the telephone number wasn't a surprise. Crucially, Maycross hadn't seen – or being preoccupied, perhaps he just hadn't registered – the emptying of the canister.

"It rang this time." Maycross stared accusingly at Paul. "Someone answered too."

"Was it Shannon?" Paul said, pouring milk into his coffee. He put the jug down. "What did she say?"

"It was a library!"

"What library?"

"The National Library in Pretoria. A pre-recorded message told me the opening time – which it isn't yet."

Paul shrugged, affecting bemusement. He frowned thoughtfully as he sat down and reached for another peanut cookie. The telephone number was one of a few he'd obtained from Directory Enquiries yesterday, for use as a ploy to distract Maycross. He'd asked for the telephone numbers of the largest libraries in Pretoria. "I suppose it makes sense," he said, lifting his cup to take a sip.

"In what way?"

"Shannon must have been using the library, and expected to still be there when I returned her call."

"Nonsense. I doubt that they allow members of the public to use the office telephone. Nor are they likely to hail a reader on a loudspeaker if someone calls. It's a library, not a hotel!"

"She must have a contact there."

"A contact? You better have something more insightful to say when Blackwood interrogates you. He'll send someone there to make enquiries, if need be," Maycross said, moving away from the door. "It sounds so implausible, I'm not sure that I will mention—" Pointing towards Paul's briefcase, Maycross suddenly asked, "What's that contraption?"

Paul had forgotten to close the briefcase after taking out the canister. Maycross's increasing agitation was endangering the plan. The coffee was going to go cold soon.

Paul took the interlocked sheets of lead out of the briefcase. "It's not a contraption. They're pieces of lead. I use them in the field from time to time. You would too if you worked around radiation." He held them out for Maycross to inspect. "They won't harm you, unless you lick them, of course."

Maycross took hold of the dull-grey pieces of metal. Each had a thickness about three times that of a plastic credit card.

"They bend easily," Paul said.

Maycross twisted the sheets in his hands. "So they do," he said, evidently surprised.

"Look, Patrick, that telephone number... Perhaps I misremembered it. I don't think so, but it's possible. At least, it is a clue of sorts. As you say, Blackwood can look into it."

Handing back the lead sheets, Maycross said, "I can't protect you from him." He turned and walked to the other side of the table, where he'd been sitting earlier.

Paul felt convinced now that Maycross knew or suspected the truth surrounding Benedict's death – maybe not the gory details, but enough to know how vulnerable he was himself. "I understand that he can hurt me, but he needs me. And as you're my boss, that means he needs you too."

Maycross sat down. "Go on."

"The one aspect of the project that at our first meeting you forbad me from being curious about... Well, having since been to Atlantic City, I can appreciate what's at stake there. An endless river of money is going to flow through the new casino. But first, Blackwood must have the Altabrite site cleared in a way that doesn't attract publicity or the attention of local officials. That's his contribution as the facilitator. However, I learned he's under intense pressure from his powerful business partners. That's at least partly why he sent Shannon to Johannesburg. But we – me, you, Tom, the colonel and Max – will give him what he needs. From what I've seen in South Africa, I'm convinced that *your* three-dimensional chess strategy is going to pay off, Patrick."

Chapter 41

The unrehearsed flattery and the conjuring of a world where the fearsome Blackwood truly admired, as opposed to just hijacked, the moving pieces of everything he had set in train ensnared Maycross, who became so seduced he hardly noticed the gritty awfulness of the coffee. To the extent that he did notice, the brittleness of the peanut cookies, the inexplicable muck in the sugar and the presence of fine coffee grounds proved to be effective distractions.

He didn't start coughing until they had nearly finished their final discussion of the shipment details. His handling of the small lead sheets had made vivid to him the manner in which the shipment containers were to be shielded against gamma radiation leakage. There was almost enthusiasm in his expression as he listened to Paul describe the deepest of technicalities and the nature of the potential officialdom-related snares that had to be avoided.

As they finally packed away their papers, Paul said, "Given how well the staff here looked after us, I'll pop the tray back to Reception for them. I'll just be a moment, Patrick." This seeming act of civility was a ruse so that Paul could rinse the cup Maycross had used. The door to the Men's toilet was in the corridor leading back to Reception.

"Dirt in the sugar and broken biscuits was hardly looking after us," Maycross sneered as Paul left the chamber with the tray.

***

Heathrow Airport was about twelve miles away. Thirty minutes would be the typical time for the car journey, but not during rush hour. It was 8.25 a.m.

Maycross's coughing was becoming steadily worse as they folded themselves into the E-Type Jaguar. Paul wound down his window a few inches to vent the radon accumulating in the air around him. Maycross's bag and Paul's cases were in the back of the two-seater coupé, where storage space was roomier than Paul had imagined.

"Are you sure about driving me, Patrick? I can ask Reception to order a taxi."

"I want the satisfaction of telling Blackwood that I personally dropped you off at the airport. Anyway, taxis are not always... not always available at short notice round here, particularly at this time of the day. It's essential that you make your flight. It wouldn't surprise me if Blackwood collects you at the other end. Don't be shocked if he does."

Paul engaged his seat belt. Maycross, after several failed attempts, gave up trying to do likewise.

"It's the law. You must put it on," Paul said. "This car turns heads. If you're pulled over by the police, I'll definitely miss the flight."

This warning, with its allusion to Blackwood's wrath, was sufficient to motivate Maycross to persevere. He eventually secured his tight-fitting seat belt at the expense of his comfort.

Paul had a different reason for wanting Maycross restrained in his seat. In the event of the poisoned Maycross becoming incapacitated and crashing the car, the seat belt would prevent him from impacting the windscreen. The man was going to suffer enough without that.

The rate of the onset of radiation sickness was impossible to predict. About a hundred minutes had elapsed since Maycross drank the coffee. How far they'd actually get was the problem Paul had wrestled with yesterday afternoon, which is why as back-up he'd left his motorcycle midway between the institute and the airport, close to where the three most likely routes they would take converged.

From Maycross's hoarseness and perspiration, Paul guessed that they indeed wouldn't make it farther than a few miles. If they were to stop within two miles of the motorcycle, he could walk to it in about half an hour, leaving the bogus suitcase luggage behind. A hike much farther than that could make it impossible for him to catch the flight to Tel Aviv. On the other hand, Maycross might permit him to take over the driving to complete the journey. Under any other circumstances, that would be an experience to savour.

Fifteen minutes later, near Langley, on the London-bound side of the M4 motorway, the coughing Maycross pulled over abruptly from the slowly moving inside lane into the breakdown lane. He flung open his door and vomited. Following a struggle he released his seat belt and staggered from the car, leaving the engine running. The blare of a horn from a passing articulated lorry stopped him from straying on to the carriageway. A passenger in the car behind the lorry shouted something that incorporated the words "nice car" and "posh plonker". Maycross turned and vomited again, this time with his hands supporting him against the corrugated-steel crash barrier that lined the breakdown lane.

Paul got out and went round to the driver's side. By this time a concerned commuter had pulled over in front of the sports car and was reversing his vehicle towards them. Driving off in the E-Type Jaguar would be pointless as the traffic was moving so intermittently that even an ailing Maycross might be able to catch up. Instead, Paul reached behind the driver's seat and activated the mechanism that he'd observed Maycross use earlier for releasing the rear-door catch.

As he opened the rear door, which swung up from right to left, he caught sight of the driver in front who'd got out of his car.

"I'm a doctor," the bearded man said to the collapsed and groaning Maycross, whose chin was flecked with blood.

During this exchange Paul grabbed his briefcase and Maycross's bag. He clambered over the steel barrier and scrambled down the slope.

"What about your friend?" the shocked doctor shouted.

Taking advantage of the screen formed by a line of trees, Paul knelt to open the two cases. He found Maycross's annotated copy of the waste shipment plan and put it in his briefcase. He did the same with the receipts from his trip to South Africa, and then he checked for any other paperwork Maycross had brought that connected them. Once satisfied, he closed Maycross's bag and slid it under a bush.

Paul continued down the slope, arriving at a tarmacked parking lot, which extended to his right for as far as he could see. A few of the nearby painted bays were occupied. He guessed these vehicles belonged to people working in the overlooking metal-sided building, which had the appearance of a factory or a warehouse. He felt exposed here and wanted to quickly put more distance between himself and the doctor attending to Maycross.

To his left, about sixty yards away, was a wire fence that angled away abruptly towards what could be an exit. As he approached the fence, it became clear that it was a continuous barrier connecting to the side of the building. Beyond the fence was a lawn of tended grass, criss-crossed by paths. He squeezed between the endmost concrete post of the chain-link fence and the bushes at the bottom of the motorway embankment. After emerging into the park-like area, which he could now see extended under the elevated motorway, he crossed the lawn and took the first footpath leading north. This path intersected in the distance with a gravel track that formed the northern perimeter of the park. The far side of the gravel track was lined with block-like rows of garages that served nearby houses. The white up-and-over doors of the garages faced on to the park. Behind the garage blocks there had to be a road and the chance for Paul to get his bearings from the street signage. He looked at his watch. How far was it to his motorcycle?

Paul continued to the end of the footpath, crossed the gravel track and went through the opening separating two blocks of garages. He came to a long street that also ran parallel to the motorway. Choosing westwards, as in that direction the surroundings looked as if they were more residential and less industrial in nature, he came to a sign with the street name: Common Road. Balancing his briefcase on his left forearm, he opened the case and took out the pages that he'd stripped from his map book last night. Using first the M4 and then the airport as reference points, he managed to orient himself. Common Road would intersect with the broad High Street. At that junction, he had to turn right and walk north to the Langley Memorial Ground, a recreation park. He estimated the distance as about one mile.

A lot of activity proceeded around him – cars leaving driveways, buses going by, children in school uniform, articulated lorries throwing up dust from the road. It was a far more metropolitan community than that of rural Oxfordshire. No one would look out of place, unless they were wearing a clown costume or were naked, he told himself. Nonetheless, thoughts of the bearded and doubtlessly observant doctor describing him – his curly blond hair, his blue suit, his briefcase – to a motorway policeman were hard to dispel. The incriminating evidence in his jacket pocket came to mind. At the junction with the High Street, when the busy traffic permitted, he crossed over, first to the central reservation and then to the other side. He took the still radioactive canister from his pocket and dropped it into a litter bin, where it would wait for conveyance to landfill.

After walking for a further ten minutes, he came to the housing estate abutting the southern perimeter of the recreation park. He had been here, full of trepidation and indecision, at around 8.00 p.m. last night. He barely recognised the place now and feared he wouldn't find his parked motorcycle. Yet there it was, to his left, standing at the end of a row of communal parking bays. He'd chosen the spot because it was overlooked by houses. As far as any curious resident would know, it belonged to someone who was visiting one of their neighbours. What surprised him now was how exposed these bays were to the High Street. He thought he'd gone deeper into the estate last evening. In reality, thousands of people had passed by, travelling northwards along the main road during the last twelve hours. The restored machine was a magnet to motorcycle enthusiasts, including, potentially, thieves.

After briefly checking that the motorcycle was untouched, Paul walked down the cut-through that connected the housing estate to the southern side of the park. Using a lamppost as a reference point, he knelt to retrieve his crash helmet from the bushes. He left the two sheets of lead in its place. Without Diplomatic Privilege, his briefcase might be checked at the airport; the presence of impenetrable lead would have invited needless questions.

He folded his suit jacket and tie and put them in one of the motorcycle panniers. With elasticated cord taken from the other pannier, he strapped his briefcase to the rear seat. Although the motorcycle would be able to ease between the slow moving lanes of cars on the motorway, the possibility of police gathering around the E-Type coupé was too high to risk going that way. Maycross could have revived sufficiently to mumble something incriminating. Officers might already be searching the embankment now. Riding past them on a motorcycle in shirtsleeves would be as conspicuous as waving a white flag. After looking once more at his watch, Paul decided to take a longer detour, one passing through Uxbridge, Hayes End and Harlington.

The departure times for the New York and Tel Aviv flights were only fifteen minutes apart, but the check-in period for the latter was shorter, only two hours instead of three. Nonetheless the detour to the airport was so long it was going to be tight. If he were to miss the flight, he would have to go into hiding until he could get hold of Sundial again.

An image of a smirking Andrew Higstead, his office rival, came into Paul's mind for the first time since the afternoon he visited the Altabrite site with Shannon. *Now that Benedict and I am out of the way, it's all yours, isn't it?* Paul thought. *I wonder if our paths will cross again.*

***

Paul's pulse was still racing following the weaving ride through rush-hour traffic, the abandoning of his precious motorcycle in the drop-off lane, the stress of presenting the fake passport – he'd nearly shown the Diplomatic passport bearing his real name – and the dash through the large terminal to the departure lounge. Not having luggage to check in had saved him. There was just enough time left to do one more thing.

From where he was standing by the payphone in the wide corridor between the rows of boarding lounges, he could see the passengers for his flight stand up and commence walking towards the gate. The number he'd called was ringing.

"Radiation Watch," a man said gruffly.

"I have an important message for Stewart Burnham."

"This is he. Who's speaking?"

"I won't have time to repeat this. You must investigate the Willingham Corporation. It is claiming to be conducting a test into the storage of low-level radioactive waste. This is just a cover for the real activities. Ask Charlie Halliday, a South African government official, to explain what is happening at the Kop Mine outside Johannesburg. Get the South African Nuclear Energy Corporation involved. Don't do this without backup. You have press contacts. Use them."

"I didn't catch your na—"

Paul put the receiver down.

Despite the terrible thing he'd done to Maycross, Paul felt purged of guilt. Without Halliday's political cover, the dumping planned for the Kop Mine would be impossible to carry out. Cantrell and Barnaby would have to make other arrangements – perhaps even confess to the regulator what had happened years ago at the Hartling Springs plant. As for Blackwood and the mobster owners of the Altabrite site, they'd either need to find someone else with credentials to "launder" the contaminated soil or wait years to have the decontamination undertaken by the Environmental Protection Agency, risking ruinous publicity and the imposition of post-clean-up land-use exclusions.

Regarding the sensitive nuclear missile negotiations, the British government alone shouldn't be held responsible for the collapse of Programme COLOURLESS, a programme that officially never existed and no government representative would be able to openly defend. Implicated employees from *both* sides of the Atlantic would have mysteriously disappeared, after all. And a linked Whitehall figure whose precise activities no one will admit to sanctioning will be on indeterminate and unexplained sickness leave. Auberon Morrison will doubtlessly keep on doing what he does as a ghost-like fixer, apparently having moved on to aerospace deal-making. Only Tom, the self-described "good soldier", who would find himself cut adrift by Head Office, was worth worrying about. He would need to reinvent himself one more time. Perhaps it would be fitting if he retired to Cornwall and actually learned the dialect.

Paul joined the back of the boarding queue. During the flight he would have to rewire his priorities, jettison regrets, and persuade himself that what lay ahead would be everything he could hope for under the circumstances. He was safeguarding Ann's and his mother's lives and saving Shannon's.

He looked for the tenth time at his boarding pass. First Class. An auspicious omen for a fresh beginning. She would be waiting for him in Arrivals, just as she had at JFK. But that time they had been strangers.

The queue was shuffling forward along the boarding tunnel. Two hours ago, he'd been hoping for a delay in the departure time. Now he was impatient to be in the air. So much hand baggage to be crammed in overhead lockers, but he was carrying only a briefcase with little in it apart from the now-defunct shipment plans for Programme COLOURLESS.

Inside the plane, a few feet beyond the open door, a female flight attendant was spraying something on the front of a female colleague's olive-drab jacket. Then she began rubbing the fabric with a cloth. After a few seconds, all seemed to be well. Smiles exchanged. A quick hug between the attendants, the protruding light-blue collars of their blouses merging and parting like leaping fish. Everything spick and span again, and the crew ready for take-off. The mark had been wiped away...

His mind leapt back to the morning he'd made love to Shannon. Her hair had dropped away from the right side of her arching neck. Delicate, blemish-free skin, matching the white of the cotton pillowcase on which her head lay. For a distracting moment he'd been surprised that the cruel cigar burn could have healed so quickly. He effortlessly reasoned he must be looking at the wrong side. After all, he'd only seen the welt once – in her car outside ***Sandy's*** diner in New Jersey. He'd been in the front-passenger seat and must have been looking at her *left* side that evening.

Except he now – during this glacial advance of the queue – found the remembered world rearranging itself. The car passenger seat in which he'd sat would have, unlike in the UK and South Africa, been on the *right* side. The burn truly had gone without leaving behind the faintest scar. Was it ever there in the first place, or had it been faked with make-up to win his sympathy and compliance?

He looked again at the expensive airline ticket. The people she had been working for were masters of counter-intelligence and disguise. "You shouldn't be so honest with me, Paul. I'm used to being around liars," she warned him after they'd left President Square and its statue of Stephanus Johannes Paulus Kruger. Was Blackwood playing the Israelis, and to what end?

"Are you boarding, sir?" a male flight attendant called out.

Paul looked up. He was fifteen feet from the aircraft door. The other passengers had boarded. He was quite alone.

THE END

AUTHOR'S NOTES

The terms "Deep State" and "Continuity of Government" have been omitted from the narrative as neither were in common usage at the time of the story, 1983. The former term was perhaps first coined in the 1990s by the Canadian academic and poet Peter Dale Scott. The latter term originally related to the classified development of governmental infrastructure to survive nuclear war, but since its inception has been applied more widely, particularly in the USA, for example during and after the 9/11 attacks. Its existence came to public attention during the 1987 Iran-Contra hearings questioning of Colonel Oliver North.

The author has extrapolated from calculations of radiation exposure associated with radium paint ingestion as tabulated in "Radium Timepiece Dose Modelling Final Report Revision 1" by A.J. Boerner CHP and M.A. Buchholz (Oakridge Institute for Science and Technology, 2007). The connection between absorbed dosage and the likely harm arising (such as the risk of developing radiation sickness) has been based upon available online tables that compare widely differing exposure scenarios. Nonetheless the incidents described in this novel are purely dramatic contrivances and may differ from real-world exposure outcomes, which are probabilistic in nature.

Edward L. Lanner
Suffolk 2025

Also by Edward L. Lanner

The Brilliance of Matt White

The Leap into Sunlight

An Evening with Nicholas and Martin

Printed in Dunstable, United Kingdom

72283470R00179